Praise for the novels of Jane Porter

She's Gone Country

"I've always been a big fan of Jane Porter's. She understands the passion of grown-up love and the dark humor of mothering teenagers. What a smart, satisfying novel *She's Gone Country* is."

—Robyn Carr, *New York Times* bestselling author of the Virgin River novels

"A celebration of a woman's indomitable spirit. Suddenly single, juggling motherhood and a journey home, Shey embodies every woman's hopes and dreams. Once again, Jane Porter has written her way into this reader's heart."

—Susan Wiggs, *New York Times* bestselling author

"Richly rewarding."   —*Chicago Tribune*

"Strongly plotted, with a heroine who is vulnerable yet resilient . . . engaging."   —*The Seattle Times*

Easy on the Eyes

"An irresistible mix of glamour and genuine heart . . . *Easy on the Eyes* sparkles!"   —Beth Kendrick, author of *The Pre-nup*

"A smart, sophisticated, fun read with characters you'll fall in love with. Another winning novel by Jane Porter."

—Mia King, national bestselling author of *Good Things* and *Sweet Life*

Mrs. Perfect

"With great warmth and wisdom, in *Mrs. Perfect* Jane Porter creates a richly emotional story about a realistically flawed and wonderfully human hero who only discovers what is important in life when she learns to let go of her quest for perfection."
　　　　　　　　　　　　　　　　　　　　—*Chicago Tribune*

"Porter's authentic character studies and meditations on what really matters make *Mrs. Perfect* a perfect summer novel."
　　　　　　　　　　　　　　　　　　　　—*USA Today*

"The witty first-person narration keeps things lively in Porter's latest. Taylor's neurotic fussiness provides both vicarious thrills and laughs before Taylor moves on to self-awareness and a new kind of empowerment . . . a feel-good read."
　　　　　　　　　　　　　　　　　　　　—*Kirkus Reviews*

Flirting with Forty

Basis for the Lifetime Original Movie

"A terrific read! A wonderful, life- and love-affirming story for women of all ages."
　　　　—Jayne Ann Krentz, *New York Times* bestselling author

"Fits the bill as a calorie-free accompaniment for a poolside daiquiri."
　　　　　　　　　　　　　　　　　　　　—*Publishers Weekly*

Odd Mom Out

"Jane Porter must know firsthand how it feels to not fit in. She nails it poignantly and perfectly in *Odd Mom Out*. This mommy-lit title is far from fluff . . . Sensitive characters and a protagonist who doesn't cave to the in-crowd gives this novel its heft."
—*USA Today*

"[Porter's] musings on balancing work, life, and love ring true."
—*Entertainment Weekly*

"The draining pace of Marta's life comes across convincingly, and Porter's got a knack for getting into the heads of the preteen set; Eva's worries are right on the mark. A poignant critique of mommy cliques and the plight of single parents."
—*Kirkus Reviews*

The Good Daughter

JANE PORTER

BERKLEY BOOKS, NEW YORK

THE BERKLEY PUBLISHING GROUP
Published by the Penguin Group
Penguin Group (USA) Inc.
375 Hudson Street, New York, New York 10014, USA
Penguin Group (Canada), 90 Eglinton Avenue East, Suite 700, Toronto, Ontario M4P 2Y3, Canada
(a division of Pearson Penguin Canada Inc.) • Penguin Books Ltd., 80 Strand, London WC2R 0RL,
England • Penguin Ireland, 25 St. Stephen's Green, Dublin 2, Ireland (a division of Penguin
Books Ltd.) • Penguin Group (Australia), 707 Collins Street, Melbourne, Victoria 3008, Australia
(a division of Pearson Australia Group Pty. Ltd.) • Penguin Books India Pvt. Ltd., 11 Community
Centre, Panchsheel Park, New Delhi—110 017, India • Penguin Group (NZ), 67 Apollo Drive,
Rosedale, Auckland 0632, New Zealand (a division of Pearson New Zealand Ltd.) • Penguin Books (South
Africa), Rosebank Office Park, 181 Jan Smuts Avenue, Parktown North 2193, South Africa • Penguin
China, B7 Jiaming Center, 27 East Third Ring Road North, Chaoyang District, Beijing 100020, China

This is a work of fiction. Names, characters, places, and incidents either are the product of the author's
imagination or are used fictitiously, and any resemblance to actual persons, living or dead, business
establishments, events, or locales is entirely coincidental. The publisher does not have any control over
and does not assume any responsibility for author or third-party websites or their content.

THE GOOD DAUGHTER

PUBLISHING HISTORY
Berkley trade paperback edition / February 2013

ISBN: 978-0-425-25342-7

An application to register this book for cataloging has been submitted to the Library of Congress.

PRINTED IN THE UNITED STATES OF AMERICA

10   9   8   7   6   5   4   3

For my father, Tom Porter
I was fifteen when I lost you,
but you'd already given me the gift of words
the ability to dream
and the hunger to tell my stories.

Acknowledgments

Thank you to everyone at Penguin, with special thanks to my editor, the brilliant Cindy Hwang. I am so very grateful for the support.

And thank you to my family, my friends, and my readers, who have also become my family and friends. I would not be here, published and dreaming of new stories, if it weren't for you.

Part 1

Kit

One

Make a wish.

And just like that, wishes sprang to mind. One, two, three.

But it wasn't Kit Brennan who was supposed to be making wishes. It was Cass's night. The Brennan family had gathered to celebrate Cass's thirty-sixth birthday at Kit's childhood home in San Francisco's inner Sunset district.

There were ten at the table in the Edwardian-period dining room, with its high ceiling and elaborate wainscoting, the lights still out, the last of the happy birthday song dying away. Kit. Her parents. Her sister Meg and her family. Her brother, Tommy, and his wife, Cass, whose birthday they were celebrating.

"Make a wish, Cass," Mom said from her seat at the head of the table. She'd become painfully thin in the last month but looked happy tonight.

"Make a wish, Aunt Cass," Meg's eleven-year-old daughter,

Gabi, echoed, crowding in close to Cass, unable to contain herself, the flickering candlelight reflected in her shining brown eyes.

"Make a wish, babe," Tommy Jr. said, patting his wife's back. "Before your cake catches fire."

Cass Brennan crinkled her nose and tucked a long blond curl behind her ear. She'd married into this family eleven years ago and they'd immediately made her one of them. "Not too worried," she said lightly, even with her candles ablaze. "I've got two of the city's finest firefighters here."

Dad lifted his hands. "I've retired, hon, and we don't know how good Tommy is. Better make a wish and blow out those candles."

"Come on, Aunt Cass," Gabi shouted, trying to be heard above the good-natured laughter. "Wish for a baby. Wish hard!"

The laughter immediately died.

Cass froze.

Tommy's shoulders squared aggressively. "We don't need a baby."

"Yes, you do, Uncle Tommy," Gabi argued. "You've been wanting a baby for a long time!"

"Time to wish for something else. Like a vacation. Or winning the lottery."

Cass flinched, as if struck. Tears slowly filled her eyes.

All pretense of happiness was gone. Kit could feel Cass's grief, was sure everyone else felt it, too. The endless sorrow hung in the air, heavy, aching, a tragic specter weighting the room.

Tommy reacted first, his strong jaw—Dad's jaw—tightening, his blue eyes snapping. He didn't do this. Didn't break, grieve, mourn. Not in public. Not even in front of his family. He clapped his hand impatiently on Cass's slender back, between her shoulder blades. "Come on, babe. Blow out the candles."

The edge in his voice brought Cass to life. She gulped a breath, leaned toward the tall coconut cake with the fluffy icing, staring at what was left of the candles, formulating the wish before blowing out the flames in a broken rush of air.

Everyone clapped and the kids cheered. Meg rose and rushed to get the knife and delicate porcelain dessert plates. Meg's husband, Jack, asked if anyone wanted coffee or tea. Mom wanted tea and Jack headed to the kitchen to make it, and all the while Dad was talking loudly, carrying the small stack of presents from the sideboard to the table, making a big deal about which present Cass would open first. Everyone was talking, busy doing something, but Tommy.

Tommy sat stiff and silent and grim in his chair at the corner of the table. Kit refilled water glasses but kept an eye on her brother. She knew Tommy well, could tell from his expression that he was angry, resenting Cass, maybe everyone, for making him into the bad guy. Because that's what he was thinking, feeling, that they'd all turned him into the villain in the story, and he wasn't the villain. He was just being honest. Practical. After six years of trying unsuccessfully to have a baby, Tommy was done. He didn't need a baby. He wanted peace. He needed to stay sane.

As Cass cut the cake and Meg assisted by passing the plates around, Kit wondered what Cass had wished for. Was it a baby? Or was it for Tommy to want a baby again? Because their marriage was suffering. Both of them were suffering. Kit wasn't even sure a baby would solve everything anymore.

She suddenly ached with wishes of her own . . .

For Mom's cancer to go into remission.

For Cass to have her baby.

For Tommy to be happy with Cass again . . .

Later, after cake and presents, Meg's three kids were excused to watch television in the living room, while Jack and Dad headed outside with Tommy to look at Tommy's new car, which was really an old car, a 1960 Cadillac he bought on Craigslist for next to nothing and was determined to restore himself.

"Just us now," Meg said, sitting back in her chair with a soft, appreciative sigh. "The girls."

Kit was glad, too. She was tight with her sisters, and they were all close with Mom, so close that for the past ten years they had all taken an annual girls-only trip together, calling it the Brennan Girls' Getaway, spending a long weekend or week at the family beach house in Capitola.

On their getaway they'd eat and drink, talk, read, sleep. It was a time to let their hair down, a time to celebrate family, and hopefully a time to feel safe, although the last couple of getaways had been tense because of friction between Brianna, Kit's fraternal twin, and Meg. Cass had missed the last getaway, too, back in May, as she'd been in the middle of an IVF cycle and her doctor wouldn't let her travel so close to the egg retrieval.

Mom shifted in her high-back chair and focused on Cass. "How *are* you?"

Mom wasn't making polite conversation. She was genuinely concerned about Cass, and now that Tommy was gone, this was a chance for Cass to open up . . . if she could. No one was sure that she could, or would. It'd been almost three and a half months since she'd miscarried and this miscarriage had been the worst . . . not just for her, but the whole family. It was her fourth miscarriage, and it'd happened later than the others, this time at twenty-four weeks, just when Cass had let her guard down. Just when she'd started to get excited about the baby.

The entire family had grieved with Cass. All of them had been so happy about the baby, and then their hearts were broken. But this time Tommy didn't want their meals or phone calls or visits. This time Tommy announced that he and Cass wanted to be alone, and he asked that the family give them space and privacy to deal with the loss their way, in their time.

Kit's baby sister, Sarah, who lived with her husband and children in Tampa Bay, had been on the phone immediately with Kit and then Meg, hurt, even outraged that Tommy would push them away, but Mom and Dad backed Tommy, insisting that his sisters respect Tommy and Cass's need for space. As Mom reminded them repeatedly, having children, or not having children, was a part of marriage and no one's business but Tommy and Cass's.

Of course the Brennan sisters couldn't ignore Cass, not when they knew she was hurting so much. Without consulting one another, each of them quietly sent Cass private e-mails and text messages, letting her know she was loved. Tommy could refuse meals and visitors, but he couldn't expect his sisters not to reach out to Cass. They loved Cass, and they told her so, repeatedly. Cass didn't answer all, or even most, messages, but later in December, just before Christmas, she sent her sisters-in-law a group message thanking them for their amazing support and constant love. She hadn't had sisters, only two younger brothers, and she told them that she felt incredibly lucky to be one of the Brennan girls.

"I'm good," Cass said softly now, two spots of color in her cheeks. "Well, better than I was in October." She paused, studying the blue, white, and gold pattern on her dessert plate with the half-eaten slice of birthday cake. "October was bad. And November." Her full mouth quirked and one of her deep dimples appeared. "To be honest, December wasn't much better either."

Kit knew Cass had been in a very dark place and yet there had been nothing any of them could do for her then. There was really nothing they could do now. Kit hated feeling helpless. "We've been worried about you."

"I know. And I was kind of worried about me, too," Cass admitted with a strangled laugh, pushing back the same wayward curl that had slipped out of her ponytail. She had long loose curls and big blue eyes like an innocent shepherdess from a Mother Goose nursery rhyme. In reality she was a labor and delivery

nurse at a hospital in Walnut Creek specializing in high-risk de-
liveries, and far from helpless.

"Are you doing better?" Mom asked, a deep furrow between
her eyebrows. Mom had been a nurse, too, before she earned her
master's degree and became a hospital administrator.

Cass toyed with the lace edging her white linen napkin. "I
don't know. This last time broke something inside me. Here I
had this beautiful, perfect little boy . . . and my body rejected him.
Killed him—"

"Cassidy!" Meg choked, horrified, glancing toward the hall to
make sure none of her kids were listening. "Don't say that. You're
not responsible. You can't blame yourself."

"But I do." Cass looked up, the grief clouding her eyes. "How
can I not? He was twenty-four weeks old. Thirty-six percent of
babies can survive premature birth at twenty-four weeks. Instead,
my body—" She didn't finish, pressing a hand to her mouth to
keep the words in, but her eyes were enormous with sorrow and
pain.

Kit slid out of her chair to wrap her arms around Cass's shoulders. "I'm so sorry," she whispered. "So very, very sorry."

Cass covered Kit's hands with hers. "I want him back. I want
to save him."

"It's not fair, is it?" Kit murmured.

"It's not," Meg echoed. "Nor does it seem fair that people who
shouldn't have kids pop them out, and those who should have
them struggle."

"I think about that all the time," Cass said.

"Did you have a name for him?" Mom asked.

Cass nodded. "Thomas. After Dad. Thomas Joseph Brennan."

"Your own baby Tommy," Mom said, understanding.

For a moment no one said anything, and then Gabi ran into the
dining room, asking if she could please have another slice of cake
since her piece had been small. Meg cut her a sliver. Kit asked if

she could have another sliver, too. It was good cake. Meg was an excellent baker.

After Gabi left, Mom circled her teacup with her hands. "You won't ever forget your Tommy," she said quietly. "I know I've told you this before, but I've never forgotten the babies I lost. There were three between Meg and the twins. I never knew if they were boys or girls. Back then they didn't tell you those things. I wondered, though."

"What did Dad do when you lost them?" Cass asked, brow furrowing.

"Told me he was sorry. That he loved me." Marilyn paused, looking back, remembering the years of being a young wife and mother. "That I would conceive again. And then he'd go to work. Escape to his beloved firehouse. To his boys." Her voice held the barest hint of bitterness. "He was lucky. He had somewhere else to go. I was here alone with a toddler."

The clock in the living room suddenly chimed nine. It caught them by surprise. No one knew when it'd gotten so late, and it was Sunday night, a school night. Meg said she'd need to get the kids home soon. They lived in Santa Rosa. And once Meg and Jack left, everyone else would go, too. Tommy and Cass to Walnut Creek. Kit to her small house in Oakland.

"I'd try again," Cass said in a rush when the clock stopped chiming. "I've met with a new specialist, a doctor who thinks he can help me, but Tommy has said no. Says he can't go through that again."

Kit opened her mouth to speak but then thought better of it. She wasn't married. Had never been married. Wasn't her place.

Instead, Mom said carefully, "Maybe he just needs more time—"

"It's our eleventh wedding anniversary this year. I want a baby." Cass's voice dropped, deepening with emotion. "I don't want to wait. I can't wait. I'm ready to be a mom now."

"Have you two considered using a surrogate?" Kit asked, feeling Cass's desperation and aware that her brother didn't want to adopt. He'd wanted a son to follow in his footsteps, just the way he'd followed in his father's. The Brennan men had been San Francisco firefighters for six generations, all the way back before the Great Earthquake and Fire of 1906, and Tommy Jr. was proud of this legacy. Maybe too proud.

"Tommy says the Church is against it."

"The Church doesn't support IVF either," Meg pointed out.

This was greeted by uncomfortable silence, which stretched until Meg added, "Maybe it's time you and Tommy revisited the idea of adopting—"

"He won't," Cass said shortly. "It's our baby or nothing."

Meg gestured impatiently. "But when you adopt, that baby becomes your baby."

"I know, but Tommy won't even discuss it. He wants—" Cass broke off as the front door opened and the men's voices could be heard in the hall. She pressed her lips together, frustration and resentment in her tense expression. "Let's just let this go. Okay?"

They did.

But in the car, driving home, Kit played the evening over in her head. The cheerful dinner conversation where everyone made an effort to be light, kind, funny, and even Meg and Jack seemed to put their differences aside for the night. The fluffy coconut cake on the heirloom. The dimmed lights. The golden glow of the birthday candles. Her dad's big baritone singing "Happy Birthday." The bittersweet chorus of "make a wish" . . .

Hands flexing against the steering wheel, Kit thought of the wishes that had come to her. Wishes she'd make if it were her birthday . . .

For Mom to live.

For Cass to have her baby.

For Jack and Meg's marriage to survive this rocky transition.

And for Kit herself? What did she want personally? What was her heart's desire? That was easy. She was selfish. Wasn't wishing for world peace or clean water for Third World nations. No, she wanted love. Marriage. Babies. She wanted to have her own family. She'd be forty in a couple of weeks. It was time. The clock was ticking.

And yet, if she had only one wish . . . and if that one wish could come true . . . what would she do?

She'd save Mom, of course.

The oncologist was astonished that Marilyn Brennan had lasted this long, but couldn't imagine her making it through the spring. It was January 8 now. That meant Mom had what? February? March? Maybe Easter? Easter came late this year, mid-April. Would Mom be with them then?

The thought made Kit's insides churn. She wished she hadn't had that second sliver of birthday cake. Wished she was already home in bed instead of still driving at ten o'clock at night.

Kit's phone rang. It was Meg, her oldest sister. "Home safe?" Kit asked, answering.

"Just got back a few minutes ago. Sorry we left you with all the dishes."

"Not a big deal. Dad helped. Gave us a chance to talk."

"He's okay?"

"Seemed like it. But it's hard to tell with Dad. He doesn't ever complain."

Meg sighed. "He doesn't like to burden us."

"I know. But I almost wish he would. It'd make me feel better. Make me feel as if I was helping him somehow."

"Maybe it's a good thing you didn't help him. Now you can help me."

"What's wrong?"

"I'm upset. I've been upset ever since leaving the house."

"Mom?"

"No. Cass. Tommy. The whole baby thing."

"It's a mess, isn't it?" Kit said.

"I'm worried about them. I can understand why Tommy doesn't want to do the IVF anymore, but his stand on adoption is ridiculous."

Kit changed lanes to let a faster car pass her. "I agree."

"He'll lose Cass if he's not careful."

"I know."

"Now's the time for them to explore all their options if they want to become parents. But I don't think Tommy wants to be a parent at this point. I think he's decided that he's okay without kids."

Dad had said something similar to Kit while they washed dishes. Apparently Tommy had told Dad tonight that he was ready to move forward and just get on with life, as he'd come to terms with Cass's infertility and he was good without kids. "He's worn out," Kit said. "He needs a break from the focus on making babies."

"Which is great, but Cass is a labor and delivery nurse. She wants a baby of her own. Needs to be a mom."

Kit understood. She loved kids. It's one of the reasons why she'd become a teacher. She'd been in the classroom seventeen years now, the last sixteen at Memorial High, a Catholic school in east Oakland, not far from San Leandro. She'd recently been promoted to head of the English department, which would look great on a résumé, but wasn't much of an honor if you knew there were only three English teachers at Memorial. "What do you think about them using a surrogate?"

"I don't have a problem with it," Meg said. "Do you?"

"No."

"I don't think anyone in the family does. I wish they'd look into it. It's expensive, but Cass and Tommy already have the frozen embryos."

Remembering her conversation with Dad, Kit rubbed at her brow, easing the tension headache. "I just can't see Tommy ever agreeing to it. I don't know if it's a control thing, or a society thing, but Tommy's against taking any more extreme measures to make a baby."

"Adopting isn't extreme. I'd adopt, if I couldn't have kids."

"I would, too. Let's just hope Cass can convince Tommy to reconsider all their options."

Monday was Kit's least favorite day of the week. It was hard to rally Monday morning after a weekend away from school. She knew her students felt the same way, and so she made a point of making each Monday morning's lessons interesting, trying to hook her students' attention quickly, painlessly. Or as painlessly as possible considering that most of her students were sleep deprived and school started early.

Fortunately, as the head of her very small department, Kit was able to pick the classes she wanted to teach and she chose to teach everything—from basic freshman English to the very advanced AP British lit. It meant she had six different preps, but she liked it that way, as the varied curriculum held her interest and allowed her to teach far more novels, poetry, and plays every year than she'd be able to teach otherwise.

Kit loved books. Reading was her thing. But being a teacher wasn't just about sharing great books with young, bright minds. It was also about managing, controlling, organizing, disciplining, advising, as well as assuming extra duties to keep the school's overhead down. At Memorial, the faculty all had duties outside their classroom. Yard duty, cafeteria duty, extracurricular jobs, adviser jobs, coaching positions. Teachers wore many hats. Kit was spending her lunch hour in her classroom wearing her Drama Club adviser hat now.

Kit had founded the Drama Club her first year at Memorial High, and for the past fifteen years it'd been one of the school's most prestigious clubs, putting on wonderful, if not extravagant and exhausting, productions every spring.

But this year she was beginning to think there wouldn't be a production. The club was small, with less than a dozen students. Her die-hard thespians, the most talented kids she'd probably ever worked with, had graduated in June, and she—and the club—missed those nine kids. The seven students who'd remained in the club had managed to recruit only one new freshman, and the eight club members couldn't agree on anything.

"You're running out of time," Kit said from her desk, raising her voice to be heard over the rustle of paper bags and crumpling plastic and conversation taking place at the student desks. "You don't meet again until next month, and then it's auditions. So you really need to discuss what kind of production interests you and get some consensus. If you can't agree, then I think it's time you accepted that there won't be a spring show."

"What kind of show can we do again?" one of the sophomore girls asked.

Irritation beat at Kit. She hadn't slept well last night, had woken late, and had dashed to school without breakfast and was starving right now. Her gaze fell on her sandwich. It was looking bruised inside its plastic baggie but it made her mouth water. But she couldn't eat it here, in front of them. She might get grape jelly on her white blouse. She might need to answer a question. She might choke . . . and these kids, helpless as they were, might let her die. Or worse, they might try the Heimlich maneuver on her.

Better to go hungry.

"You can do virtually anything," Kit said, hiding her exasperation with a wry smile. They were just teenagers, after all. Fourteen-, fifteen-, and sixteen-year-olds searching for identity, meaning, and clear skin. "Remember the list you brainstormed last month? You could choose a comedy, musical, drama, a series of one-act plays . . . it's up to you. Perhaps you'd like to take a vote?"

Alison Humphrey, the current president of the Drama Club, and the only senior in the club this year, came to life. "We're going to vote now," she said decisively. "It'll be anonymous. Write down on a slip of paper what you'd like to do for the spring production, fold the paper up, and pass it to the front, and then we'll tally the votes. Okay?"

The classroom door opened while the students were scribbling down their preferences. It was Polly Powers, one of Memorial's math teachers and Kit's closest friend, in the doorway and she gestured to Kit.

Kit left her desk and stepped out into the hall.

"Are you going to be stuck in there all lunch?" Polly asked.

"Looks like it. They can't agree on anything."

"Which club?"

"My little thespians."

Polly rolled her eyes. "No wonder." She didn't get theater, or theater kids. Thought they were weird.

And perhaps they were, but Kit liked that. "How was lunch? Anything interesting happen in the staff room?"

"Lunch was boring. Fiona stayed in her room, too."

Fiona Hughes was one of the science teachers, and Polly's and Kit's close friend. The three of them hung out together a lot. "Why?"

"Chase is being a dick. She was crying. Didn't want anyone to see her."

Kit frowned. Fiona and Chase had been married for only eighteen months but it'd been difficult from the start. "What's he doing now?"

"I don't know. The usual. But she needs some cheering up. Think we need to take her out after work. Have a drink. Are you free?"

"Yes." Kit peeked into the class, saw that Alison was now recording the votes, and turned back to Polly. "Let's head out as soon as the staff meeting's over."

Two

They met at Z's Cocktail Lounge in Alameda after the school staff meeting ended. It was one of their favorite places to go since it was far enough from Memorial High that they didn't risk bumping into other teachers or parents, and quiet, as Z's was a bar that only locals knew about. The outside was nondescript and drew little attention from the street. Inside, it was small, cozy, and upscale, with just a few tables along the walls, the stools at the bar, and the requisite piano.

"I don't think I could do it again, not knowing what I know now," Fiona was saying, her Irish accent pronounced as she pushed her empty beer glass around on the table. "It's too hard, this blended family thing. I was so naive thinking I could make it work. Thinking that we could all get along."

This wasn't new news. Kit and Polly were aware that Fiona, a Dublin native and brilliant science teacher, had been struggling for a while. The problem was the kids. Chase's kids. She'd never been married before, but he had, and he came into the marriage with three children, two teenagers and a preteen. Fiona knew that the kids had been scarred from a bitter divorce and a poisonous mom, but she'd thought that with patience and love they would warm up to her. They hadn't.

"I'm trying so hard," Fiona added, blinking back tears. "I honestly couldn't try harder."

Polly couldn't contain her frustration any longer. "That's the problem," she said tartly. "You're too good to them."

"No," Fiona protested, but unconvincingly.

"Yes!" Polly slammed her fist onto the table, making the glasses bounce. "They're little shits, especially the youngest, Alexander. They're trying to break you and their dad up, and they're winning. It's time you fought back. Turned the tables. Taught those brats a thing or two."

"Polly!" Kit choked on smothered laughter. She'd taught with Polly for years now, and loved her sense of humor, but to call Fiona's stepkids brats and little shits?

Polly shrugged. "I'm right," she said, successfully catching the eye of the waitress and indicating that she'd have another round. She'd already finished two strong key lime daiquiris but was by no means drunk. Polly could hold her liquor. "Those kids totally manipulate you, Fiona, just as they manipulate their dad, their mom, and everyone around them. It's time you turned the tables. Put them in their place. Taught them a thing or two."

Fiona's forehead wrinkled. "But wouldn't that just give them more ammunition?"

Polly rolled her eyes. "They're already armed and dangerous. You're the one who's vulnerable. You have to stop playing nice."

Kit's phone suddenly vibrated from within her coat pocket and quietly she retrieved it and checked the message under the table.

It was from Sebastian.

Kit's heart fell. She didn't enjoy being mean. She was the proverbial good Catholic girl, and she'd grown up to be a good Catholic schoolteacher, but Sebastian Severs would not take a hint and his frequent, flirty texts were driving her crazy. Tonight's text was just like the others:

Hey, gorgeous, you're a sorceress and you've got me under your spell! Let's get together Friday night and make some magic happen.

Kit shuddered rereading it. There were so many things wrong with the message—and Sebastian—that she didn't even know where to begin. She should never have given him her cell number. Why hadn't she realized that once you gave a man your number, he could, and would, haunt you for the rest of your life? But then, why had she thought that meeting men online was a good idea either?

Annoyed with Sebastian, angry with herself, Kit turned off her phone, slipped it back into her purse beneath the table, and kicked herself yet again for joining Love.com in the first place.

She couldn't imagine what had possessed her to join back in September—

No. Not true.

She knew exactly what had possessed her.

Desperation.

In September, three months after the end of her ten-year relationship with Richard, a relationship that had probably stalled out eight years earlier, Kit did some serious, if not panicked, soul-searching, and concluded that action was needed. *Desperate* action. She was closing in on forty—the big birthday was January 28—and Kit couldn't wait for love to find her. She'd have to find it for herself. And so, after watching a late-night TV commercial promoting Love.com, she signed up for a one-year membership, since she had no idea how long it'd take to find true love.

At first it'd been exciting poring over profiles, exchanging messages, setting up the first few dates. But it had taken only a few dates to realize many men weren't truthful on their profiles. They either used photos from ten or twenty years ago, or padded their height while decreasing their weight. But weight and height discrepancies weren't a serious issue. The personalities were. Or lack of.

Kit had never thought of herself as particularly difficult to please—after all, she ended up staying with Richard for ten years—but her dates from Love.com were invariably uncomfortable. Some were boring. Others made her uneasy. And then there were the few that were plain humiliating. But Kit, Irish Catholic and from a sprawling opinionated family, was made of stern enough stuff that she attempted to endure all, determined to at last find the Real Thing. The Real Thing being love, marriage, and babies—and preferably in that order.

But after three months of online dating hell, Kit no longer craved True Love. She just wanted to be left alone.

So in December, after a particularly horrifying date, Kit closed her account at Love.com, and her profile promptly disappeared. But the damage was done. A dozen different men had her number and e-mail address. And while most of those dozen men had moved on to greener, fresher pastures, there were a few like Sebastian who couldn't.

Kit suspected it was time to change her number. Such a shame since she loved the order of the digits. It'd been her cell number for twelve years now and the numbers looked good together. They suited her. But difficult times called for difficult measures.

Resolved to take action, Kit forced her attention back to the conversation.

"Now I'm supposed to go home and make dinner and smile and act like everything is okay," Fiona was saying. "But I can't. Everything isn't okay and I'm sick of acting like it is."

"Then don't go," Polly answered.

Kit frowned. Polly wasn't helping. Of course Fiona had to go home. Fiona was married. "You can't avoid going home, but you can, and should, talk to Chase. You have to make him understand how you feel. Does he know how unhappy you are?"

"I'm sure he does," Fiona answered. "All we ever do is fight."

Kit and Polly exchanged swift glances again. "But does he understand *why* you're fighting?" Kit persisted, having just gone through a six-month roller-coaster ride with Meg when her eldest sister derailed her marriage by having an affair with her boss because she felt unloved at home. "Guys aren't like us, Fiona. They don't read between the lines very well. You have to let him know that the kids are wreaking havoc on your relationship."

Fiona's blue eyes flashed. "He knows, but he just makes excuses for them. Says that they've been through a lot with the divorce and that they'll eventually grow out of it. But it's his fault that they treat me like rubbish. He doesn't set any boundaries with them. Doesn't insist that they respect me," she added, her Irish accent growing thicker. "But then, of course, he knows everything about kids because he's a father. I'm just a teacher. He forgets that I spend eight hours a day with kids, and have for the last ten years of my life!"

Her words died away but the pain and bitterness in her voice hung in the air, mingling with the mournful minor chords of the piano.

Times like these, Kit was glad she wasn't married. Marriage was not easy. And after months of uninspiring dates, she was no longer sure men were the answer. If anything, they were the problem.

"You know this isn't about you, Fiona," Kit added with a rueful twist of her lips. "He's compensating. Feeling guilty for leaving their mom. For breaking the family up—"

"So better to break my heart! Better to let his children tear me apart because I had the audacity to fall in love with their father!"

"Just shoot the bastard and get it over with," Polly said grimly.

Kit slapped Polly's arm. "Shut up. We don't need Fiona in jail. She'd lose her green card. Get sent back to Ireland. And we don't want that, do we?"

"No," Polly agreed. "Fiona is the only one who can drink me under the table. I like that about her."

Fiona laughed. Kit was relieved to hear the sound. It'd been a while, which was tragic, since Fiona had a wicked sense of humor.

"You and Chase just need some time to yourselves," Kit said, finding it hard to believe that it was only two years ago that Chase, a San Francisco investment banker, spotted Fiona in a bar in the Marina district, and fell for black-haired, blue-eyed Fiona on the spot. There had been an immediate connection between the two and things moved quickly between them after that. "But I know it's hard when there are always kids around."

"Which is why we're going away this weekend," Fiona answered. "I'm trying to hold on to that. Otherwise I think I'd go mad."

Polly frowned, confused. "Is it already Martin Luther King weekend?"

"It is," Kit said, sitting back as the cocktail waitress delivered a tray of drinks to their table. "And you and I are going to the beach house in Capitola this weekend."

"That's awesome." Polly sighed. "I'd completely forgotten."

Fiona glanced at the pint of beer set before her. "I'm sorry, I didn't order another one."

"Neither did I," Kit said as another glass of chardonnay appeared at her elbow.

"You didn't," the waitress said. "They're compliments of those guys at the table over there." She pointed to a small table not far from the front door where two men sat smiling at them.

"Wish they hadn't done that," Polly muttered as the waitress walked away. "I don't want another drink, and I definitely don't want to talk to any men right now."

"Me either," Kit agreed.

"And I'm married," Fiona chimed in, stealing a peek in the direction of the men at their table. "Even if unhappily." She scrutinized the two men. "But they're not bad-looking."

Kit glanced over her shoulder, sizing up the pair, noting that they both wore blue dress shirts and were drinking beer. "How can you tell? All I can see are the back of their heads."

Abruptly Polly pushed her untouched cocktail glass away. "Sorry. Not to be a party pooper, but I need to get out of here. You two mind if I call it a night?"

"Not at all," Kit said, reaching for her wallet. "I've got grading to do."

"And I guess I have to face the music, too," Fiona added, with a quick glance at her watch.

They paid the bill, gathered their coats and purses, and headed for the front door, but one of the men rose from the table and intercepted them. "Polly?" he said, putting a hand out toward her.

"Jon?" she said, blinking with surprise.

He nodded. "I thought that was you. Wasn't sure. How are you?"

"Good. Really good." Polly turned to introduce Kit and Fiona. "These are my friends Kit Brennan and Fiona Hughes. We teach together at Memorial."

"You're teaching now? No more pharmaceutical sales?"

"No. Got my credential a number of years ago." She looked at Kit and Fiona, and explained: "Jon and I used to work together at Pfizer. First job right out of college." She glanced back at Jon. "You still with them?"

"Yes. Doing well there. It's been a good fit." He gestured to his table. "Would you like to join us? I can grab some chairs."

Polly grimaced. "I'm sorry, but it's late, and Fiona's husband is expecting her—"

"Do you have a second, Polly?" Jon asked, interrupting her. "I'd really like to talk to you, to apologize—"

"It's not necessary, Jon." Polly was blushing. "That was years ago."

"Maybe. But I'd feel better if I could apologize. Can we just step outside?"

Polly nodded and went outside with him, and Fiona slipped out, too, needing to get home, leaving Kit to hover uneasily by the table, aware that Jon's friend was sipping his beer and watching her.

Unable to avoid the inevitable, she turned and smiled tightly. "Hi."

He smiled back. "I'm Michael Dempsey," he said, stretching out a hand.

"I'm Kit," she said, shaking his hand.

"Have a seat," he offered.

She took Jon's chair, not knowing what else to do.

"You didn't touch the drinks," Michael added.

Kit glanced at the table she and her friends had just left. Their three drinks were still sitting there. All three glasses were full. "We were just getting ready to leave when they arrived," she said, feeling extremely awkward. Michael Dempsey had to be somewhere in his mid to late thirties. And he wasn't bad-looking. In fact, he was rather good-looking, in an athletic sort of way, with his tanned skin and thick, wavy, dark blond hair. His eyes were a light blue and almost the exact color as his cotton dress shirt. "Do you work with Jon?"

"No. Just friends." He smiled at her, and little creases fanned from his eyes. His teeth were very straight and white.

It struck her that he knew he was attractive and that he'd

worked his charm—and that particular smile—on countless women before her. "Do you know Polly?" she replied.

His smile grew, as if he recognized the ploy. "No. But Jon was just telling me about her. He speaks very highly of her."

"She's amazing. She's one of my best friends."

"So you are all teachers."

"Yes. We"—Kit broke off to gesture to the table where she, Polly, and Fiona had been sitting just a few minutes ago—"all teach at the same school. A Catholic school in Oakland."

"That's nice."

"We didn't know each other before we started working together but we've become really close. I've known Polly almost seven years, and Fiona for the past three."

"You girls go out a lot?"

"Just once or twice a month. Keeps us sane."

"You always come here?"

"Usually. It's familiar, and convenient, since Polly lives close by. What about you?"

"I'm still new to the area. First time here. But I like this place. It's mellow. Has a good vibe."

"It does." Kit looked at him more closely, wondering if it was fair to be prejudiced against him simply because he was good-looking. Or was she prejudiced because he was good-looking and he knew it? Either way, she wasn't sure she liked him. "Where did you move from?"

"I've moved around a bit with work, but I'm from Houston."

"I thought I heard an accent."

"Not too strong, I hope."

"No. So what do you do?"

"Work in the oil business."

"You're with Chevron," she guessed.

He nodded. "Just got transferred here a month ago."

"Which office?"

"San Ramon, but I live not far from here so I'm close to offices and operations in Richmond and San Francisco."

"What do you think so far?"

"Still finding my way around. But I like being close to a city and you've got all the professional sports, too."

"My dad and brother love that about the Bay Area, too, although my dad roots for the San Francisco teams while Tommy has become an A's and Warriors fan."

"Who do you root for?"

"Niners. Grew up watching Montana, Young, and Rice make history. Loved Jerry. Loved Ronnie Lott. They were incredible. And then the Niners fell apart and sucked for a while—"

"A *long* while."

She shrugged, feeling cocky. "But they're back. We're in the play-offs. And I think we've got a good chance against the Saints this weekend."

"So who is your favorite player?"

"Patrick Willis, middle linebacker. He's a playmaker. He makes things happen."

"I have to say I'm impressed by Alex Smith this year. He's proven himself to be quite a quarterback—" He broke off as Polly appeared at the table with Jon right behind her.

Kit could tell from Polly's expression that she wanted to go, and quickly. Kit got to her feet. "It was nice to meet you," she said to Michael. "And good luck settling in. I hope you'll like living here."

Kit glanced at Polly as they walked silently to her car. Polly wasn't happy. "What was that about?" Kit asked her. "Why did Jon want to talk to you? What was so important that he needed you to step outside with him?"

"He wanted to apologize for a shitty thing he did a long time ago."

"What did he do?"

They'd reached Kit's car and Polly faced her. "He took credit for something I did, and then stole my biggest account from me, earning him a big fat bonus and a promotion, when both should have been mine. Schmuck."

"And he feels bad now?" Kit asked, unlocking the car doors.

"Apparently so."

"He is a schmuck," Kit agreed as they both climbed into her car.

"I know." Polly was silent a moment as Kit started the engine and merged with traffic. "Worse, we were seeing each other back then. He was supposed to be my boyfriend. I thought he was the one."

Three

The *one,* Kit silently repeated, after dropping off Polly at her condo complex and heading for home, a charming 1895 Queen Anne in Oakland's Highland Park.

She'd owned her house only since June, and it still needed a ton of work, but she didn't mind. Her dad and uncles had helped with some of the bigger home improvement projects, while she'd tackled other do-it-yourself projects on her own after getting inspired by HGTV. Some of the projects hadn't turned out so well, but just trying to do something outside her comfort zone had been rewarding. Exciting.

Her love affair with her house had helped her unplug from Love.com. She didn't need a man to give her stability and security, not when she was doing it for herself, and she was so happy in her little house, with its high ceilings and big windows and red dining room with the glossy white trim.

There were moments when a little voice niggled inside of her, teasing her with possibilities . . . Wouldn't it be even more wonderful to share her beautiful little house with someone else? Wouldn't she love to have men's shirts and coats hanging in the closet with hers again? Kit had liked seeing Richard's suits and button-down shirts across from dresses and blouses in their condo. His clothes gave the closet a sense of order. Purpose. She felt more grounded somehow, seeing his starched blue shirts and white shirts in close proximity to her coral and peach and burnt-cherry sweaters and dresses. Kit loved color. Warm, lush color. Maybe redheads weren't supposed to embrace color, but Kit couldn't stay away from it.

And, of course, Richard, the engineer, hated color. He was always asking Kit to tone it down . . . her laugh, her voice, her curls, her personality. Why had she stayed with him? How could she have imagined that she'd be happy with a man who would decorate their condo only in shades of gray, taupe, and beige?

Were those even real colors?

She rubbed at her forehead, disgusted with herself for wasting ten years on someone who hadn't ever truly loved her, and didn't really want her. Ridiculous. She'd never had great self-esteem, but still.

Kit parked and swiftly climbed the steps to her front door, grateful that over the summer Dad had installed automatic lights on her front porch so that she never came home to a dark house.

Dad was so good about doing little things like that. He'd always put his family first, and their safety was number one. He was generous with his time, too. Kit had thought all men would be like Dad. *Wrong.*

She was just shutting the front door behind her when her phone rang. It was her sister Sarah calling from Florida. Sarah was raising her children in Tampa Bay, as her husband, Boone, was a designated hitter for the Rays. "Hey, girl," Kit said, locking the door behind her. "How are you?"

"Fine. Am I catching you at a bad time?"

"No. Just arrived home. What's up?"

"Heard that Cass's birthday dinner was kind of intense."

"Kind of." Kit dropped her leather satchel stuffed with books and student papers on the couch in the living room and kicked off one shoe and then the other. "Tommy was all over Cass last night, too, never leaving her side. At first I thought it was because he was being protective, but then later, after the whole make-a-wish thing, I realized he was trying to keep her from talking about the miscarriage."

"Do you think it was that, or do you think he just didn't want her talking about babies in general?"

"Both. He's over the baby thing. And you know Tommy: when he digs his heels in, he's stubborn. Nothing can move him."

"Sounds like he needs time."

"I don't know, Sarah. I get the feeling he's really, truly done."

"He can't be *done*. What about Cass? She wants to be a mom."

"I know. Cass is struggling. It wasn't a great birthday."

"Speaking of birthdays . . . you've got one coming up."

Kit walked toward the kitchen, flicking on lights as she went. "It's not one I feel like celebrating."

"Forty is not bad anymore."

"Because you're heading there yourself?"

Sarah laughed. "I still have six years."

"Lucky you," Kit sassed, opening the refrigerator in the kitchen. Yogurt, yogurt, yogurt. Carrots, wilted lettuce, an old container of hummus. Nothing very appetizing. She closed the refrigerator door. "How are the kids? Boone? Is he looking forward to spring training?"

"You can't change the subject."

"I just did." Kit opened a cupboard, scanned the crackers, popcorn, and cereal boxes before grabbing the box of Special K with strawberries. She had no milk, so she'd eat it dry. "And I'm hoping to get tickets for their first season appearance in the Bay Area. Do you know when that is?"

"I'll send you his schedule, but you haven't distracted me. We're going to do something special for your birthday, Kit."

Kit returned to the living room with the box of cereal, plunked down on the couch, and turned on the TV, muting the sound. "This isn't the year to celebrate, Sarah. Not with Mom . . ." She couldn't finish the thought. Didn't even try.

"But it's Mom's idea to celebrate your birthday, Kit. It's what Mom wants," Sarah said sternly.

And if that was the case, Kit was defeated.

"If it makes you feel any better, Kit," Sarah added, softening her voice, "it's not just for you. It's for you and Brianna. Mom wants to celebrate that her twins are turning forty—"

"Brianna will hate the fuss, too."

"—by going on a cruise."

"A *cruise*?"

"Mom's never been on one and thinks this is the perfect way to celebrate with the entire family."

"You're not serious."

"I am."

"Sarah!"

"It's what she wants, and she's really excited about the idea, and she asked me last week to handle the logistics. She was going to announce it Sunday night at her house, but then didn't think the timing was right with Cass so upset." Sarah paused, and Kit could hear her rustling through a stack of paper. "Mom suggested mid-February as a possible date. She thought you had a few days off next month around Presidents' Day weekend and asked me to look into different options. There's a seven-day cruise out of L.A. on the eighteenth that goes to the Mexican Riviera. And before you say it's too expensive, it's Mom and Dad's treat. I'm to book five cabins. You'd share with Bree, of course."

Of course, Kit thought, because not only was Bree her fraternal twin, but Bree was also the only other single in the family. "Does everyone know?"

"I sent an e-mail to the others a couple of hours ago and heard back from Meg and Cass, but haven't heard from Bree yet."

Kit wasn't surprised, finding it impossible to picture her bohemian, rebel twin, who worked as a tropical disease nurse in Africa, on a cruise ship. But if the cruise was for their mom, it'd be very hard, if not impossible, for Brianna to say no. "Cruises aren't exactly Bree's thing."

"Not exactly my thing right now either," Sarah confessed, "as the timing is terrible for us, especially Boone, who is training hard right now, but as it is for Mom, we can all suck it up for seven days."

"You're right."

"So get a substitute teacher lined up for February eighteenth to twenty-fifth. Boone's trying to get permission to arrive at spring training a day late. He was supposed to report to Port Charlotte on the twenty-fourth, but hopefully Joe Maddon will allow him to join us. It's probably the last time we'll all be together."

For a moment Kit couldn't speak. "I'm holding out for Easter. I think Mom can make it until then."

"That's three months from now."

"I know. But Mom's hanging in there—"

"You're not being realistic."

"Maybe you could be a little more optimistic!"

"And what? Not be prepared for the call that you've moved her into hospice care? That I need to jump on a plane and come say good-bye?"

"Why are you even talking like that?"

"Because it's real."

"I *know* it's real. I spend every weekend at the house with Mom. I can tell she's weaker. Frailer. But I'm not going to let her go without a fight—"

"You make it sound like I'm pushing her into the grave!"

"Well, aren't you?"

"No! I'm planning a damn cruise, Kit!"

"You don't need a cruise to see her, Sarah. Just get on a plane and come out here. Come see Mom. Sit with her. Spend a weekend with her, like I do."

"You don't think I want to? You don't think I look at my calendar all the time, trying to figure out which days I could go, how many days I could be gone, who I could get to stay with the kids so I could see her?"

"Never mind. Let's just forget this—"

"She's my rock, Kit. Mom has been everything for me." Sarah drew a short, sharp breath. "When things get crazy with Boone, I call her. When I need her, she comes. When I need someone to talk to, Mom's there. Mom is a saint—" She broke off, and Kit could hear her breathe over the line, inhaling hard, exhaling just as hard. It was like a fish pulled out of water. She was gasping for air. Fighting to breathe.

"She *is* a saint," Kit said softly, gently, surprised but not shocked that things had escalated so quickly. Losing Mom was absolutely devastating, and Sarah was the baby. Sarah had been Mom's little girl the longest. But then, from the time she was born, she'd been everyone's favorite. Sarah was that lucky girl who'd been born beautiful and grew up into an even more stunning woman. Tall, slim, golden, she didn't favor her sisters. No red or auburn hair for her. No freckles. No pale skin that wouldn't tan. Sarah was decadent. She shimmered through life, all amber, honey, and bronze. Tommy had once teased her that she was so pretty she must have had a different father, and Dad had rolled his eyes, but Sarah had cried.

"How can she leave us?" Sarah whispered, her voice pitched low. "I need her, Kit. I need her more now than ever and yet Boone won't let me talk about it. The kids won't let me talk about it. Somebody has to let me talk about it. Somebody—"

"You can talk to me," Kit said, knowing she'd once been a good listener, and the family peacemaker. But lately, she wasn't as patient, or as tolerant, as she used to be. Lately, she didn't enjoy endless discussions and pointless conversation. How could she, when they would all soon lose Mom? "And you should talk about Mom. There's no shame in that, Sarah."

"Thank you." She hiccuped on the other end of the line. "And I'm sorry about jumping on you."

"It's okay."

"No, it's not. I'm just so mad. And sad. I want to be there in California. I want to be close to her, like you and Meg are. Instead I'm stuck here in Florida, with another season of baseball about to start. I hate it. I'm so over baseball running our lives, ruling our lives. And now I'm planning a cruise Mom might not even be able to go on." Sarah's voice was hoarse. "Earlier today the travel agent asked if we wanted travel insurance for the five cabins in case something came up and an emergency interrupted our trip, and I just lost it. Had to hang up. Because we do need the insurance, but let's face it, all the insurance in the world won't matter if she's gone."

K it was back in her classroom early the next morning even though it seemed like she'd only just left. Sometimes she felt as if she lived at Memorial High School, and the teacher staff room was her sanctuary.

She was in the staff room now with Polly and Fiona during the brief morning break between third and fourth periods. It was their daily ritual. Five minutes to rush in to the staff room, exchange quick greetings while Kit refilled her coffee cup and Polly zapped her green tea and Fiona turned on the kettle for yet another cup of Irish Breakfast tea.

"I have a terrible headache," Polly said, opening the microwave to retrieve her steaming cup.

"Need Advil?" Kit offered.

Polly shook her head. "Already took some a half hour ago. Just need them to kick in."

Kit glanced at Fiona, who was unusually quiet this morning. "You okay?"

"Fine."

But Fiona didn't sound fine. She looked blue. "How did it go last night when you got home?" Kit asked her.

"Not so good," Fiona answered, turning off the white kettle and filling her cup with boiling water. "Chase was distant. Barely said two words to me. I think he was upset that I'd stayed out so long."

"But you were home by six-thirty—"

"I know. But I should have called him, warned him. He thought I was just out pouting."

Kit tried not to take sides, but she'd had it with Chase right now. "I think he's being a little hard on you."

"A little?" Polly snorted and then winced. "God, that hurt. But honestly, Fiona, if he doesn't want you avoiding going home, then he might want to make it more pleasant for you *at* home."

The warning bell rang, and as Kit headed back to her classroom, keys jingling in her hand, it crossed her mind yet again that maybe she was lucky. Lucky to be single. Lucky to have no one at home waiting for her, angry with her, demanding an accounting of where she'd been and who she'd been with. Because at forty, she didn't feel like answering to anyone anymore. She was an adult. Mature. Responsible. She enjoyed having freedom. Enjoyed her autonomy.

It was a good thing she'd closed her account at Love.com because she didn't need a man in her life right now. She wasn't all that interested in being a wife.

Perhaps her little house didn't need men's shirts and shoes filling its closets. Maybe what her house needed was a nursery.

Maybe all she wanted was to be a mom.

Thursday night Kit was at home sitting on her couch researching adoption on her laptop instead of grading papers that needed to be graded. If she didn't tackle the essays now, she'd be doing them over the weekend in Capitola. Unfortunately, she didn't feel like grading papers tonight. She was curious about how adoption would work for a single woman and so far she wasn't particularly encouraged. Many organizations wouldn't even look at her application if she filed as a single woman. Others might if she'd be willing to adopt an older child, or a toddler with special needs.

Kit didn't want to adopt an older child. Or one with special needs. She'd waited a long time to be a mom and she wanted an infant. A baby of her own.

She was glad when her phone rang, diverting her attention. She didn't recognize the caller. It was an out-of-state number. "Hello?"

"Kit?" It was a male voice, and slightly familiar.

"Yes?" she said, closing her computer and placing it on the coffee table.

"Michael Dempsey. We met at Z's in Alameda Monday night." He paused. "I'm a colleague of Jon's. You were with your friends."

Kit knew exactly who he was but was so stunned he'd gotten her cell number that it took her a second to speak. Being a teacher, she had an unlisted number. How did he track it down? "Yes, hi," she said finally. "How are you?"

"Good. And you?"

"Fine." She heard the reserve in her voice and wondered if he heard it, too. "Great," she added, struggling to think of something to say. "How did you track me down?"

"I have my mysterious ways." He laughed. "Especially when it comes to beautiful women."

The compliment struck her as slightly cheesy and she flashed to Sebastian Severs. But there the similarity ended. Sebastian was of medium height and medium weight and had slightly thinning hair. Michael Dempsey was tall and handsome, with blue eyes and a hint of a Texas drawl. Sebastian made her skin crawl. If she were honest, Michael's smile made her pulse race a little. "You do remember I'm the redhead . . . the one with freckles on my nose."

"Just a couple of freckles. And I love redheads."

Kit's mouth dried. Wow. Not as cheesy this time, just brazen. He was certainly putting himself out there.

"Nothing to say?" he teased her.

She glanced at the TV screen, watched Steven Tyler's eyes close as he got lost in a song. "Um, no."

Michael laughed, pleased. "Good." She could feel his smile across the line. "And I was calling, Kit, because I hoped you were free Saturday night," he continued. "I'd love to take you to dinner. As you know, I'm still new here, don't yet know my way around, but I've looked up a few places, and thought maybe you might even have a suggestion.

He'd caught her completely off guard. She'd pretty much written off men in December after that horrific date and she wasn't feeling the need to begin dating now. Hot men like Michael

Dempsey didn't call out of the blue and ask her out for dinner. "I'm heading out of town this weekend," she said, grateful she had a real excuse. She wasn't good at rejecting men. "Polly and I are going to Capitola for a few days."

"Capitola? Where's that?"

"On the coast. Just a few miles south of Santa Cruz."

"I've never been there."

"It's beautiful. My family has a beach house there. It's been in the family for three generations now."

"Sounds fun. Can I tag along?"

Something in his tone made her flush. "You'd hate it. We give ourselves manicures and pedicures and watch sappy old movies."

"Not sure about the sappy movies, but I can give a good pedicure."

It created an uncomfortable picture in her head, Michael bent over a woman's foot, painting toenails. "Seriously?"

"I had a girlfriend that injured her hand and so I'd paint her nails for her. Made her feel better while she healed."

"That's amazing. My ex-boyfriend would rather have cut off his arm than do that."

"Guys get hung up on gender and job descriptions."

She didn't want to like him, but he was intriguing. "They can, can't they?"

"So when do you come back?"

"Monday night."

"Monday?"

"It's a three-day weekend. Martin Luther King holiday."

"That's right. So what about the following Saturday? Or is that already booked, too?"

Kit hesitated. She didn't know him, wasn't entirely comfortable with him, had little interest in dating him, or anyone. And yet, what if he was a good guy? What if he was the right guy? Adoption agencies didn't love single woman, much less women in their forties. Was she really in a position to shut him down? "I think I'm free."

"You think?" he repeated.

She heard the slightly belligerent note in his voice and wondered if she'd heard him wrong. "Let me check my calendar." She checked the iCalendar app on her phone, and as she expected, her schedule was wide open for the following weekend. "I am open," she said, wondering why she couldn't, wouldn't, just tell him no. She'd gotten off Love.com for a reason. She'd gotten burned, and burned out, dating. She didn't have to go to dinner with him just because he asked. But Kit had never found it easy to say no. From birth she'd been the soft one. The one determined to please. "I'm free."

"Great. Will you save Saturday night for me?"

"I'd love to," she said.

"Great. I'm looking forward to Saturday."

"Me, too," she fibbed, and hated herself the next second for being not just a liar, but a pushover.

"Have fun this weekend," he said.

"I will."

"But not too much fun."

She laughed. He laughed with her. They hung up.

Kit lay back on the couch and stared up at the ceiling, filled with self-loathing.

This was the reason she'd stopped dating.

This was why she'd pulled her profile from Love.com.

And this was exactly why that guy in December took advantage of her. Because she let him.

Just like she let Richard take advantage of her for ten miserable years.

Kit chewed on the inside of her lip. Thank God Brianna wasn't here. Brianna would have a fit. Brianna never got taken advantage of because Brianna was the one who did the exploiting.

You've got to learn to set boundaries, Kit told herself. *Have to learn how to tell people no. Back off. Leave me alone.*

But she couldn't. She didn't know why. For whatever reason, she felt as if she owed everyone something.

Horrible, Kit thought, and rather alarming. Especially as she was an adult now. A forty-year-old woman.

Four

Friday noon and Kit was counting the minutes until freedom. There were 184 of them. Essentially three hours. Three hours until school was over and she'd be on the road to Capitola with Polly.

Three hours until Kit could spend three blissful days at the Brennan family beach house in Capitola. Three days without bells, taking attendance, collecting assignments, or yard duty. Three days to sleep in, stay up late, and curl up with a good book. A book she wasn't required to teach.

Heaven, she sang to herself, stabbing yet another leaf of her wilted Caesar salad with her plastic fork. But first she had to survive her lunch hour, which had never been an hour at Memorial High but forty-two minutes in which she usually graded papers while choking down a soggy salad or sandwich. Today lunch was more frustrating than usual because Bob Osborne, the computer science teacher, had decided to join the half-dozen teachers sitting at the wooden lunch table in the staff room rather than at his desk.

Kit would have preferred it if he had stayed at his desk.

Bob was a noisy eater and she was trying to ignore the whistling, wet sound he made as he ate his sack lunch at the far end of the table, but it was impossible. He was loud. Worse, he ate with his mouth open.

The quintessential Catholic school computer science nerd, Bob was ruddy-faced, balding, and heavyset, particularly in the hip area, which was never a good look on men, but he was a bachelor and didn't know better. Kit had come to view him as an original. She'd come to find his mustard shirts, his claret ties, his baffling mix of plaids and prints charming. She told Polly he was eccentric. Encouraged Fiona to see the best in him. But the chewing sound he was making right now . . . that wasn't charming. But Kit couldn't, wouldn't, say anything to him. It would be far too rude.

It wasn't easy, but she forced her attention back to the essay before her. Unfortunately, it was an incoherent essay, with no thesis or conclusion and endless padding of random thoughts to reach the required word length. Depressed by the student's lack of effort, Kit made notes throughout, marked it with a D, and added a "see me" note on the bottom near the footer, before moving on to the next one.

The faculty room door opened with a bang and Polly entered the staff room at a run.

"I hate cafeteria duty," Polly gasped, peeling the plastic off her Cup Noodles and then the paper top, so she could fill the foam container with water. With a glance at the clock on the wall, she thrust the cup into the microwave and hit buttons. "I hate the noise. The smell. The greasy food. It honestly makes me want to hurl."

Polly was a reformed vegan who periodically toyed with a macrobiotic diet when she wasn't doing a juice fast. Fried anything offended her organic sensibilities. But her healthy lifestyle didn't stop her from enjoying a good drink, or three.

Kit grinned up at Polly, delighted by her appearance. "You can swap cafeteria duty for parking lot duty. Spend forty-five minutes every day after school in the parking lot waiting for the little darlings to be picked up and you won't mind the smell of fried food quite so much."

"At least you get fresh air," Polly answered darkly, getting a spoon from the drawer. "The cafeteria smells like eau de throw-up."

"I wouldn't be surprised," Shelley Jones, the PE teacher, volunteered from the far side of the table. "We do have a number of students who are bulimic."

"Or, you could be pregnant," Bob said, looking up from his tuna fish sandwich on white bread. Bob ate tuna fish Mondays, Wednesdays, and Fridays and egg salad on Tuesdays and Thursdays.

Polly rolled her eyes as she retrieved her shrimp-flavored Cup Noodles from the microwave. "I'm single, Robert, and teaching at a Catholic high school."

"It happens," he answered, delicately blotting his mouth with a paper napkin.

Polly tipped her head, giving him a hard look. "I know it happens, but I'm not pregnant. It's just the food we serve here *sucks*. I don't know why we can't offer more fresh fruits and vegetables and less secret meat."

Kit ducked her head and took another bite of her salad.

"I've always loathed Taco Tuesdays," Polly added, grabbing a spoon from the drawer, "because the taco meat smells like cat food, but today's Meat Loaf Medley was even worse. I swear to God, today they were serving cat meat."

"They eat cat in China," Shelley volunteered cheerfully, happy to have something to discuss. Lunch had been awfully quiet today. "It's supposed to be a delicacy."

Polly looked at her. "I heard that."

Bob cleared his throat. "I don't know what you're talking about. I've had the meat loaf in the past, and I found it quite tasty."

Polly's eyebrows arched. "Did it taste like cat?"

Bob adjusted his glasses. "I wouldn't know what cat tasted like."

"How about horse?"

"Of course I don't eat horse."

"Do you think you'd know if you did?" Polly retorted sweetly, too sweetly, carrying her steaming cup to the table and taking a seat opposite Kit's. She had the coiled tension of a cat before it pounced.

Kit exchanged glances with Shelley, aware that Polly would soon annihilate Bob if he didn't back off. But Bob didn't understand women, and he never backed off. He was too besotted with Polly to do anything but engage.

Everyone on the staff knew that forty-something-year-old Bob had a thing for Polly. He'd harbored the crush for years. The staff also knew that beautiful, brainy, irreverent Polly always had some rich, successful, impossibly good-looking boyfriend, which put her firmly out of Bob's reach. But Bob couldn't let the dream of Polly go, and like the awkward teenage boy he must once have been, he forced her to acknowledge him by inserting himself into all her conversations.

All the time.

"Heard the girls' basketball team has a big tournament this weekend," Kit said to Shelley, trying to change the subject, hoping she could distract Polly from toying with Bob. He wasn't a mouse, she'd told Polly more than once. There was no reason to torment him.

"Yeah, in Sacramento," Shelley agreed. "We're leaving right after school. Five games tomorrow. Three more Sunday if we're in the winning bracket. Four if we're in the losing bracket. Kids are going to be exhausted."

Kit had taught with Shelley, a Walla Walla native, and a former softball all-star at the University of Washington, for fifteen years now and was one of Kit's favorite faculty members. They rarely saw each other outside of school, but every now and then they'd all go out for drinks and Kit enjoyed Shelley's mellow personality. Shelley was cool, all-around company. "I wish I could attend some of the games, but I'll be in Capitola. Too bad you're not closer. Like San Jose. I could have driven over for some games there."

Polly allowed herself to be diverted. "Less than three hours now until we go. Thank you, Jesus. So ready for a break. I can't focus today. I'm sleepy, and restless, and keep staring at the clock."

"Oh, the joys of being a teacher," Bob sonorously intoned, closing the lid on the little plastic container he brought his sandwich in. "But as you know, one doesn't teach for the money. It's a calling." He launched himself with difficulty onto his feet. "Like the priesthood. Not everyone can do it."

"This is madness," Polly muttered, dropping her face to just inches above her steaming cup. "I should have gone back to my room."

"It's okay," Kit whispered back. "He's on his way out."

"Thank God. I want to punch him."

But then Bob dropped back into his chair, apparently having second thoughts about leaving. "We have to rise to the challenge," he said. "This isn't just a job, it's a mission, a—"

"Calling," Polly finished impatiently. "Like the priesthood. Got it. And I don't want to be rude but I really don't want to do this right now, Bob."

"Do what?"

"This." Polly waved her hand in large circles. "The lecture. Or inspirational address or whatever you call it. I'm tired. Hungry. And dying to have a little girl talk with Kit, so . . ."

His chest puffed out. His ruddy cheeks turned crimson. "Am I intruding?"

"No, of course not." Polly smiled and her expression turned feline. "Not at all. I just wanted to warn you that the topic was going to get personal. I have terrible cramps because it's that time of the month and I'm not sure everything's all right down there with my plumbing—"

"Oh, no." Bob shot to his feet, bumping the table. "If you'll excuse me, I need to have a look at a malfunctioning printer in the computer science lab."

Kit suppressed her laughter until the door banged shut behind Bob. "Polly, that was mean. Plumbing problems down there . . . ?"

Polly grinned, unapologetic. "It worked, though." She fished a noodle out of her cup, managed to get it in her mouth before snapping her fingers. "Almost forgot. Sounds like we might have a new student soon. Heard Vera on the phone," she said, referring to the school secretary. "Our classes are already so full. Can't believe we'd take another midyear."

"We can't. One of my sophomore comp classes has thirty-eight students in it. Thirty-eight. Way too many."

Polly shrugged. "Vera didn't discourage the mother. She told her where to buy uniforms and what the girl would need in terms of a supply list."

"So it's a girl?"

"Mm."

"What grade?" Shelley asked, sitting back in her chair, arms folded across her chest.

"Not sure. I got the feeling she's a freshman or sophomore, as there was no mention of graduation requirements or testing dates."

Kit wasn't happy about the news. Her freshman and sophomore classes were her biggest. "Let's be honest. There's no way I can effectively teach writing, and properly grade all the necessary essays, with thirty-five-plus kids per class. There aren't enough hours in the day."

"That's why I teach PE," Shelley said, balling up her paper lunch bag and rising. "I just make them run."

Fiona entered the lunchroom as Shelley left and took Shelley's empty chair at the table. Her pale face looked blotchy and her eyes were pink. "What did I miss?" she asked huskily, taking a seat at the table and opening a plastic baggie filled with slender apple slices

"What happened?" Kit asked.

Fiona selected an apple slice and toyed with it. "Nothing," she answered, breaking the apple into two pieces.

Polly leaned forward, concerned. "Did Sister Marguerite complain to Sister Elena about your messy room again?"

Fiona struggled to smile but couldn't. "Wish it was that. But it's Chase. He sent me a text that we've got to postpone Carmel so he can take the kids to Tahoe this weekend to ski."

"What?" Polly cried.

Fiona shrugged. "Apparently Julie got invited to go to Cabo with some girlfriends and Chase wants to show her he's a good guy, so he told her we'd take the kids and she could take her trip." Fiona flung the apples down, furious. "It didn't even cross his mind to call me and see what I'd like. Why didn't he stay married to Julie? She's more important to him than I am!"

The five-minute warning bell rang shrilly. They all ignored it.

"So what are you going to do?" Kit asked.

Fiona shrugged again. "Go to Carmel."

Kit wasn't sure this was the best plan. "Without him?"

"Why not?" Fiona said hotly. "The hotel's already booked and paid for. I've always wanted to go there—"

"Because you know Chase won't take it well," Kit interrupted. "It'd be a slap in his face."

Fiona's eyes flashed. "And canceling our weekend together so his ex-wife can go to Cabo isn't?"

She'd made a good point, and after a moment they wordlessly rose and headed back to their classrooms.

The light was fading as they reached Highway 17, the twenty-six-mile-long highway that wound through the Santa Cruz Mountains, and gone by the time they reached the exit for Capitola off Highway 1.

The Brennans' narrow two-story beach cottage, built in 1903, was one of six identical houses facing the beach on Esplanade and known to locals as the Six Sisters. The clapboard cottage had been in the family since the late 1930s, and growing up, Kit and her sisters and brother had spent virtually every summer and holiday there. As Polly parked on the street adjacent to Historic Lawn Way, Kit felt a little thrill of pleasure. She was back. Home.

Kit was upstairs in the girls' bunk room, changing out of her teacher clothes into something more relaxed when her phone rang. "Hey, Dad," she said, answering her cell and hitting the speaker button so she could tug up her favorite old Levi's jeans and button the fly. "What's up?"

"Just checking to make sure you girls got in safely," he said.

"We arrived a few minutes ago." Kit glanced at herself in the dresser mirror and dragged a hand through her hair. "And we're just about to head out for dinner. We're starving."

"Where are you going?"

"Probably Margaritaville."

"That's a meat market. Go to that wine bar place. Nicer for you girls."

Kit rolled her eyes. He'd never liked Margaritaville since he caught Sarah making out in the hallway with a guy she'd just met. Sarah wasn't a kid, she'd been twenty-one, and drop-dead gorgeous, but Dad had still hauled her back to the cottage and sent her up to the girls' room. Kit and her sisters still giggled about it, although Sarah had been mortified at the time. "We're hungry, Dad, and we want to eat unhealthy things like nachos and quesadillas."

"Be careful."

"Dad, I'm always careful. I'm a middle child, remember? Give Mom my love. I'll call you on Sunday after Mass."

Polly had stepped from the bathroom to catch the last of the conversation. "Your dad is the sweetest. I love how he still worries about you."

Kit grabbed her coat and purse. "He forgets we're all grown up."

Polly grinned as she wrapped a black scarf around her neck and tugged on her coat. "I don't think he's forgotten. I just don't think it matters to him."

K it and Polly were enjoying their second round of margaritas at Margaritaville when Polly's phone rang. Polly checked the number. "It's Fiona," she said, flashing the phone at Kit before taking the call. "Did you make it to Carmel okay?"

Polly frowned, listening to Fiona for a few moments, before covering the phone to speak to Kit. "Fiona's miserable in Carmel. Doesn't want to be there by herself. Can she come join us here?"

"Yes!" Kit put down her drink, nodded vigorously. "Does she need us to go get her?"

"She's got her car."

"Tell her to come."

"How long will it take her?"

"Depends on traffic. If the roads are good, she could be here in forty-five minutes to an hour."

Polly got back on the phone and was trying to give Fiona directions, but Fiona was getting so confused it exasperated Polly. She shoved the phone at Kit. "You tell her," she said. "She's not listening to me."

On the phone, Kit tried to explain that it was simple getting to Capitola, she'd just take Highway 1 north all the way from Carmel, but Fiona kept interrupting to talk about how beautiful and romantic the hotel was and how angry she was that Chase wasn't there to enjoy it with her.

Kit covered the phone and leaned toward Polly. "She's buzzed!"

"I think she's been drinking for a while."

"Then she can't drive tonight."

"Tell her to sleep it off and come up in the morning."

Fiona didn't like the idea but eventually Kit managed to convince her that she wasn't missing anything in Capitola since she and Polly were heading to bed soon, and that Fiona should just go to bed, too, so that she could wake up early and be ready to drive up in the morning.

"That was good," Polly said when Kit finally hung up and handed the phone back. "You were really patient and calm. How do you do that?"

"I've had a lot of practice. There's always drama in my family."

"Like last summer when Meg took a walk on the dark side?"

Kit shifted uneasily. Meg's affair had been so painful, and even though Meg and Polly knew each other, Kit couldn't discuss the details with Polly. It had been a heartbreaking summer and the only good news was that it was over and Jack and Meg were still together. "Mm."

"Do you think she ever thinks about Chad?"

Kit did wonder if Meg was completely over Chad, but there was no way she'd ask her. If Meg brought it up, fine, but if she didn't, Kit wasn't about to poke or probe what might still be a tender wound. "I think it was just sex," she said casually, taking a sip of her margarita.

Polly's eyebrow arched. "As if sex is nothing."

"Sometimes it is nothing."

"And sometimes it's everything."

"I disagree."

"Kit, you can't have a great relationship without good sex."

Kit suddenly thought of her years with Richard. Richard had never been particularly sensual, but he got the job done. He was an engineer, for Pete's sake. He was excellent with the mechanics, knew how to make her orgasm. He'd also reminded her of that more than once when she expressed dissatisfaction with their relationship. *At least you have nothing to complain about in the bedroom,* he'd say, smirking and puffing out his chest.

Kit didn't argue the point with him. What could she say? That she'd rather he marry her than make her come? That an orgasm didn't necessarily make one feel loved? That frequent sex didn't answer her need to have a family . . . to be a mom?

"Maybe," Kit said, taking another quick sip of her cocktail. "But sex is strange. I think it's weird."

"Weird?"

"Don't you think so? I do. And maybe it's just me, but when it's right, it's so right, and yet when it's wrong . . ." Her voice drifted off. She wrinkled her nose. "It's just yuck. Horrid."

"I agree with you. Bad sex . . . ugh. There's nothing worse." Polly fell silent, mulling the thought over. "So, Meg and Jack are good now? They've worked everything out?"

"I think so," Kit answered, knowing only that the two of them put on a united front for the family. Kit wasn't sure what was really happening at home but hoped her sister and brother-in-law were doing well. She liked Jack. He was an architect and historian and, best of all, a book person like her. "I hope so. They seem okay now."

"I guess they'd have to do the unified front for the kids."

Kit was protective of all her sisters, but of Meg in particular.

Meg had a lot of responsibility growing up, probably too much, while Kit acknowledged now that she herself had probably had too little. "That's a good thing, though, because they're awesome kids, and they love their parents. They want them together.

"Do you still see the kids a lot?"

"Not as much as I did over the summer, but I try to get up to Santa Rosa at least once a month. They're only an hour or so north of me, so it's not a long drive, the problem is finding the time. It's harder now that I'm spending every other weekend with Mom, but I expect when baseball starts up again, I'll drive up more often. I love going to JJ's games. He's good. He reminds me a lot of my brother, Tommy, at that age."

"Tommy played baseball, too?"

"All the way through college. Got drafted by the Brewers but after a couple seasons in minor-league ball, gave it up, got a 'real job.'"

"As a firefighter," Polly said knowingly.

"The family business," Kit agreed, knowing that her father could trace his genealogy straight back to County Clare, when his great-great-great-grandfather Seamus Brennan headed to America to find his fortune in the gold and silver rushes of California and Nevada. Seamus panned for gold and worked the mines for six dirty, dusty, backbreaking years before accepting that he wasn't going to strike it rich, and ended up in the beautiful new city of San Francisco, where he worked in a hotel and part-time as a volunteer fireman. Within five years the volunteer job turned into a permanent job and every generation of Brennans since had at least one son follow in Seamus's footsteps. "Six generations of San Francisco firefighters, and before that, God knows what they were doing in Ireland."

"Starving?"

"Hopefully not. Although I don't really know a lot about the Brennans in Ireland. We knew my great-great-great-great-grandfather emigrated from County Clare, but that's about it. Meg was going to do some genealogy research but I don't know how far she got, or if she discovered anything relevant."

Polly gave her margarita glass a swirl, mixing the slush. "You're lucky to know that much. I'm a mutt. A little bit of everything and not enough of anything—"

"Except beautiful," Kit reminded her.

"Yeah, whatever." Polly swirled her cocktail. "Did you like having a dad who was a firefighter?"

"I did. My friends always had a crush on my dad—"

"He is hot."

"He's sixty-five."

"And still hot."

"Hands off. My mom's crazy about him," Kit teased, but as soon as the words left her mouth she pictured her mom, frail and fragile, little more than skin and bones, and she didn't like it, didn't want to think of her that way.

"And now he's finally retired."

"After forty years."

"That's a serious accomplishment."

"Couldn't happen now. Younger guys have to retire earlier. Dad was grandfathered in on the old charter. He could have worked until seventy, if he could have passed his physical, and that was never a problem for him. At sixty-three, he was still stronger and faster than most of the probies last year."

"Probies?"

"Rookies."

"You are proud of him."

"I loved it when he worked. I always liked calling the firehouse and asking for Firefighter Brennan, and then they'd say, which one? Tom, Pat, or Joe? Because my dad worked in the same house with his brothers. Talk about stories. They had so much fun working together. It was a guys' world."

"Would you want one of your sons or daughters to follow in his footsteps?"

Kit paused to think. "If he or she could work with someone like my dad, or Uncle Pat or Uncle Joe, definitely. Because my dad and his brothers were physically strong. Incredibly strong. But even more important, they were mentally tough. And that's the part you can't teach someone."

Five

Kit had a hard time sleeping her first night back in Capitola. She wasn't sure if it was the two and a half margaritas she'd drunk at Margaritaville, or talking about her father retiring, or her mother's cancer, but she woke repeatedly in the night, anxious and uneasy, and each time the same question returned: what would she do when Mom was gone?

She'd have so much more free time. She'd need to fill that time. Adopting a child would be a good thing.

Would the rest of the family agree?

What would Tommy and Cass think? Would Cass mind?

Of course she'd mind. Cass wanted to be a mom, too.

At seven, Kit gave up trying to sleep and headed down the house's steep staircase to the small kitchen to make coffee.

Plopping down on the sole kitchen stool, she waited for the coffee to brew. Her head hurt and the worried, uneasy feeling lingered.

She shouldn't have had the rest of the second margarita, much less the first half of the third. She wasn't much of a drinker and should have known her limits, but after talking about Meg and Jack, then Mom and Dad, she had gotten a little too serious, and Polly had made it her personal mission to make her laugh. And she had. So Kit had drunk what was placed in front of her and was regretting it this morning.

Liquor never solved anything and sometimes just made everything worse.

Coffee in hand, she grabbed her long fuzzy sweater the color of Irish oats from the hook by the front door and stepped outside to the cottage's front porch. The morning was cool and misty and she pulled her sweater closer as she leaned on the white-painted railing and stared off across the street to the beach, where the dark green surf crashed on pale, damp sand.

Not all the beach cottages on Esplanade had an amazing view of the bay, but theirs did, and this morning the fog clung to the craggy bluffs and evergreens. Capitola lay ten miles south of Santa Cruz, and in the summer tourists and beach bunnies swarmed the town, but as it was mid-January, the motels, streets, and stores were nearly deserted except for the odd coffeehouse and surf shop.

Some people hated the low gray soupy fog but Kit liked it. She'd always found it romantic. Mysterious. The fog made her think of Byron and Venice in winter and love. Foggy days made her want to curl up with a book. But then, she curled up with a book any chance she could. She loved books. Loved reading. Loved it so much she'd studied English literature at St. Mary's and then had gone on to teach it.

She'd imagined that as an English teacher she'd be sharing her passion for great literature—opening doors to the world, lighting a fire in young people's minds. She'd pictured her students with rapt expressions as she read aloud from *Hamlet* or recited her favorite William Butler Yeats poem, "An Irish Airman Foresees His Death." It was naive of her. She should have known better.

She didn't. Probably because she lived in her head more often than in the real world.

But seventeen years of teaching had set her straight. Most students preferred Facebook, online chats, texting—oh, and losing their virginity—to reading great literature.

Smiling ruefully, Kit smoothed a thick strand of auburn hair behind her ear and listened to the wind snap the flags flying across the street at the beach park. It was a rather wild morning. Gray, foggy, breezy, and the fog made her hair wild, turning loose waves into fat curls. Years ago she'd given up trying to straighten her hair at the beach. It didn't work. Inevitably it proved to be a waste of time.

A half hour later the cottage door opened and Polly joined Kit on the small wooden porch. "You got up early," Polly said.

"It felt like *The Princess and the Pea* last night. Couldn't get comfortable."

"I slept like a baby," Polly said, lifting her slim arms over her head, stretching the fleece sweatshirt she wore over her thin aqua-blue running shirt. She was dressed for a run, in nylon shorts and white-and-neon-yellow running shoes. "Feel great."

Kit made a face at her. "I hate you. You know that?"

"I do. That's why I'm here with you." Polly scooped her hair back into a ponytail and secured it with a rubber band. She glanced up at the sky as she put her foot on the railing to stretch her hamstring. "The fog will burn off, won't it? I'm craving some sun."

"It will. By ten or eleven, the sky will be blue." Kit momentarily wished for Polly's legs. As well as Polly's butt. And stomach. And face. No, not Polly's face. Kit liked her own face. But the body, she'd definitely swap. "Since you had a comfy bed, and slept like a baby, why are you up early?"

Polly switched legs and tugged on her toes to flex her hamstrings further. "I got a text from Jean-Marc . . . the guy we met last night."

"The French model?"

"He only models part-time. The rest of the time he's a sales-man in suiting at the men's Macy's in San Francisco."

Kit gurgled with laughter. Polly was not easily impressed. "And what did he want?"

"He was hoping I'd meet him for breakfast at Zelda's."

"Are you?"

"Maybe. I don't know. No, I don't think so. I'd rather just hang out with you."

"I thought you liked him."

"Oh, I did, I do, a little bit. I think. Or maybe it was the mar-garitas talking . . . hard to say. But I don't think he was exactly the brightest lightbulb, was he?"

"Last night I don't think that's what you were interested in."

Polly laughed and peeled off her sweatshirt before adjusting the mini iPod already attached to her sleek biceps. "Want to join me for a run?"

Kit glanced toward the tranquil beach, which seemed far more appealing than a vigorous run. "How far are you going?"

"Not far. Three. Maybe four miles."

Kit shuddered. She used to try to keep up with Polly, had even entered 5Ks with her last summer, but she had hated it, and she continued to run now only because it kept her butt from taking over the rest of her teacher's chair. "No, thank you. I think I'll just go for a walk around the village."

"I thought you wanted to start training for some 5Ks again."

"Changed my mind. So go. Get." Kit made a shooing motion, gesturing for Polly to scram. "Good-bye."

"You're sure?"

"Yes. You're exhausting me with all your stretching."

Polly laughed and wiggled her fingers before skipping down the front steps and taking off across the lawn.

Kit watched her for a moment, a smile playing at her lips. Polly

Powers was awesome. Truly the best friend she had outside of her sisters.

Grabbing her cup, Kit entered the house, left the empty mug in the kitchen, and headed upstairs to change, retrieve her camera, and head back out. She had always enjoyed photography but had gotten more serious about it this past fall after finding a living social deal for an Oakland Walking Tour class from Katrina Davis Photography. She loved the class so much she signed up for several more nature photography classes, and with each one became more adept at using her camera, loving how one could frame or change the world through a camera's lens.

With her camera slung around her neck, Kit walked along the misty beach, looking for that which was intriguing or unusual. For angles, textures, colors. Perspectives.

Sea foam bubbling on sand. The break of a wave. Weathered wood.

Founded back in the 1870s, Capitola was originally just a summer camp filled with makeshift tents. Later stables and a wooden stage had been added for dancing. Eventually the tents were replaced with cabins and the dance floor became a dance hall. For Bay Area residents, Capitola-by-the-Sea was a camp rather than a place, a spot where folks craving sun and sea could be close to nature and have some fun while they were at it. Once summer ended, camp closed until the following June.

Kit snapped away as she moved from the beach up onto Stockton toward Capitola Avenue and back down, making a loop, happier than she'd been all morning.

Whenever something caught her eye, she lifted her camera, focused, zoomed in or out, and snapped.

Pausing, she focused on the rusted curve of a blue bicycle fender, a red cotton dress on a mannequin in a storefront window, an older woman in a pink fuzzy sweater walking two little dogs wearing matching sweaters.

Coming to Capitola was always bittersweet. Familiar. Layered with memories. First swim in the ocean. First kiss. First break she'd attempted surfing. First time she'd had sex.

Kit cringed as she crossed the street and stepped onto the opposite curb. She didn't want to remember that one. So bad. Totally humiliating. He hadn't even liked her. Just wanted to do it to say he'd nailed one of the Brennan sisters.

And then brother Tommy heard the rumor and went after Joe Di Sosa and beat the hell out of him.

The Brennan sisters still got nailed but no one bragged about it afterward.

Crouching on the curb, Kit raised her camera to capture the burnt-orange bike parked in front of Bluewater Steakhouse, the big bike's huge ape hangers reflected in the restaurant's frosted glass window as fog swirled around the body and wheels.

Working swiftly, she snapped another half-dozen shots. First of the front tire, and then a close-up of the stark handlebars, and then another of the dark brown leather seat with its image of a sexy half-naked woman wrapped in the embrace of one scary snake.

She was still snapping the intricate leatherwork when a faded-denim-clad leg swung over the seat, hiding it.

Kit jerked her head up and lowered the camera just in time to get a glimpse of long black hair, bronze skin, dark eyes, and the slash of a high cheekbone before a black helmet came down, obscuring his face.

Impulsively she raised the camera, snapped another photo even as he turned his head and looked directly at her.

Gorgeous, she thought somewhere in the back of her brain. *Dangerous,* she thought in a more logical part. He looked like trouble. Tough. Hard. Physical.

Sexual.

And then he started his bike. It sputtered once, twice, before roaring to life, low, rough, loud.

God, her mother would hate the biker, the bike, the noise. Kit bit into her bottom lip even as the bike lurched forward and then did a quick spin, turning in the middle of the quiet street to come straight at her.

She stumbled backward, thinking the rider had lost control, but then he stopped the bike mere inches from her ankle and tugged off his helmet.

"You took a picture of me," he said, looking into her eyes, his voice nearly as deep as the engine's growl.

She opened her mouth and then shut it.

"Why?" he demanded.

Her brows tugged, and her shoulders twisted. "I liked your bike. Thought it'd make an interesting picture."

His dark eyes narrowed and his head tilted, glossy black hair sliding over prominent cheekbones. "You a cop?"

She nearly laughed. "No."

"What do you do, then?"

"I'm a teacher."

"And what do you teach?"

"High school English."

He sat back on his seat and placed the helmet between his thighs. "Then why are you taking pictures?"

"It's a hobby. Gives me something to do when I'm not grading papers."

He looked at her a long moment, expression shuttered and impossible to read. "How do I know you're really a teacher?"

"Why would I lie?"

"People do all the time."

"Well, not me. I'm a *Catholic* schoolteacher," she said, emphasizing *Catholic*. "I have to be moral. It's my job."

He seemed to fight a smile. "You took a vow of morality to teach English?"

She wondered about his background. He looked part Greek, or

perhaps it was Armenian or possibly Native American. He was very dark, and hard, and altogether too intimidating. "No. But what kind of example would I set if I went through life lying, stealing, and cheating?"

"I didn't know women like you still existed."

"The world is full of good women," she said crisply.

"I haven't met any."

"Then you're hanging around with the wrong crowd."

"You don't like me."

"I don't know you."

"But you're still forming opinions. Making judgments. You know you are."

Kit's cheeks grew hot. "I've met men like you back when they were just boys in my classroom," she said, trying to sound flippant but failing. "You go through life breaking hearts and causing trouble."

He smiled slowly, almost lazily, and the long dense lashes fringing his eyes lowered as he looked her up and down. "Left your wedding ring at home?"

"Not married."

"Divorced?"

"Never married."

"Too busy teaching the sacraments?"

"Too busy teaching hoodlums to read."

He smiled again, knowing she was referring to him. "Where do you teach?"

"Memorial High."

"The one in Oakland?"

She nodded, pulled a tendril of hair from her mouth, and pushed it behind her ear. "I've taught there for years."

"So you don't need the photos for anything."

"No."

"Can I see them?"

It wasn't a question, she thought. He expected her to hand over the camera. He was that confident, that controlled, that strong of a guy. "Are you going to delete them?"

"Depends."

She looked up into his eyes. He was serious. And dangerous. She avoided men like him. Knew that there was no room in her life for rebels. Or trouble. Silently she handed him her camera, which had turned off while they talked, and he turned it on without fumbling and then pressed the review button and clicked through the photos she'd taken.

The first one was a close-up of him on the bike, all long hair, intense dark eyes, and chiseled cheekbones. The second was a shot of his torso and denim-clad thighs against the orange of the bike. The third was the bike seat. The fourth, more bike, and then more bike. And more bike. And then a lone daffodil against a white picket fence and all the rest of the pictures she'd taken since leaving the cottage for her walk.

"You're good," he said flatly, no emotion in his voice and yet there was something hard enough, deep enough that made her look up at his face, that made her want to take her camera back and shoot him here, like this, up close.

Rough. Edgy. Callous. Her gaze fell to her camera in his hands. His hands were scarred. She could imagine him fighting.

"Can I have my camera back?" she asked quietly.

"What's your name?" he said, handing it to her.

"Kit."

The corner of his mouth lifted. "Short for Kit Kat bar?"

She almost laughed. Instead, she rolled her eyes. "*No.* Katherine."

"Katherine what?"

"Katherine Elizabeth."

"Good Catholic name."

"I come from a good Catholic family."

"What's your last name?"

"Brennan."

"Irish, of course. Which means your dad's a cop. Am I right?"

Her eyebrows arched. He wasn't far off. "Running from the law, are you?"

He shrugged. "Don't need trouble."

So he was like some of those tough kids she'd taught—boys who were too bright, too curious, too wild for their own good.

Boys who ended up lying and stealing and cheating.

Boys who ended up in jail or running from the law.

"What do you do?" she asked.

"This and that."

Which could mean gangs and drugs, or just that he was a drifter without anyone or anything to tie him down. "I was right. I *have* taught kids like you." From the corner of her eye she caught a flash of blue. It was Polly, and she was heading toward them, her long blond ponytail bouncing. "My mom's brothers are police officers. My dad's a fireman."

"I've spent time in jail."

Of course he had. She took an uneasy step away. "I better go."

"Smart girl." He turned the key in the ignition and his bike roared to life.

As Polly approached he set off, bike and man hurtling dangerously down the street. Polly turned her head and watched him shoot pass and then pulled the iPod's buds out of her ears. "Who was that?" she asked, looking at Kit.

Kit watched the bike disappear from view. "I don't know."

Six

B ack at the cottage, Polly headed upstairs to shower while Kit took a seat in one of the old rattan chairs in the living room, intent on recording grades from last Tuesday's vocab quiz into her laptop. Instead, her eye fell on her camera lying on the coffee table next to the stack of faded *National Geographic* magazines no one ever read.

Kit flashed to her walk, and her encounter with the motorcycle guy. The whole thing had been surreal. He certainly wasn't like the men she normally met. Wasn't building himself up, trying to make himself sound good. If anything, he'd done the opposite. Told her he was trouble. Said he was bad news.

Too bad more men didn't come with warnings.

Kit smiled, imagining warnings on men's profiles at Love.com.

Handsome, charming, passive-aggressive doctor.

Fun, sports-loving, narcissistic family man.

Successful, fit, explosive business executive.

Wouldn't happen. Most people buried their faults, denied their weaknesses. The biker had done the exact opposite. And it intrigued her. Not that she should be interested, or intrigued, by a guy like him. Kit had encountered her fair share of predators and weirdos in her time and she didn't need another weirdo shadowing her now.

But that didn't stop her from reaching for her camera and reviewing the photos she'd taken, examining each shot as objectively as possible, lingering on the shots of the orange bike, and then stopping on the two of the biker.

He was even better-looking in the photos than she'd remembered. Broad shoulders, big chest, neat hips, thick biceps beneath the cotton thermal shirt he wore under the leather vest. No, she definitely had never dated a guy like this. Nor been attracted to a guy like this. Now Brianna had. But then Brianna liked trouble and in high school she'd made it a point to only see guys Dad would detest. Kit had been the opposite. She'd only dated boys who were nice. Boys Dad approved of.

Her thumb stroked the LCD screen, touching the biker's big shoulders. Dad definitely wouldn't approve of this guy. Dad would say he was bad news.

Trouble.

She rolled the word *trouble* around on her tongue as she studied the biker's fierce expression, trying to understand who he was and what he did for a living and why something inside of her felt as if it was moving, humming.

Smart girl, he'd said when she told him she needed to go.

And damn him, but that had caught her imagination. Kit didn't just love books, she loved words, and she found herself replaying their brief conversation, repeating his words. They were charged. Dangerous. Like him.

So what did he do, this biker guy? This and that, he'd said, but what *was* this and that?

His bike was impressive, he didn't appear to have a lot of money, and she couldn't imagine him at a desk job. He had to be a mechanic or someone who had a trade, worked with his hands. And while his leather vest, combat boots, and ratty jeans made him look mean, tough, she liked his face.

In terms of shape and structure it was a good face. Handsome. Arresting. Broad brow. High prominent cheekbones. Strong jaw with a squared-off chin. Long, straight nose. A man's face. No boy left in it.

How old was he, then? Thirties? She covered the lower half of his face and was drawn to his dark intense eyes and the faint creases at the corners. She covered his eyes and studied his mouth. Faint lines there, too, bracketing his lips. Midthirties. Somewhere between thirty-two and thirty-seven. Definitely younger than her.

Kit removed her thumb and his enigmatic expression tugged at her imagination. Outlaw. Pirate. Rebel. And like most rebels, he wouldn't be stupid. He'd simply chosen to play by a different set of rules.

Like Brianna. Brianna had been a rebel even as a little girl.

Kit wondered what the biker had been like as a boy. She could see him as a one of those bright busy kids who had a hard time sitting still in elementary school, and he would have grown into one of those bright, sarcastic kids who sat in the back of middle school classrooms, angry, frustrated.

By the time these troubled kids got to her in high school, it was nearly impossible to reach them. They'd been ignored and bored for so many years that school was nothing more than a holding pen, with teachers as their jailors. These teenagers, who had once had such eager, hopeful, inquisitive minds, had come to loathe books and learning, and eventually they either got kicked out of school or chose to drop out because the system didn't work for them. Schools weren't designed to cater to individuals. It was about educating the masses . . . cramming the biggest amount of information into the largest group of people for the least amount of money.

With a shake of her head, aware that she was procrastinating, Kit turned off her camera and focused on getting the rest of the test scores inputted into her online grade book, hoping to be finished with schoolwork before Fiona arrived.

Twenty minutes later, she was finally nearing the end of the roster when a motorcycle with a deep, distinctive roar approached the house. She looked up from her computer and stared out the living room window to watch the big burnt-orange bike slowly cruise past.

He's come back.

Kit felt a quivery spike of fear followed by a rush of adrenaline as the bike turned around at San Jose Avenue and slowly cruised back to their house, a corner house hugging Lawn Way and Esplanade.

With the beach deserted, he had no problem finding a spot in front of the house and nosed into the curb. He turned off the engine and the morning grew still.

He took off his helmet, swung his leg over the seat, wiped his hands on the back of his jeans, and headed up the lawn toward the front porch.

Polly gave a shout from upstairs. "Looks like your Hell's Angel is back."

Kit's stomach leaped and fell. "I know." She wasn't sure if she should lock the door and hide, or open it and stand on the porch like a brave frontier woman facing an Indian war party.

Not that it was PC to think in those terms, of course.

Although when she was thirteen she loved the western historical romances in which a beautiful young white woman was kidnapped by a hostile Indian war party and forced to marry a handsome savage against her will and live happily ever after. But the lurid western romance had fallen out of favor decades ago and she'd grown up. Being kidnapped and held hostage by a man wasn't romance.

Kit opened the front door and stepped outside just as his boot hit the porch's bottom step.

"Hi," she said, voice slightly tremulous. She was nervous. This bad-boy, badass biker guy was on her doorstep and she didn't know what he wanted. "How did you find me?"

"Wasn't hard. I asked around. Apparently everyone knows the Brennan sisters."

She didn't know where to look, what to focus on—his black hair, his long nose, his unsmiling mouth. He had to have Native American blood because he was making her think of that whole *Twilight*-Jacob-werewolf craze her students were into a couple of years ago. And her Twi-hards would have loved him.

"My family's owned the house for years," she said, not knowing what to say. He wasn't helping things by standing so close to the door. His feet were planted wide on the porch and he took up space, sucking all the air and energy into him.

His dark gaze narrowed, swept the house, the porch. "I've been here, to this house, before."

"You have?"

"I sat there," he said, pointing to the right of the covered columned porch with its jumble of painted wicker furniture and antique rocking chairs.

Kit saw the old pieces through his eyes. Mom never replaced old furniture and so every couple of years Sarah or Meg would spray-paint the wicker and add fresh cushions, striving to give the porch the look of shabby chic rather than thrift-store leftovers.

"On that little couch," he added, nodding at the wicker love seat that could use fresh paint now, "but it was aqua not white."

The wicker set had been a darker aqua, almost teal, in the late eighties and early nineties. Aqua paint paired with peach floral cushions. Back then, a massive grapevine wreath with silk colored flowers and seashells had hung on the wall. It was supposed to look French Country. Kit nodded, masking her surprise. "It *was* aqua."

"Had lemonade." The corner of his firm mouth lifted. "Your friend or sister or whoever it was wanted me to spike it. But I didn't have any vodka on me."

So he'd met Bree. They'd probably partied together. Maybe even slept together. Kit tried not to feel judgmental. Brianna wasn't exactly promiscuous, but she'd certainly enjoyed sex. "Sounds like my sister. So how did you meet Bree?"

"Bree?"

"Brianna."

He shook his head. "That wasn't her name."

"You're sure?"

"Positive."

"Petite redhead . . . slim—"

"No." His forehead creased and a straight inky lock of hair fell forward. Impatiently he pushed it back, behind his ear. "She was dark blond, very tan, tall, great body. Killed it playing beach volleyball."

Kit's heart fell. *Sarah.* He hooked up with Sarah? Sarah liked to flirt, but she'd never been easy. "That's my younger sister. Sarah."

"Sarah. That's it." His frown cleared. "So did she become a lawyer?"

"No."

"But she did graduate from UCLA?"

"Yes." Kit hesitated, wanting to understand the nature of his relationship with Sarah, but not at all comfortable imagining him with her baby sister. "Did you two . . . date?"

"No. She was into my friend, and I was the wingman. Was

supposed to keep her girlfriend happy but I can't even tell you what she looked like."

"Who was your friend?"

"Charlie Altman."

Kit shook her head. She didn't know him.

"Charlie worked at that pizza place on the beach one summer," he said, shifting his weight, folding his arms across his chest, and Kit's attention went to his big chest before dropping to his lean hips.

It took her a second to realize she was staring at the bulge at his crotch. She flushed and jerked her head up. "Pizza My Heart," she said faintly, hoping he hadn't noticed.

"Yeah. I noticed it's still here in town."

She nodded, unwilling to think about anything but Pizza My Heart, a Capitola institution. When she was growing up, some of the most gorgeous guys on the face of the planet worked there, and, of course, they had every girl in Northern California eating out of their hands. Kit had no idea that Sarah had been one of them, but then Kit had gone off to college and Sarah had finished growing up without all her big sisters hovering around.

"So can I help you with something, Mr. . . . ." Her voice trailed off as she realized she didn't even know his name. "Mr. . . . ?"

His lips curved in a slow amused smile. "No mister. It's Jude. And I just wanted to talk to you. Haven't been back in a long time."

"Sarah's married now," Kit said flatly. "A mom of two."

"Not interested in Sarah. Wanted to talk to you."

"Why?"

He laughed softly and his teeth flashed white. "Why not? I don't often meet women like you."

"Go to church and you might."

Laughing under his breath, he shook his head. "My mom would love you."

Kit didn't trust herself to answer. He was beautiful and un-predictable and dressed all in black, which scared the hell out of her.

"Want to go get coffee?" he asked.

"Coffee?" she repeated.

"Yes. It's a beverage. Some people drink it hot. Others like it cold."

His humor surprised her and she swiftly looked up into his face. Dark eyes. Crooked smile. He was funny. Sexy. Engaging. Alarming. Seriously alarming in his black leather and heavy com-bat boots.

Curiosity and desire warred with common sense. She wanted to talk to him. Was seriously tempted to get that cup of coffee. But she was also the girl who'd made some dreadful decisions when it came to men. According to Bree, Kit totally lacked the self-preservation gene. And apparently that was a really bad gene to miss.

Now she struggled to see past Jude's leather and biker boots, but there was nothing soft or pretty or malleable in his long hair, hard chin, and dark eyes. She couldn't manage him. He'd be call-ing the shots. And that wouldn't be a good thing. Not for her. "I shouldn't," she said. "I'm here with friends. We're hanging out, doing girl things."

"You can't sneak away for half an hour?"

He would use the phrase *sneak away*. He was that kind of guy. And yet Kit was truly tempted. She didn't even know why she was tempted. He wasn't her type. She preferred clean-cut, educated, corporate. *Successful.*

As if sensing her indecision, he added, "We'd just go across the street to Toots. It's safe. Public. Not even a two-minute walk." He nodded, indicating the door. "Which should reassure your friend hiding back there with a butcher knife that my intentions are hon-orable."

Kit jerked around, expecting to see Polly with a meat cleaver in her hand. Instead, Polly was clutching a spatula, wielding it as if it were a sword. "What are you doing?" Kit hissed.

Polly's mouth compressed. "Don't worry. I've got your back."

"I'm not worried, and put the spatula down. You're not Michael from *Halloween*."

"I'm not going anywhere until he's gone." Polly's voice dropped even lower. "Good God, he looks like a Colombian drug lord."

Kit was mortified. Polly was impossible and embarrassing but also her very best friend. She just hoped Jude didn't hear her. Blushing, she turned back to Jude. "It's just a spatula," she said awkwardly.

For a moment he was silent, his dark gaze shuttered. "Not Colombian," he said. "But close. French, English, and Choctaw."

"That's not close," Kit said.

His smile didn't reach his eyes this time. "I know, but some people don't know the difference between a peace pipe and a baggie of cocaine."

Kit flushed. He didn't like Polly. Fair enough. Polly didn't like him. But at least Kit had been right about the whole *Twilight*-Jacob-werewolf vibe. Jude was part Native American. Choctaw. Oklahoma Territory and the infamous Trail of Tears.

Kit struggled to think of something to say but couldn't. In the end she apologized. Again. "Sorry. And I don't think I can do coffee today."

Jude's dark eyes rested on her hot face. For a moment he said nothing, then shrugged. "Maybe another time," he said. Then, with a nod, he headed down the steps, back across the lawn to where he'd left his bike.

Kit couldn't take her eyes off him. Jude had a long, careless stride that fit his long hair and black embroidered vest. He walked like he didn't care what others thought, and before she could regret letting him go, she stepped inside the house and closed the door, moving to the window to watch him slip on his helmet, start his bike, and take off.

"Good riddance," Polly said, joining her at the window. "He was a total druggie scumbag."

"No, he wasn't."

"Yes, he was."

"He was a friend of Sarah's."

"He wasn't her friend. He probably stalked her."

"Polly!"

"I'm serious. Were you really considering going with him for coffee?"

"No. Maybe."

"*Kit.*" Polly's features tightened in disgust.

"He's actually nicer than he looks," Kit said, defending Jude even though she didn't need to. He was gone. He wouldn't be back. Problem solved.

"No, he's not. And this is where your romance novels get you in trouble. That guy isn't one of your wounded heroes. You do not find him appealing. He isn't interesting. You can't save him. He's hard-core. Mean. Didn't you see those tattoos?"

"What tattoos?"

"Kit, they were all over his arm and then there was one on his neck—"

"He had long sleeves and I didn't see anything on his neck."

"Because his hair was hiding it most of the time, but it was there, and it was ugly. It was one of those gang symbols. He's dangerous, Kit. He's not a good guy."

Kit shook her head and sank down in the rattan chair she'd been sitting in earlier grading papers. "I think you're being a little harsh."

"And you're naive." Polly perched on the edge of the old coffee table, facing Kit. "And I love you, you know I do, but you've got to wise up. Men totally take advantage of you. You let them walk all over you, and I'm sick of assholes breaking your heart."

Polly was right, and she didn't even know half of it, Kit thought, pulling her fuzzy oatmeal sweater over her legs. "It's not like I enjoy being hurt."

"Maybe not, but as Meg has even said, you're a magnet for losers. You draw them to you as if you've got this massive beacon over your head, lighting up the sky, announcing that you're sensitive and compassionate and have absolutely no common sense, no self-esteem, and no boundaries whatsoever."

Kit grimaced. "I'm not that bad."

"Pretty damn close." Polly glared at her. "The problem is that you are so good, Kit. And sweet. You're the most selfless, giving person I know. But unfortunately, men see this as a weakness and they'll just use you, and abuse you—"

"You don't mean men, plural," Kit interrupted, grateful Polly knew nothing about her date with Parker in December. "You mean Richard. And I'm in total agreement that he wasn't good for me, and that I'm in a better place now without him—"

"It took you ten years to see that!"

"Because I didn't want to see it. I wanted it to work. I wanted him to be the one." Kit plucked at her sweater, teasing a loose thread before looking up at Polly. "I *know*. It was laziness. I was stupid. But I just hate dating so much. I'm so bad at it." But just talking about this made her think of Parker, and she'd been successful at blocking out the date for weeks, but she was remembering it now, far too clearly.

She'd told only one person about the date and that was her sister Brianna, because Brianna might be hard on Meg, but she'd never been tough on Kit. If anything, she was always protecting Kit, and maybe that's because they were fraternal twins.

But the date with Parker had been bad from the beginning. Like her other dates that fall, she'd met Parker on Love.com and she wasn't sure how he stumbled across her profile, but he had, and he'd sent her a message saying he thought her photo was adorable—was it recent, and did she really look like that?—and he hoped to hear from her soon.

Kit was a little thrown by the way he'd asked questions about her photo, seemed so shallow, but at the same time she understood. Many of the men she'd met on Love.com had padded their height, or changed their weight, or even used a decade-old photo from a time when they had no paunch and far more hair. She'd told herself that Parker just wanted to know if she was being real. Honest. She told herself that she appreciated his directness and his lack of guile. And so she answered him that the photo was taken just months ago, at the end of the summer, and she could send him a more recent one if she wanted.

He wanted. So Kit sent him one from Thanksgiving at her parents' house, cropping out her sisters.

Parker answered immediately, saying she was stunning, a fresh-faced Rita Hayworth, and he couldn't wait to get to know her.

Instead of doing all the preliminary coffees, Kit agreed to dinner. She'd agreed in a moment of impulsiveness and it was a mistake. The entire date had been a giant mistake.

He'd had a forceful manner communicating via e-mail and text messages, but he was even more domineering in person. He talked a lot about his career during dinner, about his power and success. They left the restaurant and he suggested a nightcap. They were walking at the time, and Kit had no idea he meant to take her home, but his apartment was close by and they ended up there.

Yet another mistake.

Inside his apartment everything changed. He became surly and aggressive. He wanted sex. Kit told him she wouldn't, that she didn't, not unless she was in a committed relationship. Parker cornered her in his living room, accusing her of playing him, leading him on. What kind of woman did that? What kind of woman treated a man this way?

Kit tried to make her way to his door. He blocked it, pushed her back. She struggled to reach her phone in her purse. He tossed her purse across the room. And then he grabbed her, his hand at the base of her throat. Looking into his face, Kit didn't even recognize him anymore. He wasn't the date from dinner. He was someone else. Someone violent, someone frightening.

With Parker's hand at her throat, she could think of only one thing—and that was to do what she had to do to get out.

She'd been hurt badly once before and her survival instinct screamed to life, telling her that the most important thing now was to keep him calm so he wouldn't strike her, strangle her, rape her.

She didn't want to be raped. Couldn't be raped. And so, even as Parker ripped her blouse open, she did everything she could to soothe him, to deflect his anger and aggression. It worked. When he took her, he wasn't violent. He acted like a lover. She let him believe they were making love. It wasn't making love, though, and as soon as she could escape, she did, racing out his door, running down the steps of his apartment, hailing a cab as she pulled her coat closed over her torn blouse.

She didn't cry in the cab. Didn't cry in the shower. Didn't cry the next day.

Kit couldn't. She was too ashamed of herself, too sickened by what had happened. A little voice in her head said she was easy and bad and deserved what she got because she didn't fight Parker harder. And then another voice whispered that it was okay to do what she did, because she did what she needed to do to be safe, to survive.

Still horrified, and deeply ashamed, Kit called Brianna a few days later and confided in her. Brianna didn't like that Kit couldn't recognize a predator and told her to let this serve as a wake-up call. Assholes abounded. Wolves lurked in sheep's clothing. Kit had to be smarter in the future. Kit agreed.

It'd been five weeks now since that date, and Kit had told no one else, just as she'd never told anyone about what had happened when she was little. Because there were some things you didn't talk about. Some things you couldn't tell your sisters, or even your best friend.

"You just need confidence," Polly said, reaching out to catch Kit's hand in hers in an effort to stop Kit from winding the thread any tighter around her finger. "You need cojones. Balls."

Kit nodded, smiled, eyes stinging because, truthfully, she knew she needed a lot more than that.

"Set limits. Define your goals. Be clear on what you want," Polly added. "Look at me. I only go out with guys I like. I don't do pity dates. If a guy rubs me the wrong way, he's out of here. If the date isn't going well, I bail. If a dude I don't like keeps calling, I tell him I'm not interested."

"Straight out like that?" Kit whispered.

"Hell yeah. This isn't the UN. I'm not a diplomat. Not interested in winning Miss Congeniality. I'm trying to meet the right guy, and I refuse to waste time on the wrong guy."

Tears filled Kit's eyes. She blinked hard, hating her secrets, hating how weak she was. The Brennan women were fighters. They were proud and smart and survivors. Why hadn't she fought Parker? Why hadn't she smashed her fist into his face, stomped on his foot, put a knee in his groin? That would have been the admirable thing to do. That would have been brave. "You're amazing," she said to Polly.

"No, not amazing. I just had a jerk of a father and he's helped me recognize the jerks of the world. Thanks to Daddy, I can spot them a mile away."

"He might have been a jerk, but he made you strong."

Polly sighed and dragged a hand through her still-damp hair. "Strong? I'm not so sure about that. Sometimes I think I'm broken. Because all I know for sure is that I don't want kids. I'll never be a mom. I won't even date a man with kids. Total deal breaker."

"You don't think you'll change your mind? Down the road . . . when you meet the right guy?"

Polly jumped up off the coffee table and paced the room. "Jon Coleman was the right guy, but I didn't want marriage, didn't want babies, and so that was that."

Kit watched Polly march back and forth, trying to burn off nervous energy. "We're such opposites. You want a man, but no kids. I want kids, but not the man."

Polly dropped down onto the bottom step of the stairs. "You used to want to get married. Last year you were desperate for Richard to propose."

"Yeah. But I've learned my lesson. I'm not waiting around anymore for a man to want me or love me and marry me so I can have kids. I don't have to have a man to have kids. I can do it on my own."

Polly's eyes widened. "You mean with a sperm donor?"

"No! I wouldn't do that."

"Good. I was going to have to hit you upside the head."

Kit laughed. "You still might."

"Why?"

"I'm thinking about adopting."

"*What?*"

Kit nodded, her smile wavering, before disappearing. "I'm seriously considering it."

Polly's brows pulled. "How serious is serious?"

"I've begun filling out paperwork with two different agencies."

"Wow."

"I want to have a family."

Polly seemed to be choosing her words with care. "Don't you think you're rushing into this? You and Richard only broke up six months ago."

"It's been seven. And I don't think I'm being impulsive. I think I'm being practical. I love kids. I'm a great teacher, and if I can handle thirty-some hormone-charged teenagers at one time, why can't I have a child of my own?"

"It's not that simple, is it?"

"How is it complicated? I'm almost forty. My mom's dying. Everyone else is married. I want a family of my own."

Seven

Fiona arrived just before noon, and after she dropped off her suitcase and things in the upstairs bedroom, they walked across the street for lunch at Paradise Beach Grille with plans to catch a matinee movie afterward at the Capitola Mall.

Fiona didn't mention Chase during lunch, and neither Kit nor Polly brought him up. They talked about everything else, though, from the weather to school to travel plans over the summer before heading over to the movie theater to see *The Artist,* a black-and-white film that had been nominated for a number of Academy Awards. *The Artist* hadn't been Polly's first choice—or second choice; she liked action films, thrillers, but even she ended up loving the (mostly) silent film.

They grabbed coffee and tea afterward at the Capitola Book Café and discussed the movie and how utterly gorgeous the French lead was, but none of them could remember his name. Fiona was going to look up his name on her phone but got distracted when Mary Dillon approached their table.

Kit was the first to recognize her and she rose to greet her. She'd taught all five of the Dillon kids at Memorial—Sean, Conor, Siobhan, Aileen, and Patrick—with Patrick having graduated the year before last. "Mrs. Dillon, how are you?"

"I'm well. Thank you," Mrs. Dillon answered.

"You know Polly Powers and Fiona Hughes from Memorial?"

"I do. And it's nice to see the three of you on holiday together."

"Would you like to join us?" Fiona offered. "I can get you a chair."

Mrs. Dillon smiled but shook her head. "Thanks, love, but can't stay. Just popping in to get a book for my sister. I'm living with her right now. In Aptos. Quite a change from the East Bay."

"I didn't know you'd moved," Kit said, remaining on her feet. Mrs. Dillon had been one of the most warm and supportive parents she had ever met in her career. The Dillon children had been just as wonderful—polite, kind, and good-humored like their parents. "Did Mr. Dillon finally retire, then?"

For a moment Mrs. Dillon couldn't speak. "Frank died this past summer. Just a week before his retirement." Her voice cracked and she struggled to find her voice. "My sister thought a change of scenery would be good for me. But sometimes I think it's been too big a change. I miss the house we raised the kids in. Miss the memories. There were so many good ones."

"There would be," Kit agreed.

"It is nice here, though. Just different."

"Have you found a new parish church?"

"I go to Mass, but it's not the same."

"Of course not."

Mary Dillon said good-bye then and Kit hugged her, and while hugging her, she was reminded of her father's sisters. Solid, kind women with big hearts.

Kit sat back down at the table after Mary left. "That's such a shame about Frank," she said huskily. "He was lovely. They were such a close couple, too."

"The whole family is wonderful," Polly said. "I taught four of the five. All of them but the oldest."

"That was Sean," Kit said, supplying his name. "He was one of my favorite students. He loved to ask questions, get me talking, get me on a tangent. The kids think they're being so clever when they get you off topic, but they don't realize that you know you're off topic and you're choosing to talk about other things."

"I only taught the youngest," Fiona said. "Patrick. He was gorgeous, wasn't he? All the girls fancied him."

Polly removed her tea bag from her glazed mug. "You know Patrick's in Afghanistan."

"I didn't know that," Fiona said.

"Me either," Kit said.

"Joined the army last year. Just hope he makes it home."

Kit exhaled slowly. "Me, too."

Kit couldn't stop thinking about Mary Dillon, and, returning to the beach house, she disappeared into the kitchen to call her mom, suddenly compelled to check in with her. Dad answered Mom's phone.

"Mom's sleeping," he said. "I'll have her call you when she wakes up."

Kit glanced at her watch. It was nearly six. Dinnertime. Mom never slept this late. Or had she only just fallen asleep? "Is she okay?"

"She's been sleeping a lot this weekend. But isn't in too much pain."

But she was in pain. "Poor Mom."

"She's in good spirits, Kit."

It was Dad's way of saying don't get maudlin. She's not in the grave, yet. "What are you doing tonight, Dad?"

"We'll probably just watch a movie. I was thinking of renting *The Help*. Your mom had said she wanted to see it, and she read the book, didn't she?"

"She did. I did, too, and saw the movie. It's good, but it's a tearjerker. At least for me it was."

"Anybody die in it?"

"Yes. But Mom already knows the story and the acting is fantastic. It's well done—"

"Chicky movie, isn't it?"

"Chicky?"

"You know, one of those girl movies."

"Because it's written by a woman and stars women?"

"Just want to know what I'm watching."

"It's good, Dad. And it's not all weepy. There's some really funny parts. You'll be all right. Trust me."

He made a grumpy sound. "I never said I wouldn't be fine. I was just gathering information."

Kit suppressed a smile. "Are you all right for dinner?"

"Your aunt Megan dropped off a lasagna earlier today," he said, still sounding grumpy.

"That's nice. You love lasagna," she said, knowing that the whole Brennan family would rally around Dad when Mom died. They'd visit with him and bring him food but eventually he'd have to move forward, single, like Mary Dillon.

What would he do once he was alone? How would he manage? Would he keep the big family house, or would he want to downsize to something smaller?

"I'll be there next weekend," Kit said.

"That'll be nice, Kit. It's always good to have you around."

"Give Mom my love."

"I will."

Kit hung up and leaned against the kitchen counter, so full of emotion that she couldn't breathe. The emotion wasn't bad either. She was lucky to be born a Brennan. Lucky to have her family and their love and their loyalty and their humor.

It was good. Life was good. Everything was good.

Polly entered the kitchen, spotted Kit leaning against the counter, and closed the door behind her. "You okay?" she asked.

Kit took a quick breath, tucking hair behind her ears. "Just checked in at home. Everything's fine."

Polly unfolded the kitchen stepstool that served as a seat. "But . . . ?"

Kit shook her head. "There's no but. I'm blessed. I've got so much. Shouldn't want anything else."

"But you do."

Kit didn't know if she should laugh or cry. "So I guess there is a but."

"It's not bad to want things, Kit. Doesn't make you a bad person."

"Don't want to be selfish."

"You're not selfish!"

Kit ducked her head, studied her fingers, which she'd laced tightly together. *Here's the church, here's the steeple . . . open the door . . .* "I never, ever expected to be single at forty. I thought by thirty I'd be married, and by thirty-five I'd have three or four kids. I wanted a big family. Planned on a big family. Didn't plan on this life."

"Your life's not over. Tons of women get married at forty, and most of them go on to have children."

"I'm honestly not trying to feel sorry for myself."

"I know that. You're just talking things through. And that's good. You need to think things through before rushing into adoption—"

"Why are you so against adoption?"

"I'm not against adoption. I think it's wonderful for couples who want to have children, but I don't think it's the right thing for singles—"

"Are you serious?"

Polly nodded somberly. "I grew up with a single mom. It was hard. And she was a dedicated mom, but it was a struggle."

The kitchen door swung open and Fiona stuck her head around the corner. She was smiling so broadly that her dimples were showing. "Can I come in? Or am I interrupting?"

"Come in," Kit said, pushing away from the counter, glad for Fiona's arrival. The last thing she wanted was to continue this adoption discussion with Polly. Polly had a valid opinion, and Kit wasn't discounting her experience, but there were a lot of single moms in the world who were doing a great job.

Fiona checked her smile as she entered the small kitchen. "You don't look very happy," she said, cautiously glancing from one to the other.

"But you do," Kit said. "Did you finally talk to Chase?"

Fiona nodded, her smile returning. "They're coming home early. There isn't much snow and he says he's missing me. I'm going to meet him at the house at noon and we're going to have a date."

Kit hugged her. "That's great news!"

"Glad he got smart," Polly added.

Fiona's forehead creased. "So what's going on in here? Didn't sound very good."

Kit shrugged. "We're just having a difference of opinion."

Fiona looked from Kit to Fiona. "About what?"

"Kit adopting," Polly said bluntly.

"*What?*" Fiona turned to Kit.

"That was my reaction as well," Polly said.

Kit was livid with Polly for dropping the news on Fiona like that. "It's no one's business but mine," she said, folding her arms tightly over her chest.

Fiona's nose crinkled, her expression worried. "I think now's an excellent time for a glass of wine. I saw a bottle of chardonnay in the fridge. Shall I open it?"

Wine poured, they settled in the small living room, Polly and Fiona on the couch and Kit in the rattan chair that had been hers all weekend. Polly stretched her feet out onto the coffee table and focused on the toes of her shoes. Fiona moved the cushions around her, trying to get comfortable. Kit just stared down into her wineglass.

"Don't be mad, Kit," Fiona said finally, breaking the silence.

Kit couldn't immediately speak, too busy wrestling with what she wanted to say and what she shouldn't say. She didn't want to fight with her best friends. But at the same time some things were private. Personal. "It wasn't Polly's place to tell you that I'm thinking about adoption," she said at last. "I'm only in the early stages and it's all still very new to me. No one but the two of you know, and I'd like to keep it that way."

"I won't say anything to anyone," Fiona promised.

"Me either," Polly said, meeting Kit's gaze, "but I wouldn't be a real friend if I didn't tell you I'm concerned, and that I don't think it's a good idea. At least not yet."

"Not yet?" Kit echoed.

Polly reached for the bottle on the table and topped off her and Fiona's glasses. "I know you want a family, Kit, but this isn't the way to go about it, and I can't help but think your family wouldn't be happy."

"At least not your mum and dad," Fiona said. "They might be Americans but they're very Irish. They want you to be a mum, but they'll want it done properly. You know, a man, church wedding, all of that."

Kit set her wine down untouched. There was no way she could drink when she was so upset. "But there's not going to be a man or a church wedding—"

"Not if you're off adopting kids like Angelina Jolie!" Polly interrupted. "Most men aren't like Brad Pitt. They don't want to raise someone else's child."

"That's ridiculous," Kit snapped

"It's not ridiculous. It's true. Most men don't want a ready-made family. I saw it happen time and again with my mom, and it hurt her badly. She had me but she was still lonely. And can't you see, Kit, that I don't want that for you?"

"I'm trying to be practical," Kit said hoarsely.

"But raising a child on your own isn't all that practical," Fiona said gently. "It'd be a hardship financially, and you'd always be torn between wanting to be home and having to work."

"Lots of women raise children on their own."

"True. But you're not lots of women," Polly retorted. "You're you. And you're traditional and sentimental and hopelessly romantic. And this might come as a shock, Kit, but I actually love that about you. So don't give up on your dreams. Life's full of surprises. Let me introduce you to some nice guys. Go out on a few dates. Mr. Wonderful might be just around the corner—"

"I've got a date for next Saturday," Kit interrupted. "Happy?"

Polly and Fiona exchanged glances.

"You really do?" Polly asked.

Kit frowned. "Yes."

Fiona bounced on the sofa. "Why didn't you tell us?"

"Because I didn't want you two getting all excited." Kit glared harder. "Like you are. So stop it."

Fiona couldn't help bouncing again. "Tell us about him. Do we know him?"

"You've met him. Michael Dempsey." She saw his name meant nothing to them. "Jon Coleman's friend from Z's."

Polly's eyes widened. Fiona's eyebrows arched.

Kit shrugged. "He called me last week, asked me out. I said yes, but I'm so tempted to cancel—"

"Don't cancel." Fiona's glass thudded on the table. "Go out with him. And if he's not right, don't get discouraged. Keep dating. Be positive. That's what you always told me."

Polly was nodding. "She's right, Kit. Stay positive. Stay open to whatever possibilities are out there, because the truth is, even if you adopt a baby, you're still going to want more. You're going to want a man . . . someone to be that partner, husband, lover, and father to your child. The need for that relationship isn't going to go away. You were never meant to be a single mom."

Eight

Kit didn't cancel her date. And when Michael called the following Thursday to confirm their plans for Saturday night, she reminded herself that dates were good things, and that she needed to keep an open mind

Kit forced a cheerful note into her voice as she told him she was looking forward to their date Saturday.

He said he was glad. He hadn't stopped thinking about her all week.

There'd been a time when Kit would have embraced such a compliment, savoring the promise, building expectations. She didn't anymore. And she couldn't blame her date with Parker. She'd always been cautious around men. Maybe that's why she'd moved in with Richard after she met him. He'd felt safe. Nonthreatening.

She'd liked that he wasn't passionate, hotheaded, emotional. He wouldn't snap and hurt her. Wouldn't lash out or play games or manipulate her.

And it'd been a good relationship. At least in the beginning. But as the years went on, Kit wondered if she'd sold herself short. Because a relationship without passion . . . a relationship based on convenience . . . didn't feel like much of a relationship at all.

"So I'll pick you up at six," Michael said, dragging Kit's attention back to their conversation, "since our reservation's for six-thirty at Millennium. I just need your address."

"I was thinking I would just meet you at the restaurant," Kit said, "as I need my car. I'm heading to my parents' house after dinner."

"Your parents?" he repeated.

"My mom's not well," she explained, wondering if she was imagining the sudden chill in his voice. Was he offended that she wanted to drive herself to Millennium? Or was she projecting? "So after dinner I'm going to her house to be with her for the rest of the weekend."

"She has no one else to take care of her?"

"My dad's there, but he needs breaks."

"What's wrong with her?"

Kit opened her mouth but for some reason couldn't bring herself to talk about Mom's cancer. "She's . . . ill. Has been dealing with something for a couple of years." And then before he could ask any more questions, she changed the subject to sports, and the play-off game on Sunday. Michael liked talking sports and then he segued into his work and traveling. Kit was content to let him carry the conversation and then they were saying good-bye.

Hanging up, Kit felt a flutter of nerves. Dating was so not her thing. But Michael seemed nice enough and Millennium was one of San Francisco's most elegant and romantic restaurants. Best of all, her parents' house was just a short drive from Union Square.

* * *

With the semester ending next week, Kit had a lot of work to do, including mountains of student journals to read and lengthy essays to grade for her junior and senior AP English classes. She spent Friday reading essays and then continued Saturday morning, hoping to be done by noon. Instead, she was still hunched over the kitchen table at four-thirty, her hand cramped from hours of writing in her tiniest handwriting in the margins of the paper.

Catching sight of the time, Kit threw down her red pen and gave up grading for the day. She gathered her work and computer into her leather satchel to take to her parents' house with her tonight and then headed to her room to pack pajamas and clothes for Sunday Mass.

With her overnight bag ready, Kit showered and dressed for her date. She did her hair and makeup without thinking too much about the evening, slicking her dark red curls into a smooth ponytail and adding big gold hoops to her ears. Dark eyeliner, mascara, nude lips. She'd dressed up to give her confidence and then she shied away from thinking about the night. No need to psych herself out.

In the car, she tried not to fret about traffic. It was heavier than she expected approaching the Bay Bridge. She told herself it'd lighten up once she made it past the tollbooths, and even if it didn't, she'd be fine, as she'd grown up here, learned to drive on the city's steep hills, between buses, cabs, cable cars, and jaywalking pedestrians. Dad had made sure Kit—like the rest of his children— knew all the side streets and less traveled routes and could navigate San Francisco any time of year whether there was sun, rain, or fog. And with Tom Brennan for your father, you couldn't help but love this city. This was his city. His lover. His mistress.

And it was ironic, Kit thought, dodging city buses in her little white Prius, that she needed cool, unemotional men when her father's strong convictions and passion for life had shaped her, coloring her world, giving it definition, meaning.

Luck was with her tonight and Kit found parking just a block off Geary. Locking her car, she dashed to the restaurant, the heels of her black boots clicking against the pavement, her bright coral-red cashmere scarf flung casually about her neck, her camel wool coat open over her black knit dress. She skipped between cars as she crossed the street, too impatient to wait at a corner.

Michael was already at the restaurant when she arrived. She found him waiting on the curb, his hands in his trouser pockets. He was looking away from her, his gaze fixed on a point across the street. He'd dressed for dinner, too, in a civilized, crisp white button-down shirt and chinos. His dark blond hair was shorter, now cropped close to his head.

He turned at the sound of her footsteps. His narrowed gaze swept over her, from her dark auburn ponytail to the gold hoops in her ears and down to the hem of her black knit dress where it hit two inches above the top of her black knee-high boots.

He smiled appreciatively. "Very sexy."

She blushed and tugged on her coat. "Everybody wears black in the city."

"All I know is that your students are lucky. I never had a teacher look like you."

She shook her head, aware that she was blushing all over again, but it went with the red hair and sprinkling of freckles. "Hope I haven't kept you waiting long."

"Just a few minutes," he said. "Did you have trouble finding parking?"

"I found a spot around the corner. How about you?"

"I valeted it. But I still think I should have picked you up. Would have given me someone to talk to in all that traffic. Why so much traffic for a Saturday night?"

"There was a lot of traffic tonight. Probably a Warriors game or something."

He reached for the front door and held it open for her. "So you're staying at your mom's house tonight?"

"Yes." She began unbuttoning her coat as she entered the restaurant foyer. "I try to stay with her a couple weekends a month. We go to Mass on Sundays and have breakfast. It's become our tradition."

Michael gave his name to the hostess, who said their table was almost ready.

"Have you eaten here before?" he asked as they waited to be seated.

"No. But my oldest sister, Meg—a total foodie—loves it. The winery she used to work for did an event here and she said it's an upscale French bistro with environmental sensibilities. But I had no idea what that meant."

"I do. Apparently they're all about sustainability. The food, as well as the design. I was reading up on the restaurant online and the aged fishnet chandeliers are actually paper sacks, and the curtains were woven from recycled plastic bags. Even the upholstery is faux leather to be cruelty-free."

"How knowledgeable."

"I did my homework."

"That is impressive."

"What's the song . . . 'Hot for Teacher'?"

She tensed, incredibly uncomfortable when he said things like that. Perhaps he thought he was being funny or charming, but she found it offensive. But then, Kit seemed to find most men offensive these days. Clearly, she had a problem. Clearly, she needed to lighten up. It was ridiculous to take every compliment and twist it into something dark and insidious. "Don't know that one," she said lightly.

"I'll sing it for you, then."

"Mm, don't. Otherwise I'll have to sing one for you."

"And what would you sing for me?"

Her nose wrinkled as she struggled to think of a song she actually knew the lyrics to. "'Itsy Bitsy Spider'?"

"Yikes. No, thank you."

The hostess was before them, menus in her hand. "I can seat you now," she said, smiling directly at Michael, giving him her most dazzling smile.

Kit was amused, but not surprised. Michael was handsome. The hostess clearly liked him, and for some reason this relieved Kit, and she exhaled, relaxing, as they threaded their way through the restaurant's warm, handsome interior.

They were seated along the back wall, where the tables covered with long white cloths were close together. Kit slipped into the booth side and she watched Michael sit. He was a big man, well over six feet, with broad shoulders, and he drew attention as he sat down, both men and women glancing at him as he took the chair opposite hers.

"Would you prefer a cocktail or a bottle of wine?" he asked, reaching for a menu.

"I'll probably just have a glass of wine."

"Not a cocktail?"

"No. I'm a lightweight and I'm driving, so one glass of wine and that's it."

"But I understand the cocktails are really good here." Michael was smiling, his expression friendly and easy. "And one cocktail won't hurt you."

She hesitated, annoyed, and then aware that maybe she was getting her back up over nothing, relented, and scanned the cocktail menu. Her gaze settled on a house cocktail called Zots, made with pomegranate juice, lemon juice, muddled cucumber, and tarragon. It wasn't what she normally ordered, but when the glamorous ruby drink arrived at the table, she was glad she'd ordered it.

It was a beautiful drink in a beautiful restaurant, and she sat back, determined to enjoy herself this evening.

Michael kept the conversation going during their starters. "You're close to your family?" he asked as they shared an oyster appetizer.

Kit dabbed her mouth with her napkin. "Very."

"You mentioned your sister Meg earlier. She lives in Napa?"

"Santa Rosa, but she used to work for a Napa winery."

"Is she single, too?"

"No. She's been married for eighteen years. Has three kids." Kit sipped her tangy cocktail. "She has great kids. Love them to bits."

"You dote on your nieces and nephews?

"I do."

"Is that because you don't have any children of your own?"

"Well, that, and my nieces and nephews are some of the best people in the world and I love them dearly."

"So is all your family here in California?"

"No. One sister is in Africa, and the other is in Florida. Sarah's the one in Florida and she's married to a baseball player."

"Baseball, as in professional baseball?"

She nodded. "Boone's with the Rays now—"

"You don't mean Boone Walker?"

"You've heard of him?"

"Of course. He was a first baseman with the Houston Astros. A great player."

"I'm partial, but then he's my brother-in-law."

"Nice."

She nodded again, proud of Boone. "He's in the final year of his contract with Tampa Bay. It'll be interesting to see if they renew his contract or if he'll be going somewhere else."

"You know baseball."

"My younger brother, Tommy, played growing up and I went

to most of his games. He had a scholarship to Fresno State and then was drafted by the Brewers, but after a couple years bouncing around the minor leagues, he left ball to become a fireman. Like my dad."

"Four girls, one boy," he said, counting up her siblings. "And the sister in Africa? What does she do?"

"She's a nurse."

"Impressive family."

"What about you?" Kit asked, turning the focus on to him. "Big family, small family? Brothers, sisters . . . ?"

"Two sisters. No brothers. Haven't seen the girls in a couple years. One's married to a guy in the military and they move around a lot. The other . . . she's got some problems."

The waitress cleared their plates and cutlery and returned to set fresh silverware in front of them for their entrées.

"Have you ever been married?" Kit asked after the waitress moved away.

Michael drummed his fingers on the table, nodded after a moment. "Yes. Until recently, as a matter of fact."

"I'm sorry."

"It's been hard."

His expression was troubled—grieved—and Kit's heart suddenly went out to him. The divorce had clearly been painful. "How long have you been divorced?"

He hesitated a long moment. "It's actually not final yet."

"You're still married?"

"No, we're separated, and papers are filed, but it hasn't been finalized."

Kit's brows tugged. Which meant he was still legally married. "When does that happen?"

"Soon. End of this month." He studied her, his expression regretful. "I've made you uncomfortable."

"A little," she admitted. "I'm Catholic."

"And divorce is a sin?"

"Divorce isn't good."

His blue eyes locked with hers and held. He looked frustrated. "I shouldn't have called you. I should have known better." He got to his feet, dropped his napkin onto the table. "Let's forget this. Call it a night before—"

"What are you doing?" Kit whispered, aware that people were looking at them.

"I'm not going to make you uncomfortable."

But he *was* making her uncomfortable. He was so tall and there was so little space between tables and everyone could hear everything that was being said. "Please sit down," she urged him.

"I didn't invite you out tonight to make you uncomfortable or to compromise your values."

Kit reached out to him, her fingers brushing his forearm. "Michael." Her voice dropped. "Sit. Please."

"I don't take advantage of women, Kit."

"I never said you did." She glanced left, right, and then up at him. "Sit . . . please?" Her voice had dropped to a whisper. There wasn't much more she could say or do. She hated the scene, hated this awkward, uncomfortable feeling. Conflict had never been her strong suit.

But fortunately, finally, Michael did sit, though he wouldn't look at her. Instead, he stared off, his jaw set, his gaze narrowed. He was upset. She'd upset him. She hated that, just as she hated the way her heart pounded and her stomach was nervous, filled with tumbling pebbles.

"Talk to me," Kit murmured, wanting to leave but unable to walk away from someone who was unhappy with her. *"Please."*

He took a slow breath and then looked at her. "You make me feel like a criminal . . . a murderer or a rapist. I'm just going through a divorce, and it's not an easy thing. I don't enjoy this. I'm not happy that my marriage ended."

"I'm sorry."

"And maybe I should have told you about the separation sooner, but it's personal. Private. I'm not proud of my situation and wasn't raised to air dirty laundry in public."

"I understand." And she did. Her family was private, too. You didn't discuss family matters with outsiders. "I'm just glad you're telling me now."

He nodded once, and then again. "But I should have known. Should have realized. So many women don't care. They don't have your morals and scruples. They just want a lay. A good time. You're different. I like that about you."

She drew back, discomfited by his reference to a lay and a good time, thinking it was such an odd choice of words for a man to say to a woman. No male in her family would speak that way in front of a woman, but the men in her family were old-fashioned, and traditional, protective of women. "So when is the divorce final?"

"Couple weeks."

Couple weeks. Fourteen days.

"You still don't like it," he said.

No, she didn't, not at all, but she didn't think it would help anyone, or anything, to focus on that now. "Friends don't judge, right?"

"We're more than friends."

What an awkward evening, she thought.

"Kit?" he murmured, looking for confirmation.

She couldn't give it to him. They'd only just met. And she didn't understand how he could want so much from her. It didn't help that he was staring at her so intently. "This is just our first date, Michael."

"But I feel such a connection with you."

"You're married."

"Not for much longer."

"But as long as you're married, we're just friends."

"No more dates?"

"No."

His lips curled. "You're that good?"

"It's not about being good. It's my faith."

"Your faith rules your life?"

The knot of tension in her shoulders eased. She breathed a little deeper, growing more comfortable. When it came to her faith, Kit knew who she was, knew what she believed, and finally felt as if she was standing on solid ground again. "I wouldn't say *rules,* but my faith shapes it. Faith is a huge part of my life. I grew up attending parochial school. Teach in a Catholic school. I still go to Mass every Sunday."

"By choice?"

She laughed, amused. "Of course. I take it you don't go to church."

"Not recently. I used to. I was raised in the Church. My mom was very religious. A little too religious, if you ask me." He studied her for a long moment, his blue gaze assessing. "You like teaching?"

"I love teaching . . . most of the time."

"What would you do if you didn't teach?"

Kit considered the possibilities. At twenty, the world had been full of so many possibilities. At forty, there seemed fewer opportunities. "I used to think I'd enjoy being a librarian, but now it's all about technology and I'd hate that. So I don't know."

"Jon's ex teaches at the same school you do?"

"Jon?"

"Coleman. He's my neighbor. I was out with him that night at Z's."

That's right. Jon, Polly's schmuck boyfriend who took credit for Polly's success and stole her biggest account from her all while sleeping with her. Nice. It was all Kit could do not to roll her eyes. "Yes," she said instead. "Polly and I teach together at Memorial."

"Why teach?" Michael persisted.

Kit shrugged. "Why not change the world?"

They dropped the discussion of marriage, divorce, and faith there, but later, while they were finishing dinner, Kit couldn't stifle her curiosity. "Do you still love her?" she asked. "Your wife?"

Michael looked at her blankly a moment. "My wife? What about her?"

"Do you love her?"

"You're like a dog with a bone," he retorted, smiling tightly.

"Sorry . . . I was just wondering what she was like."

His fingers tapped against his water glass, making it ping. "She's sweet."

"Why didn't the marriage work?"

He didn't answer right away and she got the sense that he didn't like the questions. Didn't like talking about his marriage. She couldn't blame him. She knew she was being nosy. She was asking personal questions, but wanted to understand Michael, wanted to know why this good-looking man with broad shoulders and clear blue eyes was about to be single again.

"It's complicated," he said roughly.

She nodded, waited.

"She was married before," he added. "Has a teenage daughter. Missy has custody of Dee, so it's not easy. Teenage girls aren't always easy." He looked up into her eyes and smiled wryly. "But then, I'm sure you understand this better than me. You're a teacher. You're with kids all day long."

"You don't get along with Dee?"

"I used to. When she was younger."

Kit heard the wistful note in his voice. "How old is she?"

"Fifteen."

Her eyebrows lifted. That explained a lot of things. "That's a tough age," she said.

"Yeah."

"I've always said my sophomores were the hardest group to teach. As freshmen, the kids are still relatively cute and eager to please, but they come back the next year and think they know everything."

"*Exactly*. She's so mouthy."

"Mouthy or withdrawn. I have students who don't talk at all. And if they do, they act like they're doing me a big favor."

He fell back in his chair, stunned. "You *know*."

She smiled sympathetically. "So you see, it's not you. And I know it doesn't help, but this isn't about you. She's a teenager and full of hormones and hopes and dreams."

"She needs to learn it's not all about her."

"She will eventually. It won't always be this way."

"That's what Missy says."

"I have a friend who married a man with three children, two of whom are teenagers, and they're giving her a really hard time."

"So what is your friend going to do?"

"Try to be patient. Keep talking through things. Hang on to that sense of humor."

He made a rough sound. "You're suggesting I get back with my wife?"

"I just think if you still love her, don't give up on your marriage."

"And if I don't?"

"That's easy." Kit shrugged. "Don't do anything and your divorce will be final in a couple weeks."

After dessert and coffee, Michael walked her to her car. "I really enjoyed tonight, Kit. Thank you for staying with me and having dinner."

She fished in her purse for her car keys. "I'm glad I stayed, too."

"Even though I'm an evil, married man?"

She knew he was teasing her but she got that uneasy feeling in her gut again. "I never called you evil."

"You made me feel like I was evil."

"I never meant to do that."

"Well, I forgive you."

"Thank you."

"So does that mean we can get together again soon?" he asked.

Kit frowned and looked up at him, seeing how the streetlight illuminated his straight nose and high brow. He was athletic and handsome and attractive, but he left her cold. He was too confident. Arrogant. "You're married, Michael."

"Not for long."

"You're still in love with your wife. Work it out with her."

"You're rejecting me?"

"I'm telling you to focus on your family."

He took a step closer to her. His head dropped, and the corner of his mouth curled. "Maybe I want to focus on you."

He was really tall and he was now standing so close that she felt crowded. Kit took a step back, bumped into her car. "Good night, Michael."

"That is not an answer."

"Yes, it is."

He reached out to touch her arm. "I give you permission to go out with me again."

Kit arched an eyebrow. "Now, that's strange."

"Come on. You know you women never make a decision without consulting a half-dozen girlfriends. You've got to get everybody's opinion, need everybody to weigh in. I'm just saving you time and energy."

"That's very thoughtful of you."

"I am a very thoughtful person."

He was smiling at her in a way that said he liked her, that he found her desirable, but underneath the playful banter she sensed that he was serious. He'd like to make decisions for her. He probably liked to make decisions for everyone. "I have to go."

"So next Saturday?"

"No."

"You want to."

"I don't."

"Yes, you do."

"Michael."

"I'll call you."

"Michael."

"I'll call you," he repeated, and then winked. "And then we'll make plans for Saturday."

In the car, Kit clutched the steering wheel, feeling more than a little dazed and confused as she drove to her parents' house.

What had just happened?

What a strange night, and an even stranger date. The evening had been uncomfortable at times, and mildly enjoyable at others, but it was by no means a great evening. She certainly didn't feel compelled to see Michael ever again. But Michael certainly seemed compelled to prove her wrong.

Weird.

Arriving at her parents' home, she discovered the house was dark. Kit quietly let herself in through the front door with her key, but once inside, found her dad in the den watching TV. "Hey, honey," he said, rising from his big leather La-Z-Boy chair when she entered the room.

He gave her a kiss on the cheek.

"Mom sleeping?" she asked.

"She went to bed a couple hours ago."

"She okay?"

"She's fine. She just doesn't have a lot of energy."

"Is this cruise a good idea?"

"It's what she wants."

"I worry that it'll be too much for her."

"Where did you go for dinner?" he asked, sitting back down, changing the topic. Dad didn't talk about things he didn't want to discuss. He never had. He never would.

"Millennium. On Geary."

"They used to be in a different location, didn't they?"

"Apparently."

"Good food?"

"Very good."

She sat down on the couch, curled her legs under her, and watched her dad watch TV. He appeared engrossed in the show and she wondered if this was how it'd be later, when Mom was gone. If he'd sit here every night and watch TV, allowing himself to be absorbed in whatever was on so he didn't have to think about being alone. And maybe he'd be fine. Maybe he'd do better than any of them.

She watched him for another moment and then rose. "I'm going to go to bed."

"Tired?"

"I am. Nine-thirty Mass?"

"And then we'll go to brunch after."

"I was going to make breakfast."

"Let's see what the weather's like. If it's nice, I think your mom would enjoy getting out. She's feeling a little cooped up lately."

"Just let me know in the morning. I can always grab some groceries on the way home from church." She kissed the top of his head, grabbed her overnight bag from the hall, and headed up-

stairs to her childhood bedroom, a bedroom that somehow managed to make her feel like that little girl who preferred fairy tales
and happily-ever-after endings far more than reality.

Kit slept so deeply that she overslept the next morning, and it
had been a rush getting out of the house to make it to Mass
on time. But now she was at St. Cecilia, seated between her parents in the pew.

St. Anne was closer to their house, but St. Cecilia had been her
father's parish church when he was a boy and he'd wanted to raise
his children there, too. Even today the church retained much of its
Irish flavor, despite its Spanish Colonial design with the stenciled
oak-beamed ceiling and rich red stucco walls.

With the hectic rush to church behind them, Kit exhaled, at
peace. She knew the service forward and backward—every word,
each pause, every prayer and response. And because she'd just attended Mass on Friday with her students, she didn't feel guilty
allowing her thoughts to wander, and wander they did, jumping
from Mass to Michael and then, suddenly, the biker from Capitola
popped into her mind.

Jude. Just Jude. No last name.

She almost smiled remembering, and she could see him sitting
on his big burnt-orange bike with the massive handlebars, picture
clearly his firm mouth and chin, his worn denim jeans, and the
scuffed toe of his black boots. He was definitely sexy in a disrepu-
table sort of way, and not the sort of man she'd date, but she had
found him intriguing. Appealing. He was different. She liked that.

But Jude wasn't someone she could ever bring home. No one in
her family would approve. Well, Brianna might, but that's only
because Bree loved being contrary.

No, her family would definitely choose Michael over Jude for
her. They'd like Michael's clean-cut, all-American-boy good looks,

his successful corporate career, his love of sports, and she doubted he would have any problem winning them over. Provided he didn't talk about his ex-wife or divorce. Dad and Mom didn't believe in divorce. Kit didn't either, but it was hard, if not impossible, to meet a man in his late thirties or forties who hadn't been married before.

But she'd felt no chemistry with Michael, not that chemistry was everything . . .

With the reading finished, the congregation sat for the sermon. Dad smiled at her and she smiled back, and Kit tuned in to the sermon for the first few minutes before letting her thoughts drift again.

She hadn't been to this church since Christmas morning when the entire family had gone to Mass together. They'd filled two pews—Mom, Dad, Meg and Jack, Tommy and Cass, Sarah and Boone, Kit and all the children. The only one missing was Brianna, as, at the last minute, she couldn't find a replacement for her at the hospital and couldn't fly home.

The rest of them were together, though, and it'd been a beautiful service, poignant, but heavy with meaning. During the service, Kit, Meg, and Sarah had caught one another's gaze time and again. Each knew what the other was thinking. No one needed to say aloud what the other was feeling. It was their last Christmas as a whole family. The last Christmas with Mom.

After the service, they'd returned home and opened packages and had their traditional Christmas-morning brunch. Later Dad's brothers had arrived—Uncle Joe and Aunt Megan, and Uncle Pat, who'd never married but had been with his girlfriend Rosie for almost twenty years—and Mom's only living brother, Uncle John, and his wife, Linda. There'd been more packages and more food, phone calls from Dad's three sisters, who lived in other parts of the country, and then carols and games, and they'd stayed together in the living room until late, not wanting the day to end.

But of course it finally did end with Mom reaching for Dad's hand at ten, quietly telling him she was tired, and she hated to break up such a wonderful evening but she really needed to go lie down. She'd been so apologetic at breaking up the party and it'd almost broken Kit's heart. Mom was so strong, with such a beautiful, fierce spirit.

Kit turned her head to look at her mother now. It'd been only three and a half weeks since Christmas but Mom was already smaller and frailer, her brown eyes too big above cheekbones that had become too prominent. Kit's breath caught in her throat. Mom was disappearing before her eyes and there was nothing she could do about it. Nothing she could do but love Mom till the very end.

Kit's throat ached, and her eyes stung, and she had to look away, to the tall windows with the sunlight pouring through the stained glass to hold the tears back.

How could Mom be defeated by cancer? How could there be no cure?

Suddenly Mom's hand covered hers and held tight. Kit's heart squished in her chest. Her mother's hand felt cool and frail, her skin delicate and thin, and yet her grip remained tight. But wasn't that Mom?

Her mother was both angel and warrior; she'd lived her life with dignity and grace, and now she was dying the same way. It would be hard, if not impossible, to let her go at the end, but at the same time Kit knew she'd been blessed.

Gently, she squeezed her mom's hand, letting her know how much she loved her, even though she couldn't look at her, not now, not when tears made it impossible to see, and so she did the one thing she'd done her whole life when overwhelmed. She prayed. *God is good. God is great.*

* * *

Mass over, they escaped the parishioners still milling in the courtyard and on the front steps and went to brunch. Kit had wanted to cook, but it was such a beautiful morning, the kind of morning that made San Francisco utterly unforgettable with its deep blue sky, cloudless except where the blood-orange towers of the Golden Gate Bridge jutted against the blue, that Dad insisted they go to the Cliff House.

The Cliff House, perched high on the bluff overlooking both the bay and the Pacific Ocean, was one of San Francisco's crown jewels and famous for its elegant Sunday brunch. And because Dad was also Firefighter Brennan, he knew everyone, literally *everyone,* and was able to book a last-second reservation for eleven-thirty.

Seeing as it was a last-minute reservation, Kit had expected a table in a corner, or hidden behind a massive palm, but they were seated at a spacious table in a prime location at one of the big windows with a stunning, unobstructed view of the sea and rocks.

"How nice to be Firefighter Brennan," Kit teased her dad as the waiter poured them champagne while they perused the menu.

"I'm retired now."

"But look at this table. They still remember you."

"It's the Brennan name. They remember my dad, Thomas. And your great-uncle Pat, the one your uncle Patrick was named for."

"Not your uncle Liam?"

He folded his arms across his big chest, leaned back, getting comfortable. "If they remember Liam, it was for the wrong reasons."

"But wasn't he a fireman, too?"

"That doesn't make you a saint, Kit, just means you're strong and you don't mind when things get hot."

"Tell me about him," she said, encouraging him to talk, knowing he loved telling stories, especially if they had to do with his firefighting days or his family.

"He was a hothead. Drank a lot. Took offense at everything. And nearly destroyed this place one weekend after someone made the mistake of chatting up his girl."

"I can see why he didn't like that."

"Only she didn't know she was his girl. He'd only just met her himself, and from what we learned later after getting ahold of the police report, the girl preferred the other fellow."

Kit leaned forward. Her favorite stories seemed to revolve around Uncle Liam. "Did Liam know she liked the other guy?"

"My uncle Liam wouldn't have cared. He didn't play by any rules but his own. He did what he wanted and the rest be damned."

"Sounds like Brianna." Kit laughed.

Dad grinned. "I've told your mother that many a time. When Brianna was a toddler and she'd have one of her tantrums—and no one had tantrums like your sister's; they lasted for hours—I'd look at your mom and say, 'We've got a little Liam here.'"

"He did," Mom agreed. "And scared me to death."

Dad's blue eyes were twinkling. He was happier than Kit had seen him in a long time. "The only person who could manage Liam was his brother, my uncle Pat. Uncle Liam was a damn good fighter. But your uncle Pat was better. Whenever Liam got into trouble, they'd call my grandfather, Malachi, and Grandfather Malachi would send Pat to collect Liam. Liam didn't like it."

"I wouldn't think so."

"You know, Liam had two inches on Pat, but Pat had a mean right hook, and the only way he could sort Liam out was by knocking him out cold."

"He hit him?"

"*Hard.*" He saw Kit's face and shrugged. "Kit, somebody had to. The family couldn't let Liam go around picking fights, breaking furniture, getting carted off to jail. That's how we've always done it in this family. We look out for each other. Never leave a man behind." He abruptly stopped talking, and a wistful expression crossed his face.

Kit exchanged glances with her mom. Marilyn shook her head but Kit wanted to know why her dad had grown quiet. She wanted to know her family history. It was an important history. It was her history. "What are you thinking about?" she asked him.

He didn't immediately respond. She waited. Her mother waited. One of the uniformed servers stopped by the table and topped off the champagne, then silently slipped away.

"Are you thinking about your dad?" Kit persisted gently, wanting to hear more about her grandfather, her father's father, Thomas Brennan—never Tom or Tommy—and the one person her father never discussed.

Her grandfather Thomas Brennan had perished in a hotel fire when Kit's father was fifteen and just a freshman in high school. Three firefighters, Thomas Brennan a twenty-year veteran with the fire department, and two young firefighters, one still just a probie, died that day. The entire city of San Francisco had turned out for the funeral. The family never discussed the fire, and so Kit had only learned that her forty-three-year-old grandfather Thomas had died a hero by reading newspaper clippings in a scrapbook her late grandmother had made.

Kit had found the scrapbook while in high school. She'd been helping clean Gramma's house and had been determined to organize some of the clutter. And Gramma was a pack rat. She kept everything—old magazines, newspapers, wrapping paper—and so at first Kit didn't even bother to look at the scrapbook, but then as she dusted the leather cover, a card fell out. And then more cards. She sat down with the scrapbook to put it back together and that's when she began reading the newspaper articles and poring over the photographs and sympathy cards and letters—dozens and dozens of letters—nearly all from strangers, people who felt compelled to reach out to her to say that they wished they'd known him, that they were so terribly sorry, that they were praying for her and the children and holding them in their hearts.

"We never do leave a man behind," her father said roughly, breaking the silence.

Kit nodded.

That summer, at her grandmother's, she discovered the truth about her grandfather—that he'd had a choice. He could have saved himself that day. But he hadn't. Instead, he went deeper into the fire to try to rescue the two younger men from his engine. Because those men weren't just men to him. They were his team, his brothers, his responsibility. His other family.

Kit cried when she'd read all of the articles and condolence letters from friends and strangers, and they'd been tears of anger. She wasn't proud of her grandfather for sacrificing himself. She was angry with him. He'd made the wrong decision. How could he sacrifice himself when he had six children? How could he do that to his wife? How could you allow your work family to come before your own family?

And yet how could she say any of that to her father? He'd followed in the family footsteps. He'd become a fireman, too.

They talked then of other things, and as Kit sipped her champagne, it was easy to imagine people sitting here, in this very same spot, one hundred years ago, looking out on the same glittering water and wind-whipped waves. A true city landmark, the Cliff House first opened its doors in 1863 and immediately became a popular destination until a fire destroyed it in 1896. Adolph Sutro, the "Comstock King" and a wealthy San Francisco entrepreneur, rebuilt the place, turning it into a stunning eight-story four-spire confection that survived the devastating 1906 earthquake, only to burn down in 1907 in less than two hours.

The Cliff House was reborn in 1909, this time in a neoclassical design, and was the same Cliff House they were enjoying brunch at now.

"So what are your plans for next weekend?" Dad asked in his big booming voice, a voice that would carry in the firehouse whether he was browning onions in the kitchen or lifting weights in the gym.

Kit smiled and looked from his mouth to his blue eyes. She and Tommy were the only two to have inherited his blue eyes, but no one had Dad's bright color. "Polly and Fiona are taking me out Saturday night, and Meg was talking about having me up to her house on Sunday for dinner, but I told her let's just wait until we're on the cruise and we can celebrate as a family together." She glanced at her mom. "That is, if we're still doing the cruise?"

"*If?*" Mom said. "There's no if about it. I have confirmation numbers for five cabins. We're going."

"So tell us about last night," Dad said. "How was your date? What's he like? How did you meet him?"

"He's a friend of Polly's ex-boyfriend," Kit said.

"Oh?" Mom's expression brightened. She'd always loved Polly. "Which boyfriend?"

"Jon Coleman. I don't think you know him. He's from way back in the past."

"But you liked this boy?" Mom persisted.

Kit gurgled with laughter. "He's not a boy, Mom. Michael's in his forties. And he's . . . okay . . . but there were no sparks."

"Sometimes those develop later," Dad said.

"Or not at all," Kit answered.

"But you will see him again?" Dad asked hopefully.

"I doubt it."

"Oh." Her father's face fell, disappointed. "Well, if you change your mind, you know we're always happy to meet your friends. Feel free to bring him around anytime."

Nine

K it drove home to Oakland grateful she had a sense of humor, and rather amused by her father's desperate desire to see her married. It was far better to be amused than offended. Dad meant no harm. It had always been his goal to see his daughters settled, married, with families. In that order. Dad wouldn't be happy about her becoming a mother without being a wife first. Not even if she did it through adoption.

But Kit was serious about adoption, and after letting herself into her house, she changed into sweats and dug through the caddy on her bedroom desk to find the fat adoption application, which she carried to the kitchen table.

It was a sixteen-page document and she'd filled out the easy stuff already: name, address, age, height, weight, language spoken at home, employment history, residential information, personal history (Arrested? Felony? Psychological/psychiatric treatment?), ten references from your community—thankfully that had also been easy, as she'd filled in her teacher friends' names, and then all the short essay questions . . .

Tell us about the people who raised you. Who were they, and did you get along with them?

She'd smiled reading that. The *people*. Dad and Mom, Tom and Marilyn Brennan. The best of the best and her very own parents and she absolutely got along with them, saw them every other weekend still.

How did you get along with your brothers and sisters when you were growing up?

Great. Awesome. Loved my three sisters and brother. I was the one who got along with everyone.

Which of your family members are you still close to? How often do you see or speak with them?

All of them. My family gets together at least once a month for dinner, and I talk to my sisters almost every day. My sisters remain my best friends.

Has any member of your family ever been arrested or charged with a violation of the law?

That one had given Kit pause. Brianna had been arrested twice . . . once demonstrating for or against something at city hall, and then there was the night in New Orleans when she had one too many Hurricanes on Bourbon Street and ended up spending the night in jail.

Kit had ended up answering that her fraternal twin sister, now an infectious disease nurse in Congo, had been a free spirit in college, and did have two arrests for disorderly conduct during that time, but now ran one of the most respected medical clinics in Central Africa.

Has any member of your family/household ever been in foster care?

No.

And then all the childhood questions, and there were many. Some she breezed through, like: *Growing up, which family members were you closest to? And what made them special to you?* And: *What were you usually punished for, and how were you punished?* To the one that had tripped her up last time: *What was the hardest part of growing up for you?*

She hadn't known how to answer. Compared to most people, she'd had an idyllic childhood and had grown up knowing she was loved.

But that didn't answer the question.

What was the hardest part of growing up for you?

Not feeling good about yourself. Feeling bad. Feeling ordinary.

She hadn't been gifted or special at anything . . . well, except for reading. She did win Reader of the Year in fourth grade by turning in the most book reports. When Kit was awarded her blue ribbon by Sister Sylvia, her fourth-grade teacher, on the last day of school, Brianna had laughed so hard she'd been sent to the principal's office.

Kit smiled crookedly, remembering. She and Brianna had been such opposites all through school. Kit was studious. Bree couldn't care less. In junior high, Brianna disappeared with boys, while Kit would steal away with books. But it hadn't mattered. They were all different in her family, each one unique. Bree was fierce and funny. Meg, driven and ambitious. Tommy, athletic and popular. Sarah, smart and beautiful. And Kit . . . well, Kit had simply been good. As her dad used to say, it made Kit happy to make everyone else happy.

Kit sat down at the table, picked up the pen, and wrote in the lined section, *I was a middle child and very ordinary and not special at anything, with the exception of reading. But being a good reader isn't something you brag about, and I desperately wanted to able to brag about something.*

She reread her answer, wondering if it was the wrong one, then felt frustrated by how little she'd accomplished and moved on to the next dozen questions.

Finally she reached the section called "The Single Applicant," which she was, and skimmed the pages of questions about her sexual orientation, her partners, her dating patterns, the history of her relationships, her social life the past six months, her sex life, her views on men, her views on women, her views on homosexuals, heterosexuals, her views on race, religion, everything.

Kit had just finished filling in the part about her sex life and views on men when Sarah called. She answered the phone, happy to take a break from sharing her sexual history with complete strangers. "Hi, Sarah."

"Heard you had a date last night," Sarah said brightly.

No secrets in their family, Kit thought, leaning back in her chair and stretching. "I did."

"And . . . ?"

"It was fine."

"Just fine? So you won't see him again?"

Kit's gaze fell on the question *Do you want to be single or is there an ideal partner you're still looking for?* She rolled her eyes, pushed the application away from her. "I doubt it."

"Why not?"

"He's married."

"*What?*"

"Correction. He's going through a divorce, but it's not final, won't be for another couple of weeks."

"But you like him?"

"Not sure."

"What does he do?"

"He works for Chevron. Is an engineer, I think."

"How old?"

"A little older than me."

"Attractive?"

"Very."

"Tall?"

"Extremely."

"Build?"

Kit laughed and shook her head. *"Athletic."*

"Nice, Kit!" Sarah said warmly.

"You are as bad as Mom and Dad," Kit groaned.

"No, I'm not. They're discussing a June wedding. I personally think you should insist on a yearlong engagement—"

"You're all going to be disappointed, then. I'm not into him. And I certainly would never think of him as marriage material."

"Why not?"

"Because . . ." Kit's voice drifted off as she pictured Michael— tall, dark blond, blue-eyed—and then thought of how she felt after the date. Annoyed. Played. And it bothered her still.

"Because . . . ?" Sarah prompted.

"He was just okay, and I've been there, done that. Richard was a warm body and it wasn't enough. I don't want to be with someone just to be with someone. It doesn't make you happy. And I'm not going to settle, not ever again. If I'm going to get married, he's got to be amazing. I want to have what you have with Boone . . . from the first time you guys met, it was fierce and intense, and it's still that way with you guys today. I love that. I love that you have so much passion and sex and crazy love—"

"Be careful what you wish for, because intense love and crazy love can make you crazy, too. Since I fell for Boone, I've never been the same."

"Better intense and crazy than to feel nothing."

Silence stretched across the line. "I guess it depends on how much you need control. I need it, Kit. I miss it. I'm sick and tired of crazy."

"But you love Boone."

"I do. So much that sometimes I find myself wishing I'd never met him."

After they hung up, Kit reached for the application, pulled it back toward her. *What do you think the hardest part of raising a child on your own will be?*

Her eyes suddenly burned. This had never been her plan. Never.

She shook her head, gathered the pages, put them back in order. She'd had enough questions and reflection for one day.

Fiona popped by Kit's classroom Monday morning, juggling hot tea and a stack of papers and a big pink-frosted cupcake. She placed the cupcake on the corner of Kit's desk with a flourish. "Six days until your birthday!" she sang. "Six days until we spoil you rotten!"

Kit followed her into the hall, called to her departing back. "Six days is a long time, Fiona."

Fiona lifted a hand and waved. "Not when we're celebrating all week!"

"We're not!"

"Oh, yes we are. You know we Irish like a good party!"

Back in her room, Kit eyed the tall, heavily frosted cupcake all morning, determined to save it for after school, but it smelled so good, the vanilla in the frosting tantalizing her taste buds, and she ended up eating half at break and then the other half at lunch. It was delicious and decadent and probably a thousand calories.

"I loved the cupcake," she told Fiona after school as they stood in the parking lot, monitoring traffic and making sure everyone was following the rules, including the younger student drivers who tended to race toward the exit, thrilled to be behind the wheel. "But don't bring me any more. I can't resist them. I'll be fatty pants soon if I'm not careful."

*   *   *

Kit hit the gym on her way home, ran the mandatory two miles and, once home, showered, put on her pajamas, and sat down at her kitchen table with a Lean Cuisine, intending to answer a few more questions on the adoption application, but the more she thought about the questions, the less motivated she was to fill out the paperwork.

Was she crazy, wanting to adopt? Was she crazy, thinking she could do it on her own?

Tommy and Cass were the ones who should be filling out the application. They were the kinds of people adoption agencies wanted—loving, strong, stable, committed. They'd be far more likely to be approved, too, than a forty-year-old teacher who couldn't keep a man.

In the end, Kit chose to grade papers instead of filling out more of the application. Meg called while she was eating and working.

"I hate trying to figure out what I'm going to make for dinner every night," Meg said, the sound of pots and pans banging in the background. "Is it meat loaf, chicken, pasta, steak? Bleck."

Kit grinned and stretched. "So what is it tonight?"

"Spaghetti."

"I'm eating spaghetti, too. But mine is frozen and out of a little box and is about as big as my palm."

"Not for me, thank you." Meg was an incredible cook and didn't nuke anything. "So, hey, this weekend. Your birthday."

"Not you, too!"

"Knock it off. You're such a spoilsport. We're all so happy to celebrate your birthday and you're being no fun at all."

"Meg, when you turned forty you were married, a mother to three kids, and in the best shape of your life. When I turn forty Saturday, I'm a single bookworm with aging ovaries."

Meg gurgled with laughter. "Oh, Kit, the visual on that one! You're too funny."

"Yes," Kit answered drily, "hilarious."

"So what is happening this weekend? Are Polly and Fiona still taking you out Saturday?"

"They are."

"Can I join you guys?"

"Yes!"

"You really don't mind? I know I'm the boring older sister—"

"Shut up. You know I love hanging out with you. I'll have Polly call you and she can tell you the plan since they're keeping it secret from me."

"They haven't told you anything?"

"Just that we're meeting up at seven, but I don't know where—" Kit broke off hearing the beeping sound of another caller on the line. "It's Michael," she said. "The guy I went out with Saturday."

"I thought you weren't sure about him."

"I'm not."

"Well, take the call, tell Polly I'm in, and I'll see you Saturday."

Kit said good-bye to Meg and answered Michael's call. "Hello?"

"I can't stop thinking about you," he said, his deep voice practically purring in her ear. "I hope you're thinking about me."

She rolled her eyes. "How are you?"

"Great. Better now that I hear your voice."

He was very slick with his lines. "I wish I could believe that."

"I'm totally sincere."

"Really?"

"Yes, and I want to see you again."

"You're still married, Michael."

"We'll go as friends."

"We'll go as friends after your divorce is final."

"I'm lonely."

"Maybe you should call Jon Coleman."

"That's mean."

"I'm not being mean. I'm trying to be helpful."

"Let's have dinner Wednesday, and you could invite your girl-friends so it wouldn't be a date."

"I'm busy Wednesday."

"You don't have to play hard to get with me."

Kit laughed, uncertain whether she was amused or annoyed by his persistence. "I'm not. I promised my freshman girls that I'd go to their basketball game Wednesday evening."

"Can't you miss the game?"

"No."

"There'll be other games."

"I'm looking forward to it and they know I'm coming."

"Tell them you got sick."

"I'm not going to lie to them. I'm their teacher. What kind of example would that be?"

"It's not like they'd know."

"I'd know."

"You've got to put yourself first, Kit."

She sighed, realizing she was definitely annoyed instead of amused. "I can't. And you need to take a hint."

"That's harsh."

"Then stop putting me on the spot—"

"I thought you were compassionate."

Kit gritted her teeth. "I need to go. Have a good week—"

"Why are you being a bitch?"

Wow. Kit pulled the phone from her ear and looked at it, blinking in shock. Did he really just say that? She shook her head, appalled. "I'm sorry, Michael. I need to go."

She hung up.

And then she was mad. Who did that? Who acted like that? What kind of man had a tantrum when he didn't get his way?

K it was late to school the next morning due to a series of non-event events and her students were already gathering outside her room when she reached her door. They heckled her for being tardy and Kit laughingly pleaded guilty and unlocked her door.

Turning on her lights, she headed for her desk and stopped short at the ridiculously enormous floral arrangement filling her desk. They were the kind of flowers a girl died to get—the most romantic mix of pink and coral tulips, lilies, and roses. Had to be another birthday gift, Kit thought, opening the card.

Instead, it was an apology from Michael.

Forgive me, he wrote. *I'm an ass. Go to dinner with me tomorrow night and let me make it up to you.*

Kit sighed and lightly touched one delicate, pale pink tulip. The flowers were breathtaking and the apology was appreciated, but she didn't like the attention. It felt suffocating. And he seemed to be getting obsessive.

Polly stuck her head into Kit's room, her pale blond hair caught up in a high swishy ponytail, her black turtleneck turning her into a young coed. "Somebody likes you," she said with a nod at the lavish arrangement taking over Kit's desk.

"It's from Michael," Kit said.

"I know. I saw him in the school office. He brought the flowers by a half hour ago and asked if I'd put them on your desk for you."

The final bell rang and Kit waited for the noise to die down to ask, "He delivered them personally?"

"Yep. I think someone likes you."

"Maybe too much."

"Really?" Polly looked surprised.

Kit nodded. "I'll tell you later."

Polly nodded and disappeared and Kit grumpily moved the flowers to the corner of her desk, and then eventually off her desk onto the table in the corner—she didn't want them on her desk. In fact, she didn't want them in her room. Frankly, she didn't want anything to do with Michael.

But Michael didn't know that, and he texted her during fourth period, her junior AP American lit class. She glanced down at her phone as she turned the page in a novel and read his text. *Hope you like the flowers. Hope we're good. Call me soon.*

Kit simply turned off her phone. She wasn't going to call and she wasn't going to be drawn in to this constant contact with him either.

She went home without calling or texting him back, but she was uneasy. She knew Michael was waiting for her to reach out to him. She knew he expected to hear from her. He'd sent the flowers and the text and she knew that, in his mind, she owed him a call.

Owed him.

Just like Parker had felt that she had owed him something. But Kit didn't owe either of them anything and she was not going to do this anymore. She was done being bullied and intimidated by men. Done feeling cornered and trapped.

Hunted.

It definitely wasn't what she wanted to feel. Not after Parker. And Richard. Not after a lifetime of feeling shame about sex and her body and men.

Kit was making dinner, broiling a salmon fillet and sipping a glass of wine, when Michael called. She almost didn't answer. She was enjoying the wine, savoring the smell of the teriyaki and brown sugar glazing the salmon, feeling happy. But not taking the call made her feel like a coward. She wasn't a coward and she was better off dealing with Michael now than dodging his calls in the future.

"Hello, Michael," she said briskly, answering the phone.

"You didn't call me," he said.

"The day's not over yet, Mr. Dempsey."

"It's almost seven. I've been waiting twelve hours to hear from you."

"Twelve?" she said, peeking into the oven to check her fillet.

"I left the flowers with your friend at seven-thirty this morning. I texted you, too."

"I was teaching."

"You're not still angry about last night, are you?"

"No. I'm just tired. It's the last week of the semester and I've a lot of work to do." Kit put on her oven mitt and pulled the pan from beneath the broiler, setting it on top of the stove. The salmon looked gorgeous. While she might not cook often, at least she knew how.

"But you liked the flowers?"

"They're gorgeous. Thank you. I'm the envy of the school. Half the teachers stopped by my room today to see them."

"So I am forgiven," he said smugly.

"Thank you for the flowers."

"So . . . dinner tomorrow?"

"Michael—"

"Not the married stuff again!"

"It wouldn't work, even if you weren't married." Kit drew a quick breath, relieved she'd said it, and she waited for him to say something.

He didn't.

He was quiet so long that she had to look at the phone, make sure they weren't disconnected. They weren't.

"Maybe I'll just come over," he said, finally breaking the silence.

Her eyebrows arched.

"Maybe I'll just show up on your doorstep," he added. "What would you do then?"

"Call the cops," she said drily, aware that if she ever needed help, her brother would be at her house in a heartbeat. Tommy lived in Walnut Creek, but he worked for the Oakland Fire Department and had quite a few friends in the Oakland Police Department. Tommy wouldn't tolerate anyone harassing her. Nor would the other firefighters or police officers who were his friends.

"Very funny." Michael was silent a moment. "What *would* you do if I just showed up?"

"I'd wonder how you got my address," Kit snapped, losing patience. "And I'd be really upset that you were interrupting my work." She paused, before adding firmly, "Speaking of work, I need to eat before my dinner's cold and then get back to grading. Good-bye."

Kit lingered in her classroom late Friday afternoon, grateful the first semester was officially over. The grades were all in, the report cards finished, all she had to do now was get organized for Monday.

She liked being in her classroom when school wasn't in session. It'd been her room for all but one of the sixteen years she'd taught at Memorial and it felt like home.

She was crouching next to a carton of books, counting class sets, thinking about the surprise birthday lunch the teachers had thrown for her in the staff room today. It had been a potluck, and as no one had assigned dishes, they'd ended up with desserts and casseroles and no salads. Thank goodness Shelley always brought a big bucket of Kentucky Fried Chicken. Kit loved the Colonel's chicken and Shelley knew it.

But now it was almost five and all the staff had gone home for the weekend. Kit heard the distant hum of a vacuum and the periodic metallic clang of trash cans being emptied. The custodians had begun their nightly cleaning.

Her door opened, and she glanced up, expecting to see one of the janitors. Instead, it was Michael.

Suppressing a ripple of unease, she got to her feet and wiped her hands on her gabardine trousers before tucking a wave of dark red hair back behind her ear. "Michael."

"Bad time?" he asked.

"Just finishing up," she said, shocked that he'd found his way up to her room. The front door of the building was always locked at four and it was nearly five now. "What are you doing here?"

"Came to see you." He wandered slowly through her room, hands in his pockets as he took in the rows of desks, her desk, the whiteboard, the bulletin boards, the cross at the front of the room, and the windows along the wall. "I thought the classrooms would be nicer," he said, closing the distance between them.

"It's an old building."

"And not at all secure. Which makes me wonder what you're still doing here on a Friday afternoon when everyone else is gone?"

She didn't like how he said it. As if she'd done something foolish. Dangerous. But she wasn't vulnerable here. This was her space, her domain. "I'm not alone. Javier and his crew are here," she said crisply, angered by his tone. "And I wanted to make sure everything was ready for Monday."

"And is it?"

She leaned over, picked up the books, and stepped around Michael. "Yes."

"So dedicated."

"I love what I do."

"So you say." He stepped in front of her. "Here, let me have those." He took the box out of her hands. "Where do you want it to go?"

She pointed to the counter running beneath the windows. "Beneath the window is fine."

Michael set the carton down and took a seat on the edge of the counter next to the books. "You seem . . . distracted."

"It's Friday. Last day of a long semester."

"You don't seem happy to see me."

"I'm surprised."

"Why?"

"Visitors aren't the norm."

"Friends aren't allowed to drop by to see you?"

"We try to limit guests and friends. It's to protect the children. Keep them safe."

His jaw hardened. "I'm not going to hurt anybody."

"I didn't think you would. I was just explaining school policy."

"Maybe the school should do a better job locking doors."

Kit's heart did a funny little beat. "Maybe."

Michael stared at her a moment, expression brooding. "I wanted to tell you something, thought I should tell you in person. Thought it'd be the nice thing to do. Didn't realize I'd get such a cold reception."

Kit suddenly wished that Javier or Pauline or one of the others from the janitorial team would open her classroom door, begin cleaning her room so she wouldn't have to be alone with him. "What did you want to tell me?"

He continued to stare at her, forehead creasing, mouth pressed thin. And then he shrugged. "I'm reconciling with Missy."

"You are?"

"There's one more thing. I told Missy all about you and this school and we've decided to enroll Dee here."

Kit blinked. "At Memorial?"

He nodded and wagged his finger at her. "So no more of this stranger stuff, or giving me the cold shoulder, because now I have the right to be here. Got it, teach?"

He was trying to be funny but she didn't feel like laughing. She didn't want Michael's stepdaughter at Memorial, and she definitely didn't want Michael Dempsey dropping by her room. "Who does she have for English?"

"You." He pushed off from the counter and stood, towering over her. "At least it's your name on her schedule. Katherine E. Brennan." His lips curved but his expression was cold. "What does the *E* stand for? Elizabeth? Elaine?"

"Elizabeth," she said faintly.

"Well, Katherine Elizabeth Brennan, you can expect Dee on Monday, the first day of the new semester."

Part 2

Delilah

Ten

Another first day at another new school.

Fifteen-year-old Delilah Hartnel held her breath, teeth clenched, overwhelmed by nerves. She'd felt sick all morning, but now that they were actually in the car, driving to school, she was dangerously close to puking all over the back of her stepfather's Lincoln Town Car, but that would be a disaster. You didn't puke around Howard Michael Dempsey, much less in his pristine car.

Howie loved his car. And his fine clothes. And his fine face.

Queasy, Delilah tipped her head against the car's leather seat and squeezed her eyes closed, hands clenched at her sides.

She hated him.

She hated him more than she'd hated anyone and she was good at hating, too.

She hated her dad for leaving them when she was a baby. She hated her mom for only falling in love with losers. She hated her grandpa for looking the other way when Mama's loser boyfriends put their fists in Mama's face.

Men shouldn't hit women.

But they did. All the time.

"You've got your lunch money, hon?" Delilah's mom, Missy, asked, glancing over her shoulder at her daughter.

Delilah nodded, hunching deeper into her seat, and tried to ignore her mother's brittle, bright smile. Her mom had never been exactly steady, but lately she looked positively skittish, as if any moment disaster could strike. As well it could.

"Did you hear your mom, Dee?" Howie demanded.

"Yes."

"Then answer her."

"I did."

"I didn't hear you."

Delilah ground her teeth together. "I said yes," she said shortly, turning her head to look out the front window. Instead, her gaze fell on Howie's hands on the steering wheel. She was always looking at his hands. Fascinated and yet repelled at the same time. He had big hands—no surprise, as he was six three and a half—but his fingers grossed her out. His fingers were thick and too pink and she hated thinking of them on her mother.

Nauseated, Delilah tugged on the red-and-black pleated skirt that hit just above her bony knees, trying to cover more of her skin.

She didn't like her new uniform but at least it wasn't as bad as St. Joseph's in Bakersfield. That one had been cheap gray and royal blue. She looked hideous in royal blue. Fortunately, she attended St. Joe's for only four months before they ended up moving abruptly to the Bay Area for unfortunate reasons.

But why uniforms in the first place? She was fifteen. A high school freshman. Way too old to be wearing pleated skirts and cardigans and white blouses with little round collars.

In Mineral Wells, she'd never had to wear a uniform, but then, she'd gone to public school there and things had been fine. Well, maybe not fine, but better than they were now that Mama had married Howie.

Within months of marrying Mama, Howie had them packed up and settled in Houston. They were in Houston just a year and a handful of months before they were driving across the desert on their way to Bakersfield, California. Bakersfield had been a disaster from the start. All the brown dirt seemed to put Howie in a perpetually nasty mood. And now they were here in the East Bay, and Delilah was starting a new school, *a good school*, and Howie thought he was God for making it happen.

But Howie wasn't God. He was the devil. And she heard him with Mama in their room at night, bed banging, Howie groaning, his voice louder and louder until he came. He screamed every time they had sex. Which was pretty much every night. In the beginning her mom tried to shush him. *Remember Delilah*, she'd whisper, *not so loud*. But then later, as Howie took over, Mom got quieter, protests swallowed the same way she swallowed him.

Why did her mama marry him? And worse, why did she stay? How could anyone need a man more than self-respect?

"Excited?" Howie asked now, glancing at her in the rearview mirror.

Delilah shook her head, and then catching Howie's blue eyes in the mirror, she forced herself to speak. "No," she said, hesitating before adding, "sir."

"You'll make friends in no time," her mom added with false cheer. "Just be yourself."

Delilah closed her eyes, feeling sick, so very sick on the inside. "Sure."

Her mom stretched an arm back to pat Delilah's knee. "First days are always stressful."

Howie sighed impatiently. "Missy, don't put ideas in her head. She's already a drama queen. Dee's fine. She's got it made."

Delilah bit down, grinding her teeth to keep from asking just how he thought she had it made. Instead, she fixed her gaze on the slow-moving traffic around them, the tangled traffic like the knots of dread and anxiety in her stomach.

Ten minutes later they pulled up to a large two-story stucco building with a red-tiled roof and an adjacent bell tower behind. There was probably a chapel tucked somewhere, too, Delilah thought, annoyed by the fake Spanish mission style.

"Here we are," Howie said, parking, turning off the engine.

Missy flashed Delilah a quick, nervous smile as they climbed from the car. "Doesn't it look nice, Dee? And look at that pretty statue in the garden right there."

Delilah looked. It was just a silly little white plaster monk. "Nice."

Howie shot her a swift glance. Delilah smiled up at him, showing teeth so he'd think it was a real smile. As if she'd ever give him a real smile.

Together they entered the school office.

A thin, frazzled-looking secretary with short gray hair sat behind the front desk, a phone pressed to her ear as another phone rang insistently on her desk. A half-dozen uniformed students hovered in the entry waiting for her attention, but Howie pushed through them, as if they didn't matter, and in his world, they didn't. Delilah squirmed as he loudly announced that Sister Elena was expecting them.

Mrs. Dellinger covered the receiver's mouthpiece. "I can help you as soon as I'm off the phone."

Howie's mouth pressed inward, disappearing. He didn't like being told to wait, especially not by skinny fifty-seven-year-old women in ugly orange–and-brown-striped sweaters.

"We were told we'd be given a tour at eight," he said, his face screwing up. "It's eight."

"I've got it, Helen, thanks," a big plain woman with short hair and weathered skin said, emerging from the hallway behind the secretary's desk. She moved to the counter and extended a hand to Howie. "Mr. Dempsey?"

"Yes," Howie said gruffly.

"I'm Shelley Jones, the PE teacher and girls' softball coach—"

"I bet you are," he muttered.

Delilah wondered if Shelley Jones had heard him, but if she had, she gave no indication. "Sister asked me to show you around."

Howie's eyes narrowed to slits. "She's not here?"

Ms. Jones's gaze slid over him but she didn't answer his question. "We only have fifteen minutes. Let's get going."

The tour was too short and too fast for Delilah. There were too many halls and stairwells and dopey bulletin boards for her to keep straight. Classroom. Classroom. Classroom. Upstairs. Downstairs. Outside and down a covered walkway. More classrooms. Library. Cafeteria. Another covered walkway. Science lab. Gym. Computer lab.

The day passed in a similar blur. She fumbled with her slip of paper that told her what classes she'd been given and wandered hallways until she found the right room. She took the open desk the teacher indicated, although in history it meant sharing the back table with another student. She opened books to the right pages. She stared straight ahead at the old chalkboards. She wrote down what the teacher assigned for homework. But she didn't really hear anything. Couldn't really understand. Didn't want to understand either.

She didn't want to be at Memorial High in Oakland.

Didn't want to live in a crummy white house in a crummy San Leandro neighborhood, which still apparently cost Howie a fortune because real estate was outrageously expensive in the San Francisco Bay Area. But she didn't care about the crummy, outrageously expensive house and she didn't want to live in California. She wanted Texas and Mineral Wells. She wanted people and places that were familiar. More specifically, she wanted Shey Darcy, her only real friend, even though Shey was older than her mom. But Shey had looked out for her. Shey had given her a place to go. A place to escape.

There was no escape here in San Leandro.

After school Delilah grabbed a bottle of black nail polish from her room and chugged down a glass of chocolate milk in the kitchen as the TV blared in the living room

Dr. Phil. A guest cried. Dr. Phil's voice rose. Audience erupted into applause.

Great. Dr. Phil was making someone else feel like crap. Some things never changed.

Wiping her mouth, she put her glass in the sink and headed for the door.

"In the dishwasher, Dee," her mom called from the living room, where she was ironing Howie's shirts while watching TV. Howie liked everything ironed, and he meant everything—T-shirts, dress shirts, trousers, jeans, even his tighty-whities. And he liked everything on the outside sharp. Heavily starched. Which meant Mama sprayed and ironed, sprayed and ironed. It took her forever. Most of every afternoon.

Dee put the glass in the dishwasher. Headed for the front door.

"Where you going, Dee?"

"Outside."

"Don't you have homework?"

"That's what I'm doing," she answered, ignoring her school backpack to step outside. It was blue-gray and hazy, the sun already at an angle in the sky. It was beginning to stay lighter later. She was glad. She dreaded being cooped up inside the house with Mama and Howie.

Sitting down on the front steps, Delilah kicked off her shoes, peeled off her socks, and began carefully painting her toenails black.

Her mom hated it when she painted her nails purple and silver or black and electric blue but it made Delilah happy. She liked defying her mom and she liked doing it while watching the neighbor take apart his bike, which he was doing now.

Howie couldn't stand the neighbor, Jude-something-or-other, a low-life, unemployed good-for-nothing living off welfare.

Delilah looked across the fence at Jude, the low-life, unemployed good-for-nothing and ran the tip of the brush over her pinkie toe, the last toe on her right foot, turning the small pink nail into matte black. He might be a low-life good-for-nothing but he was drool-worthy, even for an old guy, a fact that probably hadn't escaped Howie's attention either.

And so as she turned her attention to her left foot, she watched Jude from beneath her lashes as he worked on his bike, and she wondered what he was really like. Howie had forbidden her to talk to him, and so far she hadn't. But maybe today she would.

Maybe today she should. They'd been here almost a month now.

Left foot finished, she stretched her legs out in front of her to let her nails dry and stared at Jude as he picked up one tool after the other to tighten this and unscrew that. He'd been working on his bike for days now. She'd only seen him ride it once, and that had been right around New Year's. The bike was loud, really loud, and Howie had gone charging out of the house. Delilah didn't know what he said to Jude that day, or what Jude said back, but it couldn't have been good because Howie stormed back into the house and nearly killed Mama.

Flexing her foot, Delilah watched Jude lift the engine into the big bike's orange frame and begin to secure it in place.

"You actually going to get that thing running?" she shouted across the fence to Jude. "You've been working on it a long time."

Jude-the-lowlife sat back on the heels of his boots and pushed long black hair away from his face before looking at her, black eyebrow lifting. "It was running a couple weeks ago. Took a ride over to Santa Cruz."

"Sure you did."

He just shrugged and returned to work.

Delilah wanted him to talk to her again. She liked his voice. Liked his face. Liked that he wasn't afraid of Howie. "So why isn't it working now?"

"Broke down again Sunday."

"Maybe you should get a new bike."

"I like my old one. It gives me something to do."

"Huh."

"A man can't have a hobby?" he asked, looking at her over the top of the chain-link fence that divided the two yards.

"Not if he doesn't have any other form of transportation," she answered.

"Who says I don't have any other wheels?"

"Do you?"

He gestured to his small detached garage. "There."

She glanced at the Pepto Bismol–pink garage that looked every bit as decrepit as his matching house. Inside was an old white convertible Cadillac with blue leather seats. "Does it run?"

"No."

She nearly smiled. "Didn't think so."

"You're quite the smart aleck, aren't you?"

"No need to get your panties in a wad. Just making conversation."

"Nice of you."

Delilah laughed. She hadn't meant to. But now that she'd laughed, she was glad, because she liked Jude's deep, rough voice and how his jet-black hair hung in his eyes and a beast tattoo on his shoulder was inked so that some of its barbed tail circled his biceps. He was the opposite of Howie. Messy, sweaty, untidy. His voice was the same. Deep, untidy, rough. He talked like he needed a throat lozenge. Delilah liked that.

Jude had made a mistake making her laugh. He shouldn't engage her. Certainly shouldn't encourage her, especially as it wasn't the first time she'd sat on the front steps to watch him work. She was a teenage girl after all. And teenage girls were a dangerous mix of hormones, curiosity, and attitude. And this one, with her shaggy blond hair and rebellious pout, more than most.

"Your dad wouldn't like you talking to me," he said, wiping greasy hands on a tattered white rag dangling from his back jeans pocket.

She shot to her feet. "He's not my dad."

"Stepdad," he corrected, watching as she sauntered barefoot in her red-plaid pleated skirt down the walkway to cross the tidy lawn and approach the chain-link fence.

"He's my mother's husband. That's it. She married him. I didn't." She glared at him as she leaned against the fence.

Jude cocked an eyebrow. She had attitude all right. Probably didn't get her real far with the old man. "Either way, he wouldn't want you talking to me. You should get back into the house before he comes home."

She tossed her head. "I'm not afraid."

"No?" he asked softly, watching her face. She wasn't a happy little girl. She had purple patches beneath her eyes and her whip-thin body hummed with tension. Some scary shit probably went down in that house of theirs. Not that it was any business of his. He'd already been warned off by her daddy-o. As if Jude wanted a little girl that way. Freaking creep.

"I'm Delilah," she said, running the palm of her hand across the metal links.

"Nice to meet you, Delilah. Now go inside before—"

"You men are all the same. Always telling women what to do."

"You're a woman?"

"I'm sixteen."

"No, you're not."

"Am, too."

He gave her a hard look and she struggled to hold his gaze. And then she shrugged her slim shoulders. "Almost."

"When?"

"August."

"That makes you fifteen and a half."

"What are you, an accountant?"

He shook his head. "Your daddy really won't like you talking to me."

"I already told you, he's not my daddy and I don't care what he thinks."

"But I bet he can be plenty hard on you when he wants."

She abruptly averted her head, stared down the street with its row of small, square homes built post-WWII. For the most part the landscaping was as tired and spare as the neighborhood's plain, practical architecture. And then she jerked her chin to look back at him. "Do you have a last name? Howie calls you Jude-the-lowlife but I wasn't sure if I was supposed to call you that, or by another name."

Jude smiled reluctantly. "Is that what he calls me?"

"Yes, sir." Delilah smiled sweetly. "But maybe that's what you prefer . . . ?"

The girl was trouble with a capital *T*, he thought, but he liked her fire. "It's Knight," he said, walking to the fence and extending a hand over scraggly rosebushes. "But you can call me Jude."

She lifted her face, her brown eyes assessing. "Jude Knight."

"That's what my mama named me."

And then it was her turn to smile. She put her hand into his.

"Nice to meet you." Her grin split her face. For a moment she was half woman, half child, and bubbling with life.

She froze the next second when a shiny gray town car pulled into her driveway.

"Howie," she said lowly, swiftly letting go of his hand and burying her fingers in the pleats of her skirt.

Jude saw the hard, hollow look return to her face.

Some serious shit went down in that house, he silently repeated, waiting for Howard to emerge from the car. Jude had met a lot of men like Howard in his life and he'd never liked one of them.

Howard didn't waste any time. He slammed the car door behind him and came charging across the lawn. "Shouldn't you be doing homework, Dee?" he said, closing the distance between them. "First day of a new school and all."

Delilah lifted her chin. "It's done."

"Then you should be helping your mother with dinner." Howard looked at Jude and curved his lips into a thin, unpleasant smile. "Is there something I can help you with?"

At six two, Jude was tall, but Howard had another inch on him. But Howard could have had a foot on him and Jude wouldn't have worried. He'd earned his hard-core reputation by being good with his fists. And knives, guns, fishhooks, and razor blades. He didn't mind pain. He healed fast. He had nothing to lose. So he didn't lose.

"No," Jude said, smiling lazily at his neighbor. "Can I help *you* with something?"

Howard opened his mouth and then shut it, seething. He reached for the girl, hand clamping down on her thin shoulder, making her flinch. "Don't let us keep you," Howard said, his fingers tightening on Delilah's shoulder. "Looks like you've still got a lot of cleaning up to do."

The girl twisted and slipped free of Howard's grasp and, after shooting Jude an indecipherable look, ran back to the house.

Jude was glad she'd escaped, and he glanced over his shoulder to his front yard with the sprawl of tools and motorcycle parts. It *was* messy. It was always messy. "Oh, I'm not cleaning. Just puttering around."

"Maybe you should think about cleaning up."

"Why? I like it this way. Can find everything I need just where I left it."

"No wonder I got the house so cheap," Howard said scornfully. "No one wants to live next to you."

Jude's lips curved but the smile didn't touch his eyes. "I've lived here almost ten years, and no one in the neighborhood has a problem with me. You're the one they're talking about, pal."

"Me?"

"Sometimes things get a little crazy over at your place. Folks on the street can hear everything. Might want to shut your windows when things start getting loud."

"Mind your own business."

"Happy to. Just as long as your business doesn't become my business."

Eleven

Friday morning Kit watched Delilah, her new student in freshman English, shoulder her black-and-purple backpack with the skull on the little pocket and prepare to leave her classroom. "Delilah," she said, stopping the girl before she reached the door. "How's it going?"

The girl shrugged, looked away, long blond bangs falling in her eyes.

"You survived your first week here," Kit continued, determined to engage her, wanting to know why Delilah, or Dee as Michael had called her, made absolutely no effort to participate in class this week. "What do you think so far?"

Another shrug, a flick of her hair. "It's fine."

"Things becoming more familiar?"

"Yeah. I guess." And still without making eye contact, she tugged her backpack higher on her shoulder and stared pointedly at the door.

Kit knew she wanted to go, but wasn't ready to let her escape quite yet. "Have you ever read Shakespeare before?"

"Yes. Last year."

"So you're not having any problem with the reading assignments?"

"No."

"You failed the pop quiz, though, yesterday."

Delilah just looked at her, said nothing.

"We're going to have another pop quiz on *Twelfth Night* early next week. Do try to get caught up with the reading, all right?"

The girl tugged on her backpack strap. "I have to go. If I'm late to gym, I'll have to run extra laps."

"But if you are struggling with the reading, please come see me, okay?"

Delilah nodded, put her head down, and disappeared out the door.

Kit watched her go, and all she could think of was a small, bruised peach.

During lunch in the staff room, Kit ate her chicken sandwich while skimming the last chapter of Edith Wharton's *The Age of Innocence,* which she'd be discussing with her junior lit class right after lunch. Kit had taught the novel for the past seven years, but its last chapter still made her restless and unhappy. Newland Archer had made the wrong choice. He should have seized that second chance.

Kit was still engrossed in the fading light of Paris and Newland's decision to let Ellen remain part of his memory—abstractly, serenely—something that did not make her feel serene at all, when Polly appeared in the staff room, a bottle of water and an organic protein bar in her hand. She took a seat next to Kit.

"Fish Friday," Polly muttered under her breath. "That's just plain evil."

"Don't let Bob hear you," Kit whispered, closing the book. "He was raving about the delicious moist fish fillet earlier."

"*Fillet?* It was minced! Fish guts!"

Kit stuffed her sandwich into her mouth to keep from laughing aloud. "You're killing me," she said when she could finally talk without food in her mouth. "I hate that you're so funny."

"I know. I feel bad for you. I wish you could be funny, too."

Kit laughed softly again, aware that Bob Osborne was staring at them, probably trying to decide how he could work his way into their conversation, when Shelley Jones stuck her head into the staff room. "Kit, have a second?"

Kit pushed away from the table, met Shelley just outside the door. Down the hall in the workroom, copiers hummed and student voices wafted from the front office asking for a late arrival slip, wanting to call home, wondering if there was a Band-Aid.

"What's up?" Kit asked.

Shelley folded her arms across her chest. "Delilah Hartnel was late to class fourth period and she said she was with you. Just wanted to verify her story."

"I was talking to her, yes."

"Send a note with her next time when she's that late."

"How late was she?"

"At least fifteen minutes. Closer to twenty."

"But I only kept her a minute or two."

Shelley shrugged. "Just telling you the excuse she gave me."

Kit nodded and returned to the table in the staff room as the bell rang. Polly's eyebrows arched. "What did Shelley want?"

"That new freshman, Delilah, is going to be a challenge." Kit grabbed her lunch bag, tossed it, and put what was left of her Coke in the fridge.

"What did she do?"

"Told Shelley I'd kept her, which is why she was fifteen minutes tardy to PE."

"Did you keep her after class?"

"Just for a minute or two. If that.

"I don't know," Kit continued as they left the staff room and walked through the office and out into the hall. "There's definitely something going on with her."

The first bell hadn't rung yet, so the hallway was still empty. Their footsteps echoed on the tiled floor.

"I don't think this is the right school for her," Polly said, keys jingling in her hand. "She's not even trying in math. Hasn't turned in a single homework assignment yet."

"She hasn't done much in my class either," Kit admitted. "But I can't tell if it's because she doesn't understand the assignments or if she's overwhelmed—"

"Or if she just doesn't care." Polly's lips pursed. "I'm thinking she doesn't care."

"I wouldn't go there yet," Kit said. Delilah was obviously struggling. But with what? "She's still brand-new."

"I won't coddle her. This isn't a public school. You have to do your work. You have to keep your grades up. And you have to follow the rules."

Saturday morning, while doing laundry, Kit found herself thinking about Delilah, which made her think of Michael, who was the last person she wanted to think about. She didn't like Michael. Didn't trust him at all.

And Delilah . . . what was the deal with her? She was puzzling, too.

Michael had said he didn't get along with Delilah, and looking at the girl, Kit could see why. Michael was clean-cut, Mr. Corporate, and Delilah was surly, and moody and emo, but then, she was a teenager. Teenage girls were chock-full of hormones, and fifteen was notoriously difficult . . .

So was Delilah to blame for the problems between her and her stepdad? Or was Michael being the problem? Hard to say at this point, but Kit was interested in finding out.

By noon, though, her attention was diverted away from Michael and Delilah to Meg's and Sarah's texts about the cruise. Kit hadn't even thought about packing for the trip yet, but Meg and Sarah were demanding to know what she planned to wear for the formal night, and if she'd take a costume for the theme night, and whether it made sense to invest in a new swimsuit and cover-up for the pool.

Before long Meg and Sarah added Cass to the group messages, and then Mom. Soon Kit's phone and e-mail in-box were swamped with messages about shore excursions and weather forecasts and Dramamine for seasickness. Cass was worried about continuing reports of violence in Mexico and Sarah was nervous about Boone taking the kids ATV riding in Cabo. Mom wondered if any of them had heard from Brianna yet and when she'd be arriving in California. This prompted another flurry of e-mails that now included Brianna, asking her for her flight number and the date and time of her arrival.

Because of the time difference between California and Africa, they didn't hear from Brianna until Sunday. Kit saw the e-mail in her in-box just as she was walking out the door for the 8:30 A.M. Mass at St. Margaret Mary. She paused to read the message and ended up never making it to church.

Apparently her fraternal twin had been sick ever since Christmas. That's why she hadn't come home after all. But Brianna being Brianna hadn't wanted to worry her family, so she was only now sharing her "adventure."

Kit had to read the e-mail three times to understand the facts, as Brianna had cleverly glossed over the pertinent ones in her brief, cheery mass e-mail, explaining that she wouldn't be able to join them on the cruise since she was still recovering from a crazy night in Namibia in the company of a button spider.

I have a lot in common with Little Miss Muffet, Brianna added, *but sadly my little spider, when he sat down beside me, didn't scare me away. He just climbed in my pants, and bit me on the ass, and I've been on IV antibiotics ever since.*

Brianna ended her e-mail saying she was finally back home from the hospital and "almost well" but tragically not strong enough to travel, and she hoped that they'd have a great cruise without her.

After the third reading, Kit glanced up to the top of the e-mail to see all the addresses Brianna had included and there was Mom's. Marilyn was an early riser and she would have seen it by now.

Kit reached for her phone and called her but got her voice mail. She left a message. "I got Brianna's e-mail. Can't believe she's been so sick. Think I should go to the Congo instead of on the cruise so I can kick her butt."

Apparently everyone else in the family was having the same thought. Dad, Meg, and Tommy all offered to get on a plane and head to Africa to make sure Brianna was okay. Kit looked up flight options but it was Tommy who actually reserved a ticket.

Brianna's humor deserted her when she learned that in less than twenty-four hours a concerned family delegate, most likely Tommy, would be en route to see her. *ABSOLUTELY NOT,* she e-mailed them all in another mass message. *DON'T EVEN THINK ABOUT IT,* she continued shouting (yes, just like that, in caps) that she would disown all of them, her entire Brennan-Roberts-Walker family, if even one of them barged in on her when she was trying to rest in the privacy of her own home.

Brianna's group e-mail devastated Mom, and so Meg shot Brianna a curt (private) e-mail telling her that this wasn't the time to be selfish when Mom had so little time left. Brianna responded (in a group e-mail) that she was perfectly aware that Mom's time was limited, and thanked Meg for reminding her, saying she didn't know what she'd do without her to depress her and make her feel like shit.

Kit was still reading—and cringing from—Brianna's brutal response when her phone rang. She knew without looking it was Meg calling. "I was just reading the e-mail," she said to Meg as she answered.

"What's wrong with her?"

"She's been really sick."

"But why send that e-mail to everyone? Why not just send it to me?"

"Because Bree was making a point. She doesn't want us there, doesn't want us fussing. And this is her way of making us back off." Kit sighed, thinking of Bree in her little apartment in Kinshasa, Congo's capital. "And you know, it'll work. Everyone will back off. They'll leave her alone. And she'll become invisible all over again."

"It's like she doesn't want to be part of the family."

Brianna had gone to Africa as a medical volunteer when she was twenty-six. She'd just earned a graduate degree in infectious diseases and had joined the six-week program to get some practical field experience before taking a job with a hospital in Miami. But she never returned. She cashed in her airline ticket, applied for a permanent job in Congo, and stayed. "I just think she's been gone so long now that she forgets what it's like to be part of our family."

"She makes it hard to love her."

"Yeah," Kit said quietly, thinking of her twin. "That might be intentional."

Hanging up, she made herself a cup of tea and returned to the living room, with the stack of notebooks piled high on the coffee table. It'd been two weeks since she last read student journals, which meant she had dozens to review today.

The student journals were quite personal. Some students wrote very little. Some wrote a lot, filling page after page with teenage anger and angst, hopes, dreams, and irritations. The sophomores were the most arrogant. (They'd survived their freshman year and thought they'd made it.) Juniors were focused on getting into college. Seniors could taste college. And her freshmen . . . her freshmen felt everything so intensely.

Kit identified with her freshman and sophomore students. Their adolescent emotions burned razor sharp, fueled by hormones and intense wants and needs. Love. Hate. Fear. Desire. They all wanted to be somebody. They all craved something. Attention. Sex. Validation.

Kit understood. There were still so many things she wanted, things that were becoming impossible dreams.

Summoning fresh energy, she settled down to read, scribbling notes in the margins here and there, adding a smiley face or an exclamation where appropriate. She was moving swiftly through the freshmen journals when she came to Delilah Hartnel's brand-new notebook. It was black, and plain (why was she not surprised that Delilah had chosen black for her notebook color?) and contained just the introductory paragraph Kit had asked her for three days ago.

Miss Brennan,

You asked me to tell you about myself. You asked about my family. I'll tell you. My name is Delilah Hartnel. I'm fifteen. And I'm wonderful. My family is wonderful, too. My mom and stepdad are the happiest couple I know. They are so much fun to be around. We have a great time together and we like to move a lot. We moved a month ago from Bakersfield, after moving from Houston, after moving from Mineral Wells, Texas, where I was born and where my grandpa still

*lives. But now I live in beautiful San Leandro and go to this
great school in Oakland and every morning I wake up and
think, I'm so lucky. I'm the luckiest person I know.*

Kit stopped reading and pursed her lips, stifling a sputter of
shocked laughter. She could see why Michael would describe Delilah as mouthy. She had fire. Attitude. And from what Kit knew
of Michael, he wouldn't like that.

Kit studied Delilah's handwriting a moment, noting how the
girl wrote in a jet-black felt tip with dark smudges and exclama-
tions with words underlined. Teenage girls thrived on drama, but
Kit sensed that in Delilah's world, the drama was real. She and
Michael didn't get along, and Kit imagined that her mother,
Missy, was caught in the middle. Not a comfortable situation for
any of them.

Kit touched the scrawl—*I'm the luckiest person I know*—
thinking that Michael wouldn't like his stepdaughter's journal
entry. But then, he'd already made it clear that he didn't like her.

After a moment Kit took her pen, a blue ink gel that wrote
practically effortlessly, *Tell me about Mineral Wells. What was it
like? Do you miss it? Do you miss your grandfather?*

Abruptly she lifted her pen, considered what she'd written,
wishing she could ask the questions she was most curious about—
where Delilah had gone to school for the past month, why her
parents had chosen Memorial for her, and how she felt about her
mother reconciling with her stepfather. But she didn't ask.

This was Delilah's journal. Delilah's story. And Delilah would
share when she was ready to share.

Delilah wasn't having a good day, but then, when were Mondays ever good days? Today was worse than usual, though.
Howie had left late last night for a trip, which meant that Mama

overslept this morning and Delilah ended up missing her shower, breakfast, and her normal bus. She arrived at her stop to see Bus 57 pulling away, and by the time the next bus arrived, she was already twenty minutes late.

Sister Elena spotted her in the office waiting for a tardy slip, and lectured her on the importance of being organized and on time.

Grimly Delilah headed off for her first class, math, arriving in time to be handed a test but not having time to complete it.

By the time she reached her third-period class, English, her stomach was growling loudly and the kid behind her laughed. Mortified, she slid lower in her seat, chewed on her thumb, and watched Miss Brennan pass the stack of graded journals back, returning them to each student's desk.

Delilah bit a hangnail, feigning boredom, not wanting to act like she cared about this class, or Miss Brennan, because who knew how long she'd be here? Howie might put his fist through Mama's face and knock her teeth out again and then they'd be packing up and moving somewhere new again. Someplace where no one knew them. Someplace where no one could call the cops and say Missy Dempsey has a black eye and is missing one of her nice white front teeth.

The black spiral-bound notebook dropped onto the corner of her desk and Delilah didn't look up until Miss Brennan had walked on.

She was dying to open her notebook and see how Miss Brennan had responded to her first entry. Would the teacher realize she'd been ironic? Or would she read Delilah's entry and think, *Ah, lovely, Delilah has such a lovely life?*

Delilah's upper lip lifted, curled. Adults were so stupid. So oblivious to what was right before their eyes. Only most people didn't pay attention because they didn't want to know. Because if they knew . . . if they saw . . . then maybe, just maybe, they'd have to get involved.

With a careless flick of her wrist, she flipped the notebook open to the first page with her introduction and Miss Brennan's response. *Tell me about Mineral Wells. Do you miss it? Do you miss your grandfather?*

Hot emotion filled Delilah's chest, licking at her heart, making her hurt, making her sick.

Mineral Wells was small and poor and in the middle of nowhere but it was home. It was who she was and what she'd always known. But then Howie came along and convinced Mama that better things were waiting elsewhere. Fewer fights. More money. Happier times.

Delilah picked up her pen and set it to the page. *I hated Mineral Wells until I found out that other places are worse. Like Bakersfield. We were only there four months, thank God, because that place sucks. It's ugly. And smells like shit. Even the sky is brown.*

She paused to read what she'd just written.

And then other images of Bakersfield flashed to life. Images of Mama's jaw swollen and her fingers crushed, broken. Images of Mama hushing Delilah, telling her not to cry and not to argue with Howie. Telling her that fighting back would only make things worse. Better to just take it. Better to just let him get it out of his system because tomorrow everything would be better. Tomorrow things would be good again.

Liar.

Delilah clenched the Bic pen so hard it snapped in her fist, black ink splattering her palm.

Miss Brennan was passing down the aisle on the other side of Delilah's desk and paused. "Need a pen?"

Delilah kept her eyes on the tiny ink splatters puddling across her pale wrist. "No, ma'am. I have another one."

Miss Brennan moved on and Delilah wiped the wet ink across the open journal with her wrist, smearing the whiteness of the paper with black.

Serves the page right. Nothing escapes life unscathed.

Furious, Delilah yanked the page from the spiral-bound notebook and crumpled it up.

A girl next to her looked up at the ripping sound. "You can't do that to your journal. You have to leave all the pages in."

Delilah stared at the girl with the red velvet headband, dark eyes, pale skin, and glossy brown hair. She had that money look about her. Delicate little watch. Long straight hair. Little pearls in her ears. Definitely rich. "I don't care," Delilah said, shutting the notebook and shoving it in her backpack. "It's a stupid assignment anyway."

"Journals are ten percent of your grade."

"So?"

The girl's forehead furrowed ever so slightly before she shrugged and muttered, "Whatever. Be a loser."

And then bad got worse when Miss Brennan assigned them scenes from *Twelfth Night,* and partners, too, telling them they had two days to rehearse before performing their scene in front of the class.

Of course Delilah's partner would be the Little Rich Girl with the red hair band. Delilah was going to say something to Miss Brennan, but Kendra, her spoiled-rich-girl partner beat her to it. Miss Brennan, though, refused to assign her someone else.

Delilah watched Kendra with the perfect hair flounce back to her seat and waited for her to sit down before glancing over at her. "I didn't want you either," she said, biting yet another hangnail and spitting it out.

Kendra shuddered. "That's gross."

"I know," Delilah answered, peeling off another tiny strip of skin and rolling it between her teeth.

"You're disgusting *and* messed up."

"Thank you."

"It's not a compliment."

Delilah's eyes met Kendra's and held. "Says who?"

"I do."

"And who are you? *No one.*"

Tuesday, Delilah and Kendra had to sit off in a corner and rehearse their lines. Kendra refused to look at her, so they read their lines to the storage cabinet. Delilah didn't mind. She didn't want Kendra to like her. Wasn't interested in making any friends. It was so much easier moving when you had nothing, and no one, to leave behind.

Delilah sauntered to PE, arriving a minute later, but Miss Jones had to be a hard-ass and make her run two extra laps for tardiness, and then two more for having attitude. Delilah told her she wasn't having attitude, so she had to then do ten push-ups. She couldn't do even ten girl push-ups, which made a bunch of the kids laugh. So Delilah got mad, tripped one by accident, which Miss Jones said wasn't an accident, and assigned Delilah a three-page paper—typed, double-spaced, Courier font—on respect.

Due tomorrow morning before school started.

By the time Delilah stepped off her bus and walked the four blocks to her house, she was in a foul mood. Mama didn't help things by shouting at her when she entered the house to get started on her homework right away.

Delilah went to her bedroom, slammed and locked her door, and threw herself onto her bed. She hated Memorial High. Hated Kendra. Hated Miss Jones. Hated everyone.

An hour later she sleepily opened her eyes to the sound of loud knocking on her locked bedroom door. "Dee. Dee, what are you doing in there? Open the door."

Delilah slowly opened her eyes and turned over on her back. She stared up at the ceiling, chilled. She'd had the weirdest dream. It'd been so real. Shivering, she reached for her bedspread and pulled it across her body.

"Delilah!" Her mother's voice was louder, anxious. "Howie's on his way home from the airport in a terrible mood. Get up. Get your homework done."

"'Kay."

But she didn't move. She clutched the quilted bedspread, a blue-and-green swirl of colors that made her think of the ocean, and tried to get warm. She felt strange. Her room felt strange. Unsettled, she slid from bed, grabbed her backpack, and left her room, heading to the kitchen table to study.

Mama was standing at the kitchen sink peeling potatoes. "I'd go easy on Howard tonight. He had to fly to Houston early this morning and he's had a rough day."

Delilah dropped her backpack on the table, wishing that for once Mama would ask about her day, or want to know how she was feeling. But there was no room in Mama's life for anyone but Howie. God, Delilah hated Howie. "What do you mean, go easy on him? I never do anything—"

"That's exactly what I'm talking about. That tone of voice. That attitude. It's just going to upset him and we don't need to do that. He's already going to be worked up when he gets home."

"Why? Did he get laid off again?"

Missy shot Delilah a sharp glance. "No. He wasn't laid off." She took a quick breath, her right hand swiftly working the peeler, slicing the skin off in long graceful spirals. "There was an explosion at one of the refineries. Men are missing. Two of them were Howard's good friends."

"That's too bad," Delilah answered flatly, jerking out one of the chairs, letting it scrape against the floor. "Shit happens, don't it?"

"*Delilah.*"

"It's true."

Missy clenched the peeled potato in her palm, her voice rising. "If you say that to Howard, he will just lose it. *Lose it.* Do you understand?"

Delilah stared at her, her gaze hard, understanding all too well. "Why did you marry him?"

"That's none of your business."

"It *is* my business."

"No, it's not."

"What happens to you happens to me—"

"Nothing happens to me."

"You have a black eye or broken bone every couple of weeks."

"Don't exaggerate. It's not that bad. And when something happens, he always feels terrible about it later. He's a good man, Dee. Just had a rough childhood."

"Who hasn't?"

Missy glanced nervously toward the back door as if waiting for it to open. "This isn't the time. As I said, Howard's had a bad day and he's going to need things nice and quiet."

It was always about Howard, wasn't it? Keeping him happy. Making sure he was comfortable. Smoothing things over so he could feel like The Man.

Never mind that her mama was nothing but a doormat, just there for him to wipe his feet on.

How was that fair?

Delilah ground her teeth as she watched her mother pick up another potato. How could her mother take it? Accept it? Worse, how could she make excuses for him? God, there was no justice. No justice at all. "Which of his favorite dishes are you making, Mama?"

"German pot roast and mashed potatoes."

Delilah's eyes smarted, and she shook her head and looked

away toward the living room with its brown leather couch and love seat. Howie's furniture, of course.

"So he's pretty torn up?" she said.

"Yes."

Delilah swallowed around the ache in her chest and the fear thickening her throat. "Would you like me to make my Texas sheet cake? You know he always likes that."

Missy shot her a grateful smile. "Oh, that'd be wonderful, hon. He loves your Texas sheet cake. Says it's better than even his mama's."

Delilah went to the sink to wash her hands but suddenly turned to her mother and pressed her cheek to her warm, thin back. She could feel her narrow bra strap through Mama's blouse and caught a whiff of her perfume—Fantasy, by Britney Spears. Howie had bought the perfume for her after their first date and Mama wore it whenever she wanted to make him happy.

And Mama tried so hard to make Howie happy.

Delilah squeezed her eyes shut, held her breath. If Mama hadn't met him . . . If only Mama could have been happy with just the two of them . . .

"You okay?" Mama asked.

Delilah drew a quick breath. "Mm."

Slowly Missy reached around with a wet hand and patted her arm. "I love you, hon."

"Mm."

She patted Delilah's arm again. "Everything's going to be okay."

"Mm."

"And, baby, Howie's going to love the cake."

Twelve

Jude heard the first scream from the kitchen, where he was browning ground beef for his Hamburger Helper dinner. The hair on his neck rose and he stood motionless, wooden spoon suspended over the frying pan.

It *was* a scream, wasn't it? He held his breath and listened harder, ears, senses, straining.

All was silent except for the sizzle of meat. But Jude's gut felt tight.

He knew what was happening next door in the Dempsey house, and it made him nuts. It did. Someone needed to teach that bastard a lesson.

There were rules to the universe, rules every man knew. You hit a man, or pounded a punching bag, but never a woman.

Never a woman.

Jude knocked the skillet onto a back burner and headed outside to stand on his front porch and listen.

The night was cool, almost cold, and the moon was nonexistent. In the dark he listened to the silence. And he listened to the small sounds. And he listened for what he couldn't hear but could all too easily imagine.

Crying. Whimpering. Pain.

He squeezed his hand into a fist and realized he was still holding the wooden spoon.

And then it came. "No, Howie. Howie, please!"

The pleading shriek tore at Jude. Spots danced before his eyes. His stomach rolled. He started down the steps, reached the sidewalk, and then abruptly stopped.

He couldn't get involved.

He had to get involved.

He wasn't allowed to get involved.

But God help him, how could he not? Tossing the spoon, Jude reached into his back pocket of his jeans for his phone and swiftly punched in a number of someone who *could* get involved, giving him the address for the house next door, even while still listening to see if he needed to bust through the door to borrow a cup of sugar. And then before he could hang up the phone, the front door on the neat white house next to his opened and shut. Howard Dempsey stood on his own steps, car keys jingling in his hand.

He was leaving. Heading out now that he'd been the big man and taught his woman who was boss.

The edge of Jude's mouth flattened as he stood in the dark on his sagging front porch, watching Howard climb behind the wheel and back his gleaming gray Lincoln from the driveway into the street.

Jude waited until the red taillights of the car disappeared down the street before heading over to the Dempseys' and knocking on the front door.

He heard muffled voices and crying but no one answered.

He knocked again. Waited. "It's Jude," he said through the door. "Is everything all right? Is there anything I can do?"

No one came to the door. But then, knowing what he knew, he hadn't really expected anyone to.

He returned to his house, found a sheet of paper, and scribbled: *If you need anything call me.* He added his name and phone number and then slid the piece of paper under his neighbor's door.

Back at his house, he threw himself down on his couch and pressed a fist to his forehead, hating himself for not busting in and punching Dempsey out. Dempsey deserved to hurt. Deserved to bleed. Unfortunately, Jude couldn't be the one to do it. Not until he'd taken care of a few other people first.

Wednesday morning Kit sat in a chair at the back of the classroom waiting for the next group to assemble at the front to perform their assigned scene from *Twelfth Night*. According to her assignment sheet, Delilah and Kendra were next up.

"Delilah and Kendra, are you ready?" she asked, prodding them to action, even as she glanced down at the one-page printout of the girls' assignment. In this scene the beautiful, popular Kendra would play the lovely, aristocratic Olivia and Delilah would play Viola, who was pretending to be Cesario, Duke Orsino's servant.

Kit was fully aware that this had not been a popular pairing. Kendra had not wanted to be assigned to Delilah, preferring to be paired with one of her cheerleader friends, but Kit hadn't been swayed. She knew that Kendra wouldn't blow off the assignment and she wanted to see what Delilah would, or could, do.

The girls took their places at the front of the room and Kit was pleased to see that they were both in costume, Kendra in an emerald gown with her brown hair piled high, and Delilah in tweed trousers and a men's white dress shirt and brown vest, her hair hidden beneath a jaunty cap.

Delilah, as Viola, started the scene. "The honorable lady of the house, which is she?"

Kendra, channeling an arrogant, albeit exquisite, Olivia, stepped forward, fanning herself with a pink Japanese fan she'd pulled from her sleeve. "Speak to me," she said imperiously. "I shall answer for her. Your will?"

And they were off, reciting lines with ease, holding the class spellbound. Kit was spellbound, too. While Kendra was playing to type as Olivia, Delilah was a revelation, transforming from a silent, hostile teenager into the perfect Viola, charming and yet vulnerable. Even more impressive was that she had memorized the scene, and never once referred to the script clutched in her hand. Kendra and Delilah's familiarity with the lines allowed them to nail Shakespeare's banter. It was beyond good, it was brilliant, and Kit sat on the edge of her seat as the scene came to a close with Olivia telling Viola to tell the duke that she could never love him, and Viola responding with some of Kit's favorite lines in the play:

> *Love make his heart of flint that you shall love;*
> *And let your fervor, like my master's, be*
> *Placed in contempt! Farewell, fair cruelty.*

And then Viola was to have exited. It's what Shakespeare wrote. *Exit.* But in a surprise staging move, she leaned forward and kissed Kendra. On the lips.

Kendra froze, horrified, then abruptly came to life with a scream.

The kiss, clearly, hadn't been rehearsed. Someone in the back of the room whistled. Someone else made a catcall.

Kit was on her feet, clapping her hands, taking control. "Okay, enough drama for the day," she said, moving to the front of the room.

Kendra was unraveling, though. "Why did you do that?" she shouted, red-faced in her emerald gown. "What's wrong with you? What kind of freak are you?"

Delilah shrugged. Her jaunty cap had been knocked off and her pale skin appeared almost translucent. "The kind that likes kissing girls."

"You're a lesbo?" Kendra's voice spiraled.

The class laughed.

Kendra slapped Delilah hard.

Adrenaline pumping, Kit stepped between the girls, fearing Delilah would retaliate. "That's enough," she said firmly.

Delilah shrugged a thin shoulder, ran the tip of her tongue over her upper lip, and sang, *"I kissed a girl and I liked it."*

It was a perfect Katy Perry imitation and the boys were on their feet, whistling and giving Delilah a standing ovation.

Kendra burst into tears.

The door to Kit's classroom opened and Mrs. Adams, the short, square, stodgy English teacher next door entered. "I cannot teach over the din, Miss Brennan."

"I'm sorry, Mrs. Adams," Kit answered. "We were just wrapping up our scenes."

Delilah did a little sexy shimmy and sang, *"It felt so wrong, it felt so right . . ."*

Kendra launched herself at her with a scream.

"Fight, fight, fight!" the boys chanted while the girls were making mewling sounds.

Another teacher popped her head in to say she'd just called for Sister Elena and Ms. Jones.

Sister Elena arrived at a run, her gray veil, white underveil, and gray scapular flying. The fight was over before Sister burst into the room, but Kit knew the damage was done. Sister didn't tolerate fighting at Memorial, and the punishment was always swift and severe—immediate suspension, if not expulsion.

Still breathless, Sister turned to one of the girls in the front row and demanded a brief explanation of what had just happened.

The girl, Merrie Garnier, was a cheerleader and close friend of Kendra's. "Delilah kissed Kendra," she said with a sniff. "Kendra started crying and might have hit Delilah, not sure, and then Delilah dragged her to the ground."

"It wasn't exactly like that," Kit interjected crisply. "But there was an argument—"

"After the kiss," Damien shouted from the back of the room. "So Kendra slapped Delilah silly."

Sister Elena's gaze swept from Damien in the back row, over the class, and settled on Kendra and Delilah at the front. "One more time. Who hit who?"

Kit took a deep breath. "Kendra hit Delilah."

Sister's forehead furrowed deeply. "Kendra, is this true?"

Kendra's cheeks were splotchy. "She *kissed* me, Sister! And with some tongue, too!"

"Stop exaggerating. There was no tongue," Delilah said.

Sister Elena turned to look at Delilah, her expression forbidding. "Did you kiss her?"

Delilah rolled her eyes. "It was just a little kiss."

Sister's lips compressed. "Miss Brennan, when the bell rings you will escort Miss Hartnel to her locker, where she will clear out her things and then I will see both of you in my office."

Sister Elena swept out with a weeping Kendra, and as the door closed behind them, Kit slowly turned to face her class, avoiding Delilah's gaze.

"Are you going to be fired, Miss Brennan?" Damien called from the back row.

"No, Damien, I'm sorry. I will be back tomorrow."

"And what about Delilah?" he persisted. "Will Sister expel her?"

Kit's stomach heaved. She couldn't go there, couldn't think of that now. "I don't think that's any of your business, Mr. Franco."

And then the bell rang. Thank God.

Kit's heart pounded as everyone filed out. If she was walking Delilah to her locker to empty it out, it meant that the girl was done. Gone. Kit couldn't even imagine how Michael would respond to the news.

She glanced at Delilah where she still stood at the front of the room. She hadn't moved from the spot where she and Kendra had performed. Kit's gaze rested on the red handprint still evident on her cheek.

"Why did you do that?" Kit whispered, sinking down on the stool next to her overhead projector. "Why in God's name would you kiss her?"

Delilah's gaze dropped to the floor. "Wanted to taste her cherry ChapStick," she said dully.

For a moment Kit couldn't breathe. Her heart hurt. Her head was pounding. She hated to think that Delilah was already gone and she hadn't even been at the school for two full weeks. "You know you're in trouble, don't you?"

Delilah shrugged. "Not the first time," she said, her voice wobbling, betraying her. "Won't be the last."

Sister Elena was still closeted with Kendra, getting her version of the story, when Kit and Delilah arrived at her office. The two of them waited silently, sitting two chairs apart, until Sister's door opened and Kendra emerged, her nose high in the air.

Sister called Kit in and motioned for her to close the door. "Kendra told me what happened," the principal said, "but I'd like to hear your version."

Kit swiftly recounted the events, neither embellishing nor editing details.

When she'd finished, Sister's eyebrows rose. "This is very serious."

"Delilah was just goofing around," Kit answered.

"It's sexual harassment."

"She was trying to get attention."

"She has it, and she's not going to like it."

"What are you going to do?"

"You know the consequences for sexual harassment."

Kit sat down in the chair opposite her principal, hands clasped in her lap. "Please don't expel her. She's still settling in here and I know she's having some adjustment problems, but, Sister, Delilah needs us. She needs Memorial. I can't explain it, but this is where she should be. This is where she needs to be."

"Ms. Jones has had problems with her. I've checked her grades. She's not passing anything—"

"It's so early, Sister. She's only been here eight days—"

"Only eight days and this kind of trouble. Exactly my point, Miss Brennan."

"I know, but if you'd seen her perform her scene with Kendra this morning, you would have been amazed. She came in costume—most kids didn't even bother to dress up. She knew her lines, by *heart,* and she's the only one who memorized them. She wasn't just good. She was brilliant."

"I can't permit this kind of conduct at my school."

"I agree, but—"

"I must hold all the kids to the same standards."

"Yes, but it wasn't a real kiss—"

"Not a real kiss?" Sister's eyebrows lifted. "Did lips not touch, Miss Brennan?"

Kit blushed. "No, they touched."

Kit's principal studied her. "You're fighting hard for her, Miss Brennan."

"Yes, Sister."

"But you always fight hard for your students."

"They're children, Sister."

Sister Elena continued to look at her, her lips pursed, her expression speculative.

"But Jesus said, 'Suffer little children, and forbid them not, to come unto me: for of such is the kingdom of heaven.'"

Matthew 19:14. Kit knew the verse well. "She needs us, Sister."

"And what about Kendra, who was humiliated?"

"She'll recover."

"You are playing favorites."

"I don't mean to, but think about it—Jesus didn't treat everyone the same. He gave what people needed. Love, compassion, forgiveness. Kendra's hurt—her pride's hurt, she's embarrassed—but she'll be fine. We both know that. But Delilah . . . I don't know if she'll be fine if you send her away. I don't think her home life is all that stable. Her parents have only recently reconciled."

"So what do I do?"

"Discipline them both. Give them a two-day suspension. The girls return Monday and we all move forward."

"Fine. I'll call Kendra's parents now. You handle Delilah's."

"You don't want to talk to Delilah's parents?"

"No. I'm not particularly fond of her father. I don't trust him."

Delilah chewed her lip as she sat in the waiting room outside Sister Elena's office. She could hear just little bits of Miss Brennan's conversation with Sister Elena but not enough to know what was happening.

The principal's door finally opened and Miss Brennan emerged, calm, composed, but her jaw was set. "You need to call your parents and have them come in after school. We're going to sit down together, the four of us, and discuss what happened today—"

"And am I going to be expelled?" Delilah interrupted.

"We'll discuss that when your parents are here."

"And what do I do now?"

"Call your parents, make sure they're here at three."

"And then where do I go?"

"You'll spend the rest of the day here, in Sister's office. So if you have any homework, or something to read, I'd start it now."

Miss Brennan walked out and Delilah watched her go, thinking there was no way she'd call her parents. There was no way her mom could come in, not with her brand-new black eye and swollen nose; Delilah was fairly sure that her black eyes and bruises wouldn't go over big at Memorial what with their emphasis on Christ-like love and family.

There was also no way in hell she'd call Howie. Howie would act like he was the concerned family man in front of Miss Brennan and then beat the shit out of Delilah on the way home.

So what did she do? What could she do? Who could she call?

No one. She had no one. But that's what Howie wanted. That's why he moved them from Mineral Wells.

Delilah leaned forward, covered her face with her hands, fought tears. She wouldn't cry. She wouldn't. And she wasn't sad for herself, but for Mama, because Mama was trapped. Now that she had married Howie, there was nowhere she could go.

Her eyes burned and burned and then gradually they stopped hurting and she thought of the paper that appeared beneath their door last night.

If you ever need anything . . .

Jude.

He'd said to call him if they ever needed help. And maybe he didn't mean Delilah, maybe he only meant Mama, but Delilah had to protect Mama, and that meant Howie couldn't know . . . Howie couldn't come to school.

Sniffing, wiping her runny nose, she opened the small zipper pocket on her backpack and pulled out the crumpled piece of paper. She unfolded it on her lap, smoothing the creases.

If you ever need anything.

Delilah stared at his name and number.

If you ever need anything.

Well, he offered, she thought, walking to Mrs. Dellinger's desk and asking to borrow the phone.

Jude was sitting in a bar in east Oakland, feet up on a chair, a beer at his elbow, when his phone rang.

He didn't know the number, but then he didn't recognize most of the numbers that showed up on his phone. "Yeah," he said, answering.

"Jude?"

The voice was slightly tremulous and he pictured white-blond hair and a small tight face. The little girl next door. "Speaking."

"It's Delilah. Your neighbor."

He stared at the toes of his boots. They were badly scuffed. "Yeah, Delilah?"

"I, am, um, in trouble at school. Think I'm being kicked out."

Jude said nothing.

"They need a parent here at Memorial at three," she continued in the same flat, strained voice. "But Mama can't. She's in bed with an ice pack and Howie . . ." Her voice trailed off. "Can't call him."

"What did you do?"

"Kissed a girl."

"I guess they don't like that at school?"

"No. It's not allowed."

"You like girls?"

"*No.*"

"Why did you do it?"

"Felt like it."

"So you do like girls?"

"*No!* And I don't know why I did it. Okay? It was stupid. I was being stupid. Happy now?"

He didn't answer and silence stretched across the line. Jude slowly turned the heavy silver-and-brass ring with the Virgin Mary on his fourth finger with the pad of his thumb. He wasn't Catholic. Didn't go to church. But the ring was like a brass knuckle if he had to fight.

"Please, Jude," the girl whispered. "You said—"

"At three, huh?"

"Yes." She gulped for air. "But come a few minutes early because you need to sign in at the office and tell them you're there to see Miss Brennan, my English teacher."

Jude's brows pulled. He recognized the name and tried to place it. He could picture a face, too—wild red hair, blue eyes, wide mouth—but why? Where? Brennan. Brennan. And then it came to him. Capitola . . . The teacher. The beach house. Interesting how things came full circle. He'd liked Kit Brennan. He was looking forward to seeing her again. "I'll be there."

Kit was in her classroom after school, door open, waiting for Delilah and her parents. She was tired. Out of sorts. It'd been a long day and she'd been dreading this meeting all day. She wasn't looking forward to talking to Michael and Missy about Delilah. She wasn't looking forward to seeing Michael at all.

Eager to get the parent meeting behind her, she rose from her desk and was just about to move to the table and chairs in the corner where she'd work with students, when Delilah entered the room.

Kit looked at her, and then past her, and blinked in surprise. The biker guy . . . Jude.

She stared at him, stunned. This afternoon his long black hair was caught in a ponytail, but otherwise he looked exactly the same—slash of high cheekbones, dark eyes, square chin. He was dressed in black leather, too, and holding a helmet in one hand.

"Jude?" she said uncertainly, wondering if he was Delilah's father, but couldn't see how. He was very dark and Delilah was so fair.

"Kit," he replied, extending a hand to her.

She shook his hand, still bewildered. His fingers closed around hers. His hand was firm, his skin dry and warm. "You're Delilah's father?" she said, letting his hand go and stepping behind the table.

He set his helmet on the table, pulled out a chair for Delilah, and then sat down next to her. "A guardian."

Kit sat down across from them, opened Delilah's student folder, glanced over her registration form, emergency contact form, and shook her head. "You're not on here. I need to speak with her parents."

Jude turned the folder around and, grabbing a pen off the table, scrawled his name and number beneath Howard's name on the emergency contact form and shoved it back at her. "There," he said. "I'm listed. Now what happened?"

Kit felt a bubble of indignant fury. "That's not legal, Jude"— she broke off, focused on what he'd written, reading his last name—"Knight."

"You're not a cop, Kit, your uncles are. And I'm not here because I enjoy playing school. I'm here because Delilah's mom is ill and her stepdad is out of town." He glanced at Delilah, and then back at Kit. "So what's happened? Why is she in trouble?"

Kit drummed her fingers on the folder. "Perhaps I need to call Michael, include him here in a conference call—"

"Michael?" Jude interrupted. "Who's he?"

"Delilah's stepfather."

"Delilah's stepfather is Howard," Jude corrected. "Howard Dempsey."

Kit shook her head. "No, it's not. It's Michael. I know that for a fact—"

"His middle name is Michael," Delilah interrupted coolly. "His first name is Howard. I call him Howie."

Kit rifled through the papers in front of her, flustered. "Are you sure?"

"Look at the emergency contact form," Jude drawled. "I signed beneath his name. Howard M. Dempsey."

Kit did another paper shuffle, located the form, and studied the names on it; there was no Michael. Just a Howard M. Dempsey. And a Howard M Dempsey signature . . .

Kit's heart fell and she felt more than a little sick. Glancing up at Delilah, she asked, "He doesn't ever use Michael?"

Delilah laughed bitterly. "Not unless he's on Craigslist. He'll use it then."

Craigslist, Kit repeated silently, stomach heaving, throat swelling closed. Michael was on Craigslist? Why? She shuddered inwardly, disgusted. Disturbed. But why should she be surprised? Everything about Michael—*Howard*—was proving to be disturbing.

Kit swallowed hard, collected herself. "And your mom, Delilah? You said she's ill?"

Delilah nodded briefly. "Can't get out of bed."

"And Michael?"

"*Howard*," Delilah corrected fiercely.

"H-H-Howard," Kit stuttered. "He's . . . where?"

"Traveling."

"And who is taking care of your mom?"

Delilah's chin lifted. "I am."

Kit said nothing, her gaze resting on Delilah's pale face, set off by choppy blond hair. "I'm worried about you."

Delilah shrugged. "I'm okay."

Kit's brows knit. "I'm not so sure. And the fact that neither your mother nor father—"

"Stepfather," Delilah corrected.

"—stepfather could be here troubles me."

Delilah said nothing. Jude didn't speak. Kit took a deep breath, increasingly unsettled. This wasn't going as she'd planned, and she'd planned what she'd say to Michael and Missy carefully. But without them here, and with Jude sitting across from her, acting all laid-back and relaxed, she felt unfocused and didn't think she was getting through to Delilah. The girl was in trouble. Walking on very thin ice now. No room for error.

"Sister Elena has suggested that perhaps Memorial isn't the right school for you," Kit said, looking only at Delilah and yet aware of Jude's gaze. He might be kicking back in his chair but he was watching her intently. "I disagreed with her, and I fought for you today, Delilah. I've asked her to please give you another chance."

"Why?" Jude asked softly.

Kit looked at him. His strong features looked hard, almost harsh, in the artificial light of her room. "Why would I fight for Delilah?" Her forehead furrowed. "Wouldn't you?"

He didn't answer her, just stared right back at her, his dark gaze steady, piercing, but revealing nothing.

Deliberately Kit shifted her focus back to her student, determined to reach her. "I think we are good for you, Delilah. You're obviously very bright, and I believe you can achieve a great deal, but you have to want to be here. You have to make an effort. You have to try to fit in, and get along, and do the assigned work. You need to prove to Sister and all your other teachers that you deserve to be here. Because I think you do. I saw today what you can do—" She saw Delilah's smirk. "And no, not the kiss. That was wrong. Stupid. You have to know it was stupid."

Delilah shrugged. "I won't kiss her again."

"Or anyone," Kit retorted grimly.

"Or anyone," Delilah agreed.

"There's no more chances. This is it," Kit added, looking from Delilah to Jude, wanting to be sure they both understood. "She's suspended for the rest of the week. She can return Monday. But she's on probation. Sister and the other teachers will be watching her, monitoring her behavior, and if they don't see improvement, she'll be asked to leave. It's as simple as that."

Jude looked at Delilah. "You understand?"

Delilah sighed, closed her eyes.

"Miss Brennan's trying to help you," he added, "but she can't do anything if you won't help yourself."

"So you've heard that one, too," Delilah muttered.

"What do you have to do?" he asked her.

She sank lower in her seat. "Follow the rules. Do my work. Not cause any trouble."

"That's right," Kit said, glancing at Delilah, then Jude, still unable to believe he was sitting here, in her room, across from her. What a small, small world it was, and she wasn't sure she liked it. "You've got to be on time. Have your homework done. And pass your classes. Can you do that?"

Delilah nodded once.

Kit leaned forward, stared hard at the girl. "I want to hear you say it, Delilah, and I want to know you mean it."

Delilah sighed again but she met Kit's gaze. "I'll do it," she said testily. "Okay?"

"Do what?" Jude pressed.

"Study. Pass my classes. Be on time."

"Thank you," Kit said quietly, and then glanced at Jude.

He was looking at her and their gazes locked for a moment. Kit felt a strange little flutter in her middle. His firm lips slowly curved into a crooked smile. "Thank you," he said, getting to his feet. "She'll be back Monday."

Delilah and Kit rose, with Delilah lugging her black-backpack onto one shoulder.

"You've got my number," Jude added, reaching for Delilah, and shepherding her to the door. "Call me if you need me."

Kit watched Jude and Delilah walk out the door and into the hall. Once they'd disappeared, she sat down hard. *Lord Almighty, Jude Knight . . .*

He was the last person she'd expected to see today, and yet he'd strolled into her class in bad-boy black leather as if he belonged here. And oddly enough, sitting next to pale, sullen Delilah, he did. Kit didn't know what role he played in Delilah's life, but the girl seemed to trust him. And need him. Although Kit wasn't so sure that was a good thing.

Sighing, she glanced over the emergency contact form to the place where Jude had scrawled his name and number. And it was a scrawl. A fierce, in-your-face, screw-you signature that impressed her for all the wrong reasons.

Delilah was in trouble, wasn't she?

Delilah kept glancing at Jude as they walked out of the school to where he'd parked his motorcycle in front of the building, in a parking spot painted VOLUNTEER. Of course he'd park his bike wherever he felt like it.

"Thanks for coming," she said as he fished in his leather coat pocket for his key.

"Why'd you kiss her?" he asked.

She chewed on the inside of her cheek. "Kendra, the girl. She didn't like me."

"You think she likes you now?"

Delilah stifled a giggle. "No. But everyone laughed."

"At her, or you?"

Her smiled disappeared. She felt a wave of exhaustion. "Me. Her. Both. I don't care. And that's why I kissed her. Because I don't care. I don't care what any of them think. Spoiled rich kids."

"A lot of kids are on scholarship here. They're not all rich."

"They look spoiled."

"You're wrong."

Delilah didn't like his tone. "How do you know?"

"I grew up here. You just moved here. Maybe instead of hating on everyone, you give people a chance."

"Why? We'll just be moving again soon."

He stared down at her a long moment, before thrusting his helmet at her. "Put this on."

She looked down at the black helmet. "What for?"

"I'm taking you home."

"I can catch the bus."

"I'm taking you home so I can talk to your mom."

"She's sick."

"She's hurt," he corrected. "There's a difference."

Delilah's lips pressed together. "She won't talk to you."

"Okay."

"Okay?"

He shrugged. "If she won't talk to me, I'll just have to talk to Howie."

Delilah's breath caught in her throat. "You wouldn't do that!"

"Then you don't know me."

* * *

Missy met him in the living room in her robe and slippers. Jude had taken a seat in one of the big leather armchairs, and Delilah had taken a position at the window. Together they watched her mother move toward the dark leather couch and slowly lower herself until she was sitting down.

Her brown highlighted hair was pulled back in a low messy ponytail. She had small, neat features—ordinarily she'd be a pretty woman, the cute high-school-cheerleader type—but now she just looked lost inside her pink robe, the fuzzy chenille fabric swallowing her up, and the purple and blue bruises staining her face reminding Jude of pastel-colored Easter eggs.

She didn't look at him, though, her gaze fixed on the oak-and-glass coffee table between them. "Dee said you helped her at school," Missy said, her voice raspy, as battered as the rest of her.

She'd been choked. Her vocal cords were bruised. Jude stifled pity. It was useless and time was short. Howard could pull into the driveway any minute and Jude couldn't be here. Missy couldn't handle another beating. "Delilah's been suspended," he said bluntly. "She can return Monday. But she has to make an effort. Do her homework. Not cause any trouble."

Missy glanced at her daughter. "Are you causing trouble, Dee?"

"No," Delilah said.

Jude shot her a sharp look.

"*Yes.*"

"What did you do, Dee?"

"I kissed a girl."

"What? Why?"

"Didn't like her. Didn't like the way she treated me. So I kissed her."

"But *why*?"

"It embarrassed her. She'll leave me alone now."

"Oh, Dee, Howard's going to flip out." Missy's eyes burned in her face. Her fingers knotted, twisting, frantic. "You know that, don't you?"

"Don't tell him," Delilah said fiercely. "He doesn't have to know—"

"He'll find out!"

"How?" Delilah glanced from her mom to Jude and back again. "Jude won't tell him. Will you?"

Jude shook his head. Things were so messed up here. His dad had been volatile and struggled with addictions, but he hadn't been mean. Or violent. Howard was both.

"Howard always finds out everything," Missy whispered, a hand tugging at the collar of her robe.

They heard a car pull up outside and for a moment they all froze. Missy made a whimpering sound. Jude rose. Delilah lifted the curtain to peek out the window.

"Mailman," Delilah said, relief cracking her voice.

"You should go," Missy said, her trembling hands clawing at the buttons on her robe.

Jude couldn't leave without doing something, saying something. "I know you don't know me, but I can help—"

"No."

"There are people you could go to. Safe houses designed just for—"

"You must go," Missy rasped. "Now."

"Please let me help you."

"You *can't* help me, and he *can't* find you here. Do you understand?" She couldn't scream because her vocal cords were too damaged, but her hands were clenched into fists and tears filled her eyes.

Jude left. His boots thudded on the hardwood floor and the door slammed shut behind him. He stepped from the porch to the cement walkway before taking a shortcut across the grass.

He wished the Dempseys never moved in, wished he'd never

met them, wished their pain wasn't his problem. But they *had* moved in, and he knew what was happening and he couldn't ignore it. He'd be a shitty neighbor if he did.

Jude had been in his house only a few minutes when he saw the long gray Lincoln Town Car pull into Dempsey's driveway. Standing at his sink, he watched Howard climb out of the car, jacket open, tie flapping, a dozen long-stemmed red roses wrapped in cellophane in his hand.

Howard had returned home, bearing gifts. It was his peace offering. His way of apologizing, making everything okay.

What a fucking loser.

Thirteen

Howie never found out that Delilah had been suspended because he left every day for work before she headed to school and didn't return home until she was already home, but just to make sure he didn't come home early one day and surprise them all, she took the bus to the San Leandro library and read in a corner until it was time to come home.

Back at school on Monday, Delilah made sure to be on time for every class. She'd caught up on her homework over the weekend and aced her science test in Mrs. Hughes's biology class on Tuesday. Passing back the test, the teacher praised Delilah, telling her that she was one of only two students to earn a 98 percent or higher. Delilah simply nodded, but once Mrs. Hughes turned away, she smiled faintly at her test, immensely gratified by the big red 98 percent in the right corner, along with the word *excellent* underlined twice.

It was a pleasant change not to run extra laps in Ms. Jones's

PE class and Miss Powers thanked Delilah for completing her homework every night that week.

In English, Delilah followed along in her paperback copy of *Twelfth Night*, listened to the discussion, wrote an in-class essay on Shakespeare's use of mistaken identity as a plot device, but couldn't bring herself to look at Miss Brennan, even though she knew her teacher was looking at her. But she wouldn't make eye contact. She didn't understand Miss Brennan, didn't understand why her teacher would fight to keep her at Memorial. It didn't make sense. Delilah was new. Just one of two hundred. Why should Miss Brennan care?

Then, out of the blue on Thursday afternoon, Howie showed up at the school fifteen minutes before the day was over. He'd come requesting a meeting with Miss Brennan, and Mrs. Dellinger, the school secretary, sent a note to Delilah in the computer lab letting her know that her father was in the building and that she was to meet him in Miss Brennan's classroom after the bell rang.

Delilah read the note and nearly threw up. Howie was here requesting a meeting with Miss Brennan? Why?

She asked permission to leave class to use the restroom. Mr. Osborne sighed heavily, expressing his disapproval, but let her go. He always protested but caved, and so Delilah raced to Miss Brennan's room. Opening the door, she peeked in. The class was silent. They were taking a test. Heads turned to look at her.

Delilah spotted Miss Brennan at her desk and gestured to her. Miss Brennan indicated that Delilah should come to her.

Delilah's legs shook as she walked. Her mouth was so dry that she kept licking her lips, trying to wet them. It wasn't working. She was practically panting with fear.

If Howie found out about her suspension . . . he'd kill her.

"Miss Brennan," she whispered, standing next to the teacher's desk.

"Yes, Delilah?"

"You're meeting my stepdad . . . Howard . . . after school?"

"He showed up, requesting a meeting."

Delilah struggled to swallow. Her mouth was so dry it tasted funny and her heart was beating so hard she felt it in her throat. "Miss Brennan," she squeaked, horrifyingly close to tears as she jammed her hands against her stomach to keep from throwing up. "He doesn't know I was suspended. He doesn't know Jude came and picked me up. He doesn't like Jude—"

"But Jude's your guardian."

"Noooo . . . not exactly."

"He's either your guardian or he's not."

Delilah's legs were going to give out and she crouched down next to the desk, certain that at any moment she'd puke or faint.

"Delilah?"

"He's not," she choked, her gaze fixed on the muted swirl of blue and gold in the green carpet. "He's our neighbor. Kind of a friend."

Miss Brennan said nothing.

"I didn't know who else to call," Delilah rushed on, "because I couldn't call Mama. She was sick. And I couldn't call Howie—"

"Was he really out of town?"

Delilah shook her head.

"Delilah!"

She squeezed her eyes closed. "I didn't want Howie to get mad at Mama, and he would have, if he'd come in that day. But Mama really wasn't feeling good and I was trying to protect her. She and Howie have been having problems and he blames everything on Mama even if it's not her fault." Delilah suddenly looked up at Miss Brennan, intently searching her eyes. "Do you know what I'm saying?"

Miss Brennan's brow creased. "Does your mother know you were suspended?"

"Yes."

"Are you telling me the truth? Or do I need to call her?"

"I'm telling you the truth. My mom knows I got suspended. Jude told her. But you can call her and ask. I'll give you her cell number. But we didn't tell Howard because sometimes it's just better that way."

"I don't like this, Delilah. I don't believe in keeping secrets from your father—"

"But he's not my father. He's my stepfather and—" The bell rang, a long chime of sound indicating that the day was over. The harsh sound sent a sharp pain through Delilah's chest and she gasped as she straightened. "You don't understand. No one understands. No one but Jude."

K it slowly rose to her feet as Delilah dashed out the door, her thoughts jumbled, emotions stirred.

"Tests, please," she said flatly, moving to the front of her classroom to collect the essay tests from her sixth-period students.

Numbly she accepted the essays from her departing students, replaying her conversation with Delilah over and over in her head. This meeting with Michael would not be good. Kit actually felt scared. But why? What could Michael do?

Once her students were gone, she paper-clipped the essays together and put them in her briefcase to take home and then organized her desk, clearing off clutter and filling out some forms that should have been turned in to the office earlier in the day.

A knock sounded on her open door. "Can we come in?" a familiar male voice drawled.

Kit looked up, saw Michael in the doorway, smiling at her, lean and tan and confident in his expensive business suit. Her gaze moved to Delilah, who stood at his side, pale. Skittish. Terrified.

Feeling as if she'd been sucker punched, Kit swiftly looked away from Delilah's face.

"Please," she said crisply, gesturing to the chairs and table in the corner of the room, wondering if she was to call him Michael or Howard and then decided she'd use neither. "Why don't we sit over here, Mr. Dempsey? Delilah?" she said, walking to the table and taking a seat in the same place she'd sat with Jude and Delilah nine days ago.

They all sat down, with Delilah choosing a chair as far away as she could manage. "So what can I do for you?" Kit asked Michael, thinking that it was best to be direct, as she had no desire to prolong this meeting.

"I thought I would check in with you, see how things are going. Sometimes it's hard to get information out of Delilah." Michael smiled, but the smile didn't reach his eyes. "How is she doing?"

"She's had a great week."

"The week's not over," he retorted.

"You're right. It's just Thursday. But it's been a great week so far. Delilah's brought her grades up in all her classes, has a hundred percent in her math homework, a ninety-four on her reading quiz yesterday, and a ninety-eight on her biology test earlier this week. That ninety-eight was the second highest grade out of all the freshmen, and that's to be commended."

He studied her for a long moment, and his lips quirked, as if he were secretly amused. "How about last week?" he asked abruptly. "I'd love to hear about last week."

Kit heard the faint hitch in Delilah's breathing and her insides knotted with anxiety as she understood now that Delilah needed protection, and questions from the adoption application came to mind: *Growing up, what were you usually punished for? And, how were you punished?*

How *was* Delilah punished?

"We had some bumps," Kit answered Michael carefully, "but

it's behind us, and I'm really excited about Delilah's potential. She's a very gifted—"

"Liar," Michael interrupted, finishing the sentence for her. "A very gifted liar. Isn't she?"

He said it pleasantly, with a smile, and yet the temperature in the room seemed to drop by twenty degrees, chilling Kit.

What a horrible thing to say.

In that moment her feelings for Michael crystallized. She loathed him. Absolutely loathed him.

She met his gaze, held it, refusing to be intimidated. This was her room. Her world. She was the boss here, not him. *"Excuse me?"*

With that awful smile still playing at the corners of his lips, Michael opened his jacket and withdrew a yellow sheet of paper. He put it on the table, pushed it toward her. "What is this?"

Kit recognized the yellow carbon homework form. It came in triplicate and was used for class work and homework assignments when students were absent for a period of time. Last Wednesday, she'd had Delilah's teachers assign work for the days Delilah would miss and had sent the student sheet, the yellow carbon, home with Delilah and Jude, while turning in the white sheet to the office and keeping the pink carbon for her own files.

"It's a student assignment sheet," Kit said calmly.

"For days she missed school." Michael smiled at her, before turning to Delilah. It was the first time he'd looked at her since they sat down. "What days did you miss, Dee?"

Delilah's shoulders hunched. Her voice was all but inaudible. "Thursday and Friday."

"Thursday and Friday," Michael repeated. "Why?"

Delilah's lips parted but no sound came out, and Kit, aware that Sister had documented last week's incident and suspension and fully expected Michael to know about it, broke the news as calmly and emotionlessly as possible. "There was an incident last Wednesday in English—"

"An *incident*?"

"Delilah was performing a scene from *Twelfth Night* with another student, and she ended the scene with a kiss. The kiss was clearly nonsexual, but Sister didn't think it was appropriate and suspended both girls for two days."

Michael frowned. "Delilah kissed a girl?"

Kit nodded. "It was a brief kiss, but it caused a stir. This is an English class, not a drama class, and we don't take our staging that far."

"Isn't it normal procedure to call parents when a student is suspended?"

"Yes."

His eyebrows lifted. "So why didn't you call me? I know you have my number."

"Delilah said you were traveling."

"And Missy? Did you call her?" he asked, before shifting his attention back to Delilah. "Dee, does your mother know?"

The girl hesitated for just a fraction of a second, but that fraction of a second felt excruciatingly long to Kit.

"I told Mom." Delilah's voice was but a whisper. "I told her as soon as I got home."

"But neither of you told me," he said.

The silence felt heavy, suffocating, and seemed to go on forever. Then abruptly he was on his feet, walking out the door, and Delilah chased after him, shooting Kit a pleading, desperate look while running.

Howie was walking so fast through the parking lot that Delilah had to skip every couple steps just to keep up with him. He was mad. And when he got mad, bad things happened.

And bad things were going to happen. Not to Delilah, but to her mama, because Howie touched only Mama. Howie made Mama pay for all of Delilah's mistakes.

She skipped another step and her throat swelled closed. She struggled to swallow around the lump sitting there, aching like the hot thing in her chest.

Howie was going to hurt Mama bad.

Tears started to fill Delilah's eyes. She couldn't let it happen. If Howie wanted to hit somebody, he should hit her, Delilah, because she was the one who'd kissed Kendra. Delilah was the one who'd acted up, gotten in trouble.

Howie had reached the car, opened the driver's-side door but Delilah didn't want to get in with him until he looked at her. She needed to see his eyes. When he was in a good mood, they were blue. But when he was angry, they turned to ice, and when they were ice, you started praying. Even if you didn't believe in God.

"Howie," she panted, hanging back.

He looked at her and his narrowed eyes, pale blue, practically froze her to death. "Get in the car, Dee."

"It wasn't Mama's fault."

A muscle pulled in his jaw. "Get in the car."

"It's my fault—"

"Not going to talk about it with you. Now get in the car—"

"The school wanted to meet with Mama last Wednesday after I got in trouble and I knew you wouldn't want them to see her. She had that, you know—" Delilah's hand jerked up to her nose and eye. "And so I told them Mama was sick and you were gone, but I wasn't trying to lie to you. I was just trying to make things better."

"For the last time, Dee, get in that car, or I'll put you in there myself."

She swallowed her tears and walked around the car to sit in the front passenger seat. She fought to buckle her seat belt. It was hard when her hands were shaking so much.

Howie didn't speak on the drive home. Delilah stared out the window but saw nothing.

Once they were home, Howie called Mama into the bedroom and locked the door.

Delilah hadn't even made it into her room before she heard the first slap, and then another. Mama cried out. Howie told her to shut up. And then the awful thudding sounds began in earnest. Weeping, Delilah curled up on her bed, her pillow pressed over her head, but not even the pillow could muffle the sound of Mama screaming.

K it left school not long after Michael and Delilah, walking out of the classroom with Delilah's student folder in her purse. She didn't know why she'd brought the folder but she felt panicked, queasy, and she wanted Delilah's folder, and contact numbers, with her.

But what would she do? Call Michael? Call Missy? Call Delilah?

On her way home, she stopped at the drugstore to shop for last-minute toiletries to take on the cruise, grabbing random bottles of suntan lotion, eye-makeup remover, and Advil, dropping them into her basket. It was hard, if not impossible, to concentrate on shopping when even now, forty minutes after the meeting had ended, she felt physically ill.

What would Michael do to Delilah when he got her home?

And just as disconcerting, why had Delilah lied to her about Jude, and why had Jude lied to her in turn?

Standing in the middle of the store, Kit opened Delilah's student folder for the emergency contact number.

There at the bottom was Jude's number.

She stared at the number, remembering how he'd impatiently,

even arrogantly, scrawled it on the form. As if he really was Delilah's guardian. As if he had a right to be there.

But he had no right. He was merely a friend. A neighbor. And yet Delilah had called him when she needed someone, and he had come to school for her. Stood by her. Would he be able to tell Kit anything about Delilah now?

Swallowing her misgivings, she sent him a text. *This is Kit Brennan. I need to talk to you about Delilah.*

She finished shopping and returned to her car. Jude hadn't yet replied. Kit didn't think she could handle going home and headed to the gym instead.

She normally didn't run on Thursdays but she changed into her workout clothes and ran this afternoon. She ran for miles, fast, hard, at a steep incline, trying to clear her mind, trying to forget how scary Michael had been, and how terrified Delilah had looked sitting at Kit's corner table. But running today didn't calm her. Running didn't erase the image of Delilah's hands trembling as she tried to pick up her backpack at the end of the meeting.

Delilah's fear had triggered something in Kit, tapping into her fears, and she ran even faster, arms pumping, feet pounding, aware of her own demons chasing behind her.

But Kit wasn't a distance runner and had no endurance and couldn't run forever. Gradually she slowed, resetting the treadmill to a lower speed, decreasing the incline at the same time, until she was at a brisk walk.

Was it possible she was overreacting?

Was it possible that she was projecting onto Delilah, and creating a story, and a reality, that wasn't even there?

Still trying to catch her breath, Kit mopped her forehead and replayed the meeting with Michael and Delilah once more, and this time without being so sensitive to Delilah's emotions.

If Delilah hadn't come to her before the meeting . . . if she hadn't crouched trembling next to Kit's desk and painted a picture with Michael as this really bad guy, would Kit have found Michael's behavior during the meeting so disturbing?

Not once during the meeting did he raise his voice or lose control. Nor did he threaten Delilah.

He did call her a liar, but to be fair, Kit could see where he was coming from.

Last week Delilah had proven she was an accomplished actress. Had she been acting earlier, when she came to Kit? And had she been acting during the parent–teacher meeting?

Kit wished she knew. Wished she could trust herself to know. But her judgment was faulty, had always been faulty, ever since that thing had happened to her when she was little . . .

That thing.

That's how Kit always thought of it. As a thing out there, distant, not at all part of her, and yet it was part of her. It'd happened to her. She'd been little. Three, four. Maybe five.

Kit didn't really know how old, but she remembered the shoes she wore that day to his house. Her pink Keds. And she was wearing them with ankle socks.

How funny to remember the color of her shoes, and the lace on her ankle socks, and his house, but not everything else.

But wasn't that the tragedy? That Kit still didn't fully understand what had happened to her, only that something *had*.

Thirty-five years later she could still see him—shaggy hair, dirty blond; plaid shirt, blue—he lived on the street behind theirs, and he'd told her to never, ever tell anyone what he'd done, and for years she'd thought she couldn't tell anyone that he'd pressed a coat down on her face, pressing so hard she couldn't breathe.

For thirty-some years she'd kept her secret, that she couldn't tell anyone about the man who'd put a coat over her face.

It'd never crossed her mind that perhaps there was something else she wasn't supposed to tell. It'd never crossed her mind that she could have any other secret until Richard came home drunk one night after attending a friend's bachelor party and, deciding he wanted kinky, hot sex, attempted to take her from behind. As he forced himself on her, in her, Kit felt pain, unbearable pain, and all she could hear was the sound of screaming. But it wasn't her screaming, it was a little girl. She was screaming in pain. Screaming for help.

Richard sobered up pretty fast and apologized. Kit nodded and escaped to the bathroom to shower. But in the shower, she cried, shattered.

Someone had hurt her badly when she was just a little girl.

Someone had hurt her, and made her afraid, and not just of men, but of feelings and touch. Intimacy. Sex.

Thanks to that someone, that man, she'd spent her whole life afraid . . .

Spent her whole life not feeling . . .

It was bewildering to think that for thirty-plus years she'd blocked out the actual incident, remembering not what he did, but what she couldn't tell.

Bewildering not to remember pain, but the weight of the coat on her face.

Exhausted, flattened, Kit hit stop on the treadmill, unable to take another step. The rubber belt stopped moving. She stood there swaying on her feet.

As a little girl, she'd wanted to be special. That man had promised her she was special. And then in his bedroom with all the shades down, he'd taken whatever it was that was good about her away.

Kit stepped heavily off the treadmill. Her legs shook. Slowly she walked to the locker room, and as she opened the door to the room, a little voice whispered, *Are you sure that's what happened? Or are you making it up? You've always loved stories, Kit. Did this really happen to you, or did you read it in a book?*

Kit bit her lip, and shook her head to silence the voice, and yet the mocking voice had once again successfully sowed the seeds of doubt, creating distrust.

Because that little voice was right.

Kit didn't really know what had happened. She had impressions, sensations, fragmented memories, but what were they?

And were those really her memories? Or had they come from somewhere else?

She didn't know. And she'd never know. And maybe that was what troubled her the most. If she couldn't discern truth . . . if she couldn't separate fantasy from reality . . . how could she trust herself to know what was true . . . what was right . . . what was real?

In the locker room, Kit showered and changed back into her clothes and was walking to her car when she checked her phone.

Jude had texted her back.

Working but can take an early dinner and meet you between five and six at Gaylord's Caffe in Piedmont.

Kit glanced at her watch. It was almost five now. She quickly texted a reply. *Just got your message, on way to Gaylord's, will take me 5-10 minutes. Can you still meet me?*

He answered immediately. *Will be waiting.*

Kit's heart pounded as she walked into Gaylord's Caffe Espresso, and she hated that she felt so nervous. There was no reason for her to be afraid. This wasn't a date. Jude had never threatened her. They were meeting to discuss Delilah. That's it.

She'd just stepped into the coffeehouse when the door swung open again and Jude materialized behind her. Kit jumped, and turned quickly, knowing it was him.

"You're here," she said, her voice too high and thin.

"I am."

She nodded, knowing she needed to take control, get control, before she lost what was left of her confidence. "Shall we order something?" she asked.

"I'll have a drip coffee." He reached into his pocket, pulled out a wad of bills, peeled off two tens. "And a scone or bagel or sandwich . . . whatever they have left. I'm going to grab that table." He thrust the money into her hands and headed across the café to a corner table that had just been vacated.

Kit stood in line and watched him walk to the table, his legs long in old, faded Levi's, hips lean beneath his black leather jacket. He said a few words to the girl at the table next to the empty one, and the girl, tattooed and pierced, grinned.

Kit wondered what he had said to the girl, wondered what would make her smile. She felt another flutter of unease as she carried her latte, Jude's coffee, and Jude's sandwich to the table. "Do you want sugar or anything?" she asked him as she sat down in the empty chair and pushed the coffee cup toward him.

"Nope. I'm good."

Her chair felt hard. She was tired and worried. Very worried. Things right now weren't making sense. Kit stared down into her latte, trying to summon courage to ask him the things she needed to ask him, already knowing she wouldn't like the answers.

"Spit it out," Jude said bluntly.

She licked her bottom lip, her mouth suddenly too dry. "You aren't Delilah guardian."

"Says who?"

"Delilah. She told me the truth today. Michael—"

"Michael?"

She flushed, her cheeks burning. "Howard, sorry. Howard came in to see me after school today. He found out about the suspension. Wanted a parent–teacher meeting."

"And let me guess, Delilah's mom wasn't there."

A lump filled Kit's throat. "No. She wasn't."

"Doesn't that ever seem strange to you? She's Delilah's mom, but she's nowhere to be found?"

Kit jerked, as if stung, because, yes, it was strange, very strange, but she'd avoided thinking about Delilah's mom, and until now she wasn't sure why. "It does worry me."

"Seems like a lot of things worry you."

"No. Not a lot of things. But Delilah's situation . . . yes."

"Why are you so jumpy?" he asked, his deep voice rough.

Somehow she always forgot about that rasp. "I'm not."

"Do I make you nervous?" he persisted.

"No," she said quickly, reaching for her latte, and picking it up so fast that it sloshed over the rim of her glazed mug and burned her hand. She yelped and set the mug down hard, sloshing coffee all over her hand again. "Ow," she said, pressing the scalded hand to her chest. "And yes," she added, looking at him. "You do make me nervous. Okay?"

"Do you need ice?"

"No."

"Can I see it?"

"No."

The edge of his mouth lifted. "You don't need to be scared of me, Kit Kat."

"I'm not." And she wanted to tell him her name was Kit, not Kit Kat, but she didn't think he'd listen. She had a feeling he didn't listen to things he didn't want to hear. "Why did you pretend to be Delilah's guardian?"

"Because Delilah called me. Asked me for help. So I went."

"You can't pretend to be a legal guardian when you're not."

He shrugged. "She needed me."

"Jude, the law is very clear—"

"Don't talk to me about the law."

Kit held on to her temper, just. "Can I talk to you as a teacher, then? Because as a teacher, I have very clearly defined responsibilities, and those responsibilities are to protect my students, not to in any way endanger them."

"And you think I was endangering Delilah by coming in to school last week?"

"I think if Mi— Howard finds out you came in last week, there will be hell to pay."

"*If?*" Jude's dark eyes met hers. "He doesn't know yet?"

Kit shook her head. "Delilah begged me not to say anything to him today. She was afraid he'd flip out." She took a quick breath, remembering the meeting. "It wasn't a pleasant meeting. Delilah was *trembling.* I've never seen her—or any student—so scared. I honestly don't know what to think."

"Is that why you wanted to see me? Because you want to know what I think?"

"Yes."

"Fine. I'll tell you what I think. Your Mi— Howard is an abusive prick."

"What do you think happened when they got home?"

"What do you think happened?"

The pain was back in Kit's middle, and her heart suddenly hurt. Not adrenaline hurt, but fear hurt. "I think he . . . got mad."

"I think he got mad, too."

Kit took a sip from her latte, not an easy feat when her hand was shaking so badly. "I don't like this," she whispered. "Don't like it at all."

Jude just watched her.

She put the coffee down. "No family is perfect. I realize every family has its own problems, and every family has its way of handling problems . . . as well as their own way of disciplining. But I have a problem with corporal punishment. I have a problem with people—adults—losing control. Have a problem with adults abusing their power. Makes me sick."

"The world is full of violence."

"That doesn't make it right!" Her gaze fell on the ring on his hand that he'd wrapped around his ceramic cup. It was an enormous silver-and-brass ring with a raised figure of Mary. Her brow creased. "You're Catholic?"

He glanced down at his hand. "No."

"But . . . isn't that the Virgin Mary?"

"Yep."

"Why do you wear that ring?"

He took his hand from the cup and balled it into a fist. It was a big hard fist with scarred knuckles. "Mary helps me fight."

Kit's mouth dropped open and she stared at him, shocked. "Can't believe you said that."

He flexed his fingers, briefly admiring the ornate ring before reaching for his cup to sip his coffee. "It is what it is."

"You mean, you do what you want to do."

Jude shrugged. "Pretty much."

Kit frowned. "And Delilah? She's your neighbor—" She broke off as her phone rang and she glanced down at the number. Tommy. And Tommy never called. "Sorry. I need to get this," she said to Jude before answering. "Tommy? Everything okay."

"No," her brother said brusquely. "Mom's in the hospital. Dad's been trying to reach you, but I think he's been calling your house number. You need to come."

Fourteen

The hospital room was packed with people when Kit arrived, all family. Lots of Brennans—Dad; Meg; Cass; Dad's brothers, Uncle Joe and Uncle Pat; plus Mom's older brother, Jack Donahue, a retired San Francisco city cop who'd moved from the city down to San Mateo after he'd retired, and his wife, Linda.

Kit walked in on a nurse scolding everyone that there were far too many people in the room, that patients were allowed only a limited number of visitors, and that they had more than exceeded that number, when she spotted Kit and lifted her hands in protest, exclaiming, "Oh, no! No, no, no. Half of you must go. There's plenty of chairs in the waiting room—"

"And why would we wait out there when we want to be here?" Kit's dad boomed.

"Because it's policy, Mr. Brennan—"

"Firefighter Brennan." He pointed to his brothers and Tommy. "And that's Firefighter Brennan, Firefighter Brennan, and Firefighter Brennan," and over to Uncle Jack, "And that's Officer

Donahue. As you can imagine, we all respect and appreciate policy, but there's no way we're going anywhere when my wife needs her family now."

The nurse's mouth gaped open then closed, and clutching her small computer notepad, she marched stiffly out.

"Tom," Mom croaked reproachfully from the bed. "She's just doing her job."

"She can go do it somewhere else."

"We shouldn't even be here," Mom said. "There's nothing wrong with me. Just tired."

Kit hugged Meg and Cass before pushing through the wall of Brennan men to reach Marilyn's hospital bed. She was relieved to see her mother awake and alert despite the oxygen tubing. "Mom, you okay?" she asked, taking her hand

Mom gave Kit's hand a faint squeeze. "Yes."

"What happened?"

"A lot of nonsense if you ask me," she grumbled, her voice breathy.

"Mom collapsed," Meg said, a tissue clutched in her fingers. "On the bathroom floor."

"I did not," Marilyn protested.

"You did, too," Dad said brusquely. "You were out cold when I found you."

"I fainted, Tom."

He faced her, expression ferocious. "You could have hit your head, got a concussion or worse."

"But I didn't." Her eyebrows lifted significantly, challenging him. He might be a lion but she was a lioness.

"You don't listen to me," he growled.

"I'm an adult. I wanted to go to the bathroom on my own."

"And look what happened."

"Nothing happened, Tom!" she snapped.

Dad turned away, shoulders hunching, and Kit felt a rush of sympathy for her father. Poor Dad. He took his job as husband so seriously. She could only imagine how he felt when he found her mom unconscious on the floor. Of course he'd rush her to the emergency room. The hospital represented safety.

"Did you get to ride in an ambulance, Mom?" Kit asked playfully, trying to ease some of the tension in the room.

"No, thank God. Your father knows I'd never forgive him if he put me through that."

"So what's the plan? How long are they going to keep you?"

"They're not keeping me," she answered tartly.

Meg and Tommy Jr. exchanged glances. Mom saw. She tried to rally and sit up in bed, but didn't have the strength and fell back into her pillow. Meg moved forward to help but Mom brushed her away with an irritated wave of her hand. "Stop it. Stop fussing over me. All of you." She broke off, and gasped, unable to catch her breath. Her inability to breathe just made her angrier. "I'm dehydrated and weak but not dead, and I'm not going anywhere for weeks yet. So stop treating me like an invalid. It's annoying."

Kit's lips twitched. Batten down the hatches. Mom was in a feisty mood tonight. "So what do you want, Mom?" she asked.

"I want to go home."

No one said anything. Normally Dad or Meg might have argued with her, but neither said anything now, both still sensitive from being at the receiving end of Mom's temper.

"There's no reason for them to keep me," Mom wheezed defiantly. "I'm just a little dehydrated and anemic. Anemia's nothing new. Low red blood cells. Normal part of bone cancer." She'd run out of air again and everyone waited for her to finish. Eventually she added, "They've given me epoetin alfa. I'm getting fluids. There's nothing else they can do. I'll rest better at home. You know I will."

"You always get achy from the epoetin, Mom," Cass reminded her. She shared Marilyn's brisk approach to life, death, and catastrophe, and Kit had always wondered if that was an innate part of their personalities or a result of their medical training. "If you stay here tonight, your nursing staff will make sure you're comfortable, and then the worst of the joint pain will be over in the morning and you'll be far more comfortable being moved home then."

Mom fidgeted with her blanket, glared at the IV in her arm. "I didn't want to come tonight. I've too much to do at home but Dad didn't listen."

"Dad did the right thing," Tommy Jr. said gruffly, feet planted wide, arms crossed over his chest. It was his father's stance. Solid. "It never hurts to have everything checked out, and you know that if the shoe were on the other foot, you would have done the same thing."

Mom's eyes flashed and she pressed her lips together in silent protest. Kit again fought the urge to smile. When Mom was in battle mode, she was a Celtic warrior.

"Tell me what you need to do at home, Mom," Kit said lightly, hiding her amusement, knowing this was the mom she'd always remember. Spirited.

"Have to finish packing for the cruise—"

"Marilyn," Dad said warningly.

She didn't even acknowledge him. "Clothes are packed, but not toiletries and there are still a few things in the drier."

Meg shook her head. "Mom."

"Be practical," Tommy Jr. added.

"This is nonsense," Dad said flatly, refusing to play this game. "There's no cruise, and your mom knows it—"

"Nonsense?" Mom interrupted, fighting to sit up but unable to do so. "How dare you, Thomas Brennan? I've looked forward to this trip for weeks. It's what's kept me going, knowing I'd be with all of you, enjoying my grandkids—"

"They can come see you here," Dad said, out of patience.

"And skip the cruise?" She made an incredulous sound. "Absolutely not. The children are excited about the cruise. It's their first cruise. I'm not going to take that away from them."

"Then let them go," Uncle Jack said, frowning at his sister. "But Tom's right, Lynn, you're not going. You can't travel like this. Tom would have to push you around the ship in a wheelchair—"

"Which I don't mind, and we've already discussed bringing Mom's folding wheelchair with us." Dad waved a hand. "But that was before your red count brought you to your knees. There's no way you can fly now—"

"I'll have the oxygen canisters," Mom said breathlessly, shifting awkwardly and wincing as the IV pulled on her arm. "People fly with oxygen all the time. And they have those people who can wheel you on board the plane—"

"*Mom!*" Meg threw her hands up into the air. "Seriously! Can you even hear yourself? You're sounding exactly like Gabi right now—"

"I was thinking Bree," Tommy Jr. said grimly, brow furrowed. "She's never been too troubled by logic or reason."

Cass moved to Mom, untangling the IV tube and smoothing the needle and tape on the back of her thin wrist. "Mom, the rocking of the ship isn't going to help your nausea," she said calmly. "It would be better to cancel this trip and have everyone gather up here. If we call Sarah now, they can change their flights and rebook them for San Francisco—"

"*No.*" Mom's voice shook. "I'm not disappointing my grandchildren. They're going on this goddamn cruise and so are all of you! And so help me, if one more of you argues with me—" She broke off, panting with exertion. "I'm your mother! And you *will* respect me." Again she struggled to catch her breath. Tears glittered in her eyes. She bit her lip, horrified that she was losing control. "We are taking this cruise . . . and if you fight me . . . I am done with you. Will not . . . speak to you ever again."

Meg walked out of the room. Tommy Jr. soon followed. Cass glanced from Mom to Dad and back again. She leaned over Mom and gave her a kiss on the forehead. "Okay, Mom," she whispered, before stepping out in search of Tommy.

Uncle Jack shook his head in disgust. But Aunt Linda approached the bed, patted Mom's arm. "Stick to your guns, Lynn," she said, then took Jack's hand and tugged him out.

Uncle Pat and Uncle Joe slipped out without saying anything, leaving Kit and Dad alone with Mom.

"You'd really not speak to your children again?" Dad said gruffly, eyes watering.

Mom had to concentrate on breathing for a moment. "That includes you," she rasped.

"You'd do that to me?" His deep voice cracked.

"Take them on the cruise for me," she said, looking small and flattened.

Kit pictured a blow-up beach ball that had been deflated and her eyes stung.

"Without you?" her father demanded.

Mom nodded once.

Dad swallowed hard, started to speak, then stopped himself. He walked out of the room, into the hall, and returned immediately. "I don't want to go without you."

"But you will have to go on without me." Mom's eyes met his and held. She struggled to smile but didn't quite succeed. "The family must survive without me—"

"And we will," he said hoarsely. "But you're not gone yet. There's plenty of time for cruises later—"

"I'm not going to die while you're gone, what fun would that be?" Mom said with a hint of laughter in her voice. "When I go, it'll be in grand fashion, but that's weeks, if not months, away."

"But this cruise was for you, Mom," Kit said from the foot of the bed, where she'd been biting her tongue, trying to stay silent.

Marilyn shook her head. "No, it was for *you*. All of you. To be together, as a family. To remember that there is so much strength and love in this family—" She paused, breathed, breathed some more. "And that when you're gathered together, you have me with you, even if I'm not physically present."

"Stop sounding like Jesus, Mom," Kit muttered, blinking hard. "It's terribly aggravating."

Mom barked a laugh. And then she smiled at Kit. "That felt good." Her voice was hoarse but she sounded happy. "Needed to laugh. Must do that more."

Kit exhaled slowly and managed a watery smile. "I'm going to say something, and I don't want you to get mad, and threaten to never talk to me again because that would be really lousy." She held up a finger to keep her mother from speaking. "I agree with you about the cruise. And I think everyone should go. That is, everyone but me."

"Kit!" Dad growled.

"Of course you have to go," Mom said.

Kit shook her head. "Mom, the only way everyone can go is if someone stays home with you, and I want to stay home with you."

Mom started to protest, then stopped and frowned.

"This is ridiculous," Dad said. "I can't go and leave you, Marilyn. You know I can't."

Mom held his gaze for a long time. Her eyes had become very bright. "I never ask you for anything, Tom, because you love me so much you give me whatever I ask for. And I've never wanted to take advantage of that." She needed a moment to catch her breath to continue, and a tear trembled on her lower lashes. "But I'm asking you now to please do this for me. Please take our children on this trip and enjoy them. Enjoy the family we made."

"I'll be with Mom, Dad," Kit said quietly. "She'll be okay."

A spasm of emotion tightened his face and his eyes turned a brilliant watery blue. "I'll miss you, Marilyn."

Mom looked at him steadily. "Take lots of pictures. I'll want to see everything."

K it didn't get home until eleven, and it took her another hour to unwind so that she could sleep. But it wasn't a restful sleep. She kept dreaming about Mom and Dad and the family, and it was so intense that when she woke to her alarm at six-thirty, she felt exhausted and teary.

It was a relief to get to school and know that soon she'd be sucked into the hectic pace of Fridays. Kit didn't know why Fridays were always a little more frenetic than other days, but they were, and this morning she welcomed the structure, activity, and routine.

Fiona and Polly met up with her in the office while she was collecting mail from her teacher in-box.

"All packed?" Fiona asked, juggling her tea and the handouts she'd just printed on the copier.

"All waxed?" Polly added significantly.

"Neither," Kit answered, lifting a hand to wave at Shelley, who'd come through the office with a blue mesh bag filled with basketballs. "Not going after all."

Fiona's eyes grew big. "Your mum?"

"Can't go," Kit said. "I'm staying with her."

Polly looked confused. "What do you mean, *you're* staying with her? What about the others? And your father?"

"Mom wants them to go. She wants them to have fun."

"Can they?" Polly asked doubtfully. "I think they'd feel terribly guilty about leaving their sick mom behind."

"Thank you for not saying 'dying,'" Kit said drily. "And I'm sure it won't be easy for everyone to go knowing Mom can't, but Mom's determined to make sure we stay close and focused on the big picture—which is, in this case, the family—rather than obsess about her. And it makes sense to me. You know, the sum-of-the-whole-is-bigger-than-the-parts thing."

"The whole is greater than the sum of its parts," Fiona corrected. "But when it comes to a mum . . . ?"

"I know. But you can't argue with her. She's a Donahue."

The first warning bell rang and the three quickly headed off to their respective classrooms. Kit was soon immersed in lessons and it wasn't until she was halfway through third period that it registered that Delilah Hartnel was missing. She knew from taking attendance that the girl wasn't there but figured she was just tardy and would eventually show up. She didn't.

At lunch Kit checked in with Mrs. Dellinger to see if the school secretary had heard from Delilah's mother. "Did she call in to say Delilah was sick?" Kit asked.

"No," Mrs. Dellinger said, checking her attendance records just to be sure she hadn't missed anything. "Nothing."

Kit thanked her and went to the staff room to eat lunch but couldn't stop thinking about Delilah. Why wasn't she in school today? She needed to be in school. She'd just missed two and a half days last week. Was it a coincidence that she was absent today, the day after the tense meeting with Michael—no, not Michael, Howard—or was Delilah home *because* of yesterday?

Kit didn't like what her gut was telling her, and she couldn't ignore her instinct either.

Unable to finish her sandwich, Kit returned to her classroom, pulled the folder on Delilah from her purse, and called the home number listed on a form. No one answered, so she left a voice mail, saying that it was Kit Brennan, Delilah's English teacher, and she was just checking in on Delilah since she was absent today. "Give me a call, if you would," she added, giving them the school number and her personal extension.

But leaving the message didn't make her feel better and she scanned the emergency contact form, wanting Missy's cell number. Delilah had said her mom had a cell, but no number for it had been provided on the form. Only the number for Howard's. And Kit wasn't going to call him.

That left only Jude. Again.

Kit didn't want to call him. Didn't want to involve him or depend on him or have anything to do with him. But at the same time he was their neighbor. Would it really be such a big deal for her to ask him to check on Delilah?

Make sure Delilah was okay?

That's all Kit needed to know. Homework and lessons could always be made up, but if there was trouble at home . . . She exhaled slowly, nervously . . .

Michael—correction, *Howard* . . . Howard, Howard, Howard—wasn't a fan of Delilah. He'd made it clear, that night Kit had dinner with him at Millennium, that he didn't like Dee, saying she was mouthy and obnoxious, and blaming his failed marriage on her. And Delilah clearly wasn't comfortable with Howard. So what happened to the girl yesterday after the meeting?

What had he said . . . or done, when they got home?

Kit's stomach cramped. She felt sweaty and queasy. Staring at the emergency contact form, she reluctantly called the only person who might be able to help her.

Jude picked up on the fourth ring. "Yeah?" he answered, sounding bored.

Kit's insides did an uncomfortable flip. "Jude, this is Kit Brennan, Delilah's—"

"I know who you are, Kit Kat."

Her face felt hot. Her insides flipped the other way. He rattled her, he did. "Delilah didn't come to school today."

"Uh-huh."

"I tried to call the Dempseys' house number, but no one answered."

"Did you try the stepdaddy's number?"

"No."

"Why not?"

"I think you know why not."

He was silent a moment. "Can I ask you something?"

"Okay."

"How do you know him?"

"*What?*"

"You met him somewhere, before Delilah enrolled at Memorial, that's why you call him Michael—"

"He told me his name was Michael!"

"Where did you meet him?"

"It's none of your business."

"Did you have a relationship?"

"Absolutely not!" Kit's heart was pounding and she was glad she was sitting. "He's Delilah's stepfather."

"But you knew him before Delilah was your student, didn't you?"

"I knew him all of ten days before she enrolled at Memorial."

"Did you go out with him?"

Her heart fell and her stomach followed. "I'm not going to discuss this. It's not relevant."

"Did you sleep with him?"

"Who's the cop now?" she shouted into the phone, furious. She rarely lost her temper, and never screamed at people, but he was completely pushing her buttons. How dare he question her? How dare *he* assume the worst about *her*?

"I'm just trying to understand the relationship," he answered calmly.

She swallowed hard, trying to calm herself, needing to settle down so she could think straight. "There's no relationship and there's nothing to understand. Delilah was absent today. I called her home number. No one answered. I don't have a number for her mother, so I called you."

"But you could have called Howard. You're old friends—"

"We're not old friends. We're not even friends. I don't trust him. That's why I called you. But if you don't want to help check on Delilah, that's fine. I'll head over to her house after school and look in on her myself."

"You're not going to go by her house."

"I have dropped by dozens of students' homes over the years."

"I don't doubt you have. So let me rephrase that. I wouldn't go by their house today."

"Why not?"

"Howard wouldn't like it."

"Phooey. We may not be friends, but I'm not afraid of Howard. And I'm not going to see him anyway. I'm going to see Delilah."

"No one will open the door."

"You don't know that."

"I live next door, Kit."

She inhaled sharply, frustrated, and not at all certain she knew what to do. "I'm worried about Delilah, and maybe I'm worrying needlessly, but as her teacher, I *am* responsible for her, and if something isn't right, I must help her."

He said nothing.

Kit didn't like it. "Does he hit her?" she blurted.

"Who?"

"Howard. Does he hit Delilah?"

"I don't think so."

Thank God. Kit sagged with relief. "That's good."

Jude was again silent and Kit pictured Delilah, and her pale, frightened face, and her relief faded. "I'm going to stop by after school," she said decisively. "I have to. I just need to know she's okay, otherwise I'll be worrying about her all weekend."

"I tell you what, Kit Kat. I'll go check on Delilah for you, and then I'll call you as soon as I know something. Will that make you feel better?"

"Promise?"

"I promise."

Kit's eyes suddenly burned. "Thank you."

"You're welcome."

"Jude?"

"Yeah?"

"Why are you doing this?"

"Because I'm a sucker for a pretty face?"

"No, seriously."

"I like Delilah. She's a sweet kid." He hesitated. "And I like you."

"Why?"

"You're a good person. You remind me a lot of my mom."

Hanging up, Kit left her phone on her desk during her afternoon classes, and even carried it with her to the parking lot for Friday-afternoon yard duty and traffic patrol, but Jude didn't call. And as the hours passed, she felt increasingly anxious, and she hated being anxious; it made her feel things she didn't like feeling.

Back in her classroom after traffic patrol, she tidied her desk, placing her attendance book and lesson plans in the middle, where next week's substitute would find them easily. It felt strange leaving for a week and she glanced around her room, making sure she hadn't forgotten anything.

Kit was just about to turn off the lights when she thought of Delilah again. So ridiculous to worry and wait. Why was she waiting? She was Delilah's teacher, not Jude. Kit closed her door and headed for her car, having decided to swing by Delilah's house on her way home.

J ude was crouching next to his motorcycle in his driveway, running a wet, soapy sponge over the chrome carburetor, when he spotted a white Prius slowly approaching his house. Probably someone looking for an address. Nothing unusual in that. Except that Jude wasn't most people and he trusted no one, particularly in this neighborhood.

He shifted slightly, his leather work boots creaking, and stretched his arm out to run the sponge down the chrome pipe. The change of position also allowed him to watch the car out of the corner of his eye.

The Prius, already creeping along, suddenly stopped in the middle of the street, right in front of Howard's house. Jude listened to the car humming in the street. He turned his head an inch, glanced at the driver, spotted the red hair, familiar face. Swore.

Kit Kat Brennan.

What the hell was she doing here?

Standing, he tossed the dripping sponge into the blue bucket and headed toward her, drying his wet hands on the back of his faded Levi's.

She stared at him through the closed window, chin up, jaw stubbornly set.

He made a circling gesture with his finger, motioning for her to put the window down.

She hesitated. He gave her a look.

Reluctantly she put the window down a couple of inches.

He motioned that he wanted it all the way down.

Kit rolled her eyes, rolled it down. "Yes?" she said with exaggerated politeness as he bent down, his gaze now level with hers.

"You don't listen very well," he said shortly.

"You didn't call me and I wasn't going to wait anymore." She leaned forward, peering past him. "Is that their house? The white one with the blue shutters to the left of yours?"

"Yes."

"Looks fresh . . . well maintained. Lots of new rosebushes."

"Howard likes to give her roses after they fight."

"That's . . . nice."

God, she was clueless. Jude didn't know if he wanted to kiss her, shake her, or spank her. "The one word I would not use to describe Dempsey is *nice*. He's a lot of things, Kit, but nice isn't one of them."

Her dark eyebrows arched. "Now, if you'll move aside, I'd like to park and introduce myself to Missy."

"You're wasting your time. No one's going to answer."

"You don't know that."

"I know more about the situation there than you do."

"Delilah is *my* student."

"And they're my neighbors. These are small lots and voices carry."

She glanced at the Dempsey house with the fresh white paint and new blue shutters and then at Jude's pink stucco house with the peeling paint, rusted metal chairs on the lawn, and the scattered automotive parts. "I'm sure you hear plenty. Now please move. I'm not leaving without saying hello and seeing Delilah."

He stepped back onto the curb, folded his arms across his chest, and watched as she rolled up the window, parked, and climbed out of the car.

She was wearing a pencil skirt, heels, and a cute little cardigan that made him think of a 1940s pinup.

His lids dropped, lashes lowering, as she marched up the Dempseys' sidewalk, her straight, snug skirt outlining her derriere to perfection. He was an unabashed butt man and he loved Kit's.

Tugging on her cardigan, Kit straightened her shoulders, rang the doorbell, and waited.

No one came to the door.

Kit lifted her hand and knocked vigorously. "Delilah . . . Missy," she called through the door. "It's Kit Brennan, Delilah's English teacher. Just wanted to say hi."

And still no one responded, despite her very cheerful voice. Jude felt almost sorry for her. "Try again," he said. "Shout a little louder."

She flashed him an uncertain look, lips pursing. "You think?"

"Why not? You're there."

He watched as she rapped even harder, and then pressed her mouth to the door to loudly say, "Delilah, it's me, Miss Brennan. I wanted to check on you. Meet your mom. Make sure things are okay."

"Why don't you go around the house, check the back door, try that," he suggested helpfully.

She straightened swiftly, realizing now he'd just been messing with her. Color stormed her cheeks, and her eyes blazed. "Why don't I just climb in through a window?"

"You're sure that's not too pushy?"

Heels clicking, she marched back down the stairs and flashed him a look of loathing as she headed for her car. "Dick," she muttered beneath her breath.

Jude nearly laughed out loud.

God, she was hot.

Her high heels rang against the pavement and then went silent as she sank into the dry grassy patch bordering the curb. Her nose tipped higher. "You can stop laughing at me now and go finish washing your motorcycle."

"But I like watching you."

"Go away."

"Angel, I live here."

"I feel sorry for your neighbors!"

"Why?"

She stopped, faced him, and jabbed a finger there, there, and there, pointing to the chaos in his front yard. "That, that, and that. And I just hope the inside of your house is tidier than the outside!"

"What's wrong with the outside?"

Her lips parted for a split second before she snapped them shut and walked quickly around the car. She swung the door open, slid inside, but before she could slam it closed, he was there, leaning between the door and her side.

"How far did you make it in school before you were kicked out?" she demanded, cheeks a hot pink. "Eighth grade? Ninth grade? Eleventh?"

"Actually made it through college."

"You did not!"

"Graduated with honors."

"Liar!"

He held up two fingers. "Boy Scout's honor."

"I don't believe a word you say."

Jesus, he wanted to kiss her.

She was angry and beautiful and all she needed was someone to stir her up, get her going, make her come alive.

"What did you study?" she demanded.

He wanted to tell her the truth, that he'd double-majored in political science and criminal justice, but that would give away too much about who he was and those were things he never revealed. "Poly sci," he said instead.

"Where?"

He had to bite down on the inside of his cheek. He couldn't laugh, mustn't laugh, she was already so mad at him. "UC Davis."

She studied him suspiciously, her blue eyes searching his. He liked the focus and intensity in her eyes. She had beautiful blue eyes. Beautiful face. But her lips . . . those were his favorite. He had a thing for her mouth. It was what had caught his attention that morning in Capitola. The wild dark red curls and the shape of her mouth . . . her lips a little too full, a little too wide, a little too pink. Even bare, like now, her lips weren't proper. They had a softness and lushness that made him think of tangled sheets, damp skin, and hot, slow, mind-blowing sex.

"Any other questions, teach?" he drawled, aware that his old, faded, ripped Levi's had just gotten way too tight across his groin. He loved these jeans but they didn't really accommodate an erection.

Her lips compressed disapprovingly. "I'm not amused."

"Which I find really funny."

"Can you please step away from my car? I'd like to go home now."

"You don't want to come in? Have a drink?"

"It's four-thirty in the afternoon, Mr. Knight, too early to drink."

"I've got iced tea. And we don't have to go inside. We can sit out here. Enjoy the fresh air."

"And what do you think Howard would say if he saw us?"

Jude's smile slowly faded. His amusement evaporated. "Do you care what he thinks?"

"No."

"You're sure? Sounds like you've got a bit of a sweet spot for him—"

"Get away from me and my car!" She yanked hard on the door, hitting him in the shoulder.

He straightened up but didn't move. "He's dangerous, angel."

"I'm not attracted to him, Jude. Never have been, never will be. He's Delilah's stepfather and that's all he is to me. Now back off so I can go home."

Fifteen

Kit was glad she hit traffic leading up to the Bay Bridge because it gave her time to calm down. She didn't want to arrive at her parents' upset, and right now she was upset, really upset, and it was all Jude's fault.

What a jerk. What an asshole.

And if he really was so smart, and graduated from UC Davis with honors, then why did he live like a bum?

Forty minutes later, Kit opened the front door of her childhood home and heard her mother laughing.

For a second she just stood there and listened.

Her uncle Jack was telling a story and Aunt Linda and Mom kept laughing. They must be in the family room from the way the sound traveled.

Slowly Kit unbuttoned her jacket, letting the day's frustration and anger go.

This was how she wanted to remember her mom. And this is how she wanted to remember this house. As a happy house. A house full of family and love and laughter. Because even in the most challenging of times, the Brennans and Donahues told jokes and teased and made light of their difficulties. Hanging her coat in the hall closet, Kit was glad. She couldn't even imagine growing up in a family like Delilah's.

Entering the family room, she dropped kisses on everyone's cheek. "Far too much gaiety in this house," she scolded with mock severity. "Who said you could have fun without me?"

"We are just reminiscing about your mother and father's courtship," Aunt Linda said, giggling a little as she wiped her eyes dry.

"And how my big brother Jack didn't approve of your dad," Mom said, lips twitching. "So Jack had your dad arrested one night when we were sitting in a parked car kissing."

Kit sat down on the couch next to her uncle. "You had Dad arrested?"

"He wasn't charged," Jack said, "just booked."

"And strip-searched!" Mom cried, dissolving into laughter all over again. "He was so mad at Jack when he found out he'd put the other officers up to it. I've never seen your dad that mad."

"He showed up at our apartment with a baseball bat," Linda said, glancing from Kit to Jack and back again. "Jack and I were just newlyweds and I didn't know what had happened, and Jack's in our bedroom napping—he'd just finished his shift, he was working nights then—and here's your dad on the doorstep with a baseball bat demanding Jack come out."

"What did you do?"

"I told him to come back in seven hours when Jack was awake and he could have a good go at him then."

Kit grinned. "Did you really?"

"Absolutely." Linda's eyes twinkled mischievously. "And your father did. And they went outside and threw a couple punches—"

"A lot of punches," Jack corrected, looking at Kit. "Your father was actually a lot tougher than I gave him credit for. And I was the one that suggested a drink. I needed it. I had a god-awful headache at that point. I just wanted a good pint of beer."

Everyone laughed and then Uncle Jack and Aunt Linda were saying good-bye and Kit assisted her mother up the stairs. They had to take the stairs slowly, just one at a time, so Mom could rest and catch her breath.

"Your dad was right. We should have bought one of those electric chairs that go up and down the stairs," her mother cheerfully wheezed. "Then I could take joyrides up and down."

"That would be very annoying for the rest of us, Mom," Kit teased.

"I know, but the grandkids would have loved it."

Kit helped her mom with her bedtime routine, and then once she had Marilyn in bed, settled comfortably, she handed her the water bottle and her pain medicine.

Her mom swallowed the medicine and, sinking back into her pillows, sighed. "It's going to be nice to have a girls' week. Just you and me."

Kit leaned over and kissed her forehead. "I'm looking forward to hanging out with you and playing beauty shop and doing your hair and giving you a manicure."

"How nice! I don't like how your dad does my hair."

Kit laughed, unable to picture her father doing anything with her mother's hair. "But you're going to have to be honest with me, Mom, and tell me when you're tired, or if you hurt, or if you just want me to leave you alone so you can sleep."

"Like now?" she answered, smothering a yawn.

Kit gave her another kiss good night. "I'll leave your door open and you can just ring the bell if you need me. I'll be here in a jiffy."

Downstairs Kit locked the front door, put the last dishes into the dishwasher, added soap, switched it on, and headed to the family room to watch some TV but couldn't find anything but crime and forensic shows, and she hated programs that started out with someone dying or disappearing. Solving the crime was anticlimactic. Someone was dead.

Her phone buzzed on the table, vibrating with a new voice mail. Kit muted the TV and reached for the phone, wondering what call she'd missed. But it wasn't Dad or Meg or Sarah checking in. It was Howard, still saved in her contacts as Michael:

"Hi, Kit, just called home phone to check messages and heard your voice mail. We're in Tahoe for the weekend for a wedding. Sorry we didn't notify the school. Dee will be back in school Monday. Thanks for following up. Have a good weekend."

So everything's good, she thought, reading the message a second time. Everything was fine. At least Howard made everything sound fine.

Could she trust him?

Did she believe him?

Kit didn't know, wished she knew, wondering if perhaps her imagination had gotten the best of her.

Was it possible that her personal feelings for Howard had prejudiced her against him? And, yes, he was obnoxious and overbearing, but did that make him a villain?

Frustrated, and regretting all the wasted energy, she turned off the TV and went to bed.

At home in the family living room, Delilah kept her eyes glued to the TV, pretending she didn't hear Howie on the phone, leaving Miss Brennan a message.

"Hi, Kit, just called home phone to check messages and heard your voice mail. We're in Tahoe for the weekend for a wedding. Sorry we didn't notify the school. Dee will be back in school Monday. Thanks for following up. Have a good weekend."

Her stomach heaved at the way he'd said, "Hi, Kit," as if they were old friends. So disgusting the way he turned on his charm, used his Mr. Smooth voice, acting like the good guy, the nice guy, as if by being the conscientious stepdaddy, he was the hero.

Delilah hoped Miss Brennan wouldn't fall for it. Because women always fell for it. Women loved Howie. They couldn't get enough of him. Handsome, charming, chivalrous Howard Dempsey with his megawatt smile.

That's how her mother fell for him. Howard with his nice cars and credit cards and confidence. Mama felt so safe with him. "Lean on me," he used to tell her when they were first dating. "You can rely on me."

And just like the spider and the fly, the fly only recognized she was trapped once she was stuck.

Sunday at noon Mom's favorite priest from St. Cecilia came over to bring her the Eucharist. The priest sat next to her, talking to her for almost an hour afterward, and Kit sat downstairs at the dining room table trying to get through the freshmen and sophomore journals. She was halfway through the sophomore stack when she came across Delilah's plain black notebook. So many of her students liked to decorate their covers, creating photo collages or applying stickers or doodling, but Delilah's was plain black. The only way you knew it was hers was that she'd printed her name on the back in a purple marker. *Delilah Hartnel.*

Kit flipped through the pages she'd read before and then began reading the entries that were new to her. In one entry, where the assigned topic sentence was *If you could do anything, what would you do?,* Delilah wrote:

> *If I could do anything, I would make Howie disappear, and then Mama and I could go traveling. Maybe we'd go to Paris*

*or Rome or Venice. I think Mama would enjoy going around
in the gondolas. She likes romantic things. But knowing
Mama, she'd fall in love with an Italian and then we'd be stuck
in Italy and would never get back to Texas. I miss Mineral
Wells. I want to go home.*

Delilah was homesick, Kit thought, turning the page, skimming several entries, noting the frequency with which the girl
mentioned Mineral Wells and Texas, as well as her hatred for
Howard.

Kit tried to remain detached as she read, wanting to keep a
professional distance, aware that Delilah was entitled to her feelings and that it was natural for teenagers to have issues with parents and authority figures, but it was hard not to react to some of
the entries. There was so much drama in them. So much emotion.

Kit's eye fell on the last entry. It was from this last Thursday,
the day Kit had collected the journals to bring home to read before her trip, the day Howard had shown up for the meeting after
school.

I saw Howie watching Jude.
   He hates Jude.
   I think Howie would kill him if he could.
   I think Howie would enjoy killing him.
   I don't know why I think that, but I do.

It was all she'd written, and the lines were surrounded by little
skeleton heads. It was creepy.

Kit closed the journal and got to her feet, putting it away without writing anything in it. What was she going to do about Delilah? What was she going to do about Howard?

Was Howard dangerous?

Was Delilah unstable?

Who, or what, was she to believe? And was she supposed to warn Jude? Would it be such a bad thing if Howard killed Jude?

Chastising herself for being unchristian, Kit sent Jude a text. *FYI Delilah says Howard wants to kill you. Forewarned means forearmed.*

There, she'd done her duty, she thought, putting her phone away. She still didn't know what to do about Delilah and Howard, but at least Jude was no longer her problem.

K it's phone rang at eight o'clock while she was sitting and chatting with her mom in her mother's bedroom. Her heart jumped a bit when Jude's name flashed, and excusing herself, she stepped out of the room to take the call.

"This is Kit," she answered formally.

"Who else would be answering your phone?"

"You got my text?"

"Yeah. Thanks for the warm fuzzies."

"So, Jude, what exactly happened between you and Howard?"

"Nothing happened."

"Why would he hate you so much?"

"Because he's a prick?"

"Jude, I'm serious."

"So am I. He doesn't like me because I know he's a prick and I won't treat him like he's someone special."

"Dudes and their pissing contests."

"There's no contest. I already won."

"I see."

"So when did Delilah tell you her stepdaddy wants to kill me?"

Kit sighed. "She didn't say it to me, she wrote it in her English journal on Thursday in class. I just read it this afternoon."

"Oh, if that's all."

"What do you mean, that's all?"

"She's a girl. She writes crazy shit in her diary. It's what teenage girls do—"

"It's not a diary, it's a school journal, and she wrote it during English class. I think I need to go to Sister Elena and tell her about this, but if I do, she'll tell me to go the police."

"Go to your principal? Why? It'll just get Delilah expelled."

"But what if he tries to kill you?"

"He won't. He can't."

"Why not?"

"I wouldn't let him."

"You're turning this into a joke!"

"I'm not trying to, Kit, but it's hard for me to take Howard seriously. He's an idiot."

"Maybe, but I want you to see what she wrote." She hesitated. "Just in case. Because if something did happen and I hadn't warned you—"

"Okay, fine. I'll read it."

"Thank you." She breathed a sigh of relief. "Tomorrow?"

"Can't do tomorrow. Have something going on. What are you doing now?"

"I'm in San Francisco . . . staying with my mom."

"I can come to you there."

"No." She said it too quickly and added apologetically, "My mom's not well."

"And we both know she wouldn't like me."

Kit grimaced. He was right.

"Where do you want to meet?" he asked.

"Do you know the city at all?"

"Can find my way around."

Kit pictured the Outer Sunset district. It was filled with coffeehouses and restaurants, but at this time of night, the indie coffeehouses and cute cafés would be closed or closing, leaving just the bars. But then again, Jude would probably prefer a bar. "Ever been to Durty Nelly's?"

"On Irving Street?"

"That's it," she said. He did know his way around. "How about an hour?"

"See you there."

K it told herself she was not nervous as she drove to Durty Nelly's. She wasn't nervous and she wasn't excited and she wasn't looking forward to seeing him.

Those weren't butterflies in her stomach, she told herself, parking around the corner on Twenty-fourth; she had indigestion.

Her hand shook slightly as she opened the bar's distinctive red door. *Not nervous, not nervous, not nervous.*

One of the bartenders greeted her as she entered. She smiled fleetingly and turned away, her gaze scanning the pub. It was a quiet night, with just a few people at the long bar and another few at tables.

She spotted Jude almost immediately. He was lounging by the big redbrick fireplace, his long legs stretched out before him, a glass of Guinness in his hand. Kit unwound her scarf and joined him.

"Waiting long?" she asked, hating the breathless note in her voice. Why did she do that when she saw him?

"No. But even if I had, I wouldn't mind. I like this place. Haven't been here in a while."

Kit unbuttoned her coat, slid it off, and sat down. "Haven't been here in ages either. Used to come quite a bit. Loved the Irish music on the weekends."

He sipped his Guinness. "What's wrong with your mom?"

Kit shook her head, unwilling to talk about it with Jude, thinking these meetings between them weren't good. Jude wasn't good for her. She couldn't think straight around him. There was something about him that discombobulated her. And men in general didn't have that effect on her. Men in general left her cool, if not cold.

Jude, on the other hand, made her hot.

Frustrating, distracting, unacceptable.

Kit forced herself to look at him. He was watching her. Smiling at her.

"Why are you smiling?" she asked, incredibly annoyed with him for no reason that she could think of, and yet looking at him, sitting with his long legs outstretched, totally unruffled, ruffled her.

"Why are you so mad at me?" He sounded amused.

"Because I'm exhausted and worried sick about everyone and trying to take care of everything and you don't look as if you have a care in the world!"

"Would you feel better if I looked worried?"

"*Yes!*"

He had the gall to laugh.

Kit ground her teeth, hating him, regretting calling him, regretting caring enough to call him, regretting that something in her found him interesting and appealing when she should find him horrible and revolting.

"Would you like a beer?" he asked when he had finally stopped laughing.

"Yes. *Please.*"

He smiled and stood. God, he was tall and handsome, and Kit saw every female head in the place swivel to watch him walk to the bar to buy her the beer.

He walked like he owned the place.

Walked like he owned the world.

Bastard, she thought breathlessly, trying not to admire his muscular legs, his big shoulders, his lean hips, his full-on swagger.

And she was doing a pretty good job not being overly impressed until he leaned on the counter to talk to the bartender.

Suddenly there was no air. She couldn't breathe.

The denim of his jeans hugged his hamstrings and butt, the soft fabric clinging to him like a second skin, outlining all that dense, hard muscle.

Kit had a father and a brother. She'd lived with Richard forever. Knew her way around a gym. A man didn't get a body like that by sitting around and drinking beer.

He'd worked for that body. Sweated for that body.

She tried not to think of him working up a sweat on her . . . working her . . .

Don't be sexual, Kit, not with him.

Jude returned with the beer. It wasn't a Guinness, it was a brown ale. She thanked him. She'd never developed an affinity for Guinness despite touring the brewery on her last visit to Dublin five years ago when she'd taken a six-week course at Trinity College on Anglo-Irish literature.

"Have you had dinner?" he asked, sitting down again across from her, his legs extending into her space.

Kit quickly pulled her legs up into her chair, tucking them under her. "I have. Are you hungry?"

"No. Just wanted to make sure you'd eaten."

"I'm good. Thank you." She drew a breath. "So Delilah—"

"No. Not Delilah, not yet."

"But we're here to talk about Delilah."

"No, we're here to talk about Howard. And so we're going to talk about Howard, and how you know him, because you do know him."

Kit glared at him for a long moment. "I find you very unlikable."

"I know. And I'm sorry to hear that."

Of course his lips would be twitching as he said it. Such a shithead. "Okay, fine. I'm going to tell you how I met Howard, I'll tell you everything, but don't interrupt me."

She took a quick breath and plunged on before he could say anything. "I met Howard at a bar in Alameda called Z's. I go there with Polly and Fiona, teacher friends of mine from Memorial, once or twice a month for drinks. He was sitting with Polly's ex-boyfriend. Apparently they're neighbors or something, and while Polly and Jon were outside talking, he introduced himself to me. He said his name was Michael, he was from Houston, had just moved here, and didn't know anyone. He never mentioned he had a family. If anything, he made it sound as if he was single and lonely but I didn't give him my number or encourage him in any way. And then a few days later he calls me on my cell—"

"How did he get your number?"

She'd told him she didn't want to be interrupted, but Jude had just asked a very good question. "I don't know. I even asked him that, and he made a joke out of it, saying he had 'his ways.'"

Jude said something that very possibly was obscene under his breath.

Kit swallowed and pressed on. "He wanted to take me out that weekend but I was already heading out of town to Capitola—"

"The weekend I met you in the village?"

"That's right. So we made plans to go out the following weekend, and we did. We went out only once, to dinner. I met him at the restaurant. I drove my own car."

"Thank God for small mercies," he muttered.

She ignored him. He wasn't sticking to her deal, but never mind. "I wouldn't call dinner pleasant—"

"Why not?"

"He was . . . overbearing."

"What does that mean?"

"I guess I found him rather aggressive. If I said something he didn't like, he'd try to change my mind. But it wasn't comfortable.

I felt uncomfortable. Almost like I was dealing with a teenage bully."

Jude's expression hardened. "He was aggressive with you?"

"Not physically, no, but he didn't like that I wouldn't go out with him again since he wasn't divorced." She looked into Jude's eyes. "I didn't know he was going through a divorce. Would never have gone out with him if I'd known he was still married."

"He told you he'd filed for a divorce?"

She nodded. "He said it would be final in two weeks, and he blamed his failed marriage on his fifteen-year-old stepdaughter."

"And that impressed you?"

"*No*. I never went out with him again. But he kept calling—"

"Did you tell him to get lost?"

"I tried.

"I *did*." She exhaled, rubbed at her forehead. "Then five days after that one date, he showed up in my classroom, announced he was getting back together with Missy and that Delilah would be one of my students."

"That's just plain weird."

"I know."

"Do you honestly know how weird that is? He's a freak, Kit Kat. A stalker—"

"That's why I texted you. I was warning you."

He dramatically put a hand across his heart. "That FYI you sent me this afternoon was a warning? 'Forewarned is forearmed'? I'm sorry, Miss Brennan, but I found it rather glib, and devoid of any genuine concern about my personal safety."

Kit had to fight really hard not to smile. She actually liked his sense of humor. "You have really good diction for a biker who is running from the law."

"My mom was a teacher."

Kit sat back in her chair. The way he said it completely disarmed her. "What did she teach?"

"Fifth grade. That was her favorite grade. But she taught almost every grade at one point or another. She just retired last year after forty years."

"Is she in the area or . . . ?"

"In the area."

"Where did she teach?"

"Sequoia Elementary." He said it proudly, without hesitation, and something in Kit shifted, softening.

"What is she doing now?" she asked.

"Reading. Gardening. Playing bridge."

"Bridge?"

"Maybe it's duplicate bridge. She tried to teach me once but it wasn't for me. The game went on forever."

Kit tucked a rebellious curl behind her ear. She'd tried straightening her hair tonight but not all curls seemed to have gotten the message. "I can't picture you playing bridge."

"I guess she couldn't either. She gave up after that one lesson. Suggested I stick to poker."

"Are you a good poker player?"

"No. Not real big on cards. Would rather be outside doing something."

"Like what?"

"Working on my bike. Riding my bike. Heading to the beach." The corners of his mouth lifted. "You like asking questions, don't you, Miss Brennan?"

"No more than you do."

He grinned, swigged his beer. "My mom used to call me Curious George. I used to get into everything."

"So did I."

"Really?"

"I used to be so curious about everything. I wanted to know everything, so I'd snoop in my brother's and sisters' bedrooms, opening drawers, searching their closets, looking for things."

Laughter gleamed in his eyes. "Kit Kat was a snoop."

She nodded, embarrassed.

"So what were you looking for?" he asked.

"Anything. Everything. I just liked looking. Maybe, like you, I was born curious, because I remember looking at everything, even as a little girl. Reading everything. Books, pictures, encyclopedias. I guess I should have been an investigator. I used to pretend I was Nancy Drew."

"Did your sisters and brother mind having a snoop for a sister?"

"I'm sure they did, when they found out. But they rarely found out. I was good. Discreet. And it was a great way to spend an hour, or an afternoon. My favorite room to explore was my parents'. What did they have in bottom drawers? In the back of drawers? In pockets? In coats? Hidden behind coats?"

"And what did you find?"

"All sorts of things. Coins. Cards. Unwrapped Christmas or birthday presents. Girlie magazines. Dirty handkerchiefs. A handgun—"

"A gun?"

"My dad kept one on the top shelf of his closet. But the bullets were in a lavender floral shoe box in Mom's closet behind her other shoe boxes."

He smiled, creases fanning from his eyes. "You were worse than I was."

She blushed. "And those were the safe things I found." She chewed on the inside of her lip, hesitating. "There were things I wish I hadn't found."

"Like?"

"Um. Other stuff. Adult stuff. And it's time to change the subject, I think." Aware that her face had to be bright pink, Kit took a massive sip of her beer and then another, wondering what on earth had possessed her to share so much, and how had they gotten on this topic in the first place? "So Delilah," she said, desperate to change the subject. "Let's talk about her."

"It *is* why we're here."

Kit opened her purse, pulled out the black notebook, and handed it to him to read. "Here. Read."

She watched his face as he skimmed the lines. There weren't many. It didn't take him long.

Jude looked up at her. "She's quite good at making skeleton heads."

Kit's lips curved. Damn him. She wasn't supposed to find him funny or sexy but she did. She really, really did. "You're supposed to be reading what she wrote, not looking at the cartoons."

He handed the journal back to her. "I read it all, and, Kit, I'm okay if Dempsey hates me. The feeling's mutual."

"Why don't *you* like him?"

"Because he's a snake. Bad news. Can't think of one redeeming quality."

"He has to be intelligent. He's a petroleum engineer."

"Did he tell you that?" Jude smiled but his eyes were hard and unforgiving. "Because he's not. He's a reliability manager."

"What's that?"

"He helps monitor quality in the manufacturing department. And no, you don't get there without some effort and experience but Dempsey is no genius. He's a sick SOB that preys on women. I'd take him out of this life if I could."

His vehemence startled her. He didn't sound calm now. "That's a joke, right?"

"No."

Kit blinked. "You can't really mean that."

"Then you don't know me."

Kit glanced down at Delilah's entry. "Are they back yet? Have you seen her since they got home?"

"Got home from where?"

"Tahoe."

"When?"

"This weekend. Howard called me Friday night from Tahoe, said they'd gone there for a wedding, apologized for not letting the school know that Delilah would be absent—" She broke off as she saw Jude's expression. *"What?"*

"They didn't go to Tahoe." His voice was deep and rough, as if he'd been smoking cigarettes and drinking whiskey all day. "Howard's car has been parked in the driveway since Friday evening."

"Maybe they didn't take his car."

"Or maybe he just lied to you again."

Kit ducked her head, her feelings hurt, and she didn't even know why. But then, nothing about this Jude-Howard-Delilah thing made sense.

"Kit, Howard was home this weekend. He was out mowing his lawn yesterday, planting new rosebushes today." Jude's straight black eyebrows lowered over his eyes. "In khakis and a wife beater, no less. Imagine that."

Kit looked up at him. "Did you see Delilah at all?"

"Yesterday, briefly, when she took a beer out to Howard. And then today she and Missy were out watering the rosebushes Howard had planted."

"How did Delilah look?"

"Fine." He paused, studied Kit. "It's usually Missy that's hobbling about."

"Is that because she's sick . . . or. . . .?"

Jude held her gaze. "What do you think?"

Kit slammed her beer down on the table. "I don't know what to think! That's why I'm talking to you. You're their neighbor. You're Delilah's self-appointed 'guardian.' What *should* I think? And should I be worried?"

"Hell yes. *I'm* worried."

Okay. Not good. Kit exhaled and sat back heavily in her chair. If Jude was worried, things at the Dempsey house must be . . . terrible. "Why don't you go to the police, then?"

"And what will they do?"

"Intervene. Help get Delilah out of there."

"You want Delilah taken from her home?"

"If she's not safe."

"And you think putting her in foster care will be better?"

Her heart was racing. She hated this entire conversation. "You're the one who lives next door to them. Would foster care be better?"

"Delilah wouldn't think so."

"But Delilah's a child. She needs to be protected."

"And yet Delilah thinks it's her job to protect her mother."

Kit dragged her hands through her hair, overwhelmed. Children shouldn't be taking care of their parents, not when they were still children. "So you think I should do nothing?"

"I think you need to do what you're doing now—pay attention. Keep an eye on her. Keep reading her journal. And keep in touch with me. And I'll keep in touch with you."

"It doesn't seem like enough."

He studied her from beneath his black lashes, not saying anything. Finally he said, "If I weren't in the equation, what would you do?"

She frowned. Interesting question. If she didn't know Jude, and couldn't call him, what would she do? Go to Sister? No. Not yet. Because Jude was right. Once Sister saw Delilah's journal, she'd probably want to expel her.

Kit sighed. "I'd wait, and watch . . . at least a little longer, because I don't think Sister would understand, or be sympathetic, and I can't go to the police, because I don't really have anything to take to them. Do I?"

"Depends on what you have."

Kit glanced down at the notebook on her lap. "Just this journal, and the things Delilah told me, about how she lied to Howard
about the suspension to protect her mom, and the things you've
told me about Howard." She chewed on her lip, looked at him.
"But that's all hearsay, isn't it?"

"Pretty much."

"I'm afraid no one would really believe her," Kit said.

"She has a reputation for being a difficult teenager. Her principal and her teachers all view her as hostile. I'm afraid the police
wouldn't have anything to move on. They'd look at the notebook
and think her anger is typical of an unhappy fifteen-year-old."

Kit thought of Fiona and her stepchildren and how often kids
and parents and stepparents struggled with blending families. "So
there's nothing I really can do," she said.

"Not yet. But that doesn't mean there won't be."

She nodded.

"And your mom? She's not okay, is she?"

Kit shook her head. Shook it again. Looking up into his eyes,
and something inside of her tripped. Fell. Shattered.

"You don't have to talk about it," he said gently.

She tried to smile but couldn't. Not when she suddenly felt so
sad and tired. Life could be hard and sometimes she was tough
and strong and then sometimes, like tonight, she felt bruised.
Raw. And right now she was too bruised to bullshit. "She has
cancer."

His gaze held hers, but he didn't say anything. She was glad.
She was glad he knew how to listen.

"It's terminal, and she's in the advanced stages now," she
added, trying to slow her heart, calm her breathing. "We're just
trying to keep her comfortable now."

"I'm sorry."

"I am, too. It sucks." She was blinking back tears and trying
to smile because she really didn't want to fall apart here, in front

of him. "Makes me kind of crazy, so I try not to think about how little time is left. Instead, I spend time with her whenever I can. In fact, I'm staying with her all week. My dad had a family thing to do and so I've taken the week off from school."

"Who's with her now?"

"No one. She's asleep." She saw his expression and lifted a hand to stop him. "She knows I'm here. And I told her I wouldn't stay long—"

"Then let's get you home." He drained his beer, got to his feet. "You don't live far, do you?" he asked her as they exited the pub into the night.

"No. Fifth and Judah."

"Good. You are close."

He walked her to her car. They passed his huge burnt-orange motorcycle on the way to where she'd parked. The bike had massive handlebars and fat tires and mean-looking chrome. "Does your mom like your motorcycle?" Kit asked.

"No. Says it's dangerous. That's why I've promised her to always wear my helmet."

She smiled faintly. "I thought it was California state law to wear a helmet."

They'd reached her car and Kit opened her purse, dug around for her keys.

"And your dad?" he asked abruptly as she retrieved her key ring. "What's he like? Is he good to your mom?"

"Dad? Oh, he loves Mom. Lives for her. Treats her like a queen." Her voice cracked as she added, "He's going to miss her so much. But then, we're all going to miss her. She's our rock."

"I'm sorry," Jude said quietly.

She tried to answer, but couldn't. She swiped at a tear, and another, horrified that she was coming unglued. "Better go," she said huskily.

Suddenly his large callused hands were framing her face and

he pressed a kiss to her forehead. "Don't worry so much," he said, letting her go, stepping back. "And try to take care of yourself."

Kit's heart turned over, and not because of her mom, or her dad, but because this big tough guy in leather and tats made her feel good. How did that happen?

"Good-bye," she said, opening her car door, sliding behind the steering wheel.

He was standing back from her, feet planted wide, hands in his jacket pockets. "Good night."

Blinking away fresh tears, Kit started the engine and pulled away, aware that he was still watching her.

He didn't make sense. He was scary and enigmatic and yet strangely soothing and calming, once she stopped being mad at him. But how could she feel good near him? How could she be safe with him? Wasn't he dangerous?

Or was it just an illusion . . . the result of the bike, the long hair and tattoos?

She tried to imagine Jude with short hair and clean-shaven. Pictured him in something besides denim and leather. He was a good-looking guy, he'd probably look very *GQ* if you put him in chinos and a polo shirt . . .

But who was she kidding? Jude wasn't going to ever wear chinos and a navy polo. He might shave for her, but he wasn't going to cut off his hair.

And even with his head shaved, Dad would still never like him.

Which was too bad, since Jude was interesting. And funny. Really funny. He made her laugh. He also turned her on a little bit. He had a very masculine, alpha male swagger to him, and she could see him on the sidewalk on Twenty-fourth Street next to her car, his feet wide, planted shoulder-width apart, looking as if nothing could shake him, or move him, or knock him off-balance.

It wasn't until she was dashing up the steps to her parents' front door that Kit realized who else stood that way—feet planted. Shoulder-width apart.

Tommy.

Her dad.

And every fireman she'd ever met.

Sixteen

K it didn't sleep well. She dreamed of Jude all night. She woke up early, crankier than when she went to bed, and headed to the kitchen to make coffee and try to snap out of her funk.

Fortunately, Mom woke up in a good mood, with an appetite, and Kit made her soft scrambled eggs with cheese melted on top and her mother ate every bite.

Meg called Monday morning to check in and see how everything was going. "You okay there with Mom?" she asked, sounding worried.

"Doing good. How's the cruise?"

"The kids are having a ball. It's eat, eat, eat, swim, sun, play, and then eat some more."

Kit smiled. "I heard there's a lot of food on board. Have you guys managed to hit the midnight buffet yet?"

"We haven't missed it once. I'm not kidding when I say I think I've gained five pounds already—"

"You can't in just two days."

"Oh yes you can if you're eating six meals a day plus blender drinks every hour, plus ice cream sundaes in the afternoon and then desserts like bananas Foster or baked Alaska every dinner."

"I do love desserts."

Meg's tone turned serious. "Wish you and Mom were here, though, Kit. We all miss both of you."

"I like being with Mom, and I don't think she could have managed the cruise. She gets tired so easily and sleeps most of the day now."

"What about food? Is she eating all right?"

"Cleaned her plate this morning. Couldn't believe it."

"Oh, good! Cass was telling me that as it gets closer to . . . you know . . . Mom will have difficulty swallowing food. Have you noticed that yet?"

"Sometimes." Kit could picture an hourglass, and the sand was slipping down faster and faster now, leaving the top almost empty. "Now and then, but she had a good morning, and a great breakfast, so try not to stress. And truthfully, I like cooking for her. I make her smoothies between meals, and then little tea sandwiches at lunch to tempt her appetite. Mom loves my egg-salad-and-cucumber sandwiches and I cut off the crusts and cut them into pretty shapes. We eat on her bed for all our meals now. It's like being at camp."

"I love you, Kit."

"Are you getting all mushy on me, Mags?"

"We're on a cruise eating baked Alaska while you're keeping Mom comfortable and cutting her sandwiches into shapes, and turning lunch, which I'm sure is a chore, into a tea party—" Meg broke off. "I just love you, Kit," she said when her voice was steady again. "And we all are grateful to you, not because you're selfless and perfect and some kind of martyr, but because you are you. You have always, *always,* given others the benefit of the doubt. You always try to be loving, and it's not an act, it's just you, and you have to know, we wouldn't be half the family we are without you."

"I love you, too, Mags."

"Wish you were here."

"Go easy on those sundae bars and dinner buffets . . . it's so much harder taking the weight off now than it used to be."

"Thanks, Kit."

"Anytime, Mags."

"I *hate* that name."

Kit gurgled with laughter. "I know you do."

Sometime very early Wednesday morning, between two-thirty, when Mom woke Kit for assistance to go to the bathroom, and six o'clock, when she woke up in a soiled bed, she had an accident.

The frantic ringing of the porcelain bell woke Kit and she flew out of bed, racing to her mother's side.

Her mom was still shaking the bell when Kit got there, and she took the white bell with the green shamrock from her mother and set it back on the table. Kit had bought the bell in Ireland. It was a touristy trinket but Mom collected shamrocks.

"Oh, look, look," Marilyn cried, struggling to pull back the covers to free her legs. "Look what I've done. How stupid! I can't believe it—"

"It's okay, Mom. It's not the end of the world."

"I don't know why it happened. I didn't even feel a need to go—"

"It's fine. It's happened before—"

"When I was going through chemo. But I'm not going through chemo. There's no reason for this."

But there was. They both knew it. Advanced stages . . . end stages . . . final stages . . .

Just a matter of time now before it was hospice care.

Fuck.

"Why don't we get you cleaned up," Kit said calmly, so very glad she could sound calm, nonchalant, when part of her on the inside was screaming. Panicking. She didn't like this. She didn't want to do this. Death, dying, bodily functions, the loss of bodily functions. She wasn't the nursing type. She was the reader, the teacher, the girl who loved books and ideas and escape. She'd never liked reality. Had never been comfortable with reality. This is why she got lost in beauty, poetry, fiction, fantasy . . .

"I don't want you to see me like this," her mother choked, trying to untangle her legs from the mess of the sheets and crying with shame.

"I appreciate that. I wouldn't want you to see me poop or deal with my poop—oh, wait, you did. You changed my diapers for years."

Marilyn laughed and sobbed at the same time. "But you were a baby!"

"And now you're a baby, so what?"

"Don't make me laugh, not when I'm so upset!"

"Aw, Mom, let me make you laugh. It's the least I can do for you."

"*Least?* All you've done is wait on me and help me to the toilet and now you're going to have to help me bathe and do my sheets—" She broke off, tearful and angry. "I don't want to do this, Kit! Don't want you to have to clean me, and I definitely don't want your dad to have to do it either. I don't want his final memories of me to be of him lifting my nightgown to wipe shit off my bony ass!"

Kit was shocked to hear her mother swear. Her jaw dropped and her eyes widened and she stared at her mother for the longest time, absolutely incredulous that she'd put *wipe shit* and *bony ass* together in the same sentence.

"Yes," Marilyn flashed tearfully, defiantly, "I swore. I did."

"I heard you."

"Then hear this—I don't want to die without dignity. I need to be me. Do you understand? I need to feel like me."

"I hear you, Mom."

"It's time now to bring in someone else. A nurse or nursing assistant—"

"You mean after Dad gets home?"

"No. Before Dad gets home. Then when I need help . . . like this . . . the nurse will do it and your dad won't have to be part of it."

"Okay."

"And when it's at the end . . . we'll find me a good place for hospice care. I've been looking into it for a while and there are two wonderful places . . . they're both great options. I want you to talk to the administrators today, make sure they remember me—"

"You don't want to . . . die . . . here at home?"

"No. Dad has to live in this house after I'm gone. I'm not going to have him remembering me in a bed, dead. Or me getting last rights. Or waiting for the ambulance or coroners to come. Not going to leave him with those memories. Won't become a ghost in my own house."

Kit couldn't speak. She just nodded once.

"Good." Mom managed a smile. "And now that we have that settled, I'll let you help me to the bathroom to clean this . . . you know . . . off of me."

Kit spent the afternoon on the phone talking with a service that provided nursing care at home. Mom had been very specific that she wanted around-the-clock care so that Dad was no longer tied to the house because of her, and she insisted the help started Saturday or Sunday morning so the aide could get familiar with the house, and Marilyn's needs, before Dad came home.

"Dad's not going to like walking in the door and discovering everything's changed while he was gone," Kit warned her, after hanging up from the service, who had promised to have someone at the house eight Sunday morning and then around-the-clock from there.

"It's what I want," Marilyn retorted.

"I understand, but this is Dad's home, too—"

"And it will be solely his house in just a couple weeks. But until then, he can adapt to having someone here, assisting me." She toyed with the lace on the edge of her ivory bed jacket. "I'm not doing this to hurt your dad. I'm doing it because I love him."

I t was a long afternoon.

Kit sat next to her mom's bed from two until almost four making phone calls. Her mom sat quietly, listening, as Kit talked to the agency that would provide home health care, and then to the hospice facilities her mom approved of. By the time she was finally finished, she was exhausted.

Marilyn had been dozing during the last forty-five minutes of the last call, and she woke with a start, blinking at Kit. "What did I miss?"

Kit smiled at her, patted her arm. "Nothing."

"I was sleeping again."

"It's okay. The conversation was boring." Kit drew her chair closer to the bed. "Thirsty?" she asked, reaching for the tall plastic water bottle with the flexible straw.

Her mother tipped her head forward to sip slowly. "You're taking very good care of me, Katherine Elizabeth."

"Thank you."

"You would have made a good nurse."

"Oh, I'm much happier being a teacher."

"You like your books."

"And my kids." Kit put the water bottle back on the nightstand and reached for the little tub of Vaseline to dab on her mother's lips. Her skin was always so dry now.

"Then I give you an A-plus-plus."

"A-plus-plus? That's awfully generous. Should help my GPA."

"Where are you applying to school now?"

"Life school . . . motherhood."

"Motherhood?"

Kit nodded. "I want to be a mom."

"You will be someday."

Kit heard the *someday* and knew what it meant. Someday, after she found a man and got married. Someday, when she was a wife and properly settled. "I don't trust someday," she said. "Someday is like maybe. Not very definite."

"You can't really control those things."

"I think I can."

"Do you have some news for me?" There was a flicker of excitement in her mother's eyes. "The guy you're seeing . . . the one from Chevron?"

Kit nearly shuddered. "*No.*"

"Why not? You said he was nice."

"He's also quite married."

"Oh, Kit, no!"

"Yes."

"When did you find that out?"

"When he announced he was enrolling his stepdaughter at my school."

"Oh, Kit. Yuck." Her mother made a face.

"I know."

"So how do you plan to do this? Who's your magic man?"

"He's a Chia Pet, Mom. I ordered him off TV. I just water him and he grows."

Her mother didn't even crack a smile.

"That was a joke, Mom." Kit reached for the Lubriderm lotion, squirted a little bit into her palm, and then took her mother's right hand to gently massage the cream into her soft skin. "But I'm not joking when I say I'm wanting to become a mom, and there are a lot of single mothers out there doing a fantastic job."

"That's not God's plan."

"Did He tell you that? He hasn't told me."

Marilyn pulled her hand out of Kit's. "If you just be patient, you will have everything you ever wanted."

"Is that what you tell Tommy and Cass? For them to just be patient? No. I know it's not. I know you've spoken with Cass about adoption. I know you're waiting for the right moment to approach Tommy."

"That's different, Kit. They've been married ten years. But you're still young. You have plenty of time yet—"

"I'm forty."

"Plenty of forty-year-olds still have children. And that's something you can explore down the road."

Someday . . .

Down the road . . .

Marilyn reached for the TV remote on the nightstand and hit the power button. "Let's see if we can find something to watch. I'm pretty sure we recorded *American Idol* last night."

Kit stared at her mother's profile, willing her to look at her, finish the conversation.

She didn't.

Heart heavy, Kit stood up, gathered the dishes and water bottle from the side of the bed. "I'm going to get you some fresh water and a snack. Is there something special you'd like?"

Her mother glanced at her, smiled as if nothing significant had just happened. "I'd love some more of that cantaloupe from breakfast if there is any left. I think it was the best cantaloupe I've ever had."

The best cantaloupe . . .

In the kitchen, Kit paced back and forth, fighting to box up her wild emotions so that she could return to her mother's room, calm and cool and sweet and loving . . .

But she was far from calm, cool, or loving right now. She was angry and frustrated. So frustrated.

She'd never been the type to make waves, had never argued with her parents or rebelled in high school. Brianna was the rebel. Swashbuckling Brianna, who took the risks, ignored advice, cheerfully, defiantly cutting her own path through life.

But right now Kit wished she'd been more like Bree. Wished she had just an ounce of Brianna's fire.

During childhood and adolescence, it had pained Kit to watch Brianna be punished for being a free spirit. But the discipline and consequences didn't deter Bree. If anything, she just got wilder. By eighth grade she had a reputation for putting out, and by her freshman year of high school she'd already had a couple of scrapes with the law. Being sent to juvenile court would have crushed Kit, but it made no impression on Bree.

Brianna made it clear she didn't care what her parents or the priest or the police thought. She got through school because she was brilliant. She didn't do homework, or lab work, but she had a photographic memory and would skim through her textbooks the night before an exam and then pass the test with flying colors.

It made her teachers crazy.

And so she skated through life, doing what she wanted, mocking those who criticized her, until one day she got so stoned she forgot she was babysitting a six-year-old at their house. The little girl wandered outside and was discovered floating facedown in the Brennan pool by their father, who'd come home unexpectedly early from work. He never came home early, not even he knew why, that day, he felt compelled to go home, but thank God he had. Dad jumped into the pool and performed CPR until the ambulance arrived, and the little girl eventually recovered. Divine intervention, Mom called it.

Everyone said prayers. Everyone was grateful.

Brianna shrugged it off.

And Dad flipped out. He stopped talking to Bree, wouldn't even look at her, or acknowledge her when she sat down at the dinner table.

Mom hated it.

Kit tried not to take sides—Bree was her twin—but she understood Dad's anger, understood that shame. He'd dedicated his life to protecting people and then his own daughter nearly killed a child because she selfishly chose to get high.

That whole year, from the middle of Bree and Kit's sophomore year of high school and into the beginning of their junior year, was awful. Kit hated remembering. Her parents were at complete odds. Dinner every night was excruciatingly tense. They sat around their dining room table in silence. They'd do dishes without speaking, moving swiftly, mechanically, to finish so they could escape back upstairs.

The fall of her junior year was the one and only time Kit's parents went to counseling. Dad didn't want to go, and only complied because Mom threatened to leave him if he didn't.

Brianna, she told him, was a teenager. She'd made a mistake. People were human. And if he couldn't recognize that what his daughter needed from him was compassion and forgiveness, then Marilyn no longer saw a future for them because she'd had it with his useless, stupid, destructive disappointment and rage.

Dad had choice words for Mom, blaming her for indulging Brianna, failing to enforce consequences, constantly giving her too much freedom, and Mom fought back, pointing out that Uncle Liam came from *his* side of the family, not hers, and that she wouldn't be listening to any more of his personal attacks.

Oh, Mom could be fierce. She knew when and how to fight,

and she only took on Dad when she had no other choice. They didn't battle often, but when they did, everyone else lay low. You did not want to draw their attention then, or get in the way.

And Kit, being the good daughter, had grown up lying low, trying not to draw attention, not wanting to displease her parents or cause Dad to feel disappointment.

But Kit wasn't a little girl anymore and she couldn't go through life needing approval. She was mature enough now to recognize that conflict was an inherent part of living, and while she didn't enjoy tension or creating controversy, it was impossible to avoid them altogether, especially if she planned on moving forward with adoption. Not everyone in her family would have a problem with it, but there would be some who weren't going to be happy, and there was nothing she could do about it. She wasn't going to give up her dreams just because her dreams made someone uncomfortable.

Kit carried the cantaloupe, sliced strawberries, and graham crackers up to her mom and was tidying up the newspaper and magazine Mom had been reading earlier when her phone buzzed with an incoming text.

Stepping out of the bedroom, she checked the phone. From Jude.

Do you, or your mom, need anything?

Her heart seemed to skip and she bit her lip, overwhelmed by feelings.

Yes, she thought. Her mom needed to live and Kit needed to love. But those weren't things she'd ask Jude for.

Thinking of Jude made her eyes burn and a lump fill her throat. She liked him, she did, but he didn't fit with the Brennans. He wouldn't fit in. He'd be like Brianna, always rubbing everyone the wrong way.

It'd been so hard for her to watch Brianna constantly be criticized and punished. She couldn't bear to introduce someone like Jude to her family and watch him be shunned.

Kit forced herself to text him back. *Thank you, but we're good. It was nice of you to ask.*

Jude had been sitting on his porch, using a rag to wipe the grease from his motorcycle off his hands, when he noticed the sunset. The sky was no longer blue but colored like one of those Jell-O parfaits his mom used to make him when he was a kid—layers of blush, peach, and red.

Those colors made him think of Kit and he sent her a text. He didn't expect her to take up his offer, but he wanted her to know he was thinking of her. And he was.

He liked thinking about Kit. She made him strangely happy, and happy wasn't something he normally felt.

Of course, this wouldn't go anywhere. It couldn't. Not with his work. But if he didn't do what he did . . . if he had a different life, different career, she'd be the one for him. Not just because she had a rockin' hot bod and long red hair he wanted to wrap around his hands, but because she was kind. Good. You could feel her goodness when you talked to her and it made him warm on the inside. Made him happy.

Jude's phone beeped with a text. It was from Kit. He knew it, could feel it in his bones.

He took a sip from his can of beer, crumpling the can slightly, enjoying the sound of metal bending before reading the text.

Thank you, but we're good. It was nice of you to ask.

The corner of his mouth lifted. Kit Kat Brennan. So well mannered. So very polite.

Kit would never be interested in him. She shouldn't ever be interested in him. His life was dangerous. There was no place for her in it.

And yet . . .

The red and peach were fading from the sky now, leaving it the hazy lavender gray of twilight. Next door Howard emerged from his house to stand on his front steps and survey his property and then the property next door.

Jude rubbed another spot of oil from his right hand.

Howard was looking around his yard, and then circling his car, checking for scratches or dents. No surprise there. It was his nightly ritual to come out and inspect his crappy kingdom. But tonight, instead of going back inside, he opened the car door, got behind the wheel, and started the engine up. Howard Dempsey was going out.

D elilah was glad Howie had gone out.

She heard him tell Mama he had some kind of business meeting. Mama wasn't happy about it, especially as he left in one of his starched dress shirts, smelling of his Tommy Hilfiger cologne.

Mama stood at the living room window, watching the street, even though Howie had disappeared long ago.

"Mama, come sit down with me, watch a show with me," Delilah said, patting the cushion next to her on the leather couch. "We never did see *Confessions of a Shopaholic*, Mama. Maybe we can find it on Showtime?"

"I don't feel much like watching TV."

"I know, Mama," Delilah coaxed, "but time will go by faster and you won't worry so much if we're watching something funny."

Missy heaved a sigh, dropped the window blind, and took a seat on the couch next to Delilah. "I wish he hadn't gone out tonight," she said fretfully, folding her arms across her chest.

"Try to not think about it, Mama. It'll be better if you don't."

They didn't find the movie they wanted, but *The Devil Wears Prada* was playing on another network and it was a movie they both loved. Halfway through, Delilah paused the movie to make a big bowl of popcorn, cooking it on the stove and then coating it in melted butter and salt the old-fashioned way.

Delilah poured soda into two glasses, carried the drinks in, and then went back for the popcorn. "Refreshments are served," she said, settling back down on the couch. But instead of pushing play for the movie, she talked to Mama, telling her about Memorial and her favorite teachers, Mrs. Hughes, the biology teacher, who was actually from Ireland; and her English teacher, Miss Brennan, who really loved to read; as well as the teachers she didn't like, Ms. Jones and Mr. Osborne. "I'm not sure about Miss Powers," she confided between handfuls of popcorn. "But I don't think she likes me."

"Why doesn't she like you?" Mama asked, puzzled.

"I don't know. Maybe because I never smile at school."

"You don't smile?"

Delilah shook her head.

"Why not?" Mama persisted.

"Why should I? I'd just look like a dumb-ass like the rest of them—"

"Delilah Marie!"

"Well, they are. Most kids are. They don't know anything."

"And you do?"

Delilah didn't answer right away, thinking that she knew a lot more than she wanted to know. A hell of a lot more. Like fear. She knew fear. She knew what it smelled like and tasted like.

She knew danger. She knew how to never turn her back on a door, as well as to check a room for windows, and make sure they all opened.

She knew she needed plans—escape plans, backup plans, save-Mama's-life plans.

Most of all she knew hate. And the hate was what would kill her, if Howie didn't kill her first.

"I'm just not like the other kids," Delilah said quietly, wiping her buttery fingers on her pajama pants. This wasn't the life she'd imagined when she was a little girl dressing up in princess costumes. But then, she couldn't imagine this was the life Mama wanted either, when she'd bought her baby girl pink tulle dresses and plastic gold crowns.

Mama seemed to know what she was saying and for a moment she looked so sad. "It's not always going to be like this, Dee. It's going to get better. I promise."

"Not if you stay with him."

"I'm not talking about me, Dee, I'm talking about you. When you're eighteen. When you finish high school. You'll be able to move out, get a place of your own, and it'll be so exciting, so good for you, baby."

"I'm not going to leave you, Mama."

"Oh, baby, you're growing up. You've got your whole life ahead of you—"

"Not leaving you alone with him."

Missy reached out to lift a strand of hair from Delilah's eyes. "Baby, as soon as school is over, you'll want to go—"

"No. Not if it means leaving you with him."

"Dee, honey, Howie's not going to let you stay with us forever."

Delilah set the popcorn bowl down on the coffee table with a thud. *"What?"*

"You're only here till you finish school, and then you'll go live your life, and Howie and I will live ours."

Delilah wanted to howl and scream and take the bowl of popcorn and hurl it at the wall. She wanted to break the TV and shatter the coffee table's glass top and rage the way Howie raged—violently, wildly, selfishly.

But that would only end up hurting Mama.

So after a moment of fighting with the devil inside herself, she sat back down, picked up the popcorn, and put it on her lap.

"We should finish the movie," she said, "before Howie comes home."

Later that night, with the movie finished, Delilah was in bed, drifting in that lovely place between awake and asleep, when she heard a door slam followed by quick, heavy footsteps.

Howard was home.

Would he be in a good mood or a bad mood?

She opened her eyes, held her breath, listening. The house was suddenly quiet. It seemed to be listening, too.

There were more footsteps. Muffled voices. Her mama's. His. A cupboard door opened in the kitchen and then banged loudly shut. More voices. A little louder. A little faster. Were they fighting?

Her ears strained. Her heart began to pound. It didn't feel right, the energy in the house. Everything felt heavy now, heavy and quiet.

Tense, Delilah stared up into the dark, fingers gripping her covers, waiting for the moment when everything changed, exploded, and even breathing felt dangerous. Someday she wouldn't be here, she told herself, someday she'd be out, away, safe from all this.

But Mama wouldn't be.

In the kitchen, the voices grew louder. For a change, Mama was the one shouting. Howie said something back and then Mama screamed at him, not an in-pain scream, but an in-anger one.

They *were* fighting. Mama was picking a fight. Mama shouldn't do that. Mama would pay for it.

Delilah crept from bed, sat on the floor, her ear pressed to the faded wallpaper.

"Keep your voice down," Howie said. "You don't want Dee to hear."

"I don't care."

"Well, I do."

"Who was she? Where did you meet her, Howard?"

"You're being ridiculous."

"You don't think I know, *Michael*? You left your computer open. I saw the messages—"

He slapped her hard, the sharp crack of his hand echoing, silencing her. "It was a business dinner—"

"Some business when you come home smelling like sweat and sex and someone else's perfume!" And then she was walking away from him, and Mama never walked away from him.

Howie chased after her, cornering her in the hallway.

Delilah moved to the door and peeked through the old-fashioned keyhole.

"And I told you it didn't happen," he said, flinging her around to face him.

Delilah could see her mama's chin jerk up as she played with her wedding ring, sliding it up and down between her knuckles. "I'm not stupid, Howie."

He rolled his eyes.

"I'm not," she insisted thickly. "I used to work. I have some computer skills—"

"That was called a cash register, Missy, and you sold perfume."

"It was retail and I was a manager—"

"In the fragrance section of a cheap department store."

"It paid bills."

"It paid for your cigarettes and vodka and nothing else. You needed me. You still need me. So watch your mouth."

"You want me to get a job? I'll get a job—"

"How are you going to do that when you don't even drive?"

"I drive. I just don't have a car."

"You don't have a car because you don't need a car. You don't go anywhere."

Missy wasn't backing down tonight. She stood there staring him in the eye, jiggling her ring relentlessly. She didn't speak for a long moment, and when she did, her voice shook. "Fine. I'll take the bus."

Delilah saw Howard slam his hand against the wall right next to Missy's ear, making her head bounce against the wall. "What the fuck is wrong with you tonight?"

"You said I'm not smart and I can't do anything . . . well, you're wrong. And I'll show you—"

He silenced her by putting his hand around her neck, fingers squeezing, choking off sound. "I don't need this shit now. Honest to God, Missy, I really don't. You're not going to work. You're not going to take the bus. Your job is here, taking care of Dee and me. Got that? You hearing me?"

Missy's throat worked.

His hand fell away. His mouth screwed up tight. "Didn't hear you, Missy. Can you repeat that for me?"

"Yes," she croaked.

"That's it, baby. Now kiss me. Show me we're good, that it's all forgiven."

Delilah watched Mama stretch up on tiptoe, and Delilah turned away. Shaking, shivering, she crept back into bed, and wished she were dead.

Howie was gone by the time she woke up the next morning. Missy was sitting in the kitchen at the table, drinking a cup of coffee and smoking a cigarette. Her hand was shaking as she held the cigarette to her mouth. Purple fingerprints marked her throat.

Delilah stared at the bruises as she poured milk on her cereal. Her mother exhaled slowly, blowing out a stream of smoke.

Normally Delilah would say something about the smoke. Howie hated Mama smoking, much less in the house, but it seemed kind of pointless to talk about what Howie liked when he'd gone and choked Mama last night.

Delilah concentrated on eating her Cap'n Crunch. Howie said she was too big for little kids' cereal but Delilah didn't care. She loved Cap'n Crunch. It made her mouth happy.

"It's not what you think," Mama said, stubbing out her cigarette after a long silence.

Delilah concentrated on reading the back of the box. The Cap'n needed help finding buried treasure. Every day she filled in the missing letters so he could find it. A man needed his treasure.

"He wasn't trying to hurt me," Missy added. "Happened during sex—"

"Jesus, Mama! Really?" Delilah dropped her spoon. It clattered against the rim of the bowl and milk splashed onto the faded green place mat. "You think I want to know this?"

Her mother's lips pursed, compressed. She tapped out another cigarette, studied it before sliding it back into the box. "Just didn't want you to worry that he'd been mean. He wasn't mean. Sometimes when adults make love—"

"I'm still eating, Mama."

"Okay, fine. We're fine, then."

"No, we're not fine. I'm not fine. You're not fine. But if that's what you want us to do today, play pretend, I'll do it, but only so I can keep from hurling my Cap'n Crunch all over me and you." Delilah picked up her spoon, took a mouthful. The cereal had started to get soggy. She hated it soggy. She didn't even have to chew. She swallowed the bite and spooned up another five little golden squares. "And don't call it making love. He's not making love to you when he's choking you." Milk dripped from the bottom of the spoon. "Goddamn, Mama! Even I know that." She shoved the spoon in her mouth and muttered around the milk and cereal, "Disgusting pervert."

Delilah didn't know if her mother had heard the last part, but

Missy shot her a hard look and took a sip of coffee. She drank it black. Delilah couldn't understand why anyone would drink coffee black, but then, she couldn't understand how any woman could be with Howie. And her mom did both.

Delilah took another couple bites of cereal before it was too soggy to finish. She got up and dumped the bowl into the sink so Mama wouldn't see her wasting food. "Heard you and Howie *talking* in the hall last night," she said, squirting dish soap into the bowl and washing it by hand, and trying to sound nonchalant.

"You shouldn't have been eavesdropping, Delilah. You know Howie doesn't like that."

"Kind of hard not to hear when you were both screaming."

Mama lit another cigarette and then almost immediately snuffed it out. "I'm already halfway through a pack and it's not even eight yet," she muttered, sitting back in her chair and gently touching her throat. "Anyway, what were you saying?"

"You picked the fight with him last night, Mama. You accused him of smelling like sex and sweat and somebody's perfume."

"That's between him and me."

"You know he's just going to go crazy on you when you bring stuff like that up."

Missy's fingers slid lightly over the purple fingerprints on her neck. "I'm his wife."

Delilah returned to the table, sat down. "You have a death wish, don't you?"

Missy managed a small, tight smile. "I held my own last night. You should be proud of me."

Delilah couldn't stand watching her mother touch the bruises and dropped her gaze to the middle of the wood table with its napkin holder and the little blue-and-white ceramic salt and pepper shakers in the shape of Dutch shoes.

Holland, she thought. That's another place she and Mama would go if Howie were gone. She and Mama would visit Holland

and see the tulips and the windmills. She read somewhere that everyone in Holland rode bikes. Mama wasn't much for bike riding, but she'd like the tulip fields. Mama loved flowers. "If we could go anywhere together, you and me, where would you want to go?"

"Oh, honey, I don't know. You mean, like to go shopping?"

"Or traveling. Is there someplace you'd like to visit with me? Someplace special you've never been?"

"Oh, I like Las Vegas. Howard took me there when we were first dating."

"I know, Mama, but what about me? Would you want to go somewhere with me? Just the two of us?"

Missy took another quick sip of coffee. "Not sure that would ever happen, baby, but Seattle would be nice. I hear it's real cool and green with lots of big trees and lakes and mountains."

"You don't want to go to Paris? Or Italy? You like pasta, Mama. Lobster ravioli."

"Seattle would be nice. They have ferries, you know, that take you to all these islands. There's one called Orcas Island. Learned about it on the Travel Channel."

For the longest minute Delilah couldn't think of anything to say, and then she pushed herself slowly up. "Okay, Mama. We'll go to Seattle and ride one of those ferries. Maybe go up the Space Needle, too." Then she walked out of the kitchen, went to her bedroom, and dressed for school.

Her fingers felt stiff as she zipped her plaid skirt and buttoned the white uniform blouse. Her vision blurred and it took her a minute to find her socks and shoes. Maybe she was having a breakdown. Maybe she was coming unglued.

It wouldn't be the worst thing in the world if she lost her mind. It might even be a good thing. That way if she did have to kill Howie, she could always plead insanity.

Seventeen

By Thursday morning, Kit was beginning to miss her small Queen Anne house and her routine and her students and their noise and chaos and laughter and stories. She texted Polly midmorning in between folding loads of laundry. Polly called her back at noon during her lunch hour.

"How are you, Kit?"

Kit was thrilled to hear her voice. "I'm so glad you called!" she said, curling up onto her bed in the guest room adjacent to her parents' room. "How are things at school? Can't get any info out of my sub. She just keeps telling me to relax and take care of my mom."

"How *is* your mom?"

"Some days are better than others. Today's okay. Yesterday was terrible. Mom made me call these hospice facilities and inquire about their death packages."

"They are not called death packages."

"They should be. I felt like I was booking a one-way trip for her—which insurance companies did they work with, and how did they bill, and what was their policy on pain management. Bleck."

"Your mom doesn't want to just stay put and let hospice care workers come to her?"

"That's what I thought, and it's what Dad's planning on. But Mom has control issues about the house. And I get it. It's her home, her domain. She finds it difficult to let go here. She probably would be more peaceful 'letting go' somewhere else."

"Your dad isn't going to like it."

"I know. There's going to be some interesting conversations when he comes home."

"When does he come home?"

"Saturday night."

"Two days from now. You're almost there, girl."

"I know. I'm glad. Mom misses Dad. She's anxious for him to get home."

"I bet he's just as anxious to get back." Polly snapped her fingers. "Oh, hey, before I forget. One of your students is really missing you. She's asked me twice this week about you."

"Who's that?""

"That new girl. Delilah."

"Aw. How is she?"

"'Aw? How is she?'" Polly snorted. "Same as always. Distant. Surly. Unhappy. Well, except when she's asking about you and then she just looks unhappy."

"I've been wondering about her. Things aren't good for her at home."

"She's fine, Kit. She's a little drama queen. And don't you have enough on your plate taking care of your mom without taking on Delilah Hartnel?"

"Probably."

"Speaking of your mom, I'd love to bring you two dinner tomorrow night. She might not be up to visitors, and in that case I can just drop it off—"

"What do you mean, just drop it off? Of course you're going to stay. Mom would love to see you."

"I don't want to tire her out."

"You won't. Trust me. We'd both enjoy your company."

Kit stayed up late Thursday night reading, and had just fallen asleep when she heard a strange sound, almost like a kitten mewling, coming from a room in the house.

She opened her eyes, listened. It wasn't a kitten. It was Mom. She was crying.

Leaving the bed, she stuffed her arms in her robe, tying it over her nightshirt, and rushed to her mother's room. Marilyn was lying with her face in the pillow, weeping.

"Mom," Kit whispered, leaning over and touching her on the shoulder. "What's wrong?"

"Oooo, hurts." Her voice was high and thin and faint. "Hurts, Kit."

"Where's your pain medicine, Mom?"

"Don't know."

"You took it with dinner, though."

"No."

"Why not?"

"Couldn't find it."

"Why didn't you tell me?"

"Forgot." Her mom was panting. "Help me?"

"I will, Mom. I promise." Kit turned on the bedside lamp, searched the bottles on the table, pills for everything . . . antinausea, sleeping pills, depression medicine, stool softener, Tylenol . . . but none of the powerful stuff.

She got on the ground, searched on her hands and knees beneath the bed, behind the table, in the little metal waste bin, trying to stay calm while her mother cried, the mewling sounds more like the bleating of a lamb.

She went to the bathroom, searched there, going through the medicine in the cabinet, searching in drawers, in shadowy corners beneath the sink. Nothing.

"Mom, this is crazy," she said, more to herself than to anyone else, because her mother couldn't hear her, and even if she could, she wouldn't be able to answer.

Trying to stay calm, Kit grabbed her phone, called her mom's oncologist, and as expected, got his answering service. She told the answering service that it was an emergency, that her mom was in the end stages of cancer and had run out of her pain medicine. "I need Dr. Hilbert to please call a prescription in to a twenty-four-hour pharmacy for my mother, Marilyn Brennan. She takes hydromorphone."

The answering service promised to pass the message along and fifteen minutes later Kit's phone rang. It was Dr. Hilbert. "I'm so sorry to have woken you," Kit apologized, "but we can't find Mom's medicine. She's in so much pain. I've never seen her like this."

"Do you want to take her to the emergency room?"

Kit knew how it worked in emergency. Her mother would wait hours to be seen. "No. Can you call in a prescription for her? Please."

"There isn't a lot open right now. The Walgreens on Castro in the Castro district—"

"That's fine."

"You're sure?"

"Yes, please. Just call it in and let them know we're on the way."

Hanging up the phone, Kit returned to her mom's side. There were tears on her face. "The prescription is being called in right now, Mom," she soothed. "I'll have it for you soon. Hang in there, okay?"

Kit didn't wait for her mom to respond. She was trying to think of who to call to either sit with Mom, so she could dash to Walgreens, or who could just go straight to the drugstore for her. Normally there'd be a dozen Brennans available, but right now they were all on a cruise ship sleeping soundly. She could call Polly, but it was one-thirty in the morning, and while the Castro district wasn't dangerous, it also wasn't completely safe.

And then glancing at her phone, scrolling through messages, she saw Jude's text.

Jude.

He'd do it for her. And knowing him, he probably wasn't even in bed yet.

Kit called him without wasting another second. He answered immediately. "You okay, Kit Kat?"

"Can you help me?"

"Just tell me what you need."

Her eyes stung. "It means dragging you into the city."

"I'm already here, shooting pool with friends."

Thank you, Jesus.

"Can you go to the Walgreens on Castro street and pick up my mom's pain medicine? We ran out earlier and she's in bad shape." Her voice broke. "It'll be under Marilyn Brennan. Dr. Hilbert just called it in. Not sure if they have her insurance info, though—"

"Text me your address, I'll get the medicine, and be there soon."

Twenty-five minutes later Kit heard the roar of Jude's motorcycle and ran out of the house to meet him on the curb, bundled up in jeans and one of her dad's old baseball sweatshirts.

Jude eased the bike between two parked cars and turned the engine off, silencing the throbbing noise. "Have you been waiting out here the whole time?" he asked, removing his helmet.

"No. Came running out when I heard you approach the house."

"That loud?"

"Pretty loud, but it's okay. It'll give the neighbors something to talk about tomorrow."

He unzipped his leather jacket and pulled out a small pharmacy bag from an inside pocket.

Kit glanced into the pharmacy bag at the small box and syringes. "What is this?"

"Hydromorphone, the same medicine she's been taking—"

"It's a shot!"

"The pharmacist said her doctor wanted her to do the injectable form tonight—"

"I can't give her a shot, Jude!" Panicked, she crumpled the bag in her hand. "I don't know how to give a shot. I need the pills. We have to get the pills."

"The injectable version will kick into her system faster, dull the pain quicker."

"But, Jude, I've never given a shot before. I don't know how to give a shot."

He shrugged. "I do."

Of course he did.

She shuddered as visions of him injecting heroin into a vein flashed through her mind.

He saw her shudder and shook his head, disgusted. "It's nice to see you have such a high opinion of me, Kit Kat."

"Why do you know how to do this?"

"My grandmother had diabetes. She was on insulin for years. Just because I ride a motorcycle doesn't mean I'm an addict. Now, do you want help or not?"

Kit knew she deserved that. "Want help," she said in a small voice.

"Then let's do it."

In the master bathroom adjacent to the bedroom, Jude thoroughly scrubbed his hands with hot water and the antibacterial soap on the counter while Kit helped her mom onto her side and tried to comfort her, telling her that soon she'd feel better.

From the side of the bed, Kit watched Jude in the bathroom open all the packaging, examine the glass bottle of medicine, then wipe the top with alcohol, insert the syringe into the rubber seal, and draw the hydromorphone.

He carried the syringe and a fresh alcohol swab to her at the bed. "I really can't do this," Kit whispered, lightly rubbing her mom's back.

"Yes, you can. Do a silent count, one, two, three, and put it in. Don't think about it. Just one, two, three, in, push down, and that's it."

"It'll hurt her, won't it?"

"It's intramuscular. You'll put it in her hip or butt cheek. The solution is thick. Inject it slowly." He handed her an alcohol swab. "Come on. You can do it. You need to know how, and I'm here if anything goes wrong."

Kit did exactly what he said, counted one, two, three, and then jabbed the needle in. Her mom cried out when she poked her and Kit nearly yanked the needle out of her hip, but Jude leaned forward, steadied Kit's hand, made sure the medicine got in.

"Good job," he whispered.

She shook her head, tears filling her eyes, and remained with her mom, soothing her, comforting her, until she fell asleep.

Kit was still teary when she and Jude headed downstairs once her mother was sleeping peacefully. "That was awful," she said. "Don't want to do that again."

"It gets easier."

"Never wanted to be a nurse. Never wanted to do any of this."

"But you're doing a great job. And from what I gathered at the pharmacy, your doctor plans on getting your mom on an IV tomorrow. It'll make it easier for her to get her medicine, and it won't be painful."

"Good. Because I can't do that again, and it'll kill me if we've got to poke her with needles every couple of hours." They were standing near the front door and the lights were dim. Kit dragged a trembling hand through her hair, combing it smooth, trying to pull herself together. The last couple of hours had completely shattered her. "What a day. Thank God you came."

"I'm glad I could help."

She blinked back tears, crossed her arms, shivering. "I couldn't have done it without you."

"You did good. And she's okay now. She'll sleep through to morning." He reached for the leather jacket he'd left on the hall table, slipped it on. "It's time you went to bed. Get some sleep."

She nodded but she didn't want him to go, wasn't ready to see him go. She liked his company. He was good company. "I don't think I can. Too wound up to sleep." She squeezed her arms tighter, glanced up at him hopefully. "Can I make you something to eat? Get you something to drink?"

He looked at her, dark eyes shadowed, his expression impossible to read. "Feeling lonely?"

She nodded. "When Mom's sleeping, gets awfully quiet here sometimes."

He reached out to pluck a strand of hair from her eyelashes. "I am a little hungry."

She liked the way he touched her. Carefully, thoughtfully, gently. She remembered the kiss on her forehead outside Durty Nelly's. For a big, tough guy, he was awfully tender. "What sounds good to you?" she asked unsteadily.

"Do you know how to make grilled cheese?"

Grilled cheese. Her heart turned over. He really was a sheep in wolf's clothing. "You're in luck, Mr. Knight. Grilled cheese sandwiches just happen to be my specialty."

In the kitchen he took a stool at the counter and watched her gather the bread and butter and cheese and heat the pan. He didn't try to chitchat, but let her focus on putting the sandwiches together. Kit appreciated the quiet. She was tired and her thoughts were jumbled and her emotions felt raw and intense.

She liked him here with her, watching her, being near her. He was calm and focused and his stillness steadied her. "You're a puzzle, you know," she said, cutting the hot sandwiches, toasted a perfect golden brown, then setting his plate before him. "You're not as scary as you look."

He sipped from his coffee cup and his thick biceps bunched. "I look scary?"

She sat down on a stool opposite him. "You know you do."

"What makes me so scary?"

"Your eyes, the hair, the stubble on the jaw, the tattoos, the bike, the boots, the black leather . . . oh, and all those muscles."

"Well, if that's all," he said wryly, picking up half the sandwich.

"Sorry."

"It's okay. I did the ink and the piercings, but inherited the hair, the eyes, and the body."

She looked at him, seeing his straight black eyebrows and dark olive skin. "You told me in Capitola you were part Choctaw."

"And a little bit of English, Irish, French, and Norwegian."

"Was your mom or dad Choctaw?"

"My dad. He was raised on a reservation in Oklahoma, moved to Texas for a bit, then California."

"Where is he now?"

"Died when I was ten."

"I'm sorry."

He shrugged. "Long time ago. I barely remember him."

"Where did your mom meet him?"

"They were introduced to each other by friends."

"Was it a happy marriage?"

"Could have been. Should have been. My mom's a really good woman. My dad should have taken care of her."

"She sounds nice."

"You'd like her."

"Do you see her often?"

"I have dinner with her every week."

Her eyes widened. "Really?"

"We're pretty close. After my dad died, it was just the two of us and I like to keep an eye on her. And now that her parents are gone, I'm all she has. Poor *madre*."

Kit heard the mocking note in his voice and she studied him more closely, trying to see past the shadowed jaw and the black spiky inch of a tattoo creeping above the neck of his shirt. She'd seen another intricate tattoo on his arm the night they met at Durty Nelly's. "How many tattoos do you have?"

"A lot."

"When did you get your first?"

"High school."

"How old were you?"

"Sixteen. Seventeen, maybe."

"Does your mother like them?"

He cocked a brow. "No." The corner of his mouth lifted. "Do you?"

Kit flushed uncomfortably, surprised at how easily he turned the tables on her. "I . . . uh . . . no. I guess, I don't really know people who have them."

"Your dad doesn't have any?"

"No. He's old-school. Irish. Athletic. Clean-cut."

"And you want to marry a guy like Dad, right?

"He is a good dad," she said mildly, "but not looking to get married."

"You're that age."

"*Past* that age." She made a face, remembering her conversation with her mother earlier in the week. "Now I'm focusing on other things." She shot him a swift glance to see how he'd react. "Like motherhood."

"Pregnant?"

Kit laughed out loud. "*No.* I'm looking into adopting."

"Good for you."

"You mean it?"

"Why wouldn't I? I think you'd be a great mom. You're smart, successful, terrific with kids. Why shouldn't you adopt?"

Her shoulders twisted. "You're the first to think so. No one else has been enthused about the idea. They think I need to be married before I become a mother."

"Why?"

"Because being a single mother isn't easy, and I'm from a traditional Catholic family, and apparently I'm so very traditional myself—" Kit broke off, frowned, picked at the crust on her sandwich. "But I'm actually not."

"No?"

He was smiling at her, his dark eyes crinkling at the corners, his expression amused, and she felt that funny little ache in her heart again. "I mean, I can't be, not if I . . . like you."

His long black eyelashes suddenly lifted and he looked deep into her eyes. "Did you just say what I thought you said?"

She swallowed hard, nodded, nibbling on her bottom lip.

"About time," he said, lips curving. "Took you long enough."

Jude didn't know what it was about this redheaded, blue-eyed English teacher but she really did something to him, and when she looked straight into his eyes, all he could think about was kissing her.

He'd been wanting to kiss her for a long time now.

"Am I a fool for liking you?" she whispered, her gaze falling to her plate, on which she was tearing the crust to bits.

God, he wanted to touch her and he stared at her mouth, fascinated, as she chewed on that lip. "Depends on your definition of *foolish*."

"You never do answer a question directly," she said.

"Never did like being questioned. Prefer to ask the questions."

"That's right. You have a problem with authority."

His mouth curved. "Am I supposed to think of you as an authority figure?"

"I *am* a teacher."

He laughed softly, more entertained than he'd been in a long time. "I don't find you very authoritative, Miss Brennan. In fact . . ." He paused, allowing the tension to build and intrigued by the way she responded to it . . . eyes dilating, lips parting, color heightening. Shit, she was beautiful. "If anyone was to do some teaching here, I think it'd be me, teaching you."

He heard her inhale quickly, sharply, and that soft gasp made him hard, made him hurt. He wanted to touch her. He also knew that if he reached for her, kissed her, she'd let him. She wanted him. Wanted him the same way he wanted her.

But it would be just sex. And that's all it'd ever be. She'd never have more, not with him. Jude didn't do relationships. Wasn't a boyfriend, would never be a husband. Not again. Not after Amy.

And that's when he understood the attraction.

Kit reminded him of Amy.

Jude felt sucker punched, and he pushed away from the counter, wanting his coat, wanting to go. "It's almost four," he said gruffly, glancing up at the kitchen clock.

Kit was immediately on her feet, contrite, scooping up dishes, stacking plates. "I'm sorry. I had no idea."

He rocked back on his heels, muscles knotting. Why hadn't he seen it before? Understood the attraction? Was it because Amy was a brunette, with dark straight hair, and Kit was this glorious redhead?

But now that he saw the similarity, he didn't know what to do, where to look. Kit had Amy's warmth, and Amy's heart-shaped face, generous mouth, bright, smiling eyes. Irish eyes. Of course. Amy Keegan. Kit Brennan. Irish, Irish, Irish to the core.

God.

He ran a hand over his jaw, stunned. His gut was twisting. His temper rising. He needed to go. Now. "I'll see myself out," he said shortly.

Kit threw him a bewildered glance, wiped her hands on a dishtowel. "I have to lock up. I'll walk you out."

They didn't speak as they headed to the front door.

Jude picked up his coat from the hall table. His helmet was already waiting for him outside on the bike. He prayed Kit wasn't going to say anything to make him feel worse. He honestly couldn't feel worse. He was already reeling.

"Thank you again," Kit said quietly, opening the door. "I couldn't have done any of this without you."

"You're a smart girl. You would have figured it out."

His tone was brusque and she quickly looked away, but not before he saw the sudden sheen of tears in her eyes. Goddammit.

He did not want to hurt her. The last thing he wanted to do was hurt her. Kit was everything good and sweet, but also vulnerable, achingly vulnerable, and he wanted to protect her. Which meant protecting her from him.

"Call your mother's doctor early," he said gruffly, trying to fill the painful silence. "He said he could send someone to start the IV. Make sure he does it."

"I will."

There was a wobble in her voice and he ground his teeth together. She didn't know it, but he was doing her a favor by leaving now. He swung the door open, tried not to look at her, not wanting to see what he knew she was feeling. "Go to bed."

"I will."

She'd whispered the words but it was enough.

Unable to stop himself, he reached for her, pulling her into his arms, to cover that soft, lush mouth of hers with his. She tasted like sweet coffee and tears, and her lips were cool, but her mouth was warm, and kissing her, holding her, felt absolutely right in a world that was mostly wrong.

Jude was not a romantic. Or soft. Or tender. Couldn't be, not with what he did, and how he did it. But she felt like his. Perfect and familiar.

He deepened the kiss, bringing her closer, a hand in the small of her back to hold her hips firmly to his, and the blood heated in his veins, hot.

If he were someone else, with a different career, and a different past, he would keep her forever. Love her forever.

But he wasn't someone else, and didn't have the luxury of hoping, imagining.

He lifted his head, gazed down into her bright, bemused eyes, stroked her flushed cheek, then let her go. "No tears, Kit Kat."

He walked out into the night to where his bike waited on the street.

She followed him out. He wished she hadn't. He sucked at good-byes.

Jude swung a leg over his bike, sat down on the seat. She took a step closer, her fist pressed to her chest. She wanted to say something. He could see her trying to find the words, but he didn't want to hear them, didn't want to know what she wanted, needed, was feeling.

It was pointless. What could he give her? Nothing.

He'd vowed to be different from his father, vowed to be a better man, and then what did he do to Amy? The very same fucking thing his father did to his mother.

Jude jammed his helmet onto his head, impatiently snapped the strap under his chin.

"If your mom ever needs something, call me," he said, zipping his leather coat closed. It was a cool night. The fog had moved in. It'd be a cold ride home.

She nodded, blinking. Thank God her eyes were now dry.

Unable to help himself, he stretched out his arm, brushed his knuckles across her cheek, and then over her mouth. Once, and again. "Take care, angel." And then he started the bike, the engine roared to life, and he was gone, tearing down the street, racing the devil who owned his heart, and all his memories of Amy.

I n the house, Kit locked the front door and turned out the lights, fighting the urge to cry. There was no reason to cry, she told herself, no reason to cry at all. He was awful and terrible, a low-life nobody who lived in a decrepit little house and wore far too much leather—

And she liked him. More than she'd liked anyone in years.

If not ever.

Upstairs, she checked on her mom, found her sleeping soundly, and leaned over her, kissed her cheek, smoothed her hair, kissed her again. "Love you, Mama," she whispered. Before going to her room, stripping off her clothes, and climbing into bed, she pulled a pillow over her face and gave in to tears, knowing that Jude had no intention of seeing her again.

Eighteen

Polly arrived Friday afternoon a few minutes before six. "Sorry I'm late," she said when Kit opened the front door. She was clutching a shallow cardboard box with two foil-covered pie tins. "I had a late start and the quiche took longer to cook than I thought. But they're still warm, fresh from the oven. One with veggies and one ham and cheese. I wasn't sure which one your mom would find more appealing."

Kit was so happy to see her and hugged her despite the box between them. "So glad you're here!"

Polly shot her a swift glance. "Is everything okay? Your mom—"

"Fine. Mom's fine. She's looking forward to seeing you." Kit struggled to smile as she took the box from Polly, feeling stupid for almost bursting into tears. She couldn't cry over Jude. He didn't fit into her life, and he certainly wasn't the kind of man she'd ever been looking for. "The quiche smells delicious. Can't believe you made them."

"I'm good with piecrust," Polly said, following Kit into the kitchen. "And I did a little research and in my reading discovered that your mom might enjoy quiche. It has all the things doctors and dieticians recommend for her right now, like eggs and cheese, so hopefully this will taste good, and be easy for her to swallow."

With the quiches safely stowed on the counter, Kit gave Polly another fierce hug. "Thank you. Thank you for caring and coming and making something special for Mom to eat. I'm so grateful. I really am."

Polly pulled back to look Kit in the face. "You okay?"

Kit struggled to smile and, when she couldn't, shook her head, not trusting herself to speak.

"It's been a long week, hasn't it?" Polly said.

Kit nodded. "Yeah."

"I bet you'll be glad when your dad's home."

"Yes, and no. I miss my house and my routine, but it was good for me to be here. Important for me to be with Mom, see this—" Her voice broke and she turned away, paced across the kitchen to straighten the dishtowel hanging on the oven door before wiping her eyes dry. "Shall we go say hi to her? See if she's hungry?"

They ate with Mom in her bedroom, and then as Polly chatted with Mom, Kit took the dinner trays downstairs to the kitchen, washed up the dishes, and put the leftovers of the quiches in the refrigerator. The kitchen tonight reminded her of making grilled cheese sandwiches for Jude and she didn't like that. She didn't want to think about him.

When Kit returned to her mother's room, Polly held a finger to her lips. "She fell asleep a few minutes ago," Polly whispered. "I think I wore her out."

Kit picked up the TV remote and muted the sound, adjusted the covers over her mother's legs, then gestured for Polly to follow her. They headed down to the family room, where Kit curled up in her father's La-Z-Boy and Polly sprawled on the couch and talked. Polly had started dating someone new a couple of weeks ago and told Kit she thought it could turn serious. "I really like him," she said. "It just feels right."

Kit curled her legs under her. "What does that mean when you say it just feels right?"

"Just feels good being with him. Feels good doing nothing with him. I'm comfortable with him . . . myself with him."

"That's good," Kit said. "That's what you want."

"Yep."

"So how's Fiona? Are she and Chase doing okay?"

"They seem pretty great. Happier than they have been in months."

"I'm glad to hear that. Their little date night back in January seems to have worked some magic."

"Their little date night *definitely* worked some magic." Polly paused, lifting her eyebrows. "And apparently Chase is over the moon."

It took a second for Kit to register the significance before sitting up. "She isn't!"

"She is." Polly's lips curved. "Six weeks. And sicker than a dog. No one else knows, though. Fiona's going to wait to tell Sister until she starts to show."

"So baby is due next fall . . . is she planning on taking maternity leave, or . . . ?"

"I don't think she's going to return. Chase makes a ton of money, and since Fiona wants to be home with the baby, Chase is fully on board."

"Good for them." And yet Kit suddenly found herself thinking of Tommy and Cass, who just couldn't have a baby, no matter how hard they tried. "How are Chase's kids reacting?"

"Like little shits, of course." Polly grinned evilly. "But this time Chase isn't tolerating it. Seems he's finally woken up to the fact that he's being way too permissive and he's ruining the kids, turning them into monsters. He's told them that if they can't re-spect Fiona, then they're not welcome at his home."

"Wow."

"Wow indeed."

K it stayed at her parents' house one more night to give Dad a chance to settle in and to be there Sunday morning when Mom's new nursing assistant showed up. As expected, he was not happy that someone would be taking over his nursing duties and moving into the guest bedroom on their floor.

But finally everything was calm enough that Kit could say her good-byes. She went to her mom, sat down on the edge of the bed. "Well, Mom, I'm being kicked out. Dad's told me you guys aren't going to support me any longer and it's time to get a real job."

Marilyn laughed quietly and extended a thin hand. "My funny girl."

Kit took her hand and held it carefully. "I've had a great week with you. I'm really glad I got to be here with you."

"It was a terrible week for you—"

"Not true. It was an honor—"

"Oh, Kit! Please! You sound like your sister Margaret."

Kit choked on laughter. "I can't believe you just said that, Mom."

"Where do you think you get your sense of humor from? And your good looks? My goodness, Kit, you've grown into a beautiful woman."

"Thank you, Mom."

Her mother's expression turned serious. "I hope you know how proud I am of you, Kit. I hope you know I could not be prouder."

"Oh, Mom, I've done nothing with my life—"

"You're a dedicated teacher. An excellent teacher. And a very kind person."

"Teachers don't get a lot of respect."

'Our society has its values upside down. You know what you do is important."

"I do," Kit agreed quietly, gently stroking her mother's hand even as a lump filled her throat. "I don't want to lose you, Mom."

Her mother said nothing, but her brown eyes were bright.

"Why isn't there a treatment . . . a cure?" Kit whispered.

"We tried those, they didn't work."

"I can't help thinking we didn't try everything, we didn't explore every option, and all the new drugs—"

"I didn't want to be a guinea pig anymore. I just wanted to live, to enjoy what time I had left. And I have. This has been the best nine months. I've loved every minute of being with all of you."

"God should have selected someone else."

"God didn't do this to me."

"Feels like it."

"*Katherine.*"

Kit held her mom's hand between hers. "I'm sorry, it's how I feel. There's a world full of selfish, mean, terrible people, and God takes you?"

"Maybe He has something special planned for me in heaven."

"I hate it when people say that."

The corner of her mother's mouth lifted. "I'm not afraid to die, Kit."

Kit bit into her lip. "Is the pain that bad now?"

"I'm just not myself anymore. Everything's starting to go—my strength, my control, my bladder—and you know how hard it is for me to be dependent on other people, needing to be cared for like a baby."

"We don't mind, Mom."

"But I do. And I haven't said this to your dad yet, but I'm starting to look forward . . . forward to what comes next."

"Heaven?" Kit said faintly.

"And seeing my mother and father, and Johnny. Miss Johnny. He was my baby brother. We were really close."

Kit leaned over her mother, kissed her forehead, smoothed the fine hair back from her temple. "Do you really think it'll be like that? That they'll be there, waiting for you?"

"I do."

"What makes you so sure?"

"Because love is so strong, it transcends death."

Kit was not going to cry. She refused to cry. Her mom wasn't gone, not yet. "You really think someday I'll get to see you again?"

"Absolutely. There will be a big parade when you arrive, Kit, and I'll be the first in line waving my straw hat and shouting, 'It's time for a Brennan Girls' Getaway!'"

"You're crazy, Mom."

"I know. I'm crazy about you."

Kit arrived back home just after lunch and it felt like she'd been gone a month instead of a week. She wandered around her quiet little house with its charming blue-and-white living room with the big Impressionist print hanging above the couch. Her house was sweet and petite and full of books and knick-knacks, like her rock collection and the huge jar of sea glass collected over the years in Capitola, but it was quiet.

And empty.

And right now she felt empty.

She wanted a house like the one she'd grown up in. A house with life and love and people.

Kit needed people. She needed a family and she wanted to be a mother, and she hated having to wait weeks for the adoption interview, but it's the way it worked. Adoption was slow. She'd probably still be waiting for a child a year from now.

She paced her house, exhausted, frustrated, frazzled. The little house, normally cozy, felt small and confining at the moment. She'd thought she wanted to be here, but now that she was back, she wanted to be anywhere but alone inside these four walls.

Impulsively, she grabbed her phone and sent Jude a text. *I want to see you today.*

Jude opened his fridge, stared at its contents—a couple of Miller beers, a half-eaten can of tuna, an old carton of sour cream, a jar of pickles—and shut the door.

Why didn't he ever buy groceries? He was thirty-seven years old. He could certainly buy groceries for himself, couldn't he?

Grimly Jude stalked through his house to his bedroom and checked his phone where he'd left it charging. He read Kit's message for the tenth time.

I want to see you today.

And for the tenth time, he put the phone down and walked away. He hadn't answered her, wasn't going to answer her, wasn't going to encourage her in something that just wasn't going to work.

Jude walked back to his small living room and checked the score on the basketball game. It wasn't at all close. His team was being blown away. What a lame game. He turned off the TV, walked around his house, hating Sundays.

He'd never liked Sundays—they were terrible, all of them. No, that wasn't true; when he was a little kid they'd been special. Pancake Days, he used to call them, because his mom would be at the stove with her big frilly apron making them a hot breakfast and his dad would be at the table, reading the paper, joking with her, teasing Jude, who sat near him, poring over the comic strips. Pancake Days were happy, and he remembered that kitchen and how the sunlight came through the window and his mom's and dad's laughter would blend together, light and deep, like one of those orchestras with wind and string instruments.

But later, must have been in first or second grade, it all began to change. Dad wouldn't be there, or if he was at the house, he didn't eat with them. Mom would be making a hot breakfast but Dad would be passed out in bed, or on the couch. And then the quiet would get loud because the drinking would start again and that's when Dad got mean. Mom was tough, though. She told Dad to take his bad attitude out of the house, or she'd leave.

And then one Sunday, he just never came home.

Got murdered on a Sunday morning and pretty much ruined Sundays forever.

So Jude didn't like Sundays, and was always glad when they ended, happy to see Monday roll around. But this Sunday was worse than usual. There was Kit's text earlier, which had done a number on him, and then there was the endless bullshit next door.

He'd reported the domestic violence to his department twice, back in December when they first moved in, and then again last week, and he'd been home both times the patrol car had pulled up to the Dempsey house to investigate the disturbance. But Missy and Howard Dempsey always presented a united front to the police, with Missy denying that anything had happened. When questioned about her bruises, she said they were from falling off the porch while she was sweeping. Klutzy her. The officers couldn't do anything if no crime had been committed and so the patrol car would slowly pull away and Jude would feel sick because he knew the violence would just continue.

It was starting up again now. Even with his door shut, he could hear their voices go back and forth. His. Hers. Dempsey's. Missy's. Sometimes Delilah's before someone screamed at her to shut up.

They'd fought from the very first moment they moved in, but

these past couple of weeks it'd been nonstop. Daily. Hourly. Fighting. Screaming. Weeping.

He hated living next to it. Would move if he could. He couldn't. Not because the department would stop him—hell, they didn't care what he did as long as he continued doing his part—but he couldn't move. Couldn't abandon a woman and a girl to a monster. And Dempsey was a monster. Someone needed to hunt him down, take him out.

Abruptly the raised voices went silent.

Jude opened the door, stepped outside, walked down the cement steps. His grass was scraggly, studded with weeds and dandelions. He stood on the edge of his lawn. Waited.

And still the house next door was quiet. That could mean any number of things. Good. As well as bad.

The front door of the little white house flew open and a terrified face appeared—Delilah's—before she was jerked back inside and the door slammed shut.

Delilah's expression was like a knife in his gut. He'd had it with their craziness, had it with the yelling and screaming and terrified weeping.

Jude grabbed the big trash can that was still on the curb in front of his house and hurled it across the yard, right at Howard's town car. Bingo. The trash can hit the car trunk, bounced off, leaving a dent.

The car's siren began to screech.

That should get Dempsey, Jude thought, leaning over to pick up the trash can.

The front door flew open and Howard Dempsey came running out. "What the fuck?" he shouted at Jude as Jude wheeled the trash can back to his house.

"Stupid kids," Jude said, shaking his head, "throwing shit around."

Howard circled his car. "They hit my car?"

"You weren't the only one." Jude pointed up the street. "They were doing crazy-ass pranks over there, too."

"Goddammit. Look at my trunk!"

Jude screwed up his face, faking worried. "You think they can pound it out? Or is that whole piece going to need to be replaced."

"Did you see these kids?" Howard demanded.

"Yeah. They were on bikes. Five or six of them."

"White, black, Mexican, what?"

"A little of everything."

"Really?"

"They were punks. Had attitude."

Howard fished for his keys. "I'm going to go find those bastards. Make them pay."

"I know what they look like. Want me go with you?"

"Good idea."

Jude ended up spending the next two hours cruising San Leandro and east Oakland with Howard Dempsey, and the two hours bullshitting with the man didn't make Jude like him any better.

They ended up stopping at one of Jude's favorite dive bars on the way home. Howard didn't seem to mind and they sat at the counter, drinking beers, telling stories, acting like they were old friends.

Once Jude was sure Howard had cooled completely off, he suggested they head back home. "Should we get back? Make sure those punks didn't come around a second time?"

"Good thinking," Dempsey said, slapping him on the back.

Once home, Jude showered and brushed his teeth but he couldn't seem to scrub Dempsey's evil stink off him.

He glanced at his phone between showering and shaving and found another text from Kit. *Jude, are you there?*

Jude stared at the phone, wanting her, but not wanting to want her, and wanting to protect her, which meant staying away from her . . .

But it was killing him staying away from her. He didn't like ignoring her. Didn't like hurting her feelings in any way.

Goddammit.

He wanted Kit. He wanted her, plain and simple. And he'd wanted her since first laying eyes on her in Capitola.

So why was he taking the high ground and giving her up? Did he really think some other dickhead could love her better than he could? That some other dickhead could protect her better than he could?

No.

If any dickhead was going to love Kit, it was going to be him.

Dropping his towel from his hips, he stepped into clean jeans, dragged his wet hair back from his face, and reached for his phone, sent her a text, telling her to meet him at Jump'n Java on Shattuck in Oakland at five.

She answered immediately. *Meet you there.*

Jude was heading outside to his bike when he spotted Delilah standing with a hose at the fence watering the scraggly roses-bushes Howard had been buying and planting since moving in.

"Hey, Delilah," he said to her.

"Hey, Jude." She moved the hose to another rosebush.

"You okay?"

"Yeah."

"Your mom okay?"

"She's alive."

"That's good."

Delilah shot him a knowing glance. "Saw what you did to Howie's car with the garbage can."

"I didn't do anything."

"Right." She rolled her eyes. "It was pretty stupid."

"Uh-huh."

She suddenly grinned. "And really awesome." She giggled.

"I've never seen Howie run that fast in my entire life. Looked like he was training for the Olympics."

Jude suppressed a smile. She was a funny kid. Too bad most of the time she reminded him of a young alley cat. Scrawny and sad. "If things get weird, Delilah, you get out of there, hear me?"

"Things are already weird, Jude."

"If things get weirder."

"Not going to leave my mama."

"Delilah, if she doesn't save you, you've got to save yourself."

She moved the hose to another hole, hunched her shoulders. "You better go. I can feel Howie watching."

Jude climbed on his bike, pulled on his helmet, and Delilah was right: as he backed his bike out of his driveway he saw Howard standing at the window.

Jude suggested a coffee place in north Oakland, and Kit was glad. She liked Piedmont, north Oakland, and Berkeley, and loved all the funky little coffeehouses there as they reminded her of the ones she hung out in during college.

But when Jude arrived at Jump'n Java, he walked in the front door with an edge and an attitude. Kit didn't know what was going on inside his head, only that something was. He still had that heat in his eyes when he looked at her, but when his mouth curved, it didn't look totally friendly.

"You don't seem happy to be here," she said, after ten minutes of uncomfortable conversation.

"I'm not."

She sucked in her bottom lip, chewing on it, trying to figure out what to do now. "What did I do, that night at my house, to turn you off this much?"

He was silent so long Kit didn't think he was going to answer.

And then he stretched out his long legs, putting one boot over the other, and said, "Not turned off, Kit." He dragged a hand through his thick black hair, drawing it back from his broad forehead. Muscles bunched in his quadriceps. "Not at all."

She shifted in her chair, feeling a little hotter and a little more bothered than just seconds before. "What's going on, then? It seemed like you liked me—"

"Oh, I do like you. I like you a lot. I like you so much that I'd love to take you back to my house right now and throw you on the bed and peel your pants off and take you all night long." He paused, and his lips curled, but there was a dangerous light in his dark eyes. "And maybe that sounds good to you right now, but Kit Kat, that's all you're ever going to get with me. Hard sex, hot sex, a lot of sex, but no tenderness, no commitment, and no relationship."

Kit stared at him, hearing him, but for whatever reason she didn't believe him. Something else was going on here. "What if I was good with that? What if that's all I wanted? Hot sex . . . frequent sex . . . and no commitments?"

"You don't."

"You can't say that. You don't know me. I might just be a sex addict." She leaned back in her chair, gave him a cool look, the same kind he'd been giving her ever since he arrived. "See, that's the thing, Jude. You just don't know."

Jude stared at her and it was all he could do not to crack a smile. He'd arrived here still really pissed off and yet she was making him want to laugh.

"Really?" he drawled, wondering just how far she'd take it. "Let's do a quick recap to make sure we're on the same page. You're not into relationships. You don't do commitments. You just like it raw. Hot. Hard. And sweaty."

And oh, Kit, God love her, she blushed, from her delicate little chin to the roots of her dark red hair, and nibbled on her bottom

lip, making him rock hard. Not fair. He wanted to be the one nibbling on that lip. And then sucking her tongue into his mouth
before taking her mouth—

"Yes," she said firmly, her blue gaze locking on his. "Raw.
Hard. Hot and sweaty. Couldn't pick four adjectives that describe
the way I like sex better."

Jude bit down hard on his back molars, sucked in air, fighting
with everything he had to keep from laughing. Felt like he'd ex-
plode if he didn't laugh soon. Kit was perfect.

"This could work," he said, when he trusted himself to speak.
"I think we should give it a go. Anything else you want to tell me
before our first hookup?"

"Such as?"

"Quirks? Preferences? Fetishes? Limits?"

She smiled serenely. "No. I like it all."

"Is that so?"

"Yes."

"So how old were you when you first had sex?"

Kit squirmed. "Why?"

"Just wanted to compare notes."

She stared at him, blue eyes wide. Angelic.

"I was nineteen," he said. "All my friends had been doing it for
years. But I'd wanted to wait until I married."

"Did you?"

His lips curved into a crooked smile. "I didn't make it to my
wedding night, but at least my first time was with my future wife."

"You were married?"

He nodded. "Seven years. And I've been widowed eight."

"How did she die?"

"Car accident. Died on the operating table." He dragged his
feet back under the table, miserable now, wishing he hadn't brought
Amy up. Talking about Amy never made anything better.

"How devastating."

"I'm not playing a sympathy card here, Kit Kat. I was a shitty husband. I made her life hell." He leaned forward, looked her in the eye. "And if you fall for me, I'll make your life hell, too."

She didn't flinch, didn't back away. "What did you do as a husband that was so bad? Sleep around? Take drugs? Steal? Rob? Rape?"

He leaned even closer to her and tapped the back of her hand. "I worked ridiculously long hours. Took every promotion that came along. Put in so many hours at work that I began to sleep there at night, just so I'd already be there in the morning. And before you say anything, I want you to know that I knew what I was doing, and I knew it was wrong to Amy, to our marriage, to our future. I didn't care. I didn't care that she was lonely. I didn't care that she felt like she was losing me. I took those promotions anyway. I wanted them. I needed them. It was all about me. It's the kind of person I am."

Kit stared at the back of her hand.

"I'm not going to change," he added, leaning in even closer, his big shoulders square, practically pinning her to her chair. "It's too late for that."

Her head jerked up and she looked him in the eye, her gaze unwavering even though her cheeks were a dusky pink. "I haven't asked you to change."

"No, but you will. Or you'll want to save me, because good girls like you try to save those that have fallen. But people like me aren't worth your time, angel. Leave me where you found me and take care of those who can be helped."

Her eyes searched his. He didn't know what she was looking for, but he let her look. She had beautiful eyes. He could stare into her eyes all day.

"I'm not sitting here because I want to save you," she said after an endless moment. "And I'm not here because I want to help you. I'm here for completely selfish reasons."

"Oh?"

"You don't think I can be selfish, too?"

"No."

"You're wrong. Because I'm not here for you, I'm here for me. I like you, Jude. I enjoy being around you. And I'm thinking, you just might be good for me."

"And tell me how, angel, I could possibly be good for you?"

She got in his face then, her slim shoulders touching his, her breasts practically smashed to his chest. He could see the tiny purple flecks against the blue of her eyes and the scattered silver bits, too. "I need to have some fun, Jude Knight. I'm a little lonely. I work too much. My mom's not well. And I really, really could use some of your raw, hard, hot, sweaty sex."

He cupped the back of her head, angled his mouth over hers, and kissed her.

It wasn't a hard kiss, or fierce. Had nothing raw about it. No, he kissed her slow and sexy and sweet, so slow and sexy and sweet that her mouth parted, and her lips trembled beneath his, and the air caught in her throat, and the kiss went on and on like that, the two of them making out like teenagers in Jump'n Java, as if there was no one else around, instead of folks at every table.

It was a long time before he lifted his head, but when he did, he looked into her eyes, and they looked like shimmering stars, all blue and bright like Fourth of July fireworks.

"Wow," she whispered, blinking, dazed.

His heart turned over. Wow was right. She was making him feel so many things . . . making him want things he didn't ever think he'd have again.

"That was really good," she said, her voice husky and sexy and making him even harder than he already was. "Let's get out of here and do that again."

He slid his thumb over her quivering lower lip. "Don't you want more out of a man than sex, baby?"

"Do you have any idea how long it's been since I had great sex?"

He laughed softly and shook his head. "All right. I'll make you a deal. You think about everything I've told you tonight. Sleep on it. Think about it some more. And tomorrow, if you still want to get naked with me, give me a call or shoot me a text, and we'll hook up after school."

Nineteen

K it couldn't sleep. How could she after Jude's challenge?

And no, she'd never been into one-night stands. Nor had she ever dated a man for sex. But she liked Jude. Was drawn to him. And there was some serious chemistry between them. Why couldn't she enjoy it—him—for whatever this was?

Kit showered and finished dressing for school and then shot him a text from her car: *Thought about it. Slept on it. So when do I see you again?*

Arriving at school, she emptied the mail from her box in the office, greeted the teachers in the staff room, and headed to her class to prepare for the day.

She was greeted with stacks of papers all over her desk. Her sub had been able to grade quizzes and straightforward tests, but the short-answer questions, essays, book reports, and journals were something only Kit could do and they were all there, piled high, waiting for her.

Fortunately, her students were happy to have her back, and her first period actually cheered when they filed into class and spotted her at her desk.

The day was busy and passed quickly, but Kit kept checking her phone for a reply from Jude. There wasn't one. Disappointed, she headed to the gym after school and worked out, and it wasn't until she arrived home that he finally responded.

Crazy day. Working tonight. Can I do you tomorrow?

Kit blushed as she reread the text, biting her lip. And it crossed her mind that maybe, just maybe, she was in over her head, but it was too late now. She was going for it anyway. Still smiling, she texted him back: *Only if you get a good night's sleep. I don't want to be disappointed.*

He answered her immediately. *You won't be.*

And then a second text arrived a few minutes later. *It's supposed to snow tomorrow. Be careful driving to school.*

Snow? Jude was joking, right? Kit opened her laptop, and typed in Oakland weather on the Internet, and was amazed at the report. Temperatures were dropping rapidly and there was a chance of snow for the morning.

She couldn't believe it. She'd never even seen snow in San Francisco, so even the suggestion of it was enough to get her excited.

The first thing she did the next morning after waking up was go to the window and pull back the curtain. No snow. Not even any rain.

Arriving at school, Kit heard lots of snow talk, even among the teachers, and she didn't blame them. Snow was rare in the Bay Area. According to Paul Moran, one of the social studies teachers, it'd only snowed a half-dozen times in San Francisco in the past hundred years, the last four times being in 1887, 1951, 1962, and 1976, and so for the students and faculty alike, the idea of snow was thrilling.

But first and second period passed without any flurries, and Kit put her third-period English class, her excitable freshmen, to work writing in their journals.

The room was silent with everyone writing and then suddenly someone exclaimed, "It's snowing!"

Immediately the class was on their feet.

"Snow! It's snowing!"

"No, it's not."

"Yes, it is. Look."

"Snow."

"Miss Brennan! It's snowing!"

Kit left her desk in the back corner of the room and walked to the window, where students were crowding, everyone craning to get a glimpse of this miraculous snow.

Outside, tiny flecks fell, so small they looked like white ash. But it was cold enough for the snow to stick, coating the red-tiled roof overhang below them in the thinnest layer of white.

As they watched, the flurries thickened, the flakes becoming fatter and lusher.

The kids were all murmuring, their voices hushed, even reverent.

"I've never seen snow before," Delilah whispered, and when Kit looked at her she saw the tears in her eyes.

Kit moved to her side. "You okay?" she asked.

Delilah didn't take her eyes off the swirling, falling flakes, just nodded.

"Five more minutes of watching snow, and then we're getting back to work," Kit said.

Five minutes later she spent five minutes getting the kids settled, and once they were quiet, she read to them one of her favorite Wallace Stevens poems:

> *One must have a mind of winter,*
> *To regard the frost and the boughs*
> *Of the pine-trees crusted with snow . . .*

She finished, lifted her head, looked out at her students, who were unusually quiet as the last words drifted down, much like Stevens's wind and leaves and snow. For a moment she said nothing, just looked at them, and they looked back at her, and she couldn't help feeling blessed, looking at their suddenly thoughtful faces.

Thirty-four bright young minds.

Thirty-four lives in the making.

How lucky she was to be here, doing this. How lucky she *could* do this.

Her mother was right. Teaching kids, sharing with them her love of words, of books . . . it was a gift. A passion. Not everyone had a passion. Kit was lucky she did.

"The poem is like the snow," said Andrew, one of the jocks in the back of the room. But he, like Damien, enjoyed her class, and consistently made an effort. "The poet . . . she made the words sound like snow. You know, soft, slow, like snow falling."

Kit smiled. "That's right. But the poet is a he. Wallace Stevens. Stevens was born in Pennsylvania in 1879 and is today regarded as one of America's greatest twentieth-century poets, but wasn't fully appreciated during his lifetime."

"Which probably means he didn't make much money doing it," Merrie said, unimpressed.

"Poets in general don't make a lot of money." Kit closed the book and held it to her chest. "And in the spirit of today's snow, I'm changing your homework for tonight. You still have to read the final scene in *Twelfth Night,* but you can wait on the compre-hension questions. Instead, I want you to find a poem about snow, read it, analyze it, and then write a five-hundred-word essay on it . . ." She paused as they groaned. "I want to know why you chose that poem . . . what it means to you." As they continued to groan, she shook her head. "Come on, it's not that hard. You can write about poetic devices, symbolism, meaning, personal experi-ence, whatever works for you, but proper formatting, of course. Typed, double-spaced, heading, intro, conclusion, you know the rest."

She glanced up at the clock, saw they still had nine minutes. "You can have the rest of the period free to either start your homework or watch the snow. But if you're talking, keep it down to a dull roar. We don't need Mrs. Adams in here reporting me to Sister."

Still holding the poetry book pressed to her chest, Kit walked to the window, where half the class was gathering again to watch the thick white flurries tumble down.

Delilah, she noticed, was one of the only ones at her desk, writ-ing in her journal. The rest were at the windows, watching, talk-ing, taking it all in.

Then the bell rang and the kids were tumbling to their feet, gathering their things, rushing off to the next class. As the last one left the room, Polly entered, holding a small, elegant square vase of white flowers—lilies, daisies, pom-poms, freesias. "You didn't tell me you were still seeing Michael," she said, placing the vase on Kit's desk.

Kit's skin began to crawl. "Did he bring them by the school himself?"

"No, they were delivered by a florist. Why? What's wrong?"

"I don't want them," Kit said shortly. "He's trying to buy me and I won't be bought."

"What are you talking about?"

"*Him*. Michael." Kit crossed to the window, glanced out. The snow flurries had stopped. Outside, the world glittered brightly. The light dusting of white on the red-tiled roofs and hedges hadn't yet melted, but for Kit, the magic was gone. She turned to face Polly. "But his name isn't Michael. It's Howard. Howard Dempsey."

Polly stared blankly at her.

Kit folded her arms across her chest. "Delilah's stepfather."

Polly's eyes opened wide, comprehension dawning. "Our Delilah."

"Yes."

"What's he doing sending you flowers?"

"What's he doing asking me out to dinner?"

"What a creep!" Polly's voice sharpened. "What was he doing? Why would he pretend to be single? And then, why would he send his stepdaughter here, to school?"

"I don't know. It's weird. He's weird. He's all about games."

"Have you told Sister?"

"No! Sister already doesn't like him. Told me a couple weeks ago that she doesn't trust him."

"Good woman."

"But I'm afraid to go to her because it'll come back on Delilah, and she's happy here—"

"Delilah, happy?"

"All right, *happier* here than she probably is at home."

"Undoubtedly if she has a lying son of a bitch for a stepfather." Polly reached into the flowers and extracted the small florist envelope. "Let's see what dickhead said." She opened the envelope, pulled out the card and read, "'Time to finish what you started. Where and when? Jude.'"

"Jude?" Polly repeated, forehead wrinkling as she struggled to place the name, before her fair head snapped up. "Kit Brennan!"

Kit sat down on the counter. "Yes?"

"You haven't. You didn't. Oh, Kit! Tell me it's not that Hells Angels guy."

"He's not a Hells Angel."

Polly flung the card down on the desk. "First Michael, now Jude. Have you lost your mind?"

"You told me to go out with Michael—Howard—have to call him Howard. It pisses Jude off when I call him Michael—"

"How long have you been seeing Jude?"

Kit heard the way Polly said his name, as if it were something dirty and infinitely detestable. It would have been funny if she didn't know Polly meant it. "Not really seeing him, Pol. Have just had coffee a couple of times this past week."

"And you are going to sleep with him already?"

"I like him."

"At least have him tested first! He's probably rampant with every STD out there—"

"I'll make sure he wears a condom, okay?"

Polly crossed the room, joining her at the window. "You're really into this guy."

Kit calmly met her gaze. "I am."

"Wow. Your dad is going to flip his lid."

"Here's hoping he doesn't find out."

Kit texted Jude the address to her little Queen Anne house in Highland Park. He arrived at seven on his big burnt-orange bike, and even though he was wearing his usual leather and denim combination, he'd shaved for her and his hair was still damp from washing it. When he pulled her close to give her a kiss, he smelled like soap and aftershave and tasted like spearmint gum.

She liked it. Liked him. And even though he'd said the sex would be raw and hard and sweaty, it wasn't anything like that.

He was sensual and physical and extremely patient in bed. He coaxed an orgasm from her when she was sure it wouldn't happen, and not through tricks or toys or a skillful tongue, but the old-fashioned way—his body stretched out over her, hands holding hers down, his chest to her breast, rib to rib, hip to hip, with some seriously good moves and the ability to delay his own gratification.

"That," she said later, when he held her wrapped in his arms, "was most impressive."

He smiled. "I was beginning to think it might not be raw enough, or hard enough, for you."

"Because it took me ten minutes to come?"

"Wasn't ten minutes. Maybe six."

She turned onto her side to look at him. "Did you mind working so hard?"

He smiled into her hair. "That wasn't work, angel. That was fun."

"No, but I know men don't like it to take that long."

"Says who?"

"Men."

"Not this one."

She lifted her head to better see his expression. "Can I tell you something?"

He smiled at her, smiling almost tenderly into her eyes. "I wish you would."

"That was my first O, with someone, in four years."

He wasn't smiling any longer. "Don't tell me that."

She nodded, wrinkled her nose. "That's why it was a lot of work for you."

"Kit, it wasn't a lot of work. Sex in general is fun, but with you . . . it's amazing."

"Why?"

"Because I like you." He saw her expression and traced the fine arch of her eyebrow. "But just a little bit. So don't go getting all excited about a relationship. It's not going to happen. I'm bad news . . . and still not boyfriend material."

He was saying all the things he'd told her Sunday, except now his tone was gentle, almost teasing, and Kit wiggled closer, kissing him. It had been meant to be a sweet kiss, but all it took was him biting on her lower lip and sliding his hand up her side to cup her breast and she was ready for more.

"You're a greedy little minx," he said, rolling her under him. "And I think this time I can make you come in five."

Kit saw Jude almost every night that week. He came to her house that first night, Tuesday, on his motorcycle, but the next two nights he arrived in a sedate blue sedan.

"Whose car is that?" she asked, standing on the porch Wednesday night and watching him head up her sidewalk, her insides full of butterflies. Jude was so damn hot, even climbing out of a late-model car.

"My mom's."

"You took your mom's car?"

"It's all right. I left her my bike."

Kit laughed and entered the house, knowing Jude was close behind her. The moment the door shut, he locked it, and pulled her up against him, kissing her hard, kissing her until she couldn't breathe and couldn't think and couldn't protest when he slipped her sexiest pair of silk pajama pants off her body right there in the entry hall.

Thursday night, Kit didn't want Jude to leave. She never liked him leaving, but after three nights of amazing sex, she wanted more of him. More with him. She knew he'd said there wouldn't be more, but would it be so wrong to ask?

"Don't go," she said as he climbed out of bed and stepped into his jeans.

"I have to go home. You know that."

"Will you ever stay here with me all night?"

"I don't sleep over."

"Why?"

"Just don't."

She watched him pull on his gray thermal shirt and then another shirt and then he sat down on the edge of the bed to put on his socks and boots. "Do you do weekends away?"

He glanced at her, lifted an eyebrow.

She hadn't drawn the curtains and the moonlight fell through the windowpanes of her upstairs bedroom, illuminating his firm features and strong profile.

"That's not a no," she said helpfully.

"Kit."

"We could go to the beach house. In Capitola. No one's there. You and me. Hang out for the weekend . . . eat, sleep, have sex . . ."

"I don't do romance."

"I know. And you don't send flowers and you don't make sure I climax before you do and you don't make sure I get home safe every day from school."

"You're going to be disappointed, Kit—"

"Okay, fine. I will be. But I'm not disappointed yet, so . . . come to Capitola? I really want to sleep with you and play with you and hang out with you . . ."

"You're making this a relationship."

"I'm making this fun. And you're having fun. So stop being such a hard-ass and all fierce and say, 'Yes, Kit, I'd love to go to Capitola with you.'"

He pulled her onto his lap, kissed her. "Yes, Kit, I'd love to go to Capitola with you."

"When? Next weekend."

"Can't next weekend."

"How about this weekend? We could head down in my car, tomorrow, after I get out of school?"

He laughed softly. "Sure. Why not?"

Twenty

The last time Kit had been to Capitola, it'd been mid-January and she'd gone with Polly for the Martin Luther King holiday weekend, and she'd met Jude. Now it was the first weekend of March and she was going with Jude.

If Polly knew, she'd freak out.

Kit shuffled her feet where they were resting up on the dash, feeling close to freaking out herself. This is crazy, she thought, glancing at Jude, who was behind the wheel of her Prius. He looked rather ridiculous in the car. It was like having a werewolf drive a VW bug. Just didn't work, didn't make sense.

"You are so wiggly," he drawled, stretching an arm out to play with her ponytail. "You're like a little girl."

Her feet did another nervous, excited shuffle. "Feel like a little girl," she said, wondering what he'd do if she burst into song, singing Madonna's eighties hit "Like a Virgin." "This is crazy. I don't do things like this."

He looked amused. "I know."

She liked how he touched her, his fingers sliding through her hair. It was sexy. But then he was sexy. And sex with him was, well, really sexy. She shifted again, pressing her knees together, trying to stay calm. It was almost impossible because everything about him turned her on.

Kit hadn't thought it was even possible to be this physically attracted to someone. Jude did it for her. In a big, big way.

Her gaze slid from his left hand, where it rested on the steering wheel, to his thigh, and the way his worn jeans outlined the shape of his muscular quadriceps. "You're perfectly welcome to touch me," he drawled.

Kit blushed, shook her head, looked out the window. Traffic was barely crawling along. She hoped it'd ease up soon. She'd made dinner reservations for them at Cafe Sparrow in Aptos Village. She'd gone there with her sisters a couple of years ago on one of their Brennan Girls' Getaways and she'd loved the food, and the setting—the building was historic, used to be the old post office. Its cozy two-room interior seemed so romantic that she'd vowed that one day she'd return with someone she felt romantic about. Interesting that she'd never taken Richard, but she couldn't wait to go with Jude.

"Why are you smiling?" he asked.

She turned her head and looked at him. He was everything she shouldn't want but did. "I'm just happy."

"And why are you so happy, angel?"

She couldn't stop smiling. "I'm with you."

They'd finished dinner and had driven back to the Capitola cottage, but after parking the Prius, decided to go for a walk along the beach. It was cold and a little windy but Jude had his arm around her and was keeping her tucked close to his side.

"I don't understand why you're still single, Kit Kat. I would have thought you'd be snatched up and married years ago."

"It's my own fault I'm still single. As my sister Meg used to say to me, it's hard to meet the right man when you're with the wrong one, and I was with the wrong one for a long, long time."

"How long?"

"Ten years."

"Were you married?"

"No. But we lived together. I moved in with him when I was almost thirty, moved out when I was almost forty. Talk about a decade of missed opportunities!" She was trying to be funny but instead it came out rather pathetic. "I wanted to get married, have kids . . . he didn't."

"When did he tell you that?"

"In the beginning."

"And you still moved in with him?"

"Yeah."

"*Why?*"

"I thought I could change him."

Jude didn't say anything else. He didn't have to.

B ut the next morning, after he had woken her up doing wickedly pleasurable things to her when she could put up absolutely no resistance, Jude wanted to talk about her relationship with Richard some more. "Ten years, Kit. That's forever."

"I know."

"And the whole time you knew he had no intention of getting married?"

She pulled the covers up over her breasts, feeling exposed. "I guess I hoped he'd realize how much he loved me and change his mind."

"I don't understand."

"I don't understand either. It's not something I'm proud of—"

"Was he rich? Powerful? Great-looking? A stud in bed?"

"None of the above."

"So what was it?"

"Stability?"

Jude said nothing, so Kit pressed on, trying to explain. "Richard was an engineer. He had a good job and was smart and solid and I thought that was marriage material."

"And yet he didn't want to marry you."

Kit bit into her lower lip. "No."

"Why did you stay with him?"

She shrugged, looked away. "Because I did."

"That doesn't make sense. You're a smart woman. A very smart woman. Why would you spend ten years with someone who couldn't—wouldn't—give you what you wanted? What you needed?"

A lump filled her throat. Her eyes burned. "I should have moved out. I should have. But I felt like I'd invested so much . . . risked so much . . . so I stayed, hoping things would change. They didn't."

"That's such a chickenshit way to live, angel."

Kit blinked, clearing her vision. "I know."

She stayed in bed another few minutes before throwing back the covers and heading into the bathroom to shower.

In the tiny 1950s-era bathroom with the pink-tiled shower, Kit turned on the water full force and stepped under the spray when it'd lost its chill.

She was so mad.

Mad at Richard for being a dick.

Mad at Jude for not getting it.

Mad at Mom for dying.

Mad at herself for being stupid *again*.

Goddammit, but she hadn't asked for much in life. In fact, if she thought about it, she'd never asked for anything. Was that the problem? That God didn't think she needed anything? That she was content with her life and didn't want anything?

Bullshit!

Kit threw the washcloth against the pink-tiled shower wall. *Bullshit,* she thought again, picking up the washcloth and throwing it a second time.

She was so pissed off . . . so angry that the future she'd spent her life waiting for, patiently (as well as impatiently), had never materialized.

Angry that she was falling for Jude, just one more guy who wasn't going to give her what she wanted. What she needed.

And she knew that about him. She'd known it from the first time she laid eyes on him, known it from the moment she saw his house with his rusted metal chairs on his dead lawn, known it from the time he'd kissed her at her parents' house and then walked out.

Yet here she was in Capitola with him, playing house, pretending that this was fun and good.

It wasn't good.

This was bad. She shouldn't have done it, brought him here, tried to make this—him—into something he wasn't.

Kit held the soggy washcloth to her mouth to muffle the sound of her crying.

The glass door abruptly opened. Her eyes flew open. Jude was standing outside the shower looking at her.

"What are you doing?" he asked.

Her eyes met his. She pressed the washcloth even tighter to her mouth and shook her head. She couldn't talk, couldn't tell him. He wouldn't understand.

But he didn't walk away. He reached into the shower, turned the water off. "Baby, what are you doing?"

She looked at him, fresh tears welling in her eyes. "You're right. You are completely right. You're supposed to change your mind. You're supposed to want me." Her voice broke and she buried her face in the washcloth and cried harder.

What?
      Jude stared at her dumbfounded.

Thirty minutes ago they'd had the best sex of his life. Ten minutes ago they'd been talking and had a great conversation. She'd left him to shower and he'd thought everything was fine. Then he came in here, to surprise her in the shower, and he'd been the one surprised.

But why should he be surprised by anything a woman did? After thirty-seven years of living with and near women, he'd come to think of the female gender as a completely different species . . . beautiful, exotic creatures not meant to be understood, just loved. Appreciated. Protected . . . maybe from themselves, because good God, they were complicated, never mind emotional.

He reached for a towel. "Come on, girl, let's get out of there."

"Why didn't I see it before? You're just like him." Her voice was muffled through the dripping cloth. "Just like Richard. You don't want to get married either."

Jude's jaw tightened. Why did women do that? Put two things together that didn't belong together and act like they were making sense? "I'm not anything like Richard," he said, battling to hang on to his temper. Apparently today he was going to have to practice patience a long time before he got his coffee and breakfast.

He'd been so looking forward to breakfast, too. He was

hungry. They'd made love twice last night and once this morning, and it was time to refuel.

She lifted a swollen face to his. "But admit it, you don't want to get married. You have no intention of getting married, or having children—"

He cut her off. He had to. "No, I don't." Because she was right. He'd been there, done that, wasn't going to make the same mistake again. "But that doesn't mean I don't care about you. It just means . . ." His voice faded, he didn't finish the thought, coming so close to saying, *Just means I'm not the right guy for you.* But he didn't say it, couldn't, for the same reason he couldn't stay away from her.

He loved her.

And not because she was like Amy, but because she was Kit. But that didn't change all the external factors that were making their relationship difficult, if not impossible.

He was too invested in this case. He was a man married to his work. There hadn't been time for Amy; he'd never been there for her, not even when she was dying. Christ, but he didn't even get her last voice mail—"Hey, honey, going to the grocery store, want me to pick you up anything while I'm there?"—until after she was gone.

But wasn't that the story of his life? Too little, too late.

Couldn't save his dad. Couldn't save his wife.

So there was no way in hell he'd blow this case, not after working on it for so long. Not after sacrificing so much.

He hoped that sometime in the next six to twelve months they'd make some progress, but they'd thought that last year and then the information they had, the informers they had, fell apart and they had to start over, start building their case from the ground up again.

It was painstaking work. Brutally slow at times. Violent and dangerous at other times. And you never knew when boring and slow would suddenly turn deadly. You never really knew for certain, you just lived day to day.

"Come on, Kit Kat, let's get dressed, get some coffee. It's time we talked."

They sat outside with their coffee on the deck of Mr. Toots's. It was cool and foggy and the chilly damp air meant they had the deck to themselves. Kit pulled her thick fuzzy oatmeal sweater, her favorite beach-house sweater, closer to her body and tried not to shiver or look shocked as she listened to Jude talk.

He wasn't a druggie or unemployed or a mechanic but an undercover narcotics officer with the Oakland Police Department. He'd been in law enforcement since he graduated from UC Davis and his goal from the beginning had been to do just this—put away the bad guys and the drug lords. He wasn't interested in the small guys, wasn't wanting to nail the kids or folks who smoked weed, weed was nothing to him, and Californians had been passing laws right and left to try to make it legal anyway.

No, his focus was on something bigger, darker, more destructive and insidious.

"I'm telling you this," he said, pausing and staring out at the gray mist obscuring the water, "because I do care about you. And I don't want to lie to you or deceive you, or hurt you in any way. But I'm not in a position where I can allow myself to be distracted—"

"I'm a distraction?"

"Absolutely."

"But what about when you're not working? Surely you have time off . . . surely you can have a personal life?"

"It's not that simple. The bad guys I'm chasing aren't like the bad guys in movies . . . they don't look like the bad guys. In fact, to most people they look like the good guys."

Kit studied Jude's hard, fierce profile and felt a flutter of unease. "What are you saying? That these druggies are politicians or businessmen—"

"Or law enforcement." His dark gaze held hers. "Last year we lost two detectives because guys who were supposed to be the good guys, the guys who were there to protect the detectives, betrayed them. The detectives were friends, colleagues, men with wives and children."

"Detective Hernandez and Detective Johnson," Kit said.

Jude's eyes narrowed. "You read it in the paper?"

She nodded. "And I knew the Hernandez family. Detective Hernandez's oldest daughter went to Memorial, and the younger ones went to the Catholic elementary school down the street. After Detective Hernandez's death, Teresa's mom pulled the kids out, and they moved back to Fresno to be with family."

"Hernandez and Johnson had been on the force thirteen and seventeen years, respectively. They were professional, and experienced. And yet on the day they died, they went into a building and were ambushed . . . shot execution-style. They didn't see it coming. Didn't have a clue. Didn't have guns drawn, weren't even wearing vests. Which means someone they trusted set them up. Someone on the inside, someone in my department, had them killed."

"And that's what you're working on? Trying to solve their murders?"

"No, that's someone else's job. My job is to figure out who these crooked bastards are, and collect my evidence, to build a tight case, before the crooked bastards figure out I'm a narc, too."

"So undercover narcs don't know who the other undercover narcs are?"

"Not always, no."

"And what about your boss, or superiors? How do you know they can be trusted?"

He smiled but it was glacier cold. "I don't."

She drew a slow breath, trying to process everything he'd just told her, and finding it almost impossible. "I don't really like your job very much."

His shoulders twisted. "I don't always like it either."

"So why do you do it?"

"Because someone has to."

She frowned, feeling as if there was more he wasn't telling her but sensing he'd said all he wanted to say. Still, she had questions . . . lots of them. "Your mom," she said carefully. "Does she know . . . what you do?"

"Yeah."

"Does she like it?"

"No."

"Has she tried to talk you out of it?"

"A long time ago, when I first left the police academy." He stood up, held his hand out to her. "I'm starving. Let's find something to eat."

Kit made them breakfast at the beach house, scrambled eggs with diced ham and country-fried potatoes and thick slices of sourdough toast. Jude shot her an admiring look as she presented him with his plate.

"Smart, hot, great in bed, *and* a good cook?" he said, mopping up the rest of the hot sauce on his plate with the last remaining slice of toast.

She grinned at him. She'd loved watching him eat. He ate with relish and appreciation. "I'll cook for you any day."

"Don't go teasing me like that, Kit Kat. I know you know the way to a man's heart is through his stomach."

"I do believe I've read that somewhere."

He looked up at her, expression warm. But as he held her gaze, his dark eyes shuttered and his smile faded, leaving his face naked, stark. "I told you things this morning I've never told anyone, not even my mom."

She knew what he was saying, knew what he feared. Her mother's brothers were police officers. Marilyn came from a family of law enforcement. She might not believe that cops could be the bad guys. And if she couldn't keep a secret, she could blow his cover, as well as risk the lives of others. "You can trust me," she whispered.

"I hope so. People's lives depend on me."

"I understand." The small dining room suddenly crackled with tension. She glanced down at her plate, noting how she'd only picked at her food, too nervous and excited being with Jude to be able to eat properly. "My uncle Jack retired from the department almost fifteen years ago, and Uncle John, my mom's younger brother, died in the line of duty, but we don't really talk about cops and robbers at our house. We're more about trucks and ladders and engines in our family."

She looked across the table at him, hoping he'd understand what she was trying to say. "My dad never talked about the bad stuff, or the scary stuff, at home. He didn't bring that side of work home. When he talked to us about his work, he focused on the things he loved—the guys, the loyalty, the pranks at the firehouse, his softball team and how they were the best. If there were dark things, and I'm sure there must have been, he kept it to himself."

Jude didn't say anything and now she couldn't stop talking.

Kit took a breath, exhaled, adding, "I won't ask you, or expect you, to talk about your work with me. I won't ever press you to tell me where you're going or what you're doing. That's not my business, it's yours. And to be quite honest, I don't want to know too much about your business. It scares me. But you don't scare me, Jude. You, for whatever reason, make me feel safe."

* * *

They spent the next twenty-four hours playing cards, having sex, drinking margaritas, having more sex. It felt like a honeymoon to Kit, as they spent more time in bed than out of it.

Sunday morning, instead of going to Mass as she usually did, Kit had an O in the kitchen, and then another, an hour later, back in bed.

"Don't come near me again!" she said to Jude, wagging her finger at him and trying to sound stern, which was very difficult when he was lying completely naked on his side on the bed without even a sheet to cover him. He was ridiculously gorgeous, too, with that body and that face and . . . and oh, heavens no, the first stirrings of yet another erection. "I'm tired, Mr. Knight. And sore. And sick of sex."

His laughter rumbled in his chest and he lifted a hand to push back his straight black hair, revealing his disgustingly beautiful bone structure. With his hand in his hair, his biceps remained bunched, and all the other muscles tightened and rippled. He looked like an ad for Calvin Klein underwear, and to think he was in *her* bed.

"Poor baby," he said, grinning lasciviously. "Have I been too hard on you?"

As he said the word *hard,* he grew even bigger.

Kit grabbed a pillow, shoved it in front of his hips. "You boys are all the same. Doesn't matter if you're fifteen or fifty . . . all you do is think about sex!"

"True." He didn't even sound the least bit apologetic. "Sex is fun."

"Depending on your experience."

His brow furrowed, concerned. "Have you had a bad experience?"

Kit flashed to December and Parker and the fear she'd felt that

night at his place, a fear she couldn't articulate and doubted anyone else would ever understand. Good women, smart women protected themselves, but she hadn't. She'd become paralyzed by fear
when she should have slapped Parker silly and gotten the hell out
of there . . .

"Kit?"

"Hmm?" she murmured, struggling to find her way out of her
head, and the memories, and the shame of breaking, capitulating,
when she should have been strong.

Jude reached out to touch her cheek. "What's going on up
there in that complicated mind of yours?"

She caught his hand, held it, tightly. "Nothing."

"I don't believe you."

She wished she could scoot all the way into his arms and absorb
his warmth, and there, where she was safe, tell him everything. But
she couldn't, not sure how he would react. Men didn't understand
what it was like to be a woman, and frightened of being overpow-
ered and hurt, and Jude wasn't just any man, but a tough, physical
man. He wouldn't admire or respect a woman who just capitulated
when confronted by danger.

"I was just thinking about that first time we met for coffee,"
she said, grabbing at a memory to give him, something to distract
him. "And I told you I used to snoop in my parents' room?"

The corner of his mouth curled. "How could I forget?"

She couldn't help smiling at his smile. It was so sexy and wicked.
But good wicked. Fun wicked. "I still can't believe I told you that.
I didn't even know you then!"

"So what were those . . . *adult* things . . . you found in your
parents' room?"

"You know what I found."

His eyes blinked at her, innocent. "But I don't. Can you explain it to me?"

She punched him in the chest. "You know I found sex stuff."

He choked back laughter. "You have to be more specific than that."

"We're talking about things that *scarred* me, Jude. Parents aren't supposed to have sex, or if they do, they're not supposed to enjoy it."

He was trying so hard to keep a straight face. "And what makes you think—God help us all—that your parents *enjoyed* it?"

"They had things that made it . . . enjoyable."

His chest heaved with silent laughter. "Like what?"

"You're the nosy one."

"I just like watching you talk about sex."

"All right, want to know what I found? I found a vibrator. And a book called *The Joy of Sex*. And what must have been lube— and stop laughing, because it was *devastating*. I sat there looking at that book, learning things I was not ready to learn. Even more agonizing was going to confession and not being able to tell the priest what I'd done. I needed forgiveness but I couldn't ask for it. How did I tell him that my parents were sex maniacs? He knew my parents. He liked them. How could I betray my parents like that, but, oh, I tell you, I could barely look at my parents for weeks after that."

Jude rolled onto his back and howled with laughter. "Poor Kit. You really were scarred, weren't you?"

"Yes," she agreed grumpily, allowing him to pull her toward him, onto his warm, bare chest.

"If it makes you feel any better, I was scarred, too. My parents had the book. The early edition . . . the one where the couple are hairy, long-haired hippies."

"That's the one I saw. Did they do a later edition?"

"The publishers cleaned them up for the eighties. Trimmed the hair, shaved the pits."

"I can't believe we're talking about this!"

He dragged his hands into her hair and pulled her face down

to his, kissing her very slowly, very thoroughly. "You really are a good Catholic schoolgirl," he murmured when he gave her a chance to catch her breath.

Her heart thumped so hard it hurt. "I've tried."

Kit was so happy in Capitola with Jude that she didn't want the weekend to ever end. But it did. Late Sunday afternoon they packed their things, cleaned the beach house, and headed back home with Jude driving again.

They reached her house in Highland Park at dusk. Kit had been quiet on the drive home and Jude had held her hand, comfortable with the silence, hoping she was, too. It'd been a great weekend, probably the best weekend he'd known since the early days of his marriage to Amy, and that was saying a lot.

At her house, he parked her car on the street so he could get his motorcycle out of her small, detached garage.

She stood now on her front lawn watching him back the bike out of the garage. He shut the door behind him, locking it. He might leave his house wide open, but he wanted her house, and her world, secure and safe.

He left his bike, crossed to her, kissed her hard, hungrily, trying not to feel the hint of desperation he felt every time he left her.

She was fine. She'd be fine. She'd survive quite nicely without him.

"I think I love you," she whispered against his mouth.

He stiffened, pushing her away from him. Why did she do that? Right when he was about to leave her? "Don't say that, baby."

"Why not?" She looked up at him, her blue eyes clear, steady. "Is there some rule in your little officer handbook that says no one is allowed to love you?"

"You know I can't give you marriage and family—"

"I have a family. I'm not planning on getting married. And I'm adopting as a single person, so there. Take that. Stuff your plans and rules."

Such a smart-ass. He still didn't know whether he should kiss her, shake her, or spank her and was beginning to think he never would. "So what do you want from me?"

"Just you."

"Stop it."

"I'm serious. I have a job I love, good income, close family, great friends, and I'm moving forward with the adoption. I have my interview next week."

"And what do you think the agency would say, if they found out you had a dirtball like me hanging around?"

Kit shrugged. "I won't tell them."

"You're going to *lie*?"

Her eyes flashed. "I'm not lying, I'm just—"

"Prevaricating."

"Exactly." Her nose lifted. "By the way, that was a very nice word. And it does appear on the SAT test."

He laughed. He couldn't help himself. "Ah, Kit, you're amazing, and I can't help thinking that none of this is fair to you—"

"I gave up on fair a long time ago, Jude. Now I just want whatever I can get."

"And that's crumbs, angel. You'll just be getting crumbs with me, and you and I both know you deserve a whole loaf."

"Okay. Maybe all I will get is crumbs from you, but I would rather have crumbs with you than an entire loaf with someone else. And I know what I'm talking about. I've been there with someone else."

"I think you're fooling yourself. I think you're doing what you did with Richard—hoping he'd change, hoping there'll be more—"

"God, I wish I'd never told you about Richard!"

"But you did."

Kit caught one of his hands, brought it to her mouth, pressed her lips to his knuckles. "Come on, tough guy, I don't know why I'm the way I am. I don't understand why I love the way I love, but I do. And after years of feeling nothing, I feel so much with you. I feel good with you. Optimistic about life when I'm with you—"

"I feel the same way when I'm with you."

Her eyes grew huge. He nodded, thinking this was either going to be the most wonderful thing or an utter catastrophe. "You know, Kit, no one will understand this . . . us. Your family won't approve. And it's going to be hard for you, not to tell them the truth about me. But you can't, no matter what they say—"

"I won't. I promise you."

"I've seen where you live. I know how you were raised. And I am everything your father hates. And if I were in his shoes, I'd hate me, too. I'm a scumbag, Kit—"

"Don't say that."

"—and your sisters won't like me and your brother, Tommy, will loathe me, and they are right. I am bad news, Kit. I will never give you what you deserve."

Her eyes were bright with tears. She swallowed hard, lifted a shoulder. "I don't agree."

"I guess we're not going to see eye to eye on this one."

"No, we're not, and I'm getting really tired of you telling me what I need, and what I feel and what is good for me. And as much as I love my family, I'm not here to make them happy. I have a right to be happy, too, and for whatever reason, you make me happy. That is, when you're not pissing me off."

The corner of his mouth lifted and he tugged on one of her wild red curls. On the outside Kit looked so angelic and yet she was tough as nails underneath. "Am I pissing you off?"

"Big-time. I like you, Jude. And I'm falling in love with you— whatever that means. But it's not to trap you into anything, or force you to do anything, it's just to say, hey, tough guy, I think you're pretty wonderful."

He said nothing for a long moment, too busy just looking at her, appreciating her. Crazy, beautiful, exotic creature, this Kit Brennan. She was a puzzle, and a mystery, and God help him, he loved a good mystery. "Can I come back here tomorrow night? Can I come sleep with you?"

Her smile started in her eyes and only then curved her lips. "I'll make you a key, and you just come whenever you can, for as long as you can—"

"Let's just start with tomorrow night."

"And a key."

"Are you always going to be arguing with me?"

"Always."

He kissed her, and just that one hot little kiss made him hard and want her. "At least you're honest, witch," he muttered against her mouth.

"What happened to me being an angel?"

"Changed my mind." He swatted her butt, pushed her toward the house. "Now go inside, lock the door, and stay out of trouble or I'll never get any sleep tonight."

Twenty-one

A week later, at three o'clock in the afternoon, Kit took the sturdy green tote bag of unread student journals to her parents' house, hoping she might find some time to get work done while keeping Mom company so Dad could attend a Warriors basketball game with Tommy and Uncle Pat.

It'd been fourteen days since Kit had wrapped up her week here of taking care of Mom and she was looking forward to seeing her again. Meg and Cass had spent last weekend here at the house while Kit had gone to Capitola, and they'd both said Mom was doing well and had been in great spirits. The IV pain reliever was truly a miracle drug.

"Ah, there's my babysitter now," Mom said from the bed as Kit popped her head into the master bedroom.

Kit grinned. "All clear? No one dressing? I don't want to see any naked old men walking around."

"I heard that," Dad said from the closet, emerging to show her he was fully dressed. He lifted a big arm, flexed, made his biceps jump. "Huh?"

"Not bad."

"And I'll have you know I can still do one hundred push-ups, Katherine Elizabeth."

"What about one-arm push-ups?" she teased, giving him a hug and then pulling the wing chair closer to the side of the bed. "So is there anything I should know for tonight? Anything planned?"

"Claire's here," Mom said, referring to her weekday-evening aide.

"And I rented your mom some movies that she said she wanted to watch," Dad added. "They're right there by the DVD player. She's also just been given a new IV bag of medicine. It's a nice strong cocktail that will keep her feeling good."

Mom smiled up at him. "I feel good!"

"But that doesn't mean you can have any boys over, and no parties," Dad said, leaning over to kiss her good-bye.

"So what are we going to watch?" Kit asked Mom after Dad left.

"I want to see *Julie and Julia.* Have you seen it?"

"I have. But it's a great movie. You'll like it."

Kit was fast-forwarding through the previews when Mom asked her to mute the sound because she had something to tell her.

Kit hit pause and turned to look at her mom. Mom only said she had something to say when she had something significant to say.

"I need Brianna to come home," Marilyn said quietly, her eyes meeting Kit's and holding. "I'd told her I thought she could maybe wait until Easter, but I don't think we have that long."

Kit's heart hurt. She knew exactly what Mom was saying.

"When do you need her here, Mama?"

"In the next week, just to be safe."

Wow. Oh, wow. *No.* "Is this a . . . hunch . . . or do you have some tests results I don't know about?"

"My last blood draw showed . . . things. The hospice is going to take over the nursing care soon, sometime this week."

"Are you going to one of those facilities?"

"No." She looked chagrined. "Your dad won that one. It's not fair for me to win them all."

"So you're going to stay here?"

"But not in this bed. I'm being switched to a different bed, one that's easier for the nurses to work with."

Kit knew what that meant but didn't want to go there. "That's good."

"Dad's telling Tommy tonight. We're going to call Meg and Sarah tomorrow. I'd hoped you could try to reach Brianna. With the time difference, we're finding it hard to connect with her."

"Of course." And Kit would reach her. Immediately. She didn't care if she had to wake Brianna's ass up in the middle of the night to talk to her. "I'll make sure she comes."

"We're trying to get everyone here by the weekend. Boone won't be able to make it, but hopefully everyone else can. It's St. Patrick's Day on Saturday. We'll have a little celebration with whoever can be here."

Thank goodness Mom fell asleep before they even got a quarter way through the movie, because Kit couldn't concentrate on it at all. All she could think about was calling Brianna and getting her twin on the next plane into San Francisco.

It took three calls to get through to her and now Kit was walking in the backyard, inspecting her father's flower beds with the cheerful pink, yellow, and purple primroses, listening to Brianna swear at her.

"Jesus, Kit! Do you know what time it is here?" Brianna demanded.

"Middle of the night?"

"Almost three A.M.—Is Mom dead?"

"Oh my God, Bree! And no, our mother isn't dead. Yet."

Brianna sighed. "Sorry. I don't mean it like that. But the phone kept ringing and ringing and I take stuff at night to help me sleep—never mind. What's up?"

"You need to come home, Bree."

"I will soon—"

"No. Not soon. Has to be now. This week. Unless you want to just roll in for the funeral service."

"It's that bad?"

"Getting there."

Bree was quiet. "How is she? Really?"

"Frail. Skin and bones."

"Energy?"

"Sleeps most of the day. But her pain's under control. They've got her on a cocktail of things that keeps her cheerful." Kit bent over to pluck some weeds from between the flowers. "They're planning a party this Saturday. St. Patrick's Day. She wants everyone here for it."

"That's soon, Kit. Six days."

"I know, but Mom needs you. She misses you. Worries about you."

"I know." Brianna sighed. "That's why I haven't come before now. I haven't been well. Didn't want her to see me . . . this way."

"What way, Bree?"

"I'm pretty thin. I've put on seven pounds, though. But for a while there I was just a bag of bones. People here kept asking me if I had cancer."

"Do you?" Kit whispered.

"No."

"Promise?"

"Yes."

But Kit wasn't reassured. "But there's something else wrong, isn't there?"

Brianna didn't answer for a long time. "Yes."

"Bree!"

"It's all right. I'm dealing with it. But you can't tell anyone . . . not Meg, or Sarah, or Cass. And you especially can't say anything to Mom or Dad, or I'll never forgive you. Never trust you."

"I won't."

"That's not true. You tell them everything."

"I do not!"

"Growing up, you told them *everything* I ever did!"

"Not *everything*," Kit protested. "Just the stuff that was dangerous."

"Nice of you."

"I did it because I loved you, and I worried about you, and I didn't want to see you hurt."

"And did I ever get hurt?" Brianna mocked her.

"No," Kit said, in a small voice.

"No."

And then suddenly that memory was back, the one about silence and secrets, the one that had been built to cover a little girl's pain and fear. For a moment Kit couldn't breathe, or think or feel.

There was a reason she'd never been comfortable being held too long. There was a reason why she'd never been easy around big men other than her father. There was a reason she feared feeling too much. Needing too much. Because feeling and needing might lead to losing control, and control was her friend. Control protected her, concealed her, kept her from ever completely remembering . . .

Or sharing . . .

Which kept anyone from ever knowing . . .

And Kit fought hard now, to push it away, not wanting to be

confronted by the past when there were so many other things happening now, when there were so many other important things taking place. There was no time for Kit's past, no energy to expend on unreliable little voices. She'd resigned herself to living with these ghosts—mere shadows of memory—and she of all people knew they couldn't be trusted.

She couldn't be trusted.

Because bad things didn't happen to good girls. And Kit had always tried so hard to be a good girl.

They said good-bye, and hanging up, Kit returned to the house, stopping in the kitchen for a snack. She was just peeling the foil off a Greek yogurt when her phone rang. She glanced at the number. It was Bree calling back.

Kit licked the yogurt off her thumb and answered. "Hey. Did you already book your air?"

"No." Brianna hesitated. "Remember when you told me about that date with Parker in early December?"

"Yeah."

"I think about that a lot, Kit."

"It's behind me—"

"Is it?"

"What?"

"Kit, do you remember being little?"

Kit frowned. "How little?"

"Four or five."

Kit's insides wobbled. "Why?"

"Did something . . . bad . . . happen to you?" Brianna asked.

Kit reached for a counter stool and sat down heavily. "Why?"

Brianna was silent a long moment. And as the silence stretched, Kit's heart began to hammer harder. "Bree?"

"Did someone hurt you . . . down there?"

Kit's insides felt as if they were falling out and she swallowed convulsively, trying to keep from throwing up. She couldn't do this. Couldn't talk about this. It'd make her sick. "I don't know. And I don't want to talk about this."

"Why not?"

Kit leaned forward to press her forehead against the cool marble countertop. "Because I don't know, and it's something I don't understand, and it makes me feel crazy—"

"I was asking, because it happened to me, and I wondered, if maybe it had happened to you, too . . ." Brianna's voice drifted off, and for a moment there was just empty silence on the line. "But if it didn't, that's good. That's great. I would never wish anything like it on anyone—"

"Something did happen to me," Kit whispered, dragging in air, her chest tender with every breath. "I'm pretty sure something did, but the details are fuzzy."

"What do you remember?"

"It's a feeling more than anything. I've just always had this feeling that something had happened, something bad, and then a couple of years ago Richard tried something—in bed—and it hurt me and I freaked. And I heard this screaming in my head. Terrified screaming, but it wasn't me. It was a little girl screaming. And then all of a sudden there was this flash, and in my head, I was the little girl."

Brianna exhaled slowly. "Oh, God, Kit."

"But maybe it wasn't anything," Kit said hurriedly. "Maybe it's just my imagination—"

"Can you picture anyone . . . when you think about this?"

"Yeah." Kit swallowed hard. "I can. I can see him right now. He lived on a street behind ours. He was kind of a hippie. Long light brown, dirty-blond hair. Beard. I think he had a beard. I remember he used to wear plaid shirts—"

"Flannel," Brianna finished softly. "Blue."

Kit closed her eyes. "You know who I'm talking about?"

"Yes."

"Did he . . . did he . . . hurt you, too?"

"You mean cover my face with my sweater so I couldn't see him rape me?"

Kit didn't know if she fell off the stool, she was sitting on or climbed off, but suddenly she was on the floor of the kitchen, her back pressed to the cabinets and her forehead pressed to her knees. "Is that what he did?"

"You don't remember?"

"Not what he did . . . specifically. Just that he put my coat over my face and I couldn't tell anyone about the coat, because if I did, he'd do it again, and make me disappear. And then nobody would ever be able to find me again."

"So you do remember."

"Just that." Kit's heart raced and her stomach was jumping up and down and she wanted to cry but couldn't. "I wish I could remember the rest. Makes me feel crazy not to remember."

"I'd give anything not to remember." Brianna paused, laughed. "But I can't forget."

"Why do you remember and I don't?"

"I work with abuse survivors all the time here—men and women and children who've been through hell and back with all the wars and genocide. They've been kidnapped and mutilated and raped, they've watched their families and friends be tortured and murdered, and the survivors develop different pathologies to help them cope with the trauma. Some of them remember, some of them block it all out. Either way, it's a survival mechanism, and after you were abused, your psyche tried to help you by putting up a screen and blocking off the memories to try to protect itself."

Abuse survivors. Kit repeated the phrase silently. The words fit war victims in Africa but felt alien and uncomfortable when applied to her. "And what did *you* do to protect yourself?" she whispered.

"Became promiscuous. Sexualized my identity." She laughed

and the sound was sharp, self-mocking. "Made me feel safe, strong, in control. It's how I felt loved." Brianna's voice suddenly hardened. "But you know that. You know I lost my virginity young, had that abortion in high school, and the doctor botched it—"

"I didn't know," Kit interrupted.

"Mom promised me she wouldn't tell Dad, but I figured you knew. We shared a room."

"When was this?"

"Homecoming week. Our junior year of high school."

"And Mom knew?"

"It was Mom who found me in the bathroom and rushed me to the hospital. She checked me in as 'Brianne Donahue' and paid for everything privately that day, out of her own savings, to protect me. It cost thousands of dollars. It was almost everything she'd saved and she used it for me."

Kit drew a breath. This was a lot to take in and her mind was scrambling to go back, put all the pieces together. "It was our homecoming weekend that Mom threatened to leave Dad."

"I know."

"It was because of what happened to you . . . wasn't it?"

"I don't know." Brianna's voice thickened. "I just remember that I was in bed still feeling so bad and I could hear Mom and Dad fighting and fighting. And then Sunday morning it stopped and Mom's suitcase was by the front door."

Kit remembered a suitcase the color of Dijon mustard. All the kids saw it, and Mom dressed in her good clothes, wearing her good coat, waiting in the living room for Dad to return from the early morning Mass so she could say good-bye properly. To his face.

None of the kids came downstairs that morning. Meg was already off at college in San Diego, which meant Kit was now in charge and she was doing her best to comfort Sarah, who was just eleven or twelve, and crying hysterically. Sarah wanted to fling herself on Mom and beg her not to go, but Kit wouldn't let her go downstairs, telling her this was between Mom and Dad, and for once Sarah mustn't interfere.

And then Dad came home.

Kit, Tommy, and Sarah all leaned as close to the top of the landing as they could without being seen.

And then Mom said in her clear, firm voice, "I'm leaving, Tom. I cannot stay with a man who will put his pride and his anger before his daughter. Since you can't find it in your heart to forgive her, I can't find it in my heart to love you."

Dad had been floored.

Kit didn't remember what he said, but Mom didn't go. And two days later he and Mom began seeing a counselor. They ended up attending counseling for six months and little by little Dad repaired his damaged relationship with Bree.

"Oh, Bree," Kit breathed, "this is crazy."

"Yep."

"I had no idea that . . . any of that stuff . . . had happened to you."

"You just thought I loved sex."

"Don't you?"

Brianna sighed. "No. Not so much."

Kit's head was spinning. And even though she'd learned more today than she'd ever wanted to learn, there was one more thing she had to ask. "How did we end up at that guy's house?"

"I'm not really sure. I just remember something about being special, he'd make me special, I don't know why I remember that part . . ."

"He told me that, too."

"Did he? Interesting. Wonder how many other little girls he said that to."

Kit's eyes burned. "Oh, God, I didn't even think of that."

"Let it go, Kit. There's nothing you can do."

Kit's teeth chattered. "Come home, Bree. Get on a plane now. Don't wait. Please come home soon."

"I will. As soon as I hang up, I'll book my flight."

"Love you, Bree."

"Love you, Kitty."

After hanging up, Kit reached for the crucifix that hung around her neck and clasped the cross with Jesus, clinging to the crucifix, clinging to her faith. How did these bad things happen? Where was God in all the violence and pain? Was He there with her and Brianna when they were being hurt?

She blinked as tears filled her eyes and then scrambled to her feet as Claire appeared in the kitchen.

"Your mother wants you," she said briskly.

Kit nodded, and wiped away the tears with the side of her arm. "Tell her I'm coming," she answered. "I just need a minute."

Going to bed that night, Kit was glad Jude was gone, glad that she couldn't tell him about her conversation with Brianna, not sure she could tell anyone about it.

The whole thing with that neighbor was confusing. And shameful, and the fact that Brianna remembered didn't lessen the shame. Just made it more real.

Because apparently what their neighbor did had been real.

Kit hadn't made it up. She wasn't crazy. Something bad had happened, and not just to her, but to Bree. That's the part that broke Kit's heart.

Poor Bree. Poor Bree for remembering and not being able to forget. Kit was glad now that as a little girl she'd blanked out details. Glad her young psyche had drawn a curtain over the worst of it. She couldn't imagine being Bree, going through life remembering every horrifying thing that man had inflicted on her. Little

wonder Bree had grown up acting out, trying to lose herself in sex
and drugs and everything else.

No, good thing Jude wasn't here. Kit wouldn't want him to see
her crying herself to sleep.

It was noon, lunchtime, and Kit had remained in her classroom
since the Drama Club was meeting twice a week now to prepare for their production in May. They'd scrapped doing a full-
length play this year, in favor of a series of one-acts, and the kids
had sat in groups practicing their lines, anticipating blocking
out the scenes next week. They were gone now and Kit had her
planner open, trying to remember what she was supposed to teach
next.

"Do you believe in God, Miss Brennan?"

Kit looked up to find Delilah standing next to her desk. "Yes."

"Do you believe God really answers prayers?"

Kit closed her planner, put down her pen. "I pray."

"Does it work?"

"I believe God hears our prayers."

Delilah's straight, light brown eyebrows lifted. "But that's not
the same thing as answering them, is it?"

How many times had Kit said the same thing to herself? "Faith
requires faith." She saw Delilah's puzzled expression. "Get a
chair, Delilah, bring it over here. It'd be more comfortable talking
if you didn't have to stand."

Delilah carried a chair back. She sat down, looked at Kit ex-
pectantly. "How does it work? You ask God for things and then
wait? Hoping He's going to answer?"

"We're told in the Bible to have confidence when we approach
God. In John, it says that 'if we ask anything according to His
will, He hears us.' And in Mark, we're told 'whatever you ask for
in prayer, believe that you have received it, and it will be yours.'"

"So basically God only answers the prayers that fit into His scheme of things."

Kit thought of her mom, and it hurt. "But we don't know if something is God's plan without asking. So I do think it's important to go to Him with everything, believing that what we need will be given to us."

Delilah stared across the empty classroom, her gaze fixed on a distant bulletin board. "Miss Powers said you missed school that week because you were taking care of your mom. She's sick."

Kit nodded. "She has cancer."

"Is it bad?"

Kit nodded again.

"I'm sorry," Delilah said.

"Thank you, Delilah."

"I take care of my mom a lot, too," the girl said after a moment. "When I was little, I used to be mad that I had to take care of her. I wanted her to take care of me. But maybe my mom's like your mom. She just can't take care of me anymore. And so it's my turn to help her."

Kit swallowed around the lump in her throat. "She's lucky to have you, Delilah. You're a good daughter."

Delilah turned her head to look at her. "Have you read my journal lately?"

Kit shook her head guiltily. Since she'd started to see Jude she'd been a lot less disciplined about grading and reading journals, but since Jude was gone all week, she'd planned to get on top of her work but hadn't yet, not with everything happening at home with her mom and then that phone call to Bree the day before yesterday. "No. But I can read it tonight."

"You don't have to. You probably won't want to."

"Why?"

"I don't think you're going to like it."

"No?"

"I stapled most of the pages shut. That way you won't be too upset."

Kit felt a flutter of worry, and dread. "Why would I be upset, Delilah?"

The girl shrugged, her expression lost, sad. "I guess you'll just have to read it."

The moment Kit was home from school she changed into sweats, as she intended to sit down and read Delilah's journal, but her phone rang, first with a call from Meg wondering if Kit knew when Brianna was arriving, and then a call from Sarah, who was flying in tomorrow and bringing the children and hoping Kit could pick them all up at the airport. While still talking to Sarah, she got a call that went to voice mail, this one from Aunt Linda, who wanted to take the menu and food planning over from Dad for Saturday's party but Dad kept insisting he could handle it, even though everyone knew he didn't cook.

Kit was battling through all the calls, thinking how business-like everyone was being as they made their travel arrangements and plans for dinner and scheduling visits with each other. Death was so civilizing, wasn't it?

Exhausted, hungry, and confronted by an empty refrigerator, Kit jumped into her car, went through a fast-food drive-through, and ordered a chicken burrito to take home.

Once she was home again, she sat on her couch, eating the burrito in little bites, trying to keep her mind clear so she could get the food down.

But once the burrito was gone, she couldn't ignore what she'd intended to do ever since returning from school. It was time to read Delilah's journal.

Opening her briefcase, she pulled out a stack of papers and Delilah's black notebook. She had noticed the stapled pages earlier but she'd had no idea just how many pages the girl had stapled shut..

Flipping through the journal now, she noted that page after page was stapled, signaling Delilah's request for privacy. Delilah had obviously written something personal, very personal, and didn't want Kit to read it.

Fear slithered down Kit's back, through her veins.

Kit had lost a student once, it'd been ten years ago, and it'd been devastating. He'd been a sensitive, bright, gifted boy and he didn't know where he fit in the world, didn't feel as if he had a place, and so he removed himself from it. Kit would never forget his funeral, or his parents' terrible grief. She'd cried with them, and then later at home off and on for weeks.

Kit's fingers now played over the staple in the corner of a page, the metal thin and brittle beneath her fingertips. She wanted to respect Delilah's privacy, she did, but she also had a responsibility to keep her student safe.

She couldn't ignore that responsibility, couldn't let Delilah become a statistic like Jamie.

Nervously, reluctantly, she tore the paper off the staple and unfolded the page to read.

I read about a movie called White Oleander *with an actress named Michelle Pfeiffer. Apparently the woman in the movie kills someone with oleander flowers. It's something to think about. We have oleander bushes not far from here. Last night I looked up* oleander *on the Internet and then how to kill someone with oleander. It's pretty basic. Oleander is really poisonous.*

I don't feel good reading up on how to make an oleander milkshake. It's disgusting. I feel disgusting. Part of me wants to shower or go to church, but I can't let Howie kill my mom. And he will. Sooner or later. And then he'll kill me.

Kit stopped reading. Her stomach heaved. She folded the page back down, pressing at the crease to make it flat again.

Was Delilah serious?

Was Howard truly that violent? And would Delilah really do something to hurt him?

Kit flipped through the journal, back ten or more pages to a stapled page in the middle. It seemed like most of Delilah's journal had been folded over. Hidden. Secured.

Hand shaking, she tore the page open.

This whole life sucks. Sucks so bad. Will no one help us? Does no one care? I'm so tired of being scared. So tired of feeling like this all the time. It's bullshit.

Kit scanned the rest of the page but it was all about Delilah's friends in Mineral Wells and how much she missed Texas.

She flipped forward two pages, saw something about how you could improve Catholic schools if you cut out the religion classes and Friday-morning Mass, and was relieved these entries seemed almost normal for a teenage girl; then she flipped forward to the next stapled page, peeled the paper off the staple, and unfolded the page.

Yesterday I asked Jude how much it'd cost to hire someone to kill someone, and he laughed at me. He told me I've been watching too much Vampire Diaries *and I told him to fuck off.*

What a dick. I know he knows someone who could do it. He knows those kinds of people.

But that's fine. I don't need him. I'll kill Howie myself. Not sure how yet. Can't be that hard. People kill people all the time . . . won't be with a knife, though. Don't think I could stab anyone. Or by hanging. I'm not strong enough.

Maybe a gun.

Maybe poison.

It's actually probably better if I do it myself. That way I won't get anyone else in trouble.

Kit stopped reading. She closed the journal.

Oh, God.

Jude should have told her when Delilah went to him, asked him how much it'd cost to hire someone to kill someone. How could he not tell her that? He had assured her he'd keep her informed.

Kit rubbed her knuckles across her mouth, queasy. Afraid. She wished she'd never read any of the journal. Wished she hadn't unstapled the pages. But she had read it, and she would have to report this.

It was the law.

Delilah needed help. She needed a lot of help, but the help she'd get if Kit reported this wasn't the held she needed.

Except, by law, she had to go to the police. That was the procedure. And the police would arrive, along with a social worker, and together they'd remove Delilah from her home.

Shit. Shit.

Delilah would feel so betrayed. And Kit couldn't blame her. All she wanted was to be with her mother, together with her mother, and yet once Kit reported her writing, Delilah would lose her mother.

Kit tried to look ahead, see what would happen after the social worker took her away. They'd have a psychiatric evaluation done, and once that happened, they'd put her where? Kit wasn't entirely sure where they put troubled kids . . . a foster home? A group home? A hospital?

And maybe Delilah meant none of it. Maybe this was just teenage ranting . . . an unhappy fifteen-year-old girl venting in the privacy of her journal. But it wasn't a private journal. It was a school journal, a notebook assigned for English composition and writing.

But Kit had told them to make it theirs. She'd told her students, class after class, year after year, that the journals were there for the students to be themselves, express themselves, to have a voice and be comfortable with their voice . . .

Kit pressed her hands to her face, covering her eyes. The law was clear in a case like this. But her conscience wasn't clear. Her conscience screamed for her to protect Delilah. But how? How could she help the girl without putting others at risk?

Jude.

He'd know what to do. But Jude was going to be gone for the next few days, as long as a week, and had warned her it was unlikely he'd be able to call or her even respond to texts.

She got to her feet, walked to the kitchen, walked back to the living room. She wanted to call someone but had no one to call. Too bad she didn't have Jude's mom's number. She'd call her.

As she walked in circles around her house, Delilah's words and troubled world filled her head. Kit glanced at her watch. Eight-ten.

Eight-ten. Still early. Early enough.

She went upstairs, changed into clothes, knowing that if she left her house now, she could be at Delilah's in twenty minutes at the most.

Kit wasn't sure what she'd do or say when she got to the house. She prayed that the words would come to her once she arrived. Prayed that God and Jesus and the Holy Spirit and Mary and all the saints would be with her now, because she didn't know what to do, only that she had do something to help Delilah.

Twenty-two

I was in the neighborhood and thought I'd stop by and say hello to Delilah," Kit said, standing on the porch of the Dempsey house, smiling calmly, professionally, as if it was every day she dropped by one of her students' houses at eight-thirty at night. "Can you let her know I'm here?"

Howard looked at her for a long moment, his gaze narrowed. "She's doing homework."

"That's great. She's a smart girl. Can you let her know I'm here?"

He stared at her, unblinking. "It's not a good time. My wife, Missy . . . she's not well."

"You know, I've never met her. I'd love to meet her."

"Tonight's not the night."

"Then I would definitely like to see Delilah."

Howard shifted in the doorway, so big he nearly blocked out the light coming from within the entry. "I thought you were in the neighborhood and just dropping by."

Kit met his gaze, held it. "I know she's here. And I'd like to talk to her. *Please*."

There was a moment of strained silence. "Did something happen to bring you here tonight?" he asked softly.

"Nothing specific, but I have been doing some grading and reading, and after reading Delilah's student journal, I thought it might be good for me to check in, let her know I'm here for her, and that I'm aware of what's going on."

Howard didn't blink or move a muscle and yet Kit suddenly felt afraid, the fear physical and real, and it was all she could do to hold her ground.

"What is going on, Miss Brennan?"

The softness in his voice was pure menace. And it was clear that he knew it. They were both done playing nice.

Kit locked her knees and steeled herself, aware that there was no way she could leave Delilah in this house with him. "She's my student," she said.

"And she's my stepdaughter."

"I'd like to speak with her mother."

"Her mother is indisposed."

"I'd like to speak with Delilah."

"And I'd like you to leave."

He started to close the door on her and Kit shoved her purse between the door and the frame, keeping him from shutting it completely. "I know who you are now." Her voice shook, a combination of adrenaline and rage. "I know what you do. I've read all about you—"

"In her journal?" he interrupted mockingly.

"Yes. In the journal. I've handed it over to the police," she said, fibbing brazenly, not knowing what else to say, or do, but desperate to protect Delilah in any way she could. "It's considered evidence. They wouldn't let me take it home. But someone will be contacting you in the morning—"

"Nobody's going to believe a kid."

"Maybe not. But they'll believe your neighbors and your neighbors are talking. Everybody knows who you are and what you do—"

"Get off my property."

"Or what? You'll hurt me? Hit me? What will you do, *Michael*?" She pulled her purse out of the door and turned around, walked down the steps, heart pounding, legs trembling, waiting for him to follow, waiting to feel his hand on her shoulder or the back of her arm.

Instead, he let her go and the front door slammed closed behind him.

Delilah heard the front door slam closed behind Miss Brennan's departing back.

"*Fuck!*" Howie swore, turning away from the door and spotting Delilah and Missy hovering in the hall. He slammed his fist into the wall. "Fuck," he repeated, punching the wall again.

Missy put one hand behind her, reaching for Delilah, trying to push her away, but Delilah couldn't move. She was so scared she could barely stand up straight.

"What's wrong, baby?" Missy asked, trying to sound calm, but the quaver in her voice gave her away.

"It's over," he said.

Missy nudged Delilah again with her hand, wanting her to go, hide, scram. "What do you mean?"

"We have to go. Pack your things."

"But why? She's gone—"

"That interfering bitch of a teacher went to the police. Told them God knows what. Gave them Delilah's journal." He spotted Delilah hiding behind Missy. "What did you write, Dee?" he demanded, lunging for her. "What did you put in your journal that's so bad the police are holding it as evidence?"

Missy caught at his hand. "That teacher's talking nonsense, honey. Don't listen to her."

"She's got the police talking to neighbors. The neighbors. Christ!" Howard swung his head in Delilah's direction. "And this is all your fault, you disloyal little bitch. Can't keep your mouth shut . . . you should have kept your mouth shut . . ."

Delilah knew she should move but she couldn't. Her legs were frozen, she was frozen, frozen with terror and shock. Miss Brennan had betrayed her.

"Pack your things," Howie snarled. "We're going. We're leaving tonight."

Mama's hands fluttered up, trying to soothe him. "Howard, honey—"

"You think I want this?" he roared, throwing Missy backward, sending her crashing into the wall. "You think I want to be chased out of my home? My shit-house home that still costs a half-million dollars?" His hands squeezed into fists as he grabbed for her again. "You think I like leaving my job and our house and our lives? But I'm not going to deal with any police or answer any questions. So you go pack and put the shit in car while I have a word with Dee."

Delilah saw him shove her mother away from him and spin to face her, and her legs nearly went out beneath her.

"Leave her alone, Howard!"

Delilah couldn't look away from the frost in his eyes. They were so cold they glittered. He was going to kill her. He was going to kill her finally . . .

"Howard, you promised!" Mama was screaming, her voice high and piercing. "You promised me, you swore to me you'd never lay a hand on her."

Howie didn't answer. He couldn't because he was coming for her, Delilah, and coming fast.

Delilah wished the ground would just open up and take her, swallow her, and be done with her once and forever. She was so tired of the fear and the sadness. If she was going to die, let her just die now, let her die fast—

"Go, Dee! Run!" Mama screamed at her. "Run, baby, run." And then Mama was grabbing at Howie, throwing herself before him, tangling up his arms and legs, trying to trip him. "Go, Dee, go, baby, go as fast as you can!"

Delilah saw Howie slam his fist into Mama's face, toppling her to the floor, and watching Mama crumple and fall brought her to life.

She ran to the door, flung it open, and ran as fast as she could down the steps, out into the street, past Jude's dark house, past more houses and barking dogs and TVs blaring from inside small houses. She ran and ran and ran, not knowing where to go, only that she had to go. But even as she ran, arms pumping, legs flying, she found herself wondering what would happen when she finally stopped running.

What would happen when she wanted to go home?

D elilah wasn't at school Friday morning.
      Kit didn't even wait until third period to find out. She called the office, asked Mrs. Dellinger if Delilah Hartnel had been marked absent from her first-period class, and Mrs. Dellinger said she had.

"Did anyone call?" Kit asked, her voice shaking. "Her mom or dad, to say why she was absent?"

But no one had called. And Delilah wasn't in second, or third, or any period that day at school.

Kit locked the door to her classroom at noon, sat in the dark, and fought panicked tears. What had she done? Why did she go to the Dempseys' last night? Why had she told Howard she knew anything? And most important, where was Delilah today? And was Delilah okay?

Kit sent Jude a text. She didn't know if he'd get it. Didn't know if he could respond to her, but at least he'd know sooner rather than later what was going on. *Did something stupid. Confronted Howard last night about what I knew. Delilah's not at school today. Panicking.*

Switching to her directory of contacts, she called her uncle Jack, the retired police detective. Thank goodness he answered.

"Uncle Jack, I didn't know if you could help me with something. I'm worried about one of my students. There's abuse going on at her home. I tried to speak with the stepfather yesterday and it got ugly and now the little girl isn't at school today."

"Where do they live?"

"In San Leandro. Not far from where I teach." She gulped a breath, trying to stay calm. "Do you know anyone that works on this side? Anyone who could drive over to the house and check on them?"

"You think this fellow, the stepfather, he's dangerous?"

"Yes."

"I'll make some calls. I'll let you know what I find out."

"Thank you, Uncle Jack. I owe you."

Uncle Jack didn't get back to her until after school was over. "No one was there," her uncle told Kit over the phone as she was pulling out of the school parking lot. "The house was quiet. Dark. No car. The back door was wide open, so they went in. The house was full of furniture—couches, tables, chairs, beds—but the beds were stripped bare and there were no clothes in closets or the dressers."

"No bedding or clothes?"

"No. Looked like they'd cleared out."

Kit's heart fell. "What about pictures, knickknacks, stuff like that?"

"Gone. House is empty except for the big stuff."

For a second she couldn't breathe. Oh no. No, no, no. What had she done?

"Kit?" he sounded concerned "You okay?"

"Yes."

"Anything else I can do?"

"No. That was really helpful. Thank you."

Delilah spent the first night she'd run away from her house sleeping on pieces of tree bark beneath the toddler play structure in a church playground. She slept there because the space was small and narrow and she felt safe. She couldn't imagine any other homeless person but her wanting to sleep there.

She left the next morning when she heard the first car pull up. She wasn't sure where she was. She'd run such a long way last night that she had to get directions twice to get home, and even then, it took hours.

It was almost ten when she reached her house. Howie's car was gone. The lights were off. The blinds were all down.

Delilah went in through the front door. It was open. The house was quiet. "Mama?" she called.

No one answered.

She walked back to her mama's bedroom, pushed open the door. The big bed was just a bare mattress. The dresser had nothing on it. Delilah moved to the closet, looked inside. Nothing. No clothes, no shoes, no jackets. She opened the dresser drawers, one after the other. Nothing, nothing, nothing.

Delilah backed out, went to her room, pushed the door open. Empty.

She walked through the rest of the house, and the TV in the living room was gone. The pictures of Mama and Howie's wedding were gone. The picture of Mama and Delilah and Grandpa was gone. Even the little ceramic salt and pepper Dutch shoes in the kitchen were gone.

Because Mama and Howie were gone.

They'd left. Left her.

Delilah sat down on the living room couch, chewed on her lip, trying to figure out what to do.

What to feel now. And suddenly Miss Brennan's journal "quick writes" came to mind:

I want . . .

I need . . .

I love . . .

I hate . . .

Tears filled her eyes, fell onto her fists. *I want Mama. I need Mama. I love Mama. I hate Howie.*

And Miss Brennan. *I hate Miss Brennan for doing this to me.*

After crying until she couldn't stand herself crying another minute, Delilah got up, washed her face at the kitchen sink, dried it with the sleeve of her blouse, then left her house and walked to Jude's.

She knocked on the door, but didn't expect him to answer. His motorcycle was gone. Had been gone all week.

She knocked again, just to be polite, and then knowing he never locked his doors since there was no point locking them, as he owned nothing nice, she opened his front door and went in to see if he had anything to eat and a working TV that might get some good channels.

Twenty-three

Kit would never think of a St. Patrick's Day party quite the same way. Everyone was packed into her three-story childhood home on Fifth in Sunset—a very thin, jet-lagged Brianna, Sarah and the kids, Meg and Jack and their three, Tommy and Cass, Cass's mom, Uncle Pat and Uncle Joe and Uncle Jack and their wives and their adult children.

And if that and green beer weren't bad enough, Dad had Irish music blaring out of the speakers, one folk song after another. Someone had loaded an iPod with the complete collection of Gaelic tearjerkers.

The old stuff, the new stuff, even the classic stuff Kit had once listened to, like the Chieftans, the Waterboys, Enya, and Sinéad O'Connor.

Kit wandered around the house, her sole purpose to escape whoever intended to corner her next because she'd had it with making cheerful, polite conversation. She didn't want to do cheerful and polite. She was too upset. Too heartsick.

Delilah was gone. Jude had never called her or checked in.

Brianna looked as if she was still at death's door. Tommy and Cass weren't speaking because Cass still wanted a baby and he wouldn't even discuss it. Meg and Jack were standing together, smiling like they had it all, but something about it didn't feel quite right to Kit. And then, to top it all off, Mom was not supposed to make it to next weekend.

Was there anything good in the world?

To avoid further conversation with Sarah, who seemed determined to cry all night long about Mom, Kit refilled a platter of vegetables and dip and put it back on the dining room table. Refilled a bowl of chips. Added ice to the sodas in the bucket. Then dashed up the back stairs to get some exercise.

Climbing up the stairs, she saw her aunt Linda coming down. Kit smiled, waved, and passed her quickly, trying to look like she was on a pressing errand, when in truth, she just wanted to find some peace and quiet.

Kit found it in the small bedroom off the old playroom on the third floor. It'd once been Tommy's room and it was a small room built under the eaves but it had a great big picture window, and best of all, it was dark, empty, and still.

She flung herself on Tommy's twin boyhood bed and tried not to think about Delilah, or what horrible thing was happening to her and her mom right now. She tried not to think about how she'd maybe ruined Delilah's life and that there was probably a right way to handle things, but of course Kit played the hero card and it backfired because Howard was out there being crazy when he should be locked up behind bars.

If only she'd waited for Jude to return. If only she'd asked Jude to help her handle it properly, maybe then Howard would have gotten the punishment he deserved—

Kit broke off her train of thought and sat up, hearing a deep vibration from down the street. It was a very distinctive vibration, and the throbbing hum of a very familiar motorcycle engine.

Jude.

Leaving the bed, she went to the upstairs window and looked out. Jude was nosing his bike to the curb, squeezing the big burnt-orange motorcycle between cars.

He was here.

For a moment all she could do was watch him. And she stared down at him, fascinated, as fascinated as she'd been the very first time she saw him. She watched him pull off his helmet, saw his long black hair spill to his shoulders, followed him as he climbed off his bike and casually walked to the front door.

Kit tore down the three flights of stairs, skipping around the corners, jumping onto the landings, feeling as breathless as the girl who'd once raced Brianna to the door every time the doorbell rang.

She'd heard the doorbell, knew it was Jude, and wanted to be the one to get there first. But it was Tommy who reached it first. Tommy with the short hair and no-nonsense attitude. Tommy who used to punch out the guys who didn't respect his sisters.

"Is Kit here?" she heard Jude ask.

"I'm not sure," Tommy answered. "What did you say your name was?"

"Jude."

"Jude who?"

"Just Jude."

"To be perfectly honest, Jude, we're in the middle of a private party—"

"Jude!" Kit cried, jumping down the last two stairs and pushing under Tommy's arm to wrap her arms around her man. She smiled cheerfully, brazenly, diving right into the introductions. "Tommy, this is my . . . boyfriend . . . Jude Knight. Jude, this is my brother, Tommy Brennan Jr."

"I go by Tom," Tommy corrected. "Welcome," he said flatly, before walking away.

Kit watched him go, nose wrinkling. "I think he's probably getting my dad."

Jude reached for her, pulled her into his arms. "Then lét me kiss you before my ass gets thrown out."

"You're not mad at me?" she whispered as he lowered his head to kiss her.

"Furious."

"So why are you kissing me?"

"Because I still love you."

She let him kiss her because she needed the kiss and needed him, but then she remembered Delilah.

"Delilah," she whispered. "She's gone."

"She's not gone."

"Yes, she is. Her parents left. They took her. I lost her."

"You didn't lose her. I have her." He stroked her cheek. "I came home this morning and found her sleeping at my house."

"But Howard and Missy . . . they're gone. I called the police. They checked. They said they'd cleared out."

"And they did. But they left Delilah behind."

"*What?*"

He nodded. "They packed up and left her behind."

"They abandoned her?"

"She's taking it hard, but that's to be expected."

"I want to see her. Where is she now?"

"She's with my mom, and she'll stay there while we try to fig-ure out what to do next. Delilah says she wants to go home, back to Texas. Apparently there's someone named Shey who has offered to take her. But we've got to check it out. Go through the proper channels."

"But can't Delilah come stay with me? I have room . . . and she knows me. I'd love to have her with me—"

"Don't think that'd work, Kit. She's pretty mad at you. Doesn't want to have anything to do with you right now."

Oh, of course. Kit nodded, stung, surprised, but not surprised. From Delilah's perspective, Kit understood. She'd betrayed Delilah's trust and there were so few people Delilah had trusted. "I just wanted to help her. I wanted to do something without having to report her."

"And you did help."

Kit pulled away from Jude. "No. Not if her own mother has left her—"

"I think for the first time in a long time, Missy tried to do the right thing."

"How can leaving Delilah be the right thing?"

"Missy might not be able to escape from Howard, but she wanted something else for Delilah. She wanted something better. This was her way of setting her free."

"That sounds like a nice story."

"I think it's the right story."

"What makes you think so?"

"She left Delilah a letter. She put it under my door."

Kit's eyes burned and she stood, arms across her chest, trying not to wonder where God was in all of this. She'd always had such strong faith. Had always been so sure that all things worked together for good . . .

"Why did this happen? Why did any of this happen?" she asked Jude. "I don't understand it. Howard appears in my life, and thrusts Delilah into my life, and it's chaotic and violent and scary—" Her voice broke. "And then they're gone. For what? What was the purpose of this?"

Jude leaned against the doorjamb. "My mom thinks God used you to help save Delilah."

"I didn't help her if her mother left her!"

He reached for her, his hand closing around her wrist, and tugged her toward him. "Delilah's a strong little girl. She's going to be all right."

Kit leaned against him, needing him. "How can you be so sure?"

"Because there are a lot of people who care about her. You, me, my mom, this Shey in Mineral Wells. We all care about her, and we all want what's best for her."

Voices and footsteps sounded on the stairs, and more voices came from the hall. Jude lifted his head, listened. "Sounds like your brother has summoned a lynch mob."

Kit sniffled, then looked up and saw her father and a half-dozen other men on the stairs. "That's just the family. My dad. My brother. All the uncles."

The corner of Jude's mouth quirked. "That's all?"

"Feel like being introduced?"

"Sure." Jude shrugged, planted his feet wide, and channeled his bad-boy-biker swagger. "Why not?"

"Ha-ha," Kit muttered as her dad stepped forward, looking like a bulldog. "It's about to get crazy."

Jude laughed softly. "You know I love crazy."

Twenty-four

Shey Darcy sat at the big oak kitchen table that dominated the spacious kitchen of the Texas limestone ranch house she shared with her husband, former bull-riding champion Dane Kelly, and their four kids, and watched Delilah Hartnel fold and unfold the letter her mother had written to her just before she left her.

Delilah had read the letter probably fifty times since arriving at Shey's house two days ago but so far hadn't shared its contents with her.

"I don't need to read it, Delilah," Shey said gently. "It's personal. Between you and your mama—"

"I just don't get it." Delilah kept her gaze fixed to the table. "I don't get how she could pick him over me. How can she do that?"

Shey shook her head. "I don't know. But it couldn't have been easy for her."

"She was supposed to love me! She was supposed to want me!"

"I'm sure she did. I'm sure she thought she was helping you . . . protecting you—"

"*Bullshit.*"

Normally Shey would have reproved her, but today she let it slide. Delilah had been through a lot. She had a right to be angry, and she needed to vent.

Delilah looked up at Shey, her blue gaze stony. "Would you leave your kids, Shey? Would you leave them for a man?"

Shey searched for the right answer. The police and child protective services had filled her in on what had happened since Delilah's mother married Howard Dempsey, and it was horrific. The violence was horrific. She couldn't imagine enduring months of such abuse. "No, but, Delilah, your mom was in a difficult situation. She was caught between a rock and a hard place—"

"He was a loser from the start. I knew it. I could tell. But Mama couldn't. She was sure he was Prince Charming in a fancy gray car." Abruptly Delilah shoved the letter toward Shey. "Read it." She softened her voice. "Please."

Shey searched Delilah's pale face. "You're sure?"

Delilah nodded and Shey carefully unfolded the letter and spread it open on the table in front of her.

Dear Delilah,

Remember how we talked about one day you'd move on? Baby, it's time you moved on. Not because I don't want you with me, but because you can't do this life with me anymore.

Forgive me, baby, for not being a better mama. I'm just not strong like you. But you are strong and smart and braver than I ever will be and I'm proud of you.

Study hard and do your best, and go to college.

*Promise me you'll go to college. That would make me so
happy.*

I love you, Dee. You'll always be my beautiful baby girl.

> *Your mama,*
> *Missy Hartnel Dempsey*

Shey's eyes burned as she finished the letter. "Your mother loves you," she said huskily, carefully refolding the letter and passing it back to Delilah. "You have to know she loves you."

"She should have gone with me, not him," Delilah whispered, cupping the letter in her hands.

Shey reached out and slowly, gently, pushed back a lock of Delilah's pale hair. "I don't think she stays with him out of love, honey. I think she stays with him out of fear. And she probably doesn't even know the difference between the two anymore."

Delilah's eyes filled with tears. "I hate him."

"I know you do. And you have every right to. But don't give up on your mama. She needs your love. She needs your love more now than ever before."

The tears were falling so fast Delilah couldn't catch them. "How do you know?"

"Because I'm a mother, too, and I don't think I could survive if I didn't have my children to love me."

At Kit's house in Oakland, Jude was stretched out on the couch next to Kit, watching the foreign film *Biutiful* starring Javier Bardem and trying not to look bored. One day he'd have to tell Kit he did not enjoy foreign films. They weren't his thing. Not even if they'd been nominated for, or won, an Academy Award. But he'd save that conversation for later. Kit had been emotional all evening, ever since speaking to Shey Darcy, the woman Delilah had gone to live with in Texas.

Delilah still wouldn't speak to Kit, continuing to blame her for her mother's desertion, and Jude had done his best to comfort Kit, reminding her that it hadn't even been a week since the big blowup with Howard.

"It's still so new for her," he had told her after she hung up the phone. "She's still so raw. One day she'll forgive you, she will. It's going to take time."

Kit nodded but it was obvious she was hurt, and grieving. This whole thing with Delilah couldn't have come at a worse time. Marilyn didn't have much time left. A day or two at the most. No wonder Kit was so emotional. Jude couldn't even imagine how he'd cope with losing his mom.

"You never told me how the interview with the adoption agency went," he said, dipping his head to kiss the top of hers. "How was it? Were they cool? Do you think they liked you?"

"It went good," she said in a small voice.

"Yeah?"

She nodded and turned her head to look up at him. "They liked that I was open to adopting an older child, or even siblings. Those kids are always harder to place."

"You don't mind not having a baby?"

She thought about it a moment and then shook her head. "I don't have to have a baby to be a mom. And that's the point of all of this. Becoming a family. Having a family."

Jude stared down into her eyes a long moment. "You're beautiful, Kit Brennan. Beautiful inside and out."

She opened her mouth to protest. He could see it in her eyes. And then she shut her mouth and managed a small smile. "Thank you."

"I love you, Kit. You know that, don't you?"

She nodded.

He stroked her cheek, savoring the warmth of her skin. "Would you ever want to adopt or have a baby together?"

Her eyes narrowed. "What does that mean?"

"I just . . . I don't know . . . but I kind of think I want to have a family with you."

She pushed against his chest and sat upright, facing him. "But you don't do commitments. You won't marry. You aren't boy-friend material—"

"When my case wraps up, I want to be transferred to a desk job. I'm ready for regular hours and a safe, sane job."

"Why?"

He cupped her chin, kissed her mouth. "Because I want you. And I want to come home to you. And I want to be a father to all the kids we adopt, or choose to make together."

Kit stared up into his eyes in disbelief. "That sounds an awful lot like a commitment, Officer Knight."

"Maybe it's because I consider myself committed, Kit Kat. Hope you're okay with that."

"What happened to my tough bad-boy biker dude who just wanted hot, hard, sweaty—"

"Don't worry, he's still here. The tough bad-boy biker dude will always be around to protect you."

"I don't need you to protect me. I just need you to love me."

"Sorry, angel, I'm here to do both."

And after a moment's reflection, Katherine Elizabeth Brennan nodded. Cool. She was good with that.

If you enjoyed *The Good Daughter,*
keep reading for a special preview from
the next novel in the Brennan Sisters trilogy

The Good Wife

Coming in September 2013 from Berkley Books!

Sarah sat on the kitchen island barstool, watching her brother-in-law, Jack Roberts, at the old farmhouse-style sink, carefully wipe down the glazed white surface with a pale pink sponge. He'd just spent more than an hour washing and drying dishes, putting away the platters and silver that belonged to the Brennan family, and stacking the dozens of dishes—Pyrex, ceramic and wooden salad bowls—that had been brought by neighbors and friends for the reception following her mom's funeral service at St. Cecilia's in San Francisco this morning.

Jack's commitment to the kitchen and dishes put a lump in Sarah's throat, and she squeezed the glazed mug between her hands, needing the mug's warmth. Jack had refused her help, but he'd made her a cup of tea, and told her to sit, and then he went back to work, washing and drying those mountains of dishes.

Sarah didn't know why she was so touched by Jack's dedica-tion to the dishes. Boone, her husband, did dishes. If Boone hadn't needed to jump on a plane and rush back to Florida for the end of spring training, he would be the one at the sink, soaking and scrubbing and toweling dry.

But he wasn't here. He was gone. Just as he was almost always gone.

Maybe that's why she was so appreciative of the time Jack spent in the kitchen tonight, transferring leftovers to Tupperware, putting things in order, making things better. Time was special. And it was the one thing she couldn't get enough of from Boone, who always seemed to be packing or unpacking his suitcase, which was always out, always on the bench at the foot of their bed.

But it wouldn't be long before he retired. He'd turned thirty-nine in November. He was ancient in baseball. Grandpa, the rookies called him. The rookies weren't far off. There weren't many players Boone's age in the majors who could still hit the ball like Boone. But then, Boone was special. He always had been.

She glanced down at the phone on the counter, checking to see if Boone had texted her yet. He should be landing anytime now.

"They had a late departure. He'll be landing soon," Jack said, squeezing the sponge dry.

She jumped guiltily, unaware that Jack had been watching her. "I can't relax when he's in the air."

"Nothing's going to happen."

Sarah turned the phone over, pushed it away. "I still get nervous."

"You have to be positive."

"I try."

"It was good to see him," Jack added, opening a cupboard above the refrigerator where Mom stored her oversized platters and serving bowls and carefully sliding two platters into the stack. "Heard he's hitting well."

"He had a great spring training."

"JJ said he had three home runs last week."

She nodded, trying not to be nervous, trying not to worry. "He hasn't hit like this in awhile," she said, aware that she always worried during baseball season. There was so much to worry about. Team politics, trades, injuries, Boone's performance at plate, the fickle fans, the groupies.

Sarah shuddered, not wanting to think about the girls and groupies tonight. They were part of baseball, and a fact of life, but she wouldn't let them get to her, not when there were so many other more important things to think about.

Really important things like today's funeral Mass at St. Cecilia's, and the graveside service after. The church itself was packed, and almost everyone followed to the cemetery. Dad was such a rock during both services. His eyes had teared up, but he didn't break down, at least, not until the casket was lowered at the end of the graveside service. That's when he went down on one knee and bent his head, and cried.

Those who'd remained left for the house then, everybody moving on to the reception, except for Boone and Tommy Jr., who stayed behind with Dad. Eventually, they accompanied him back to the house for the reception, and then Sarah had just enough time to give Boone a quick hug and kiss before he jumped in a cab and took off for the airport.

Now, at nine o'clock, everyone was gone. The guests. The strangers. The friends and neighbors. Only the immediate family remained—Jack and Meg, Kit and Jude, Brianna, Tommy and Cass, and the kids. Meg and Jack's three, and her two, Brennan and Ella.

Jack reached for a damp dishtowel, dried his hands one final time before crossing the floor to toss the wet towel into a white plastic basket in the laundry room next door. "I think that's it," he said.

"You deserve a medal of valor," Sarah said, sliding off the stool and stretching.

"It was the least I could do. And it felt good to do something. I haven't been much use to anyone lately—"

"You've been there for Meg, and that's what counts."

"I don't know about that."

"I do. Meg told me how amazing you've been. You've cancelled your trips to DC, and you've been managing the kids so Meg could be with Mom as much as possible. That's pretty cool."

He managed a tight smile. "It's tough, seeing her go. Your mom was a great lady."

Sarah's eyes burned all over again. She'd cried more this week than she'd cried in her entire life put together. No, not true. She'd cried for weeks when she first found out about Boone and that Atlanta woman. Jesus. That had nearly killed her. "I can't imagine life without her," Sarah said. "And Easter's coming up—"

Then she was crying in earnest and somehow she found herself in Jack's arms, sobbing against his chest as he awkwardly patted her back, trying to comfort her, but all she could see was Dad on one knee at the cemetery, his big shoulders shaking, and Ella, scared to see Grandpa crying, pressing herself into Sarah's legs, while Brennan stood stoic at her side, which was rare, when he was usually so out of control with his ADHD.

No, there were definitely more important things to worry about than groupies and girls chasing Boone. There was her widowed father, and timid, clingy Ella, and eight-year-old Brennan, who could be an incredible athlete if he'd just swing the bat when he was supposed to, instead of swinging it at other kids because he had no self-control.

Eventually, Sarah cried herself out and looked up at Jack, her face wet, nose streaming. Horrified with herself, Sarah turned away to hunt for tissue. "Okay, that was embarrassing."

"You're fine."

"I'm a mess."

"We all are."

"Yeah?" she asked, locating the Kleenex box under the sink and grabbing handfuls of tissue to blow her nose and scrub her cheeks dry.

"Yeah," he answered, taking the stool she'd vacated a few minutes earlier.

Something in his tone caught her attention and she gave him a close look. "You and Meg okay?"

He hesitated. "What do you mean? As a couple?"

She nodded.

His shoulders twisted. "I don't know. Things are what they are."

That did not sound good. Sarah frowned. "Things still rocky?"

He made a face as he shrugged again. "We have our ups and downs. Sometimes it feels like more downs than ups."

"But you haven't thrown in the towel yet," she said, trying to be encouraging.

"Not yet."

"That's good."

"Is it?"

Sarah heard the weariness in his voice, and her chest tightened. She and Boone had been through so much and yet she couldn't imagine life without him. He was as important to her as oxygen—not that her sisters thought she should love any man that much. But Boone wasn't just any man. He was Boone. And when things were good with them, things were heaven.

Her phone suddenly vibrated on the counter, signaling an incoming text.

Jack handed Sarah the phone. "It's Boone," he said.

"He's landed," Sarah said, reading the text. It was short, just one word, but it was all she needed. *Here*, it said.

Sarah texted Boone back. *Glad you're safe.*

You okay? Boone replied.

Yes. Just wish you were here, she answered.

Me, too, babe. Give my love to everyone, especially the kids.

As if on cue, Meg entered the kitchen carrying a weeping Ella. "There's your mommy," Meg crooned, kissing Ella's wet, flushed cheek. "I told you we'd find her. Your mommy didn't go anywhere. No need to cry. She's right here talking to Uncle Jack."

Ella leaned out of Meg's arms, reaching for her mother. "Momma!" she wailed. "I want Daddy. I want to go home. I want to go to bed. I hate Brennan. He's so mean."

Sarah took her kindergartener from Meg and cuddled her close. "What did he do this time, sweet pea?"

"He said he was going to bury me like Grandma—"

"He's not," Sarah interrupted sternly, meeting Meg's eyes above her daughter's head. "And he shouldn't say things like that."

"I don't want to go in the ground and be covered up with dirt. Why did they cover Grandma with dirt?"

"Because Grandma went to Heaven to be with God and Jesus and Mary and all the saints and angels." Sarah kissed Ella's cheek and smoothed her hair. "Now, stop crying, because if we cry, we might make Grandpa sad, and we don't want to leave him here tonight sad, okay?"

"Are we going home, Mommy?"

"Not to our house. We're staying with Aunt Meg and Uncle Jack for a few nights, remember?"

"Without Daddy?"

"Daddy had to go back to Tampa Bay, but we'll see him soon."

"I want to go home now."

"I think you're tired, sweetheart. I know I'm tired. It's been a really long day." Sarah glanced over at Meg, who was leaning back against Jack as he sat on the stool, and mouthed to her sister, "Do you think we can leave soon?"

Meg nodded and glanced up at Jack, who also nodded. "Let's round up the kids," she said, straightening.

"We'll go say our good-nights, then," Sarah added, grateful

that they'd soon be in the car, driving to Meg and Jack's big hand-some house in Santa Rosa.

An hour later, Meg left her youngest sister, Sarah, tucked in the guest room bed with five-year-old Ella sharing her bed, and Brennan in a sleeping bag on the floor, before moving down the hall to check on her kids.

Tessa and Gabi were both in bed talking in the dark, but JJ was at his desk, Skyping with his girlfriend, and when he spotted his mother in the doorway, he tersely signaled for Meg to leave.

"Simply saying good night," she said mildly, refusing to take offense. "Just making sure you're okay . . . with the funeral and all."

JJ's glare suddenly softened, and he said something to his girl-friend before hitting the disconnect on the computer. Springing from his chair, he went to his mom and wrapped his arms around her in a quick, guilty hug. "Sorry. And I'm sorry about Grandma," he muttered. "Sorry for you, too. It must be awful losing your mom. I would hate to lose you."

Meg, who'd kept it together for much of the day, blinked to clear the hot, stinging sensation from her eyes. "Well, I have no intention of going anywhere, and Grandma was a really good mom."

"I loved Grandma."

"I know. And she loved you."

JJ pulled away and folded his arms across his chest. He'd grown five inches in the past six months and had filled out through the chest and shoulders, showing an early hint of the Brennan brawn. Not that he was a Brennan, but he had her brother's and father's athletic ability, and JJ hoped to make it to the pros, like Boone, Sarah's husband. "Why did she have to die?" he demanded.

Meg shrugged. "Something about God's plan."

"Don't get mad at my language, but I think it's a fucked-up plan."

"Can't disagree, babe, but let's not use foul language."

"But it is. She suffered so much—" He broke off, took a step away, and rubbed at his watering eyes. "So not right."

"No."

"Grandpa's going to really miss her, won't he?"

Meg swallowed around the lump filling her throat. It'd been such a long, hard couple of months, but hopefully Mom was in a better place. Or at least, a place without pain. "Yeah. They've been together a long time."

"And they were happy, weren't they? They always seemed to be in a good mood when they were together. Always laughing and joking around."

She nearly reached out to touch his jaw with the straggly chin stubble, his facial hair still light and thin, but crossed her arms instead, not wanting to invade his space. She'd learned that it was better to let him come to her, to reach for her, otherwise she could end up rejected. "They definitely enjoyed each other."

"Did they ever fight?"

"Oh, most definitely. They had their moments. Grandpa isn't always easy to live with, and Grandma was never a pushover, but they were committed to each other, and very committed to the family. It's why their marriage worked."

"They were best friends, weren't they?"

"Yes."

JJ's forehead creased and he stared across the room, to his desktop computer. "Were you and Dad ever like that? . . . Best friends?"

Meg's mouth opened, then closed. It took her a second to think back, to the early days of her marriage, and her first thought was how new and exciting it had all been, that big move with Jack to California, her state, which then made her reflect on how different it'd been for him, and how uncomfortable he was with her big family. From the start he'd been overwhelmed by the tight-knit Brennan family, and resisted their many traditions—family summers and holidays in Capitola at the beach house, big gatherings for Thanksgiving, Christmas, and Easter, winter ski trips to Tahoe, weekly Sunday brunches, Saturday barbeques, baptisms, and ball games, never mind casual family dinners.

No, Jack hadn't enjoyed her family holidays and traditions. He'd never come out and said so, but she'd suspected that he found them a little too loud, a little too blue collar, a little too Catholic. Jack's family—the Roberts family, which could trace its ancestors to the Mayflower—had been educated, affluent, and aloof, as well as fractured by a highly contentious divorce and custody battle that lasted for years, scarring Jack permanently.

Meg had loved Jack anyway, adoring his brilliant mind and his talent for sensitive architectural preservation and design. She'd learned that he needed his space, and he was most creative when left to himself, and so she gave him his space and told herself that the space was good for her, too. She was, and always had been, very independent. She didn't need a lot of attention. Mary Margaret Brennan Roberts excelled at self-sufficiency.

"Your dad is still my best friend," she said now to JJ, which stood for Jack Jr. "He's amazing. There aren't many people as smart as he is."

"I thought Aunt Kit was your best friend."

Meg's throat worked, and she felt the weight of the last week settle in her gut, and burn in her chest. There were few people as loving and supportive as her sister Kit. She struggled to smile. "We are really close."

"So she is your best friend?"

"Can't a girl have two best friends?"

"I guess."

Needing to escape, she kissed JJ's cheek. "I'm going to bed. Don't stay up too late, okay?"

"I won't. I can't. We've got that double-header tomorrow. Remember?"

In her bedroom, Meg discovered that the lights had been dimmed, and Jack was already in bed, on his side, his back to her.

She gently closed the door, retreating to the master bath to wash her face and brush her teeth. She performed her nightly routine swiftly without looking at herself. She was too tired to look at herself, not interested in seeing her face, not wanting to see her fatigue or her sadness.

Impossible to believe Mom was gone. Mom couldn't be gone. There was still so much life ahead. Still so much time. Baseball games and ballet recitals and high school graduations and weddings. . . .

Her girls would one day walk down the aisle and her mom wouldn't be there to see it. Her mom wouldn't be there for any of it.

Meg cried, bent over the bathroom sink, splashing water on her face even as tears fell. Tired. She was just so tired. And sad. But that was natural. This was all natural. Part of life. Birth and death and change. She didn't have to like it, just accept it. And adapt.

In bed, she quietly slid into her spot, carefully fluffing and adjusting her pillows as she eased under the duvet. The sheets were cool and smooth, the softest, lightest cotton. Her favorite indulgence. She didn't care about expensive clothes or jewelry or cars, but she loved quality sheets. Good sheets made a great bed.

"You were gone awhile," Jack said, breaking the silence. His voice was clear, firm. He hadn't been asleep.

"Talked a long time to Sarah, then to JJ," Meg answered, rolling over to look at him. His eyes were open, his gaze fixed on her.

"Everything okay?"

"Sarah's a wreck, and JJ just wanted to talk."

"What did JJ have to say?"

Meg hesitated, studying Jack's strong, patrician features and unsmiling mouth. He didn't smile much anymore, and suddenly she wondered if he ever had. "He talked about Grandma and Grandpa, and how much Grandpa would miss Grandma. He said they were best friends. I agreed. And then he asked . . ." Her voice trailed off as she struggled to voice JJ's question. "He asked. . . . if we had ever been like that. Best friends. And I told him yes."

Jack didn't say anything. His expression didn't change. But Meg felt that acidic knot return to her stomach, the one that seemed to live there all the time, making her reach for Tums and Rolaids several times a day.

"What?" she prompted, trying to see into Jack's brown eyes, trying to read what he was thinking.

"A long time ago," he said finally.

She pressed the pillow closer to her cheek. Her face felt so hot and yet on the inside she felt so cold. "Not that long ago."

"Seems like forever."

"We've had a hard year."

"It wasn't good before that."

He was referring to her affair. Her affair, her fault, her responsibility. And it was no one's fault but hers. She'd be paying penance forever, not because anyone asked it of her, but because she owed it. She'd messed up, badly; and nine months later, she still found it impossible to forgive herself. Maybe one day she could. Maybe when she and Jack were good again, solid again. She looked forward to the day. Prayed for the day. It was hard living with so much self-hatred. "It'll get better."

"I'm not happy."

Meg exhaled slowly. "I'm sorry."

"Are we working?" he asked.

"I'm not unhappy."

"But are you happy?"

Her eyes stung and the acid from her stomach seemed to be bubbling up her esophagus and into her throat. "This is a kind of tough time to be talking about happiness. Mom's just died. The funeral was this morning. We had two hundred and fifty people over to the house—"

"But that's the point. We're all going to die. Death is inevitable. In fact, some would say we're dying every day."

"I disagree. As long as you're alive, you're alive. When you're dead, you're gone—"

"Unless you're not really alive. Unless you're just going through the motions." Jack's mouth flattened, and a small muscle pulled and popped in his jaw. "Like we are."

You mean, like you are, Meg silently corrected, closing her eyes, shoulders rising, up towards her ears.

"This isn't working with us, Meg."

She didn't want to hear this, not now, not today. She was too sad. Things had been too hard. "We're tired, Jack, worn out—"

"I leave tomorrow for DC, and I think we need to really think about the future, and what we want. We're not getting any younger. We deserve to be happy. You deserve to be happy—"

"I'm not unhappy, Jack!" she cried, sitting up, knocking away a tear before it could fall. "I'm just tired. It's been a rough couple of weeks, and a very long day, and I will not lose you now, not after everything we've been through. We're good together. We have the kids. We have a history. We have a future."

"But maybe it's not the one I want," he answered quietly, his voice cutting through the dark room, and her heart.

Meg's lips parted but no sound came out. She balled her hands into fists and pressed them against her thighs. She wouldn't cry. She wouldn't. Things would work out. They always worked out. She just had to be strong. Had to stay calm. "We will get through this."

"I don't think so."

"*Jack.*"

"I'm not trying to be mean, Meg. I'm just being honest."